After distinguished naval service during the Second World War, Alexander Fullerton learnt Russian at Cambridge, on a Joint Services course, then worked in Germany with Red Army units. He predicted the lowering of the Iron Curtain, a forecast that was rejected by the SIS, whose Russian desk was at that time manned by Kim Philby. After passing the interpretership exam (CS) he was at once returned to sea in submarines. He resigned and was released in 1949, and worked in South Africa as an insurance clerk, in a Swedish shipping agency and as a publisher's representative. His first novel was published in 1953. In 1959 he returned to Britain to pursue a publishing career, but abandoned it in 1967 to write full-time. He is now the author of over thirty novels.

Also by Alexander Fullerton in Sphere Books:

SPECIAL DELIVERANCE

Special Dynamic

ALEXANDER FULLERTON

SPHERE BOOKS LIMITED

SPHERE BOOKS LTD

Published by the Penguin Group
27 Wrights Lane, London W8 5TZ, England
Viking Penguin Inc., 40 West 23rd Street, New York, New York 10010, USA
Penguin Books Australia Ltd, Ringwood, Victoria, Australia
Penguin Books Canada Ltd, 2801 John Street, Markham, Ontario, Canada L3R 1B4
Penguin Books (NZ) Ltd, 182–190 Wairau Road, Auckland 10, New Zealand

Penguin Books Ltd, Registered Offices: Harmondsworth, Middlesex, England

First published 1987 by Macmillan London Ltd
Published by Sphere Books Ltd 1988

Printed and bound in Great Britain by
Richard Clay Ltd, Bungay, Suffolk

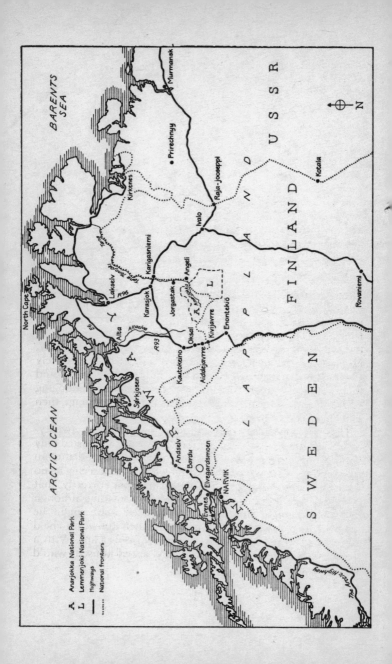

PROLOGUE

They could have been wolves, the way the skiers followed exactly in each others' tracks, thrusting out of the icy blackness of the forest into the broad, cleared strip that marked the frontier. They most likely had learnt the trick from wolves; this was wolf country and a pack often travelled in that way, each animal placing its feet in the same pug-marks so precisely that only a very experienced tracker could read the truth – and then only if the snow was soft enough – from the smudging and the depth of the impressions. When the pack split up, then you could count them.

Clas Saarinen was counting now: twenty-seven, twenty-eight . . . His surprise at the first one's showing had lasted only seconds; he was a pragmatic, plain-thinking man and after an initial jump of nerves he'd accepted what he was seeing as no more than proof that he'd interpreted the *yoik* correctly, that the girl had got it right and that he'd read its meaning although *she* hadn't, might not even have guessed there might be anything in it to understand, not even when the words she'd memorised were tumbling from her own sweet lips. With a body and a disposition like hers, he'd asked himself, who'd want a brain?

A more sensible question, on which he'd then had to concentrate his own brain-power, had been where to start, since even if he'd limited the search to points north of – say – Kotala, he'd have had something like three hundred kilometres of the desolate, deep-frozen border area to cover. He'd sought advice first from old Juffu, Martti's uncle, who lived like some old wolf himself and knew more than anyone alive about these forests and (a) whatever lived or moved in them, (b) how to kill or catch it, but the old hunter had been either unable or unwilling to assist. So then he'd decided on his own plan of action, which was first to decide on which were the more likely areas and then to disperse his team to nose around on their own, and Veili Santavuori had struck lucky in the second week, finding tracks that weren't explainable in any ordinary way. From Veili's starting point they'd backtracked, using guesswork, intuition, common sense and acquired skills and finding – here and there, sometimes at long intervals – traces as faint even to Clas Saarinen's own practised eyes as the scent of danger that freezes a wolverine in its tracks....

Thought froze abruptly as he realised they'd stopped coming; and the count was thirty-two, which might be a likely number. He still waited, motionless, making certain, knowing very well that to move too soon could blow it. Not that he could be seen from the watchtower from which MVD guards overlooked this section: he'd chosen his position with care, and he knew very well how to make himself invisible, part of the snowscape, half buried in the snow itself and white-smocked, white-hooded. Even the gun on his back, a Jati, was mostly white. He thought this *must* be the whole party on its way now. Twisting the microphone up to his mouth and pushing a switch with the thumb of his mittened left hand he told the others who were three-quarters of a kilometre from him, inside the forest and close to the track, 'Patrol of thirty-two. Let 'em go by, then Martti tail 'em. Veili, wait for me to join you.' Young Martti could move like an arctic fox when there was need to: he'd been well taught, by his uncle Juffu.

Wind thrummed in the trees. The wind-factor was holding the temperature down to not much above minus forty, and back there in the woods its erosive effect continuously dislodged crystals from the high branches so you'd imagine there was an unending crackling snowfall, icefall, even though here in the open it wasn't enough to stir the crusted surface. Still cold enough to freeze a man's balls off if he didn't take good care – which this one certainly did, not least for the reason that in Rovaniemi and more distant Helsinki, in warm houses and even warmer beds, there was not one warm-limbed girl and not two, but three, all awaiting the return of Clas Saarinen; as well as the young Sami girl, that slimy bastard Isak's niece, the kid who'd steered him on to this. She – Inga – was currently over the border in Norway, at Karasjok with her doting uncle, although her real home was here in Finland.

Frontiers didn't mean anything much to Sami – Lapp – people. Except this Soviet frontier; although it wasn't fenced – as the Norwegian section *was*, further north – there were still problems that made the crossing hardly worthwhile. The wild deer wandered across it as they pleased, of course – which was enough to attract old Juffu when he was in the mood. . . . But that little Sami lass was really *something*, he'd promised he'd visit her again and it was a promise he'd keep. Best not up in Karasjok in the uncle's house again – that had been a risk, could have led to awkward complications – but when she was at her own home and when this business had been cleared up. It was a business in which she'd helped enormously without any notion that she was doing so.

If she *had* understood she might not have spilt the beans as she had, crooning for him in that husky little voice the first lines of the new *yoik* she'd told him Isak was composing. So far as she'd known, those lines were the only ones yet completed, and she'd known them by heart because her uncle had squatted for hours, days, going over and over the same phrases. Which, Clas thought, must have been fairly punishing, despite Isak being a famous *yoik* artist, known even a thousand kilometres away in Oslo and at the Tromsø university where they had recordings of all his work. He was also known as something of a bloody nuisance, had written some books providing malcontents with some sort of historical

3

background to their grievances. A patriot, fellow Lapps of that kind called him – that kind being the 'Samiland for the Samis' fraternity as well as some lefty outsiders. It was why Clas had decided to turn his investigatory talents towards Inga, in her uncle's absence on a visit to Alta, guessing that even if Isak might be too slippery a customer to be actively involved in whatever was going on he might well know quite a lot about it. Clas had struck oil, in the *yoik* material professionally and in the niece personally.

He was remembering the warmth in her eyes, her breath soft in his face as she'd leant close, whispering the words of the new *yoik*; then he'd caught his breath, recollection of those moments of pleasure exorcised by the sight of another figure – and another, which made it thirty-four now – standing out like birch-trunks separating from the black mass of other trees. The main bunch had meanwhile vanished westward. . . . Back to these newcomers – still only two, late-comers hurrying to catch up, moving swiftly across the open, treeless strip of land.

Waiting with a hunter's natural patience, Clas was listening again in his memory to that *yoik* – Lappish song, a guttural chant. . . . *See them come, the nameless, voia voia!/ Stealing from the haunts of Rota, woolly ones padding, padding/ Then over the high vidda like Spring's white torrents rushing/ Horde of the nameless flooding to Kautokeino bloody knife!* The melody was as monotonous as any other *yoik*'s but the lyrics were very much in Isak's style, only minimally padded with the traditional *voia-voia*s and *nana-nana*s.

Clas had asked the niece, 'If you were nameless – while still as lovely as you are – and I were to ring you now, would you reward me?' Her eyes and her soft laugh had told him that she had precisely the reward he wanted right there ready for him; at that moment there'd been nothing else in her mind, while in his own the *yoik*'s phrases had been unravelling themselves.

A 'nameless one' for instance meant a bear – sometimes a wolf but usually a bear – because in past times the mountain Lapps had been very much alert to the peril of openly naming either bear or wolf in plain speech and thus offending it. The reference here was obviously to bears because of the mention

4

in the second line of 'woolly ones', yet another code-phrase for that animal which they'd long revered as well as hunted. As to his own provocative question, a Sami hunter who'd tracked a bear to its lair would proceed to 'ring' it, circling it three times on foot at some safe distance and thus establishing the right to lead the hunt to kill it. *Haunts of Rota* suggested something below ground: Rota was the god of sickness and death and lived down there, and the custom had been to sacrifice a horse if someone was ill, burying the whole carcase so Rota could mount it and gallop away through his own subterranean domain, thus removing the sickness. Presumably this was another reference to bears, since bears made their dens inside the earth. And *Kautokeino bloody knife* was the first line of a very well known *yoik* commemorating the events of eighteen fifty-two when Lapp religious fanatics went crazier than usual and murdered Norwegians in the traditional manner of slaughtering reindeer, stabbing into their hearts.

He'd had these interpretations unfolding in his brain while the girl's smile enticed him and his fingers loosened the buttons on her blouse; the nameless ones could only be Russians, and in that last line there was a suggestion of (a) murder and (b) Kautokeino as an objective, a target of the intrusions. . . .

He twisted the mike up again, and muttered, 'Two more coming. Two hundred metres behind the first lot. Sit tight till you've counted thirty-four past you, Martti.' He watched that pair until he lost them when they merged into the forest on this side, he himself remaining motionless, thinking about another Sami, a wise and knowledgeable friend whom he'd questioned about the extraordinary phenomena of recent weeks and months and who'd spoken grudgingly after a typically long, ruminative silence, murmuring, 'Not our people. Some from Kola there might be. They were as we are, at one time – well, more or less. As you'd know well enough. But for generations now they've been—' he'd spat '—under that other influence.'

These people – some of them, anyway – would open their minds to Clas Saarinen, sometimes, because they knew he had the blood of a *sápmelaš* in his veins – not such a lot of it, and through his mother's mother, but enough to make him trustworthy or at any rate more to be trusted than non-Lapps, *daččas*.

He wasn't moving yet because there could be some Ivan still to come, some smart Alec hanging back. He'd have moved at the speed of light if he'd had any way of knowing that his last transmission had given them a cross-bearing back there in the trees so they had him nailed, a Russian at this moment whispering into a radio-telephone, 'Three-sixty metres from the base-line, compass bearing from you now zero-seven-seven. Did you locate the others?'

'Yes. Get off the air, stay off.' A.N.Belyak added quietly into his own mike '*Now*, Yuri', and switched off, began moving forward and to his left over the snow with an action not unlike that of a sidewinder, from the cover of the trees – or rather tree-stumps, the forest on this Finnish side having been thinned so that it became sparser before it ended completely at the border strip. The other two Finns, this guy's back-up, were on ice metaphorically as well as literally, Yuri Grintsov having had them pinpointed for the past hour. Belyak had his own target visually now, the Finn having decided it was safe to move. He was crouching, slowly turning, studying the surroundings through some kind of – Belyak guessed – infra-red viewer. So it would have to be done quickly, instead of closing in for the neater job which the Spetsnaz man would have preferred.

He thumbed up the crossbow's telescopic nightscope – also IR, an image intensifier – and was still again, elbows like struts rooted in the snow, an eye slitted at the 'scope's rear end, target conveniently coming into profile and blinkered by its own hood. There'd never be a better moment. The steel bolt sprang away, flew, a little surface snow scattering from the bow's convulsion: a second later the bolt smashed into the side of the strong Finnish neck, the sound of impact barely audible even from this close range and Belyak already moving fast towards his kill.

Eight hundred metres away, from good cover, Martti watched the ski platoon glide by, a long file of silent figures pushing northwest along what had been one of the old Lapp migration routes. For centuries Sami nomads had driven their restless beasts along this trail and these same trees had seen them pass. Martti heard Veili Santavuori snaking over from his own hide – to be ready to slip into this one as soon as he'd left it vacant, moving off to maintain contact with the intruders. But there were still two Soviets to come, the older man should have stayed put. Martti hissed, 'Veili, for the love of God—' and an arm like a steel bar clamped his throat, wrenched his head back, while a knife stabbed frontally, its blade driving through thicknesses of cloth into the heart. Blaze of agony short-lived – shorter even than Martti, who'd never get to celebrate his twentieth birthday – and the snow already staining, black-looking blood pumping to expand the patch around the body. From a few metres away, a whisper: 'Heh – Paskar?'

'No problem.'

Gerasimov – a sergeant – grunted satisfaction as he let Santavuori's body sprawl beside the other. He called low-voiced, '*Tovarisch leitnant?*'

'Yeah. Let's have the others back. Except sentries.' Yuri Grintsov added in his Caucasian-accented rasp, 'Start stripping them, Paskar, before they freeze fucking rigid.'

Gerasimov muttered approvingly, 'Good thinking.' He whistled into the dark, the direction the patrol had taken, and a double peep came back almost instantly. Then a trill from behind, the border area. A suggestion of silver overhead in that sector was a lie, false promise of a dawn that would be many hours coming yet. A fortnight ago, this far above the Arctic Circle, there'd been only a little twilight around the middle of the day.

Andrei Belyak's voice called – surprisingly close at hand – 'Yuri?'

'*Syuda. Vsyo v poriadke.*'

'*Chudno.*' Belyak's shape, hidden in arctic clothing and with the tent-like smock over all that, loomed hugely out of the black surround. He was an athlete of distinction, a leading light of the GRU-run sporting club ZSKA and a gold medal-list at the 1980 Winter Games. He'd brought a third body, carrying it over his shoulder; he was coated in its sticky outflow. He said, dumping it, 'Had to shoot him. Stab him now, someone.' There had to be a stab-wound in the heart.

Paskar saw to it, then went back to the other job. Clothing, possessions, weapons and other equipment such as IR viewers, skis – everything – were to be sent back across the border, but the bodies had to be freighted south. All in aid of *maskirovka*, a term which embraced camouflage of the routine kind but also deception and disinformation. Gerasimov would be taking command of the party transporting the corpses while Grintsov with half a company of Spetsnazi escorted a supply convoy across the frozen Suomojoki and Tolosjoki rivers. It was all just about wrapped up, only final stages of logistical preparation – *podgotovka* – remained, and throughout these stages the security of the operation had been the responsibility of Andrei Nikolaievich Belyak, Spetsnaz commander in the field. 'Spetsnaz' being a contraction of *Spetsialnoye Naznacheniye*, literally 'special designation' but more usually translated as 'special force'.

The size of the task had seemed huge at first, but he'd licked it. Or he'd thought he had – until *this*. . . . Staring down at the bodies, lit by flashlights as the men worked on them. Corpses cooling fast, blood-flow already slowed to only seepage. Belyak was uncomfortably aware that his own outer clothing was soaked in it, his white camouflage smock stained like a butcher's apron. He'd need to change some of this gear before departure. Gerasimov said, 'Here's your guy's gun.'

Belyak crouched, flashlight between his teeth. There *must* have been a leak. He'd have liked to have been able to see some other explanation for the Finns' presence here, but there wasn't one, and it was therefore his own vital and urgent need to find the leak and seal it off. It had to be done immediately, because the Command decision whether to launch the invasion now, in January, or delay it to end March or early April, would come at any moment. Weather conditions were excellent, too. . . . All the more reason therefore to have sent back a report of this emergency situation and awaited orders; and he was risking his neck – much more than that too, but the personal hazard was the one a man saw most clearly – by keeping it to himself while he took a small, hand-picked team in to find the source and eliminate it. If he'd sent a report back now, the operation would almost surely have been called off. V.V.Rosenko, Marshall of the Soviet Union, had stressed this point, right at the start: security had to be absolute, or the plan wouldn't get off the ground. With total security it would be a walkover; but there'd be no compromise, total was to mean *total*.

Belyak remembered the Marshall leaning with his fists on the ornately carved, inlaid table which had served him as a desk and which might a couple of hundred years earlier have graced some nobleman's palace; Rosenko's dark eyes had been as hard as stones as he'd hammered the point home: 'Cross-border security, Captain, is in your hands. We entrust you with it because your efficiency in such matters has been well proven and because it's of the highest importance in an operation that's of *paramount* importance. Understand this clearly: without watertight security, the vehicle will not roll. *Ponyatno*?'

He'd understood, all right. They were jumping him up to the substantive rank of major, acting rank *pod-polkovnik*, Lieutenant-Colonel; he was being offered the chance of a lifetime, because they thought he was capable of pulling it off. If he let them down, it would have been a lot better not to have been singled out for the honour in the first place.

Paskar had two other soldiers helping him strip the bodies. Economical use of flashlights was permissible; guards had been posted on a wide perimeter in case a Finnish Frontier Force patrol should inconveniently show up. Not that it was at all likely, the pattern of such deployments having been carefully monitored over a period of months. . . . They'd dealt with the first two bodies and were starting on the man Belyak had killed – a stocky, thick-limbed Finn whose head had been almost blasted off his shoulders. The exit of the crossbow bolt on the right side of the neck had created that damage.

Gerasimov was spreading reindeer skins, one for each of the corpses which were now rolled on to them; the edges of the

9

hides were then drawn together, leather thongs tightened and knotted. Long traces also of reindeer hide were coiled ready for the skiers who'd take the loads in tow, frozen solid as logs as they very soon would be. This ultra-simple form of freight-sledge was the most basic type of Lapp *geres* or *pulka*, traditional transport since ancient times for reindeer meat and other stores.

Belyak knew a lot about Lapps – in Russian, *Laplandtsi* or *Lopari* – and their history and way of life. Or rather ways, plural, because the *Loparis*' lifestyle varied according to habitat and primary occupation. There were for instance mountain Lapps who herded reindeer, river Lapps who lived by farming and some fishing, and coast Lapps whose liveli-hood came from the sea. There were also many who'd been assimilated into the 'settler' ways and lived like their Norwe-gian, Swedish or Finnish neighbours. Belyak had studied the Lapp customs, folklore, eating and living habits and the principles of reindeer husbandry; he'd also looked carefully into the grudges and political aspirations which a few of them nursed. He and his Spetsnazi professionals had investigated the Lapp background so well that they could just about pass themselves off as Lapps when they needed to.

Yuri Grintsov was a reek of onions at his side. There'd be a moon in about an hour and its radiance would permeate the overhang of cloud, lighten the scene down here to some extent, but for the moment the world consisted of shadows etched against snow's whiteness – and muted sounds, odours includ-ing the sweet sickliness of fresh blood. The boys were clearing up, throwing clean snow over the sodden patches; snow that fell looked natural, whereas raked-over snow did not. Belyak asked Gerasimov, 'Are you clear on how you're to dispose of them, Aleksandr Borisovich?'

'Clear enough.' The sergeant's affirmative was a growl as he straightened, but Yuri Grintsov chipped in, 'Wherever they're dumped, won't their pals in the Ivalo barracks know this is where they must have been hit?'

'No.' Belyak gave him the answer quietly. It wasn't for everyone to hear. 'At Ivalo they know fuck-all.' The toe of his boot nudged one stiffening corpse. 'This one telephoned his boss. Not at Ivalo – they're not locals, they're from Rovaniemi, undercover squad. This guy's half *Lopar*, as it happens. He *was*. . . . He called in to report he'd be out of touch for a while, snooping down in this direction. Didn't say for what or why – and his boss didn't ask, for shit's sake – so I'm starting from scratch now.' He shrugged. 'Well. Not quite.'

'How d'you know *that* much?'

'His boss passed it on to us. He's our man, you see. Unfortunately, slow in the uptake. Now, look here . . .'

It was time to get his team together, and move out.

This had started for Andrei Belyak nearly a year ago, with a summons to a high-level meeting in Moscow after a sudden recall from service in Afghanistan. Ushered into the underground conference hall of the *Verkhovnoye Glavnoye Komandovaniye*, Supreme High Command, he'd found himself in company with two Marshalls of the Soviet Union, several lesser generals, a whole crowd of other senior officers and a small group of civilian officials whom he'd guessed might be GRU 2nd Chief Directorate officials. Rarified air indeed, at first gulp. Not that he himself was any nonentity, despite his junior rank: he was known nationally for his athletic achievements, and as most of the senior men glanced at the powerfully built young officer they'd have noticed that on his airborne forces' uniform he wore a para badge. Soviet air assault troops wore that uniform but they used helicopters, not parachutes, and the badge was the one thing that marked him for what he was.

Presiding over the meeting was Marshall V.V.Rosenko, who was to be the 'Representative' on this Operation *Temnota* – code-word meaning 'darkness'. Viktor Vassilievich Rosenko outlined the intention and objectives and spent several minutes on a swift review of the historical, geographical and political

11

background. Then from Lapp origins, history, present political 'subjugation' by the settler populations of Norwegians, Swedes and Finns, he expanded on the golden opportunity which Lapp dissidence in northern Scandinavia now presented. Operation *Temnota* was designed to use it, enabling Soviet forces to take possession of Finnmark, Norway's northern province, with the main object of securing the coastline from Kirkenes on the present Soviet/Norwegian border via North Cape and numerous intermediate small ports to Alta with its fine deepwater anchorages in sheltered, ice-free fjords, and all of this would be achieved without risk of confrontation with NATO forces.

On 'Lapp dissidence', Rosenko explained that where the basis for anything like an insurrectionary movement did exist, steps were being taken to nurture and develop it. Where none existed, it would be planted, created through various kinds of persuasion, or it would simply be invented. The physical takeover would then be accomplished by clandestine penetration – in preference to a swift, armed grab of that weakly defended territory – first because fighting was still in progress in Afghanistan and anti-Soviet propaganda was being maintained at such levels that a new military initiative, which would be falsely interpreted as aggression against a neighbour state, was politically undesirable, and second because it wasn't necessary, as the situation in Lappland would permit the more or less bloodless achievement of the same aims. It would be a *fait accompli*, all objectives secured, before the NATO hierarchies woke up to the fact that it was happening.

Timing: Rosenko told his audience that in order to fit in with other longer term strategic plans, all stages of preparation would have to be completed by mid-January. There would be two options then: either to attack immediately or to wait until maybe April, ie to move in advance of the NATO winter exercise deployments or after the withdrawal of those forces. There were various factors to be taken into account – including weather, snow and ice conditions.

Belyak had left the conference hall with enough reading matter to fill a large suitcase. He and other force commanders

12

were also given individual briefs detailing their own areas of planning. Language study, too, commenced immediately. Other Spetsnaz officers and NCOs, from *okhotnik* ('hunter') units in the East and *reidovik* ('raider') western-based units – Belyak himself was an *okhotnik* – were sent to special language courses in their own districts, without knowing what need they'd have of that language, those languages. Linguistic ability being one of the Spetsnaz characteristics, the desired results were achieved in nearly all cases within the time allowed, and in his own six months of study Belyak acquired not only the Northern Lapp tongue but also passable Norwegian and enough Finnish to get by – to pass for a Finn when in Norway, for instance.

V.V.Rosenko meanwhile moved west to set up a subordinate headquarters at Kandalaksha on the White Sea. He took over his command under the alias of V.V.Sidorenko and in the rank of colonel, this demotion being a standard security precaution and an element in the overall cover, *maskirovka*, as of course was the location of his *stavka* – convenient enough at this stage to the scene of projected action but not so close as to point to it. Belyak spent some time there before deploying with his Spetsnazi, also Mountain Recce Troops and a regiment of Combat Engineers, to a heavily camouflaged forward base southwest of Prirechnyy, not far off the highway from Murmansk to Raja-jooseppi on the Finnish border. Here the spearhead units were joined by a detachment of Kola Lapps. Drawn from rear-echelon units into which they'd been conscripted, they were now put through the gruelling Spetsnaz training – Belyak's NCOs watching them closely, picking only the best to join operational sections and relegating the majority to duties around the base. Later they'd help to marshal other Lapps in convincing the outside world that the takeover of Lappland had been a spontaneous Lapp initiative. V.V.Rosenko had given an illustration, at that first Moscow meeting, of how this would be put across, in newspaper and television pictures. The fast, clandestine invasion would have been through Finland, two light columns linking with air and sea insertions, and there'd be no attempt to breach the USSR's frontier with Norway; but after a Lapp declaration of independence there'd be a formal, peaceful opening of that border from the Norwegian side, Soviet troops pouring through to a spectacular welcome by cheering, flag-waving Lapps.

The two Kola Lapps who set off that night with Belyak were the only conscripts in his team of nine skiers. Five of them happened to be from the south, from states east of the Caspian: Kunaiev and Kusaimov from Kazakhstan, Pereudin from Turkmenistan, Rakhmanin the Uzbek, and Akhmatbek Tsinev who was a Kirghiz. Markov, who was from Leningrad and the only westerner in the group, was a *praporschik*, warrant officer. All were trained killers and saboteurs and all except the two *Lopari* had proved themselves in action in Afghanistan.

Personal weapons on the march were limited to fighting-knives and P.220 SIG-Sauer 9-millimetre parabellum automatic pistols – designed by SIG in Switzerland, made by J.P.Sauer in West Germany – and MKS 5.56-mm assault rifles from Interdynamic Forsknings AB of Stockholm. Within the principles of *maskirovka*, which in Spetsnaz operations forbade the trans-frontier use of identifiably Soviet weapons, the Swedish MKS was Belyak's personal choice. He'd selected the short-barrelled version with folding stock and the smaller, twenty-round magazine. Rations and spare clothing, and gear such as tents, cooking equipment and an R350M radio, were packed into another traditional kind of Lapp sledge, a *pulka* of the boat type with a keel, ribs and transom. It was a facsimile, strutted with aluminium, but to Sami or Norwegian eyes it would look like the genuine article – although that would have had reindeer, not Spetsnaz skiers, to haul it.

Belyak led them west. After crossing the main highway south of Ivalo he intended making a dogleg course alteration to the right, pushing northwestward into a frozen emptiness so vast and desolate that you could lose an army in it, let alone nine men.

1

Grey, wind-patterned waters of Ofotfjord were sliced by a jagged edge of rock foreshore, snow and ice-covered, slanting into frame as the Hercules banked, allowing Ollie Lyle that glimpse then replacing it with a sliding rush of the Evenes airfield at a distance amongst whitened mountains. Then he'd lost that picture too; his view was of much higher mountains stretching back from the other side of the fjord – south side, Narvik side, except that Narvik town was up near the fjord's top end – white mountains shiny and clean-looking against a dirty sky in which some of the peaks were hidden. The closer, less dramatic summits crowned slopes that were greyish under a stubble of fir and birch.

There'd be more snow coming soon, he guessed, by the look of that cloud-layer inland. Also coming soon would be darkness, the long night which at this latitude and time of year started at about three-thirty or four p.m. – or even earlier, among the mountains. . . . He glanced round from the little window in the aircraft's fuselage, at an RAF crewman who'd yelled at him, gesturing to him to sit down and fasten his seatbelt in preparation for the landing: and why not, indeed. He slid down, into the plastic-webbing seat which he'd occupied on and off for about six hours, the long flight from RAF Lyneham in Wiltshire to Gardemoen in the south and then northward up most of the considerable length of Norwegian coastline. The RAF crewman raised a thumb and grinned ingratiatingly as he continued aft, climbing over the top of the stack of cargo filling the centre of the hold. There were only seventeen passengers on board but there was a lot of cargo. Wings level now, condensation dripping like a rainshower as the Hercules settled nose-down into its approach run and the noise of its four engines rose to a skull-splitting scream. Ollie had flown in these C130s often enough, but on this flight even with the little yellow foam protectors in his ears the volume of sound seemed excessive.

Not that he was in any position to complain, when he was getting a free ride. Oliver Lyle, civilian, having replaced Captain Lyle, Royal Marines, of the RM Special Boat Squadron. Maybe when you became a civilian you automatically took more notice of minor discomforts like having your eardrums turned inside out.

If so, it was something he'd brought on himself; he'd been in no way obliged to leave the Corps. They'd tried to persuade him not to, one very senior officer going so far as to invite him to be less of a pig-headed bloody fool. . . . But they'd suggested, after his hospitalisation and eventual return to duty, 'You've had a good long run in the Squadron, Lyle, don't you agree it may be the right time for a change?'

He had *not* agreed. His back had been passed as OK – he'd fractured a vertebra but it had mended and the medics had assured him it would be as good as new – and he'd dug his heels in. The prospect of returning to general service had actually appalled him, because in the SB Squadron he'd found his métier – the job, life and motivation he might have been born for, might have joined the Royal Marines for in the first place. Whereas in the months before he'd been accepted for the SB training course – and passed it, despite a current failure rate of seventy-five per cent – he'd been thinking of chucking his hand in. *That* far back, when he'd been a young lieutenant; and not because he'd thought there was anything wrong with the Corps, only because he was Ollie Lyle, something of a maverick, inclined at times to buck the system – *any* system. And one of his characteristics was what he'd heard referred to as a 'high degree of taciturnity'.

It wasn't rudeness, nor was it intentional; he thought it might have been inherited from his father, who'd been a Scot and less polished socially than he'd been competent as an engineer. But he'd see sometimes in people's faces – including those of senior officers – the question, *Is this guy being deliberately offensive?* He was not – not usually – he was only being himself. OK – as the man had said, obstinate, pig-headed, and knowing it, recognising that being the way he was he probably didn't have such a great future in the Corps. So why not get out while the going was good, before you fouled it up? But they'd given him the chance of getting into SB, and there among fellow individualists with a sense of motivation so high it defied description he'd found himself completely happy maybe for the first time in his life; and consequently good at it, bucking no system because the system could have been tailor-made for him.

So what the hell. Sooner than go back to being an also-ran, he'd left. With a sense of gratitude for those truly marvellous years, and also aware that he should also be grateful for being alive at all, seeing that men whose parachutes fail to open can reasonably expect *not* to be hopping around much thereafter.

His own had part-opened. A tree had broken the resulting plummeting descent.

Bump...

The pilot hadn't handled it too cleverly. Two more bone-shaking crashes were followed by smaller bumps and side-to-side lurchings. Then the worst was over; the Hercules was taxiing towards the military terminal, the crewmen back aft were making ready with the aluminium ladder and the passengers were unclipping their belts, collecting gear and zipping up DPMs and/or other protective clothing. They were a mixed lot – two civilians who were probably technicians, an Army gunner commando major, two other Army in light-blue berets – Army Air Corps but REME insignia – three RN flyers, and

17

the rest Royal Marines, Bootnecks who would no doubt have been sick or on special leave or otherwise mislaid when the Commando had deployed to the Norwegian snows a couple of weeks ago. At which time Ollie Lyle had had no idea at all that he'd be getting an offer of a job that would bring him out in the same direction.

It had started with a telephone call from a fellow Royal, a man by the name of Barry Dark. Ollie hadn't seen him for a long time but he'd heard over the grapevine that he'd gone to the Ministry of Defence as Royal Marine PRO. Dark had called through to Mary's pad in Brighton, and Mary had answered the 'phone rather tersely because they'd been having a row and her last words had been, 'You don't have to take it out on me, Ollie. If you're going to spend the rest of your life snarling, count me out of it!'

She'd been voicing something that might have been shaping in her not inactive mind for quite a while, he thought. She was right, some of his half-suppressed anger, frustration — whatever it had been — *had* been spilling over, and each time he was ashamed of it.

He'd taken the receiver from her. 'Who is it?'

'Barry Dark, Ollie. Did I interrupt one of those golden moments?'

'Not by a long chalk. How'd you get this number?'

'Rang around, tuned in to the dirt. I mean the gossip, don't take that literally. . . . Ollie, I was damn sorry to hear about your smash.'

'Calling to say *that*, are you?'

He heard a chuckle. Then: 'Did spoil something, didn't I?'

'No, you did not.'

'I'm relieved. Look, Ollie — d'you want a job?'

He hesitated. The question touched an exposed nerve, his present lack of gainful employment being part of the frustration that had been bugging him. He explained, 'I'm marking time, at the moment. I'm hoping I may have one lined up, you see. Had an interview, chances seem fair, but they won't make up their minds before about mid-April.' He named the airline in which there was a vacancy for a deputy to the chief of

18

security, which in these days of hijacking and bombing was a post of importance and – he anticipated – interest. He'd been given to understand that he was currently the front-runner, but they had other men to interview and two of them were coming from abroad, on leave from jobs in the Middle and Far East, which accounted for the long wait and a degree of nervous tension. He asked Dark, when he'd told him about it, 'What are you offering? Some whelk-stall need a manager?'

'It's a fill-in, if you wanted one. And if you're up to it physically. Only temporary, you see – might attract you, little swan to Norway? Did your AW training early on, didn't you?'

'Sure. But—'

'They're offering two and a half grand, Ollie. For a month's free winter sports.'

AW stood for Arctic Warfare, and AWT – Arctic Warfare Training – was part of the Royal Marine curriculum. Ollie had been through it before he'd joined the SB Squadron. In fact he'd been on two Northern Flank deployments in those earlier days. Dark was saying, 'I dare say you'd have uses for some ready cash, if you're having to wait for the word on this other thing?'

There was a pension for his years of service, obviously, but he'd resigned, hadn't been invalided; there was no other kind of compensation. No certainty he'd get the airline job, and if that fell through it could take a long time to find another. It wasn't just a matter of finding *a* job, either: having had the luck to have spent several recent years in employment from which the rewards included something like two hundred per cent job satisfaction, one had high standards now. On the money angle, too, for some years he'd been helping his widowed mother to keep her head above water. So the short answer to Dark's question was yes, he'd sooner devote the coming weeks to earning than to spending.

'Basic question first, Ollie – how's the wonky spine? Reckon you'd be OK on skis?'

'No question. I'm as sound as ever.'

'So why the fuck walk out on us?'

He hesitated. Then: 'Good question. Nothing relevant to the present discussion, though. OK?'

'I wouldn't want to put your name forward if that wasn't straight-up, Ollie.'

'Christ Almighty, I just bloody *told* you . . .' He checked himself: he'd heard Mary laugh, in the bedroom. Deep breath. 'Listen. The reason I ducked out was a suggestion I should leave the Squadron. That's *all*.'

'Well.' Dark sort of half laughed, too. 'You haven't changed, Ollie, have you.'

He didn't comment. There was a silence until Dark added, 'Main thing is, you *are* fit for a skiing trip.'

Cross-country skiing, it would be, in Norway. As it happened he'd been thinking of the downhill kind, a cheap package-deal trip to Austria, to kill some of the waiting period. Then Mary had said she couldn't make it – for various reasons, or rather excuses, adding up to the simple fact she didn't *want* to. . . . And whatever this stunt of Dark's was, it mightn't be a bad idea to get away for a while, give them both time to think things over. He was pretty sure she didn't feel the same about him as she had before he'd left the Corps, and that she had some sense of guilt about this, wouldn't want to admit it although he could understand it and didn't *blame* her for any such change of heart. It was less Christian tolerance on his part than pragmatic recognition of the fact he probably *had* changed – as she would be seeing him now – and that there was no mileage to be got out of busted flushes.

Two days later, in the MoD main building in Whitehall, Dark led him to a higher floor and along a mile of corridor, into the presence of a civilian called Jarvis who ranked as an Assistant Under Secretary. The PRO then left, saying he'd return when summoned, to take Ollie back to his own department. Visitors weren't encouraged to wander around this establishment on their own.

Jarvis was a man in early middle-age. Greying hair, pale complexion, well cut charcoal-grey suit, white shirt and striped tie. His office accommodation made it obvious that the letters AUS equated with VIP. It was a suite of two rooms, one with his desk in it and this other one furnished with a mahogany boardroom table with matching chairs set round it. Jarvis pulled out a chair for his guest, then sat down beside him. Declining the offer of a cigarette, Ollie was treated to a surprise close-up of his own face – blunt, wide jaw, wide-set eyes, the nose that hadn't set quite straight after an argument with a mainsail boom at the age of fifteen – reflected in the silver box's raised lid. From that he glanced up at the contrastingly smooth-looking character who was now lighting a cigarette and asking him through the first exhalation of smoke, 'I suppose Captain Dark sketched out the basics of our problem?'

'He said some Yank professor needs a minder to escort him through Lappland. *I* was saying, as we came along, I'd have thought you'd have looked for someone from the MAW cadre.'

That they'd have picked one of the Mountain and Arctic Warfare specialists, he meant. They were the real experts, far more so than the ordinary run of Arctic-trained men like himself. Jarvis agreed: 'That was the intention, and we did indeed look for one, but it seems they're few and far between. It does have to be an *ex*-Marine, of course.'

Because it was a civilian expedition: obviously they'd hire a civvie. Royals who were still serving wouldn't be available anyway. That figured, but he thought this high-level MoD involvement did not. It didn't yet, anyway. Smoke trickled from Jarvis' nostrils, and Ollie noticed his fingers were stained with nicotine. He was explaining, 'The American – the main one, actually there are two in the party – is a professor of social anthropology, by name Carl Sutherland. If you'd made any study of Lapps or Lappland you'd have heard of him through the book he published a few years ago. He's a lecturer at Harvard. Middle forties. His aim is to update his book, revise and expand it to cover the present political, politico-social situation, of which we've been hearing bits and pieces lately. His previous fieldwork was all done in the summer, when the nomadic, reindeer-herding Lapps are at the coast or on the islands, and he wants this winter trip now so as to see them in

21

their up-country quarters.' Jarvis shrugged. 'Apparently they retire to the highlands, inland, when the snow comes. God knows why. . . . But Sutherland is being given some financial assistance from the State Department and we've been brought into it by the Foreign and Commonwealth Office. There happens to be some special interest in Lappland, you see. Result of recent disturbances?'

'The air disaster at Tromsø.'

'Yes. The bomb in that 'plane was almost certainly put there by a Lapp, we're told. Oslo's been trying to play it all down, but – well, they've had some Lapps in for questioning, as you'll have read. But then Murmansk too?'

Within a few days of the Tromsø air crash there'd been Tass reports that a bomb had exploded outside a government building in that northern Soviet city, killing one passer-by and blowing out a lot of windows. A very unusual incident: at least, highly unusual for news of such anti-Soviet activism to have been allowed out by the Soviet censors.

'Have they pinned *that* on Lapps?'

'So we're informed. They're also taking it seriously enough to be deploying MVD troops close to the Norwegian border in the Kirkenes area to counter any trouble that might develop there. The Soviet border commissioner called a meeting with his Norwegian opposite number a few days ago, to explain what they were doing in case it might look like something more sinister. Border cooperation is very close and circumspect, you know, up there. They're careful not to make each other nervous.'

'I'd forgotten there were Lapps on the Soviet side of the border.'

'Kola Peninsula.' Jarvis gestured towards a wall map. 'Reindeer farming there was collectivised just after the Bolshevik revolution. You'd have thought they'd have been dutiful commie citizens by now, wouldn't you. . . . But coming back to the wider picture, Lyle – Sweden too, the riots in Norrbotten?'

'Yes, of course . . .'

There'd been damage to property but no deaths in the

Swedish riots. But from the Norwegian air disaster, a Douglas DC9 that had disintegrated in a fireball only minutes before it had been due to land at Tromsø, there'd been no survivors.

'We've had rumours of funny goings on in Finland, too. Not that Helsinki's telling us anything – and it may be no more than rumour. Flare-ups like this have been known before, haven't they, a group in one area following another lot's lead for no obvious reason. But the Norwegians are rather concerned, now. They have no positive evidence of any general problem, but – well, they do a great deal for their Lapp population – schools, housing, encouragement of the language, training for non-Lapp-type jobs, and so on. Despite which, they've had their difficulties, over the years. It's a complex issue dating from when God was a boy, but basically the Lapps feel they're second-class citizens – which they are not, incidentally, they have full political and social rights. And of restrictions interfering with their old, traditional lifestyle. Modern technological developments – hydro-electrical schemes or oil pipelines cutting ancient migration routes, for instance. But whatever the nuts and bolts of it, it's of interest to us – to NATO and to the West in general – because of the immense strategic importance of that Northern Flank.'

Ollie nodded.

'In summary, then – if anything was likely to happen that could destabilise the area, we'd want to know about it *before* it happened. That's why the Americans are supporting Sutherland's effort now. I hear the Norwegians are also sending a representative along, someone from their Department of Lapp Affairs, whatever they call it. I don't speak Norwegian – do you?'

'No—'

'But it was our own idea that we might provide an escort – 'minder' as you called it.' Jarvis slid spectacles on to his nose; steely light from across the Thames flashed on the lenses as he glanced down, opening a buff-coloured file. 'Do you want to take it on?'

'I do have about six weeks with nothing much to do.'

'Yes. Dark explained your situation. And despite the recent

accident you're sure you're up to it physically?'

'Well, I do a hundred press-ups every morning, I've been playing squash—'

'I'm sure' – Jarvis reached to stub out his cigarette – 'that you know better than I can what sort of exertions might be called for. If you say you can handle it—'

'I can. I promise you.'

'All right. Then let's get on with this.' He'd opened the file. 'Sutherland and his assistant, whose name is ...' Checking. ... 'Gus Stenberg. They're both described as competent skiers, and they've been through some course of survival training. You'd be expected to meet them in Alta in about a week. Rather short notice, but there we are.'

'As long as transport's available—'

'Oh, we'll get you there. That's to be our own contribution. But Dark's the man for you to see, on all such details. The Americans are already on their way – by ship to south Norway, then coastal steamer from Bergen to – oh, Tromsø, I think. Sutherland doesn't like flying. He was here last week, if we'd had you then you could have travelled with them.' Jarvis spread his hands: 'You'd have thought it would be easy to find a suitably qualified candidate for this job. *I* thought it would be. But until Dark produced you it was beginning to look hopeless. I suppose you're either a serving Royal Marine or you're out of that and into some good civilian job. Case of first-class material always in demand, eh?'

Flattery. Ollie waited.

'Well.' Fingering papers in the file. 'As I've said, Captain Dark will fill you in on detail. If there *was* any problem with transport I suppose you could get yourself there and claim reimbursement later. Any special equipment, ditto.'

'I've got most of what I'd need. But you mean—'

'I mean, refer to Dark. But – wider aspects now, Lyle. And this is between ourselves now. I have to explain that your value to *us* in this expedition will be less as escort, obliging the Americans, than as an observer. We'd like to have our own eyes and ears on the situation up there, you see.'

'Although I'll be on their payroll?'

'I'm sure you'll do the job they're hiring you for?'

That was an answer, apparently. . . .

'Will they know I'm reporting back to you?'

'No reason *they* shouldn't, but Sutherland himself is – well, somewhat typical of his kind. He has what he'd call a "liberal" outlook. His book argued the Lapp case, supported their grievances – which to describe briefly one might say are the sort of thing one used to hear of in connection with Red Indians. There's a tie-up there, too, Red Indians and Eskimos see themselves as in the same boat. They and the Lapps from all the Scandinavian countries get together in some kind of world conference to chew over mutual problems. And a few years ago, after a Norwegian Lapp had tried to blow up a bridge – near Alta, I think it was – he got away across the Atlantic and some Indian tribe took care of him. Then he was extradited. He'd blown his hand off, or part of it, hadn't damaged the bridge at all – and I'm told that's typical, that they've never been martially inclined. Although apparently it *was* a Lapp who planted the bomb in that 'plane.

'But my point is, Sutherland would have taken that man's side. Which, incidentally, is why he stands some chance of getting to the roots of whatever's happening. He's very much *persona grata* with politically-minded Lapps, because of his book. Which may explain to you the interest we have in this expedition: he may get somewhere where others would not. The Norwegians have suddenly caught on to this, too. But at the same time, paradoxically, he's not the sort of man one would rely on from other points of view. I'm not saying that if he hit on some real threat to the area's security he'd keep it to himself – one hopes he wouldn't – but on the other hand this is the north of Norway we're talking about, where our interests are quite vital and a Soviet land grab's been on the cards for decades. . . .' He paused again. 'You know all about that, of course. And we've said all that needs to be said about Carl Sutherland. We're left with his assistant, Stenberg, and he's rather different – apart from being a lot younger, of course.' Jarvis found the page in his notes. 'Stenberg, August, name usually abbreviated to "Gus". Age twenty-seven. Engaged in post-graduate studies in anthropology. But he's also an ath-lete, a valued player on the Harvard ball team.'

'Sounds like CIA potential.'

Jarvis smiled. 'Because he plays football?'

'Because they wouldn't be making the investment if they weren't expecting a return on it and, as you point out, they'd hardly get much mileage out of Sutherland. Stenberg looks like the answer.'

'Logical.' Jarvis shrugged. 'Except that as far as I know the interest in all this is purely NATO's. Another point I should make is that there's no kind of rivalry involved; anything you told us, we'd pass straight to the Americans. Our interests are identical, are they not. . . . All I'm asking you to keep in mind, Lyle, is that Sutherland may identify himself with Lapp inter-ests to a degree that blinds him to the wider issues. Eh?'

'So there'll be two of us – me and the ball-player – looking over the egghead's shoulder.'

'Or three of you.' Jarvis was lighting another cigarette. 'Oslo won't be sending *their* man along for nothing. . . . And before we leave this subject – if anything cropped up that you felt we'd want to hear about quickly, you could pass it by telephone to a Major Grayling who's on the staff of COM-NON. He's a Royal Marine, on an exchange posting related to oil-platform security. I'll give you day and night telephone numbers for him – just in case. . . .'

COMNON was an acronym for 'Commander, North Nor-way', a Norwegian national headquarters near Bodø, subordi-nate to the joint national and NATO headquarters at Kolsas near Oslo.

Jarvis said, as their meeting ended and while they waited for Barry Dark to come up and fetch him, 'I'm told you were in the Special Boat Squadron.'

Ollie looked at him. Surprised that he would have been told. It wasn't a thing you advertised, and you *never* discussed it, not even with other Royals who were not in the Squadron. Presumably Jarvis operated at such a dizzy height that he was privy to every kind of information: but it still didn't seem to Ollie to be any of his business. He said, 'I'm a civilian now, anyway.'

26

The civil servant's expression showed a mixture of interest and puzzlement. As if some other question was forming behind it. And he'd looked a bit surprised, Ollie recalled, when he'd first walked in here and they'd shaken hands; he'd noticed it and then forgotten it, but now he realised it had most likely been Jarvis' reaction to the fact this ex-SB man was only five foot nine inches tall and not noticeably built like a weight-lifter. People had these odd ideas: Special Boat men, like SAS, performed what seemed to be miracles, therefore should all look like Superman – or worse. . . .

At Evenes, where the ground temperature was twenty-two degrees below zero, and the hairs in his nostrils froze into prickly bristles as soon as he emerged from the aircraft, transport in the form of a half-ton Land-rover with studded tyres was waiting outside the wooden building of the military terminal to take Ollie and some of the Marine passengers to Elvegardsmoen, where the Commando was quartered. He was sure there'd have been an onward flight within an hour or so to Alta, but the arrangement was that he'd spend the night at Elvegardsmoen and go on by road next day. There was at least one useful dividend: arrangements had been made – or should have been – for a pair of Royal Marine cross-country skis, bindings and poles to be issued to him on temporary loan from the Commando's quartermaster's store.

He sat up front beside the Marine driver, chatting desultorily about the Commando's current preoccupations and admiring the winter scenery. Towering, snow-covered mountains, fjords with ice around their shores but steaming in the centre, rock-faces laminated with pastel-green ice several feet thick. The road had been scraped clear of loose snow, and the tyres' studs hammered on a hard-packed, icy underlay over which Norwegian motorists drove at what seemed like about sixty miles per hour without even slowing for the bends. They had studded tyres too, of course, and everyone drove with headlights on, as the law required, even at midday. In fact the daylight was nearly gone by the time they were running up the side of Herjangsfjord, with Narvik's lights glittering across the dark water: then they were passing through the village of Bjerkvik and swinging left. The driver muttered, 'Not far now, sir.'

'I know.'

'Ah. Yeah. . . .'

Remembering – he'd told him – he'd been here before. . . . But until the driver had broken in with that comment he'd been thinking about Mary, wondering whether he was right in his belief that she wanted out, or whether she might only have been reacting to his own edginess. He wouldn't have wanted to be running out on her, or hurting her. Remembering the exciting times, near-idyllic hours; and that not so long ago they'd had thoughts of making the idyll permanent.

'Here we go. . . .'

Left from the main road – it was the E6, also known as the Arctic Highway – and then winding over a snowbound track, snow banked high on either side, groves of leafless birch skeletal and gloomy as the vehicle's lights swept over them. . . . It was all familiar, from way back. Then the driver had swung left again, running down a straight length of track to where it ended at the officers' mess, a grey-painted two-storey building with a few pairs of skis dug into a snowbank outside it. Ollie slung his bergen over one shoulder and picked up his holdall, went up the steps and pushed into the hallway thinking, *Home, sweet home. . . .*

The mess itself, to the left off the hall, was deserted, but tea had been set ready on a side-table – tea, etceteras, bread and a toaster – so obviously there'd be some forms of life around before long. He went through to the back and found the mess manager, a sergeant, in his office.

'You're in the Red House, sir. If you know where that is?'

'Yeah.' He jerked a thumb. 'Unless they've moved it.'

'Fifty metres, first building on the right, red-painted. There's a bed for you in room three, you'll find. But I'll give you a hand with your gear, shall I?'

'No, hell—'

28

'Other thing is, would you telephone Captain Ellworthy? You could use this 'phone. . . .'

'Right.'

He hadn't seen Tam Ellworthy in years. But he was commanding HQ Company, the sergeant told him while he was getting through to that extension for him, then pushing the 'phone to him across the desk. . . . 'Hold on, sir. Captain Lyle, just booked in. . . .'

'That you, Tam?'

'Ollie, you old bastard!'

'Half a day late, aren't I? Crabs were late getting off the ground, then we had four fucking hours stuck at Gardermoen—'

'Better late than never. Look, I'll see you down there about half-six, OK?'

'Fine. But one thing, somewhat vital – anything fixed for my onward transportation to Alta, d'you know?'

'All laid on. Norwegian Army truck. We'll ship you over to them – transport from the mess at 0600 – bit early, I'm afraid.'

'Well, it's six hundred k's, isn't it. Anyway, early night, that means.'

'Fat chance of *that*.' Ellworthy laughed. 'Several of your former chums, including me, are keenly anticipating an evening of Old Lang Syne. No early bed for *you*, my lad!'

'Bloody hell. . . .' He changed the subject. 'One other point, though. Skis – they told me in London you'd—'

'I've got them for you – the new GRP variety, too, absolutely brand new. All you have to do is sign on the dotted line and make sure we get 'em back. Look, I'll come to the Red House at six-thirty, I'll bring them then and we can go on up to the mess from there, OK?'

Ollie treated himself to tea, toast and honey in the deserted mess before lumping his gear down to the Red House. He'd had very little to eat all day, except breakfast at Lyneham before takeoff and the standard box of snacks on the aircraft. Then, down at the Red House – which was more of a shack than a house – he'd showered and changed and reorganised his gear for the next day's long drive north, and was reading a paperback when Tam Ellworthy showed up. He was the same age, roughly, as Ollie – which meant thirty, thirty-one – tall, fair, prematurely balding. They'd joined the corps at about the same time and served together as subalterns, consequently had numerous friends in common from those days of yore and a lot of gossip to catch up on.

The white GRP cross-country skis were a vast improvement on the old wooden kind which until very recently had been the standard issue, known to all Royal Marines as 'pusser's planks'. The cost of these new ones was justified, Ellworthy explained, by the high incidence of breakage they'd always had before. Ollie adjusted the bindings to fit his own Lundhags ski-march boots, while Tam sat on the bed and talked and one or two other Red House residents looked in to say hello.

'Speaking of old chums, Ollie, we had some SB characters through here last week. Not part of the brigade deployment, a special team en route to some place further north, some demonstration for the Norwegians. Guy in charge called Brabant?'

Mike Brabant was a Special Boat Squadron lieutenant with whom Ollie had served in the Falklands. He was sorry he'd missed seeing him. 'How many – I mean, who else?'

'A WO2 by name of Beale—'

'Tony Beale!'

'—and six Marines. Demo team, they were calling themselves.'

Tony Beale, then a colour sergeant, had been one of a party who'd gone into mainland Argentina to castrate Exocet missiles, during the Falklands fracas. Then they'd been ashore on East Falkland for about the last week of it, and last year Ollie had had the newly promoted warrant officer – sergeant major, warrant officer 2nd class – with him on another enterprise, elsewhere. He'd have enjoyed a reunion with old Tony: being out of it now, and having no idea when if ever there'd be another chance to meet. . . . He and Ellworthy were walking over to the mess by this time. Snow lying deep, wind cutting enough to draw blood. Tam said, 'I suppose you know the whole brigade's out here this year?'

Ollie nodded. 'For Anchor Express.'

Two Commandos — the other was in southern Norway at present but would move north later — together with the various supporting and specialist units which made up the full strength of 3 Commando Brigade RM, had deployed for this three-month stint that would culminate in Exercise 'Anchor Express' involving twenty thousand NATO troops — including six thousand US Marines , two Norwegian brigades and the Ace Mobile Force, a brigade representative of all NATO countries and currently including the British 1 Para, Italian Alpinis, Canadians . . .

'We were all damn sorry to hear you'd got careless, Ollie. You were lucky to come out of it, weren't you?'

Pushing in through the outer door, he nodded. 'Could've been a lot worse.'

'Like terminal. . . . Anyway, I'm glad you have this other job prospect. It's nice to think that if one did have to go outside—'

'Ah, Captain Lyle, sir. . . .'

The mess manager. Ollie stopped. 'Yes, Sergeant Hoyle.'

'I was just going to send a message down — telephone from a Major Grayling RM at COMNON, sir. He asked would you call him back, please. Here's his number.'

'Thanks.' He took the bar-chit with a number pencilled on it. 'I suppose I'd better use your office again.'

'Telephone's on the bar.' Ellworthy pushed the door open. 'Quiet enough, this early. But what's a Royal Marine officer doing at COMNON, I wonder?'

It was a reasonable question, since COMNON was a Norwegian national HQ, not a NATO command. Although the Norwegian general there would put on a NATO hat once any emergency broke out and Norwegian forces were committed to NATO control. Ollie explained, 'Exchange posting, I was told, connected with oil-platform security. But he's also my contact if I need one.'

The bar was at the far end of the long, narrow room. Portraits of Norwegian royals stared down from the walls. Ollie was through to Grayling quite quickly.

'Lyle here. At Elvegardsmoen. I had a message to call you back.'

Grayling must have been eating something. 'Ah, Lyle. Yes, right.' He'd swallowed. 'Fine. Good trip, was it?'

'Not really. Just as usual.' He waited, and Grayling said – more clearly now – 'I have some information for you, Lyle. It's not at all pleasant, I'm sorry to say. But you'd better let Sutherland know about it, when you get up there. In confidence – we don't want headlines. . . . When will you be joining him, incidentally?'

'Tomorrow. Probably quite late, some time in the evening.'

There was a pause while Grayling digested this, probably made a note of it. Then he began, 'This report emanates from Helsinki. Source as yet unidentified but vouched for by responsible authority in Oslo. It's to the effect that twelve days ago a Finn security patrol, a team of three men briefed to investigate the stories of Lapp unrest, just vanished. Nobody had any way of knowing where they were or had been, or what they'd been doing; they could have been anywhere in Finnish Lappland – which as you don't need telling is a hell of a big wilderness. These chaps should've reported in to their base at certain intervals, and they didn't. Their leader was a *vanrikki* – that's Finnish for second lieutenant – and despite the junior rank he was a very experienced operator, half Lapp, commissioned from the ranks. But – coming to the nasty bit – they've now been found. Somewhere in the depths of nowhere, central Finland. They were naked and they'd been stabbed, clean stab wounds into the hearts. Frozen like boards, of course, but set up in some kind of ritualistic fashion on the site of what was – repeat *was*, hundreds of years ago – a Lapp sacrificial site.'

'Sacrificial . . .'

'No clothes, weapons or any other gear. No tracks either, but there've been heavy snowfalls in that region. These Finns were armed and well trained, experienced undercover operators, should've been able to look after themselves. A final detail is that the leader hadn't only been stabbed, he'd also been either speared or shot in the neck, and if it was a bullet it may have been dumdum. The theory is it probably happened before he was stabbed, because stabbing into the heart apparently has some ritual significance – did have, way back – which could explain it having been done after this *vanrikki* was dead. Sutherland might be able to throw light on that point, from his knowledge of – er – Lappery. . . . But what strikes me hardest is – well, God's sake, a certain amount of Lapp unrest, agitation – that's one thing, it's a nuisance, even potentially destabilising maybe – oh, OK, the bomb on the Tromsø flight, that's a lot more than a nuisance, but there's no skill in it, is there, any bloody lunatic, psychopath . . . No, what I'm trying to say, the thing that gets me, Lyle, is those three Finns are described as having been professionals!'

'Nothing amateur about whoever greased them, then.'

'Exactly. *Exactly* . . .'

2

He'd been asleep, was awake again now with fragments of dream fading as he checked the time and decided the truck must now be about sixty kilometres north of Narvik. His estimate was confirmed as about right by the truck's headlights briefly illuminating a roadsign that said BANDVOLL: and the driver was shifting gear, to cope with a steepening incline. Braced back in his seat against the truck's lurching, its tyres rumbling like distant drums and the Norwegian driver a dark silhouette stolid and silent on his left; attempts at conversation had petered out somewhere around Storfossen. The driver spoke no English and Ollie had only a dozen words of Norwegian; he'd tried German — his own German being quite good — but that hadn't got him anywhere either.

Storfossen must have been roughly where he'd fallen asleep. And the lights visible ahead would be the twin towns of Bardu and Setermoen, he guessed. It was a big military area, camps and ranges, with the Bardufoss airfield at the top end, thirty kilometres up the road. The road being the E6, the Arctic Highway, which reached right around the top of Norway and as far as Kirkenes on the Soviet border. Not, thank God, that he'd be in this conveyance for anything like *that* distance, only for about — well, maybe another five hundred kilometres, to Alta. And that was going to be far enough.

Norwegian Army vehicles didn't have studded tyres. They used the same ones all year round.

The irritant stirring in the back of his mind now was the thought on which he'd dropped off to sleep last night. *No weapon* ...

Grayling's story about the murdered Finns had triggered it. Although in fact it was also a point he'd raised in London with the civil servant, Jarvis. Since he was being hired to protect these Yanks, and Jarvis himself had been open to the possibility that something very peculiar might be going on, presumably it could be fixed for him to import a hand-gun?

The Assistant Under Secretary had looked shocked.

'My dear chap, what on earth for?'

'If as you suggest there's a "threat to the stability of the area", that means trouble of some kind, surely. And if I'm supposed to look after them—'

'I see. ...' A shake of the head, faint smile accompanying it. ... 'I very much doubt that the Norwegian authorities would sanction the import of any firearm by a civilian. Of course, if you applied for a hunting licence — but there's hardly time, is there. ... In any case, Lyle, I'm sure they aren't thinking of quite *that* kind of protection!'

Jarvis wanted a pair of eyes and ears there, nothing else. Jarvis or whoever gave him his orders. Ollie had felt embarrassed for having suggested that he might need to be armed; there'd been a hint of derision in that dismissal, as if Jarvis might have been thinking *Christ, now he's trying to play cowboys.* ... So he'd put it out of mind, and the only weapon he had with him was a knife. Not the traditional Royal Marine Commando fighting knife, the dagger that had never been very useful and wasn't issued now in any case, but one he'd carried for some years and used in numerous expeditions, a survival knife with a wooden haft and a quarter-inch thick carbon steel blade heavy enough to use for chopping wood. It was in its leather sheath inside his bergen, in the back of the truck with his civvie holdall and the skis — for which he'd also scrounged —

in Bootneck terminology 'proff'd' – a supply of Swix ski-waxes suitable for all the likely snow conditions.

The driver made a refuelling stop at Andselv, beside the military airfield, and daylight arrived about an hour later when they were running downhill with an ice-covered gorge on the right and then, ahead soon after on their left, the broad head of Balsfjorden, which the road skirted for about the next twenty kilometres. They were leaving the water now, climbing again, snow deep on both sides of the road, luminous green ice decorating the sheer rock walls. Bits and pieces of the puzzle floating in his thoughts. The comment by Jarvis, for instance, that Lapps were not a warlike people – meaning that they were basically non-violent. Jarvis might re-think this, when he heard about the Finns who'd been slaughtered. Which surely had to be part and parcel of the recent pattern of violence – the aircraft bomb right in this area, and the Murmansk one, the riots in Sweden ... But on the subject of that bomb on the flight south from Alta, the Commando's second-in-command had remarked last night that if *he* was a terrorist and had been thinking of planting a bomb in some airliner, Alta was one of the two places in the world that he'd have chosen. The other was Kirkenes, close to the Soviet border. Because at neither of those small airports, he'd explained, was there any security at all. Passengers checked-in their own bags, and nobody tallied them against tickets or travellers.

'So it wouldn't have to be a resident of Alta who did it.'

'Right. Could've gone there simply because it's a soft target, no risk to the bomber whatever.'

The next fuelling stop was at Sørkjosen, in mid afternoon. By then he'd eaten all his sandwiches and drunk most of his flask of coffee, the general direction of the highway had become more easterly than north, and the light was fading. The driver had gulped food and drink during the halts for petrol, but he also ate sweets and chocolate most of the time. 'Langfjorden.'

'What's that?'

The driver gestured with his left hand, and repeated 'Langfjorden'.

They'd passed through a place called Bognelf. Ollie unfolded the map again and shone a pencil torch on it. At least another couple of hours. . . . And he could have flown the whole distance in two hours, from Evenes last evening.

The truck sped into Alta, its lights blazing yellowish on the snow-covered road, just before eight-thirty. Using the map again, he was looking out for a road junction, a point where a right turn would lead off southwards, Route 93 into the interior of Lappland and the Finnmark *vidda*, but before they'd reached it the driver braked, changed gear, swung in towards a line of flagpoles, up a cleared tarmac driveway skirting a flat area of dirty snow and broadening out in front of a long, two-storied building with light flooding out of all its windows. He hadn't expected the long day's haul to come to an end so suddenly, but he read the floodlit sign *ALTAFJORD TURISTHOTELL* and realised this was it.

He was taking a shower when the telephone buzzed in the bedroom. He went through, dripping; this would be Sutherland or the other one. He'd asked the blonde girl in reception, when he'd been filling in the registration card, to let the professor know he'd arrived.

He picked up the 'phone. 'Lyle here.'

'Captain Lyle, this is Carl Sutherland. Welcome aboard. . . . And look, we're in room 110 and we'd be happy if you'd join us when you're ready. There's no bar, you see.'

'*No bar?*'

'I was sort of prostrated too, when they told me. The truth is they'll sell wine or beer in the dining-room, and there *is* a bar — dancing-bar they call it — but for some reason it doesn't open this evening. So the only place you can get a real drink is right here, room 110.'

He dressed and went along, found room 110, knocked and walked in. They were standing with glasses in their hands, facing him as he entered, and his first sight of them, reality, as always, called for instant mental readjustment, correction of images that had been wide of the mark. Sutherland was the short guy with the balding head and ginger beard, small sloping shoulders, creases in his forehead like contours on a map. Pale eyes glinted as he shook hands. Both Americans studying *him*, too, of course, all three of them interested to see who'd be with them in the wilderness. . . . 'Glad to have you on the team, Captain.'

He thought, *Oh, God*. . . . Then forced the smile back, and nodded. 'With what sounds like Prohibition in force, I'm lucky to be on it, too. But call me Ollie, would you?'

'Ollie. Great. I'm Carl – OK? And this guy here is my sidekick Gus Stenberg.'

He'd visualised the ball-player as beefy, back-slapping, crewcut, soap-opera profile. But Stenberg had a narrow face, thin-bridged nose, deepset eyes with a lot of intelligence behind them. Thick, dark hair – no kind of crewcut – and he was tall and wide-shouldered, a skier's build for sure. His handshake was firm, but unlike Sutherland he didn't try to impress with it. Ollie recalled that Jarvis had given this one's age as twenty-seven; he'd have guessed at five years more.

Sutherland was holding up a jug with some kind of mixture and ice in it. 'Vodka martini suit you, Ollie? Happens to be what we have in this pitcher. Alternatively there's Scotch whisky, but only tap-water to put in it – if you wanted anything in it. Unless we could screw some more ice out of these good people. Gus, you're the guy with all the charm, maybe *you* could—'

'Scotch and tap-water'd be fine. Even if you had ice I wouldn't want it.'

'Because there's plenty out where we're headed, right?'

Sutherland was at the washbasin, getting water. Ollie glanced at Stenberg. 'When do we start?' But Sutherland answered, turning with the glass in his hand: 'Actually, I've started. Right here in Alta. Now – there you go. . . .' Passing him the tumbler; then reaching for his own glass again. 'To a great trip.' They drank to it, and Stenberg told Ollie quietly, 'Day after tomorrow, we expect to start south, to Kautokeino. We've rented a VW minibus and they're checking it over, fitting new snowtyres and so on.'

'Glad I haven't delayed you, then.'

'No way.' Sutherland said, 'Our Norwegian colleague has yet to show up, for one thing. Flying in tonight, supposed to land here 2140 – right, Gus?' Stenberg nodded almost imperceptibly: he was watching the professor in a detached sort of way. Critical way, maybe. Or as if he thought he was putting on some kind of act. Sutherland added, 'We did think of waiting supper, but she may have eaten on the airplane.'

'No bombs on this flight, let's hope.' Ollie did a double-take, then. 'Did you say "she"?'

'—like to get our ideas straight on this, now.' Sutherland scowling, talking fast: 'Let's forget the bomb thing – OK? Because none of that stuff fits with what we're doing or hoping to do. My opinion, it's a load of eyewash anyway. As I just said, I've made a start here, and nothing I've heard yet suggests these rumours are anything *but* rumours. Can we agree on this, Ollie?'

'Rumours about Lapp unrest, you mean.'

'*Certainly* that's what I mean!'

'I hope you're right.' Jarvis had been right about this one, anyway. . . . He added, 'Someone was saying last night that there are no security precautions at all at the Alta airport.'

'Told you nothing but the truth.' Stenberg stirred, from his observer's position on the sidelines. 'I was down there today, saw it for myself. *Incredible*. You walk in, there's an overhead sign says "Baggage Check-in", and a rack with boxes of labels for all the destinations. So if you're travelling to – well, Oslo, say, you pull out as many Oslo labels as you have pieces of luggage, write the flight number on them and tie them on, then you haul your stuff through an archway and load it into an open-top truck marked "Oslo". In point of fact the flight that bomb was on—'

'If it was a bomb.' Sutherland shook his head. 'As far as I've heard that hasn't been positively established, has it?'

40

'OK. Let's call it the flight that exploded in mid-air.' Stenberg had a slightly crooked smile. His sweater was Norwegian, mostly red and white with a frieze of antlered reindeer in the pattern. 'Flight SK 375, takes off daily at 1540. Two baggage trucks provided, one Oslo and one Tromsø – where the flight touches down on its way south. The bomb went off –' he glanced at Sutherland, 'or as I should say, the explosion occurred – a few minutes before the scheduled Tromsø landing, so the bag that *might* have had a bomb in it could've been left in either of the trucks. They bring a tractor and tow 'em out on the apron for loading, and passengers only show their tickets as they go out to board. So, once that stuff's labelled and in the truck, the guy who brought it could just go home. Or he could sit around, eat a sandwich and drink a beer – make like he's waiting for his flight and then slip away nearer takeoff when there's a crowd to confuse any surveillance. Not that I believe there is any. My guess is he'd have dumped it and walked right out.'

Sutherland said, 'You didn't tell me you were down at the *flyplass*.'

'Well, I had the time to spare, since you didn't want any recording done, and I was curious. . . . I mean, Christ's sake, this day and age, the age of terrorism, who'd *believe* it?'

'And even since the bomb they haven't changed it, eh?'

'Norwegians are very trusting.' Stenberg shrugged. 'Seem to imagine everyone else is honest like they are. There's also the theory that lightning never hits twice in one place. Nonsense, of course . . .'

'Ollie, I'd really like you to understand me on this issue.' Sutherland's tone was earnest. 'I'll accept it, there most likely *was* a bomb. But there's no valid reason to link it with these rumours of trouble-making by Sami dissidents. If indeed any such thing is happening. I flatter myself I understand these people rather better than most of us do, Ollie.'

He was going to have to get along with this guy. Even if it killed him. Stenberg was OK, anyway. He nodded: 'Your book was the definitive statement, I was told.'

'Precisely why I need to revise it now, adjust to the changes and the extent to which environmental changes have affected them. . . . You didn't read it?'

'No. I looked for a copy, but they said they'd have to order it, and there wasn't time.'

'I have one I could lend you. Put you on the wavelength?'

'Well, thanks.' As it happened, he was genuinely interested, aware of knowing nothing about Lapps. 'Are there many here in Alta?'

'It's a Lapp town. Well, it *was*. And sure, lots of them. It's also a fascinating place in terms of Sami origins. Would you believe it, they've dug out fossilised Lapp skis that've been carbon-dated as three thousand years old? And just along the road here you can see rock paintings *six* thousand years old!'

'Well. . . .'

'But Ollie,' Stenberg put in, 'you asked are there many Samis here, and while the answer is, sure, there are, the fact is a lot of them wouldn't want to have you know them as such. OK, you get a lot who're proud of their origins, who wear the traditional costume on Sundays and special occasions, have real pride in their ancestry. But plenty more who'd sooner forget it. Basically, because they expect to be looked down on. Like in the States a guy with Indian blood won't be quick to announce it, not if he's in the mainstream, competing?'

'And who's responsible for *that*, one might ask.' Sutherland reached over. 'Let me fill that glass, Ollie. We're a couple ahead of you.'

'Right. . . .'

At least he wasn't mean with his Scotch. He poured a good tot, too.

'Social and political attitudes aren't clearly separable, of course. Chickens and eggs — right? But that scenario is illustrative of the majority population's attitude to the Samis, the way it forces on them this kind of — well, you could call it class-consciousness.' He handed Ollie the refilled glass. 'Too brown?'

'Exactly the right shade.'

'Then, the majority population choose to imagine that resentments that they themselves have created by their attitudes are signals of revolt. That's the majority's guilt-complex showing through, right?' But it's taking it too damn far when some lunatic puts a bomb on an airplane and just because it happens in Lappland they all take it as read a Sami did it.' He spread his hands. 'OK, maybe it *was* a Sami. So what? In most barrels you'll find a rotten apple, or two or three. But there's no upheaval, they aren't all nuts or something, just sensitive, a lot of well-founded grievances on certain issues that are important to them. It's all in my book, you'll find. But for a correct perspective the first thing to grab hold of is the fact these people's ancestors lived here literally thousands of years before anyone even knew what a Norwegian, Swede or Finn *was*. OK?'

Stenberg said, 'The local cops did have some Samis in for questioning. *They* obviously think that's where the bad apples are.'

'They *thought*. . . Gus, they let 'em all go, right?'

'Sure.' Stenberg held the professor's glare calmly. 'Sure they did, Carl. All I'm saying—'

'Look.' Sutherland turned to Ollie. 'I apologise. You just got here, and I start right in lecturing.' He looked down at the amber glow in Ollie's glass. 'If you'd drink up now, we might see what there is to eat. Before they shut the fucking dining-room too?'

The dining-room was on the far side of reception. Sutherland told Ollie as they walked through, 'Whatever you want, any place we're staying at, it goes on the one check and I pay. OK?'

'Excellent arrangement. Thanks.'

'And on that subject, Ollie, you'll get your fee in the form of a bank draft payable in London when we're through. If in the meantime you want a float, for incidental expenses—'

'I brought some krone with me. Thanks all the same.'

'Right.' Sutherland led them to a table beside a window. 'May as well keep the same table we've been at this far. The set menu's the best value. And since wine is a crazy price in this country I'd suggest we stick to beer. All right?'

'Fine.' Ollie nodded. 'But this might be a good moment for

43

me to ask a few questions. Some things I'm not clear on. D'you mind?'

'Before I start the next lecture.' He grinned as he sat down. 'OK, Ollie, shoot.'

'The first is a very basic and broad question. What d'you want me to do on this trip, to earn my fee? Another is where are we going when we push off from here – and when . . . Oh, and when you mentioned the Norwegian who's coming, I think you said "she". Or did I hear wrongly?'

'You heard right. Is that the full list now?'

'Just to kick off with. . . . But listen – sorry, but I've remembered something more urgent – not a question, something I have to tell you, news I got last night when I landed. Rather far from pleasant, I'm afraid.'

Sutherland was facing Ollie at the window end of the table; the tightening of his expression showed that he was not a man to welcome bad news. Over the professor's left shoulder Ollie could see out through the glass doors to the foyer, to where the blonde girl receptionist was booking in some new arrivals. Skis amongst that luggage . . . Sutherland said with an effort, 'OK, we better hear this.'

'I suppose they didn't telephone you about it from Oslo or somewhere – report about the killings in Finland?'

Sutherland's pale eyes widened slightly. He shook his head. Stenberg muttered, 'Here we go. . . .'

'A security patrol, undercover unit, three men led by a half-Lapp lieutenant. All three experienced and armed, supposed to be investigating the rumours you've been talking about – the Finnish end of them, presumably. Two weeks ago they vanished, failed to report in to their base. No one knew whereabouts they'd been operating. But yesterday – could've been the day before – they were found dead. I can't say precisely where, but well down in the middle of Finland and in the wilderness, miles from anywhere. My informant made the point that it was a long way south from where he thought *you*'d be working.'

'How had they been killed?'

'Hang on a minute.' The waitress was coming with their

beers. He asked Sutherland, 'Did the Sami people at some time in their history have places where they made human sacrifices?'

Stenberg groaned: 'Oh, Jesus.'

The waitress was putting down glasses and uncapping bottles; Sutherland told her they'd pour it for themselves, and she went away. He confirmed, 'There is some evidence of it. Far more animal sacrifice than human, but – yeah, it did occur. The sacrificial sites were called *seide* or *saivo*. *Saivo* in fact referred to the Sami version of Paradise or 'happy hunting ground'. Very close to the Red Indian tradition, you see. Some of the sites were more or less public, others were kept secret; usually there'd be some outstanding natural feature like a peculiarly shaped rock, or an ancient tree stump.' He took a breath. 'Go on, then.'

'They'd been stabbed. Stripped naked and stabbed into their hearts, then set up in some ritual arrangement on this sacrificial place. The bodies were frozen solid, of course. No possessions or clothes anywhere around.' He added, low voiced because there were other diners not so far away, 'Some special significance about stabbing in the heart, I was told?'

'Sure, it's the traditional way of slaughtering reindeer.' Stenberg got in ahead of his professor. 'It's how they *used* to do it, actually. Now it's controlled – I mean slaughtering is controlled, has to be done the regular way in abattoirs. But that's the seasonal slaughtering, mind you, for the mass market, which they do in the Fall. When they're only killing an animal for their own consumption I guess they'd use the old method.'

Ollie nodded. 'The lieutenant had also been either shot or speared, in the neck, and they think he might have been dead before he was stabbed.'

'*Well*.' Stenberg looked at the professor. 'Point to you, Carl. Stabbing might have been just for show? To make it *look* a Sami killing?'

'In contemporary contexts there is no such thing as a ritual Sami killing, damn it.' Sutherland shook his head angrily. 'The records indicating human sacrifice as having occurred in isolated instances are two hundred years old – when the whole damn world was cock-eyed anyway.' He followed Ollie's glance, saw the waitress approaching with prawn cocktails. 'But this is a hell of a thing to believe, Ollie. . . .'

'These prawns were most likely swimming around in the sea not long ago. We're in prawn country, right?' Stenberg thanked the waitress, a brief exchange in Norwegian, which seemed to please her. He asked Ollie, 'D'you speak the language?'

'Wish I did.'

'Well, no sweat. We both do. And my mentor here, being the kind of genius he is, can also get along in Lappish.'

'Very difficult to learn, I'm told.'

'Difficult?' A shake of the head. 'It's *impossible*.' The waitress had gone now. 'Where did this information come from, Ollie?'

'A contact at NATO headquarters near Bodø. I had a message to call him when I arrived yesterday, and that's what he wanted to tell me. Asked me to pass it on to you, Carl. The report came from Helsinki via Oslo.'

'And those Finns—' Sutherland began to eat '—would have been looking into the same kind of research area that *I'll* be in.'

'Which was why you had to hear about it, I suppose.'

'Well, *Jesus*—'

'Wait a minute.' Stenberg pointed at him with his spoon. 'It's not the same *at all*, if you just think about it. For one thing, we won't be in Finland. Also, you're an extremely well-known authority on Samiland and the Samis – not some Finn spook nosing around where they didn't want him. Also highly relevant is that you're well established in the Sami consciousness as a friend and ally, you might say as a champion of their cause.' He shook his head. 'Nobody's going to stick a knife in you, Carl – the Norwegian government might feel inclined to, but—'

'I assure you, my government would not dream of such a thing!'

Female voice, close by. They all looked up, and the blonde from reception was saying in English, 'This is Professor Sutherland, Miss Eriksen. And Mr Stenberg and Mr Lyle.'

46

'I think *Captain* Lyle.'

She was quite tall, dark-haired, and every man in the room was looking at her. About twenty-seven, twenty-eight, Ollie guessed. Not conventionally beautiful, but – striking. . . . She was about level, eye-to-eye with him: the three of them were on their feet and she was telling Sutherland in Norwegian-accented English, 'I am Sophie Eriksen, you are kindly allowing me to join you on your tour? I just flew up from Oslo. I am most happy to meet you, professor – of course I read your book when it was first published. . . .'

Stenberg was eyeing her wolfishly, Sutherland turning pink as he pulled out the fourth chair for her. 'You'll join us, I hope? Haven't dined yet?' Ollie heard him mutter to the receptionist, 'Have someone bring us a wine list, would you?' Economy was going out of the window, it seemed. Sophie Eriksen folded her slim body into the chair; she was wearing expensive-looking soft leather trousers and a loose green alpaca sweater that wasn't quite loose enough to hide her shape. Ollie deciding that she was, in fact, terrific. . . . But what a crew to be taking into the wilderness. Stenberg would be OK, he thought. Sutherland – well, time and proximity would tell. And now this exciting-looking girl: who surely wouldn't make the trip any *less* interesting. . . .

'So, Captain Lyle—'

'No, I'm not a Marine any more. Name's Ollie.'

'Ollie.' A nod. . . . 'I was going to say I did not know you had arrived yet.'

'I wasn't far ahead of you. Just this evening, by road.'

'I was told that you had a bad accident. Parachuting? But you're all right now, obviously. . . .' Then he'd lost her to Sutherland: the waitress had brought a wine list and Sophie had turned to advise him that he might do best to go for the house wines – there, *Husets Rodvin*, if he wanted a red one. . . . 'I hope you don't mind that I suggest this – the prices are so crazy, as you can see.' Sutherland nodding like a metronome: 'Right, right. . . .' It was some Norwegian blend that she was recommending. Ollie, only half-hearing this discussion, thought back to the murdered Finns. It was the presence of this extremely attractive girl that had switched his thoughts to that atrocity: because she'd be with them and Sutherland *would* be nosing into this Lapp business, and despite Gus Stenberg's recent blather – in which there was an obvious flaw anyway – there couldn't be much doubt that there were elements around who were hostile to any displays of curiosity.

And what could he, Ollie Lyle, do to protect any of them, if the worst came to the worst? Throw snowballs?

Small-talk was still in progress. Ollie waiting, barely hearing it, wanting to talk about things that mattered: and there *were* a few. . . . The pause came, finally, and he moved in with 'Sophie, I suppose your department had the report about the Finn soldiers they've found murdered?'

'Oh.' Her expression changed. 'Yes. We did. . . . I see, you've told them?'

Sutherland said, frowning, 'We could discuss it later, maybe.'

'We *must*.' She nodded. 'I was not expecting you to have heard of it so soon.' Glancing round, seeing who else might be in earshot. 'We certainly do have to discuss it. There are some details that reached us only this morning – rather *clinical* detail, if that's the word?'

Her English was already less stilted, he noticed, just from the last ten minutes' use of it. . . . Sutherland said, 'If it *is* the word, all the more reason to leave it until we've finished our meal. OK?'

'Sure.' Ollie nodded. 'The issue that's bothering me, though – well, correct me if you disagree, Sophie, but I'd imagine those Finns would have been asking the sort of questions that Carl will be asking. Gus pointed out, a short while ago, that the professor's book has established him as an ally of the Lapp people, so that *he* wouldn't be in any similar danger, but—'

'Excuse me.' She cut in. 'That's assuming the killers were Sami people.'

'*Right.*'

It was the flaw he'd seen too, in Stenberg's theory, and he'd also noticed the double-think in Sutherland's acceptance of it,

Sutherland refusing to see the Lapps as instigators of violence but still accepting that being their champion might guarantee his safety. He told her, 'Carl has doubts of that, I mean on the likelihood of Sami involvement. Would you agree with him?'

'It comes into what I have to tell you later.'

'Ah . . . So meanwhile I'll air my own problem. I'm supposed to be responsible for this expedition's safety. At least, that's what they hired me for.' Sutherland moved to interrupt him, but he went on, 'And I'm told those three Finns were armed. It couldn't have helped them much, but you'd have thought it should have, and the point is I am *not* armed. It bothers me, frankly.'

'Yes. I understand your concern.' She'd nodded, taking the point seriously. He was surprised – having expected her, like Jarvis, to take the view that he was being unnecessarily alarmist. Sutherland also showed surprise, and Sophie added, 'Before we received the Helsinki report I probably would not have agreed, but with the circumstances as they *appear* to be . . .' She shrugged, left the sentence unfinished, sipping her glass of wine.

'Is there any chance you could help – to get me a firearm licence, hunting permit, whatever?'

'I could make enquiries. Tomorrow we might go to the *Lensmannen*.'

'Well, that'd be marvellous. . . .'

'Ollie.' Sutherland turned to him. 'Let me relieve your anxieties a little. What I was looking for was back-up of a rather more general nature. Escort, sure, in a sense, but I certainly never asked for an armed guard, for Pete's sake. For instance, we don't want to get lost out there – and you'd be good with a map, right? Also I'd hoped you'd handle the driving, or most of it. Especially when my first idea was to get hold of some kind of tracked over-snow vehicle, which I was told you'd be familiar with – although I've learnt since then that we're OK on wheels until such times as we may want to leave the main highways. But I'd be relying on your advice in facing up to adverse climatic conditions, problems of terrain when we're off the beaten tracks, all that stuff. I may as well

49

explain, while I'm at this rostrum so to speak, that it's not my intention to spend much time in the wilds, mainly to handle outlying places by short excursions from the two main centres. Most of the Sami population of Finnmark is around Kautokeino and Karasjok, after all. We'll take Kautokeino first, since that's the nearest, hole up there in some degree of comfort—'

'At the *turisthotell*?'

'Right, Sophie. No need to starve or freeze when we don't have to.'

'But some fieldwork we'll be doing on skis?'

'*Some*, sure. . . .'

'It's what I love most.' Her eyes shone with enthusiasm. 'To cross the open *vidda* on skis, you know?' Glancing from Ollie's smile to Stenberg's interest. . . . 'In winter down there, Gus, not so many people ever see it, but my God, it is fantastic. . . . One winter before I have been there, camping and stopping some places with Sami people.'

'D'you talk Lappish?'

'Oh, yes, that is how I got the job I have. . . . But the scenery, the great distances and the silence – it's another world . . .'

She began – when the meal was finished, coffee on the table: 'We should talk about this horrible event in Finland now, do you think?' Ollie lit her cigarette for her, then his own. Sutherland was cutting a cigar, and Gus didn't smoke. Ollie had given it up years earlier but since the malfunction of that parachute he'd decided he might as well start again. Sophie asked them, 'I suppose you know the soldiers were stabbed in the way Sami mountain people have been used to killing reindeer?'

'Except the leader had also been shot, or speared, possibly before he was stabbed.'

'Yes.' She frowned. 'Professor – in your research work, did you ever read that the reindeer Samis in southern Lappland used a *double* stab?'

50

'My God, *yes!*' Sutherland snapped his fingers. 'I'd forgotten that! You're damn right, though – a paralysing blow first!'

'And why then would a Sami from that part, if he wished to make a public display of these murders, make a *wrong* display?'

'He wouldn't, would he.'

'So the murderer was ignorant of this. All right, it does not prove it was not Samis who did it, because there are so many who have forgotten the old ways. As of course you know well, professor. But another detail now. In the traditional manner of slaughtering, north or south it makes no difference, the custom was to leave the knife in the heart – to stop the outflow of blood, save it for, well, various purposes. But there would always be *some* bleeding, of course. In the place where these bodies were found there was none at all, not in the bodies and not in the snow. Blood is easy to see in snow, you know?'

Ollie pointed out that according to his own informant there'd been heavy snowfalls in that area recently, so surely blood traces would have been covered.

'There had been snowfalls, as always at this time of year, but the bodies themselves were not buried by it so deep they could not be found. Huh? And in any case, you scrape away the top layers and if you continue, removing layer by layer, you come to it. Maybe stained ice by that time because of the compression of more weight on top, but whether snow or ice the bright colour remains until there is a thaw. And my information is there was not one spot of staining in that area. So it is beyond doubt that the bodies were carried there, and what *this* tells us is simply that the murders could have been committed *anywhere.*'

'Even well up to the north. Norwegian side of the border even.'

Stenberg had said it. Sophie shrugged: 'Or east, or west.'

'So what positive conclusions are you drawing from all this?'

'Really only one, Ollie – that it was not done on that spot. And if it had been done nearby, by Samis from that area, maybe it would have been the double stab. So we might guess the killing was done some distance away, and perhaps it was not Sami people who have done it. Why would they so advertise it? Only if it was to *seem* like a Sami crime would the killers do this. Do you agree, Carl?'

'Yeah. I do.' Sutherland was back in his own convictions. 'In any event, it's not in character, not in the Sami character in this day and age.'

Ollie asked her, 'Did you discuss these conclusions in Oslo?'

'Yes. There was a meeting, before I left there.'

'So your people are aware of the danger but they still let you come?'

'We do not think there would be any immediate danger to us here in Norway, Ollie. There could be, of course, we could be quite wrong, but we *think* if there is danger it must be in the future. What I am trying to say — well, the bomb, that was dreadful, but only one piece of a pattern maybe. They had the rioting in Norrbotten, and afterwards rumours of trouble all over Lappland. Such rumours gain strength and multiply since the Tromsø bomb, of course. Now, these Finns are murdered. And so on. What must follow, if such things continue, is backlash, Norwegian people looking at Samis as at enemies. So then maybe Samis are insulted, attacked even, there might be discrimination in employment or in trading, and so on. Then the Sami are under pressure and it could seem to be a fact, to the world outside, that they are being — persecuted. . . . So, they would have support — for nothing, a situation that is completely artificial — but it's a vicious circle, huh, where would it end?'

'That scenario, Sophie—' Sutherland shifted uncomfortably on his chair —'is realistic enough to scare me.'

'But you see, if it *is* the scenario, it must be what someone wants to bring about. It would have been set in motion deliberately, there would have to be some — how do you say, some impulse—'

'Some dynamic behind it.' Stenberg nodded. 'So who'd stand to gain?'

She looked at him. '*There* is a question, Gus.'

'I'd say there's a rather obvious answer to it, too.' Ollie shrugged. 'But one bomb was in Murmansk, wasn't it?'

Stenberg said, 'So we were told.'

There was a silence, then, some thinking going on. Ollie broke it finally, suggesting to Sophie, 'If it would make getting a permit any easier, I'd settle for a shotgun.'

3

Thirty-six hours later they were on the road south to Kautokeino. The sky was clear, there'd been a brilliant, orange-glowing sunrise and it promised to be a lovely day: with, of course, a bitingly low ground temperature to match. Ollie was at the wheel with Gus Stenberg beside him and the other two behind.

Southward out of Alta the road ran downhill into the whitened valley, past signs advertising summer camping grounds and through open snowfields with hay-racks visible here and there, and was then joined by the river, the Altaelva. Where the river exited to the fjord was the site of the airport, at Elvebakken, where yesterday after breakfast Sophie had steered him to the *Lensmannen*, sheriff's office, to see about applying for a hunting licence. A lot of talking and a long telephone call to Oslo had seemed to achieve the desired result, but Ollie thought it might have been Sophie's charm that had counted most. She might have pulled some rank, too; he had a suspicion that she might be quite high-powered in whatever department it was, in the capital. Anyway, he'd been issued with a licence. Armed with it, they'd taken the local bus back from Elvebakken to Bossekop, to the sports shop where he'd already decided on an AYA 12-bore ejector that was less ridiculously expensive than some of the other guns. One of the advantages of a shotgun – in preference to a sporting rifle, which would have been the alternative – was that it came apart so easily, for stowage purposes, and could be put together again in two seconds. He'd bought fifty cartridges, Remington number 4 shot.

The road was entering a gorge, with the ice-bound river on the left and a ridge behind it dark with fir trees. There was a steep rise on the other side as well, as high as a thousand feet above road and riverbed. Dipping into the gorge, they lost the sun, plunging into half-light with the glow above them, down here only hazily reflected in the sheen of ice. Scrubby trees lacking either enough soil or enough light, or both. . . . In Karasjok, Sutherland was telling Sophie, there was one man in particular, a Sami, whom he had to see and from whom he was counting on a lot of help. He was known as Isak – just that one name; he was a writer on Sami culture and history and also famous as a *yoik* artist.

'Maybe you'd know of him?'

'I read the two silly books he wrote.'

'Oh!' Sutherland chuckled, rather artificially. 'Well, I grant you some of his contentions may be a little – naive. . . . And OK, he tends to over-simplify. But he has a good brain, you know. And he gave me a lot of help, last time I was here. And there was nothing in it for him, either, I can tell you; he was simply generous enough to help.'

'I think you quoted from his writings?'

'Sure, I did, but—'

'If he's going to be of use to you again – well, fine. . . .'

There was a silence. Ollie could just about hear Sophie suppressing her real feelings about this Lapp. She added diplomatically, after a while, 'As a *yoik* performer Isak is considered to be exceptional. Have you heard him?'

'No, as it happens, I have not. I've heard others, of course. With – this may surprise you – fascination. Oh, I grant you, none of it's ever going to make the charts, but from an anthropological viewpoint—'

Gus Stenberg asked Ollie, 'Ever hear a *yoik*?'

He hadn't. Bridge ahead, and a sharp turn. Gus telling him, 'The guy squats, fills his lungs up and sort of squeezes the sound out of his throat. Very little melody you'd notice, and not a lot of words either, mostly the same ones over and over.'

Ollie eased the van into the turn, not quite sure of the snow-covered road and the snowtyres' grip yet, on bends. They were in the very gut of the gorge, with rock walls on the right of mostly solid ice, dull greenish gleaming, and huge stalactites in clusters shimmery in the half-light. The gorge's sides were steep and high enough to be shutting out a lot of the new day's light. He heard Sophie ask Sutherland, 'Have you been in contact with your friend Isak?'

'Sure. He knows I'm coming, after Kautokeino. . . . He has a snowscooter business, did you know?'

'Yes. There was an article about him, in some paper.'

'He does good business. Since the reindeer Samis mostly use scooters now, in the winters. It also keeps him in touch with them, so if anything's going on in his area you can bet he'll know about it.'

Stenberg asked, glancing back over his shoulder, 'Does this guy have only one name?'

'It's an affectation.' Sophie made a face, a disparagement of Isak which Sutherland didn't see. 'The great artist, all that.'

The road was winding as it climbed now. From Alta to Kautokeino was supposed to take about three hours: 129 kilometres, the map said.

Most of yesterday he'd had Sophie to himself, and it had been a very enjoyable experience. Gus had been with Sutherland, taping interviews with Lapps. Ollie and Sophie had seen just about all all there was to of Alta; mostly on foot, which had involved a lot of exercise because the place was strung out around the wide head of the fjord.

'Did you see that, Ollie?'

He had: a sign saying 'Kautokeino 100 Km'. The road was climbing in a series of sharp bends. Ahead, rounded hillsides were covered in a greyish fuzz of birch trees, but the summits were bare, gleaming smoothly white. Sophie said with her mouth close to his ear, 'Soon we will be up on the *vidda*, you will see how my description was right or wrong.'

'I'll let you know.'

Last night they'd danced, in the bar which for some reason the hotel called 'Aunt Augustine's'. She'd also danced with Gus, but only a couple of times, and he hadn't stayed with them long.

He called back, 'Anyone seen any reindeer yet?'

'Not yet. But don't worry, you'll see thousands!'

They'd eaten reindeer pizzas in the 'dancing bar'. And at one point she'd asked him about his past in the Royal Marines. 'You were something special, were you not?'

'Just a Bootneck.' He added, 'That's slang for a Marine.'

'But the information from London said Special Boat Squadron, I think.'

It shouldn't have. Blabbermouth Jarvis had been at work there, he guessed. But in fact it was a matter of principle more than anything else now, in his present circumstances, being right out of it as he was. He told her, 'That's no big deal. It's a specialist qualification, one of several. The one that would be really worth having on this trip would be a thing called MAW, the Mountain and Arctic Warfare Cadre, or ML for Mountain Leader – those are the real pros. They only offered *me* this job because I happened to be available.'

'But surely SBS is *very* special.'

'We're swimmer-canoeists, that's all. But we're dancers too, so how about it?'

'Commandos, parachutists?'

'All Bootnecks are commandos. And quite a few are parachutists. Others fly helicopters or drive landing-craft, and so on. The really top guys get to dance with wildly sexy Norwegian girls in pizza bars.'

'Yah?' They were on the floor and her body had begun to weave. Dark head back, eyes laughing under the sweep of lashes. 'What are they called, special whats?'

'*You*'re special, Sophie.'

'You talk balls, you know?'

'You have an impressive command of English too. And

look, there's no doubt how special you are, look at those guys' faces – in that corner. And the girls wishing they could look like you do.'

'Better we sit down, then.'

On the tip of his tongue was *Better we go to bed*. He'd held it back, thank God. Cautious old civvie, he thought, in retrospect, half-contemptuous but also suspecting that he'd been wise, that caution might succeed where the mad stallion routine – with *this* one, anyway – could surely have blown it.

The river, now they were up on the plateau, seemed to have taken the form of a chain of lakes. Cabins in the trees around them would be fishermen's summer places, he guessed. Everything was deeply overlaid with snow, the lakes iced over and carpeted. He called back, 'Sophie, there's something I've been meaning to ask about. Your mountain Sami migrate with their herds to the coast in spring, spend summer there and return to the *vidda* when the snow comes – right? Well, it seems crazy, wrong way round. Would you explain it?'

'I'll tell him.' Stenberg twisted around on the seat to face him. 'All winter, up where we're going and around Karasjok and some other places too, the deer live on lichens and a special moss. And they migrate because they have to eat. Up on the highlands they dig down through a metre or more of snow to get at the moss, but in summer it dries, has no nourishment for them. But another reason for them not to stay on the *vidda* in summer months is the mosquitoes get so bad they'd be driven nuts.'

Ollie thought Stenberg *could* have some intelligence connection. He'd thought of it when Gus had been telling him about the lack of security at the Alta airport. He'd taken the trouble to go along and study the baggage check-in routine for himself, and surely you wouldn't have that close an interest unless you were going to make some kind of report on it. The thought had been triggered again when he'd made that comment about the Murmansk bomb, that mutter of 'So we were told . . .'.

There was a lot of water on the right now. Frozen lake, more than river, and several miles of it. Then it became a mere ribbon of ice again. The road ahead rose and fell gently, snaking over ridge after ridge, low undulations of this basically flat plateau they called the *vidda*. Sophie told him, continuing his education, 'Little while ago there was darkness for all twenty-four hours up here, the sun never above the horizon, but once it starts to lift up again the daylight hours grow quickly because it is all so open and there are no mountains or valleys.'

'I thought someone said Kautokeino and Karasjok were both in valleys?'

'Not real valleys. Only lower land because there are rivers in it.'

'Nothing like the rest of Norway, is it.'

'Not at all. Or Finland either. There is no place like the *Finnmarksvidda* anywhere in the world, I think.'

The huge distances rolled away, sheeted in snow. . . . Might be about halfway, Ollie thought. Stenberg, following their progress on a road-map, said there was an agricultural settlement down on the river – the river Altaelva, which was now converging with the road on that side. He added, 'Making good time, Ollie. Be in Kauto nicely for lunch. You OK, not dozing off yet?'

'Should I be?'

'Well, I wondered. Up dancing the night away. . . .'

'You'd have been welcome to stay with us.'

'Yeah, the hell I would.'

Sophie leant forward: 'Yes, Gus, you *would*.'

'I'll believe *you*, Sophie.'

'I should hope so. . . . Ollie, there's a reindeer fence, see?'

That side of the road was mostly stunted birch, no higher than bushes, but there were open areas in it. No deer in sight at the moment. The low fence was of wire supported on rickety-looking stakes, and in places where they'd run out of wire they'd used string, a single strand of it with strips of coloured plastic dangling. It wasn't pretty. And still no deer; in fact they were nearly an hour closer to Kautokeino before he saw some.

'Hey, *there*, at last!'

Then, after a double-take: 'All males, are they?'

'Uh-huh.' Stenberg told him, 'Both sexes have antlers.' He glanced sideways at Ollie. 'Their toes click when they walk, did you know that?'

'Well, naturally.'

'For real. Little bone in the toe goes clickety-click. It's how they stay together in a white-out, by hearing each others' clicks.'

'How did I get to be thirty-two years old without knowing *that*?'

'OK, if you're not interested—'

'But I am.' He'd been looking up to the right, at a radar early-warning station, twin spheres and a mast perched up on the highest snow-covered summit for many miles around. Sitting back again, eyes on the road. . . . 'Another thing I wanted to ask – Sophie said when they stab reindeer they leave the knife in to reduce blood-flow, save the blood for some other use. What kind of use?'

'Uses, plural. They make a gruel out of it, also – believe it or not – a kind of pancake. And sausages. They make use of every bit of that animal – or they *used* to, the way they did live. Maybe not so many of them do such things now, but for instance they'd use the leg sinews to make thread – stranded sinew, that is – and hides of course for clothing and boots, tents, ground-sheets . . . Even the stomach – they clean it and use it as a bag to store food in.'

'I'm glad they clean it.'

'They're not squeamish, that's for sure. Example – when their old folk were too infirm to migrate with the rest, they had a form of euthanasia they called the Blessed Journey. They'd put the old guy in a sled – called a *pulka* – and point it downhill at a high cliff above some fjord, and let go.'

Ollie changed gear, to overtake a slow-moving truck. 'You provide first class in-car entertainment, Gus. Let's hear more.'

'Well, let me think. . . .'

They were into gruesome medical detail – such as drinking reindeer urine as a cure for alcoholism – when they were coming into the outskirts of the settlement. Stenberg was asking him, 'Wouldn't that keep you off the hard stuff?'

'I think it might. But so would Norwegian prices. . . . Lapps tend to go crazy on liquor, am I right?'

'That's their reputation. And *yoik*ing was always associated with boozing, as a matter of fact.'

Sophie leant forward. 'Two garages down there – see them, Ollie?' He nodded, braking gently, downhill. Checking the time, seeing the trip had taken just over three hours. The ground sloped down to the left too, to a sprawl of snow-covered buildings dotted erratically over low-lying land bordering the frozen river. It didn't look like any ordinary town or village, just a random scattering of dwellings. Sophie told him, 'After the second garage, turn right up the hill and you'll see the hotel on the left.'

She was in ski gear, and a red woollen hat with a bobble on it. Sutherland and Stenberg were out interviewing Lapps to whom the professor had written from Alta. She agreed, as he followed her down a cleared path to the road, 'No, it doesn't look like much of a township, but it's an important centre. Kautokeino district is the whole western half of Finnmark – and ninety per cent of the people are Lappish speaking.'

He'd heard some of that, during lunch. He could well believe it wouldn't be an easy language to pick up.

'Were those hundred-per-cent Lapps, in the dining-room?'

'Samis. Yes, most were. They don't go around in Sami costume all the time, you know. Some never dress that way now. Others just for Sundays and special occasions, weddings and so forth.'

She went on to say that while Sami women tended to average about five feet in height and the men five-three or five-four, recent years of better diet, medical care and generally improved living standards had resulted in younger ones growing taller.

'It's one of the silly complaints that that *yoik* person makes. The man in Karasjok, Isak, Carl's friend? Because the younger

62

Sami are more healthy, not so poor, have houses instead of tents full of smoke that used to make them go blind in middle age — Isak sees these benefits as his folks' right — which certainly they *are* — but still objects to the changes in lifestyle that make such improvement possible. . . . It's annoying, you know?' She pointed: 'That's the school.'

A big, stylishly designed building. . . . 'Lapp pupils?'

She nodded. 'Mostly. And this is all new, you see. As in Alta, the Germans destroyed everything when they had to leave in nineteen forty-four.'

'That church doesn't look new.'

'Oh, they left some churches. Do you want to see it?'

She told him as they walked that the Lapp religion was called Lestardianism, so named after a sixteenth-century missionary-priest who preached hellfire and damnation. 'His teachings were very extreme, so fanatical they resulted in violence and bloodshed. Only about a hundred years ago there was such an outbreak here, Samis stabbing Norwegians to death. . . . Before the missionaries came they were animists, worshipping rocks, trees, rivers and so forth — and there are still remains of the old beliefs, under their skins.'

'Like making human sacrifices?'

'*Then*, sure.' She shook her head. 'Not now. That was *not* a Sami doing.'

'And we aren't supposed to think about it — right?'

It was dark when they got back to the hotel. They'd visited a silversmith's place about three kilometres out of town. Passing the timber-built tower of Kautokeino's ski-jump, she'd referred to it as a *hoppbakke* and he'd suggested 'Let's hop up it, then.' Wooden stairs led to the top, from which a jumper's view down the slope and to the river was breathtaking. He'd said, 'I'd want a parachute,' and she'd commented that parachuting was something she'd thought of taking up.

'So why don't you?'

63

'The first time, it must be terrifying.'

'Or thrilling, you might find.'

It only got to be terrifying, in his own experience, when your 'chute didn't open. He'd asked her, back on the road and yomping towards the silversmithery, 'Do you have a lot of boyfriends, Sophie?'

'Some. . . . How about you?'

'Nothing worth mentioning.'

'Aren't you being rude to them, when you say that?'

'No. If you want the truth – well, until very recently there was one in particular, but it's over.'

'Does she know it's over?'

He nodded. 'She knew it before I did.'

Back in the hotel, collecting their keys at the reception desk – Sophie had a single room, of course, and so did Sutherland, but Ollie had found he was sharing with Gus Stenberg – the clerk told Sophie that the Alta police had pulled in another suspect in connection with the bomb on the Tromsø flight. There'd been a news item about it on radio or TV a few minutes earlier, apparently. Sophie told Ollie what the gabble of Norwegian had been about, on their way down to the bedrooms.

'Another Sami. They had some in custody before, and let them go. Now this one.'

'Carl won't be happy, will he?'

Sutherland came back about an hour later, he and Stenberg coming into the room where Ollie was lying on his bed, reading a paperback. He didn't have to look twice to see that the professor was *far* from happy.

'You look as if you heard the news from Alta.'

Stenberg grunted confirmation as he dumped the recorder on his own bed. Sutherland growled, 'We heard it, all right. *Everyone's* heard it. And they're as sore as hell. What they're saying, basically, is the *politi* don't just want whoever did it, they want a Sami to have done it, they're not looking for evidence, only for a Sami they can pin it on. And I tell you, before the news broke I wasn't getting such a hell of a lot of cooperation, but now nobody's saying a damn word to me!'

'Except some very rude ones.' Stenberg gestured towards the tape-recorder. 'Effectively, nothing.'

Ollie got off the bed. 'Maybe they'll have cooled off by tomorrow.'

'I wouldn't count on it. Plainly this development has only triggered frustrations that were already building up.' Sutherland won a battle with the zip on his coat, finally, and stuggled out of it. 'I'm going to take a shower now, and I'll see you in the bar in thirty minutes, Gus. But listen – Ollie – we're supposed to be having guests tonight. One's Sami and the other is not, but he's close to them, he married this Sami guy's sister. If it was two Samis I wouldn't expect they'd show up, the way things are now, but I'm hoping they may. . . . Sophie in her room?'

'I'd think so. She was going to use the sauna, but that was some time ago.'

'Well, look – *if* they show, Gus and I'll look after them. Sophie being from the government – well, shit, if they got to know it they'd walk out on us. So you two stay clear, OK?'

He nodded, liking this prospect. To make up for that, he said, 'Sorry, Carl.'

'Yeah.' Sutherland turned away. 'We may not grace Kautokeino with our presence much longer, as things look right now. Unless I get a breakthrough tonight, maybe.' The door shut behind him. Stenberg said, 'I'm surprised you didn't join her in the sauna.'

Sutherland's guests did come. At dinner Ollie and Sophie were given a table at the far end of the room while the professor's party was in a corner at the door end. The Lapp guest was easy to identify – short-legged, barrel-chested, with a pear-shaped face and small, nondescript features. The other one could also have been a Lapp, except that he was taller when he was on his feet. At this early stage Sutherland was doing most of the talking and it didn't look as if he was getting much response from them, despite beer and wine bottles piling up. In fact the atmosphere in the whole place was depressing: only about a third of the tables were occupied, nobody looked happy and the waitresses were noticeably on edge.

They'd reached the coffee stage when a Lapp stood up and began to make a speech, haranguing the other customers, looking and sounding angry. The wine waiter went to remonstrate with him, but others were joining in, shouting and applauding — and in anger, not for fun. A waitress hurried away, returning with a man who was obviously the manager; meanwhile an elderly Norwegian couple stalked out, the man carrying his bottle of wine. Sophie leant over: 'First they make him wait and wait, he says; although his money is as good as theirs he has to wait for the "settlers" to stuff themselves with food before he is allowed any. Then he is given a very small portion and the worst piece of meat he ever saw, a piece such as he would give to his dog if he wanted the dog to bite him. That was when some of them laughed.'

A chair and its occupant crashed over. It was a Lapp who'd been clapping, with his short legs braced against the table; he'd tilted himself back too far. Other Norwegians were leaving the room, leaving their meal uneaten. The man who'd started it all was now seated, a plate in front of him heaped with enough meat to feed the whole of that table.

Ollie put a hand on Sophie's. 'Shall we beat it?'

'Not much to stay for, is there?'

Sutherland glanced towards them as they passed, quickly looked away again. That party wasn't going any better either, by the looks of it.

'It's happening, isn't it?' Ollie followed Sophie down the stairs to the bar. He'd suggested they might have a quiet drink of *aquavit*, if the bar too wasn't full of belligerent Lapps. 'Your vicious circle shaping up exactly as you described it?'

There were no other customers down here yet. He bought the drinks and took them over to her. She said, 'I would never have believed it could change so quickly. Nobody ever saw anything of this kind before. I am ashamed you should see it. There will have to be something done, but *what . . .?*'

'If the Alta police were to go public with whatever evidence they have against this guy?'

'I don't know.' She sipped her drink, and he swallowed some of his. He was paying for it himself, not freeloading on Uncle Sam. Sophie said again, obviously deeply worried, 'What was happening up there, Ollie, I am *ashamed*. . . .'

They had a second glass, but then the place began to fill up, and in any case it was more or less time for bed. Beds, plural, unfortunately. He suggested on the way to their rooms, 'If our colleagues are working tomorrow, like to put skis on and explore those trails?'

'Why, yes, why *don't* we. . . .'

There was a notice in the foyer about the trails, called *lysløype*, which started on the other side of the river and were marked with lights so tourists couldn't easily get lost. He'd forgotten about it until now, and Sophie looked much more cheerful at the prospect of a day in the open. She was very much an open-air girl, he was beginning to realise. They were outside her bedroom door by this time: he'd glanced back down the passage, seen that they were absolutely alone, but as he turned back to her she moved quickly, forestalling him with a quick peck at the jawline and a murmur of 'Good night'.

He held her lightly. 'Couldn't we do better than that?'

She allowed him to touch her lips. Just a brush, then she'd pulled away.

'Good night, Ollie.'

He was surprised to find his own door unlocked, the lights on and Gus in there getting ready for bed. He asked him, 'What happened to the dinner party?'

'Wash out. And that's it, there's nothing to be gained by hanging around here any longer.'

'So we're leaving? Calling it off?'

A jerk of the head. . . . 'No. Karasjok – leaving right after breakfast. And let's hope it's different there, or we *will* have to call it off.'

He sat down. 'What I don't get, Gus, is why they should be so uncooperative with Carl Sutherland when he's proved he's on their side. I mean, he *is* on their side, isn't he?'

'Very much so. And until tonight I'd have asked the same question. But the answer's a simple one. These guys don't read. If you live in a tent and spend your life on the move you don't have bookshelves and you don't want a lot of weight to haul around. OK, so mostly they have houses now, but there's no reading habit, so what is or is not written cuts no fucking ice with the great majority of them. They *tell* stories, that's their tradition, they don't read 'em, the stories go from mouth to mouth and generation to generation.' He flopped down on his bed. 'We leave in the morning, Ollie. Carl asked them to call the hotel in Karasjok.'

'Must be depressing for him.'

'Say *that* again. He's worried it could be the same in Karasjok as here. Our one and only hope is this *yoik* artist. If he won't play, we really are washed up.'

'A lot of money down the drain. Mostly Uncle Sam's money, isn't it?'

Stenberg glanced sideways. 'Tell you in London, did they?'

'I was told there was some governmental support. The Pentagon and/or NATO interested in whatever the professor's researches turn up?'

'Yeah, that's – about it. . . . And you see, the Norwegians were treating it very low-key. Nothing they couldn't handle domestically, etcetera. The Tromsø bomb changed their minds to the extent they decided to send an observer along – picking *her*, one might guess, because nobody would ever believe someone who looks like she does be any kind of spook.'

'Sophie – a spook?'

'Nah. . . .' Stenberg grinned at the ceiling. 'Any kind of *official*, say. They have this sensitivity over their relationships with the Sami people, the last thing they'd want is to be accused of – you know, spying on them? No Oslo official would be likely to get much change out of 'em anyway. Hence the hopes that have been placed in *us* – in Carl, I should say – with Sophie's little ears tuned in, and naturally very welcome. . . . But the crazy thing is Washington not catching on, like Carl and me, to this thing about Samis not reading, hence not taking Carl as *persona grata*. They had him figured for about the one guy who'd be certain of a welcome, and with ideal cover.'

'Was it the Pentagon's idea that you should come with him?'

'Me?' Another sideways glance, but sharper. 'Christ, the Pentagon never *heard* of me!'

A thought hit him at that moment. He muttered, turning to the door, 'I'll let Sophie know we're pulling out. She'll want to pack.'

'Hell, yes, I should've thought of that.' Stenberg was on his back, eyes shut. 'Give her a call, why don't you?'

A call – telephone – as opposed to a tap on her door. . . .

He'd stopped on his way across the room. Caution reasserting itself as he heard again the tone of finality in that 'Good night, Ollie'. . . . Looking round at the telephone, which was between the two beds, and admitting to himself that caution hadn't exactly reigned supreme, that if she *hadn't* turned him off like that he most likely wouldn't have been here now.

He turned, moved towards the telephone. 'Hope she's not in dreamland yet.'

4

Karasjok had its river too. Approaching from the west, as they drove into the municipality they could see its broad surface of snow on ice looping away to the right and, at a distance, squeezing itself under a modern suspension bridge.

'Take the left fork, Ollie.'

'Aye aye.'

Trying to sound cheerful to offset Carl Sutherland's gloom. The professor had hardly spoken all the way from Kautokeino, except to repeat a few times that he was sure Isak would cooperate with him. It was obvious to the others that he was far from certain, whistling in the dark.

The *turisthotell* was long, low and timber-built, with an extra roofing now of snow. Ollie turned the VW into the parking area and backed up close to the hotel's front door, where a wall of scraped-up snow stood shoulder-high. Switching off the motor, he glanced back at the professor. 'Carl, I wish you all the luck you didn't have in Kauto.'

'Thanks, Ollie. I wish myself the same. Otherwise we're through.'

Inside, the architecture was impressive, a dramatic design in heavy timber. There were four rooms reserved for them too,

71

which made for another good impression, and although it was now early afternoon lunch was still being served. Sutherland told them, 'I'll pass, on that. You three go ahead. I'm just a little anxious to sort this out with Isak.' He added, 'If he's here, even.'

'Sure you don't want me along?'

'Thanks, Gus, but this better be solo. If you don't mind.'

'Well, you know the guy.'

'Right.' He explained, on the way to their rooms, 'No offence, Gus, I'm not suggesting you'd blow it, only that I believe chances are better if I keep it on a quiet, strictly personal level. I don't want to stampede him, and the personal relationship I have with him is about the only thing we have going for us now. OK?'

Sophie said when they were lunching – it was buffet-style, and better than any meal they'd had up to this point – 'He may be disappointed, you know. If the feeling here is like it was in Kautokeino, Isak is the last person who'd want to make himself unpopular with his Sami friends and admirers.'

'Wouldn't want to be seen fraternising, you mean.'

'That's what I would expect. He's not a strong character, he's – well, in *my* opinion he's a *poseur*, a nothing.'

They were leaving a lot of gear locked in the van. Arctic clothing, skis, etcetera. It seemed pointless to unload it all when it was as likely as not that Sutherland would come back in deep depression and abort the whole thing.

Ollie said, 'I suppose we'd drive back up to Alta.'

The VW would have to be returned to the garage where they'd hired it, and the shotgun sold back to the sports shop. In any case the only way out of Karasjok was by road; the airfield here, as at Kautokeino, was only military.

'Stroll around the metropolis, anyone? Sophie, show us the sights?'

'If you like.' She glanced at Stenberg. 'You like?'

Gus feigned astonishment. 'Including *me* in this?'

Sophie shook her head. '*Dum . . .*'

* * *

Carl had expected Isak to be at his snowscooter place, but he'd found it empty and locked up. Not abandoned, there were several Yamahas on display in the showroom, but that glass entrance and also the doors from the yard into the workshop were locked. So he had an even longer walk then to Isak's house, which was on the southeastern edge of town, near the Sami high school. He was fearful that he might draw a blank there too, that the *yoik* artist might be away on literary, *yoik*ing or snowscooter business. Oslo, Tromsø, any place ... It was a twenty-minute plod to the house and he was sweating inside his thermal underwear by the time he walked up the path to the front door. Scrubby birch, and long, snow-decorated grass; at one side the wreck of an old snowscooter buried under snow looked like some futuristic sculpture.

The curtain had moved, in the front window. It was one of those peculiarly Finnmark curtains, a surrounding frieze as if they'd stuck material over the window and then cut a square out of the centre, not very evenly ... The door was now opening, though. It was a girl, a rather pretty Sami kid, he guessed about sixteen: she'd opened the door just far enough for her small, heart-shaped face to be framed in the gap. Dark eyes examining him. He said in slow Lappish — wondering if maybe she wasn't a pure-blood Sami as he'd first thought: 'I am Professor Sutherland, from the United States. I'm looking for my friend Isak. I wrote him a letter saying I was coming.'

She'd let the door open wider now. She had to be more than sixteen, he thought. She raised one hand, thumb projecting: 'At the works. Where he sells scooters. Know where?'

'Where I just came from.' He smiled. 'All locked up.'

'Oh.' Returning his smile, and becoming prettier still: 'Sorry. I just remembered. They're at the river, speed-testing, he had a customer to meet there.'

'You say on the river?'

'They have speed trials on the ice. You'll find him on the bridge.'

'Oh, that bridge, sure. . . .' Carl nodded, while the layout of Karasjok's streets and the river's course returned to memory. He'd got it, knew which way to go. 'Thanks. Thank you very much.' He switched into Norwegian, which came more easily. 'Just in case I miss him, would you tell him I'm hoping to see him as soon as possible? I'm at the *turisthotell* – Carl Sutherland – would you give him that message, please?'

She nodded. Smile still there, warm eyes on his. Maybe she liked older men, he thought. Then: *Down, boy . . .*

He wondered who she was. Isak cradle-snatching? Carl wished *he* was twenty years younger. Or ten, even. . . . It was another long trudge now, back the whole distance that he'd come, right up to the road junction and then left, that long straight road to the corner where the shoe-shop was, and left past the new church. Should have taken a taxi in the first place. . . . Anxiety over the outcome of this crucial meeting with Isak was now mixed with a certain prurient interest in that Sami kid. There really had been a good strong hint of a come-on, in all that smiling warmth, he thought. But Jesus, wouldn't *that* have been a sure-fire way of blowing any chances he might have with Isak?

You'd have to be crazy. . . .

He was plodding south towards the suspension bridge, still a couple of hundred yards to go, when he heard the racket of a snowscooter screaming down the river at full throttle. He'd been hearing it off and on for some minutes past, he realised, without noticing. Thinking about Isak's little piece of home comfort, of course. But now he could see two figures on the bridge – one short and thick, identifiable as Isak, the other a much bigger man. They were out in the middle, leaning over to look down as the scooter or another one flashed past below them, doing about a hundred and fifty, Carl guessed, judging by that explosion of engine-power. He waited until his ears had stopped ringing, then shouted Isak's name through cupped, gloved hands.

No use. Too far, and a car was rumbling across the bridge. And more scooter noise, maybe the first one coming back. Isak was facing this way for a moment: Carl shouted, waving, and this time caught his attention. The big man swung round too. He was dressed roughly, more or less like a Sami herdsman – except no Sami was ever that size. . . . He and Isak faced each other, talking: then he was striding away towards the southern bank, the old wooden church beyond him in the distant, snowy background.

Isak came to meet him. Short, with a dipping, ape-like walk. . . . His greeting was warm enough – limp handshake, as always – but his small, dark eyes were shifty. It didn't bode well, and made Sutherland nervous, because if this guy wouldn't help, *nobody* would. . . . He began in Lappish, 'Delighted to see you! And thank you so much for the kind things you said about my book. . . .' He switched to Norwegian. 'You got my letter, Isak, I hope. And you can spare me a little of your time?' He pointed back the way he'd come. 'I was at your house, and before that at the *snøscootere*—'

'So it was Inga who told you where I'd be.'

'A young girl, sure.'

'My niece. A little beauty, isn't she?'

'She is – most attractive.' He didn't know whether to believe the 'niece' bit; Isak's smile could have been an expression of avuncular pride or it could have been a leer. Carl asked him urgently, 'Can we get together, do some talking as we did before? My aim is to update that book of mine. They want to reprint, mainly for academic purposes, and since nothing is static—'

'Your book does a service to my people, in bringing our situation to world attention.'

'That was my primary aim, in writing it.' They were walking north, back the way Sutherland had come. 'But the scene here has changed, *is changing*, right? One hears of attitudes hardening, social polarisation, even talk of violent solutions. . . . I need your help, Isak. Up in Alta I was talking to former acquaintances, Sami folk whom I'd met on my last trip, and none of them had the least idea of the origins or basis of this spirit of unrest. Of course they're all deeply concerned about it, and particularly about that terrible air crash – bomb, if it *was* a bomb – but they were also disturbed at the official

75

reactions to that crime, what seems to be an automatic, unreasoning assumption that the culprit is a Sami.'

'Another has been arrested, now.'

'So I heard. But hear *this* now. Yesterday I was in Kautokeino, and I found myself up against a wall of silence, even – believe me, Isak – overt hostility! What have *I* ever done that makes me those people's enemy?'

'They are – ignorant, I suppose.' Isak gestured contemptuously. 'Kautokeino people – well. . . .' He smiled, pushing that gloved hand back into a pocket of his reindeer-hide coat. His hat was also made of deerskin. 'But – well, feelings *are* running high, and you're right, it's very bad, very unfortunate. . . .' He shook his head, sighing. 'Much as I would *like* to help you. . . .'

He hadn't completed that sentence. Silent now, with his head down, eyes on his boots scuffing the hard-packed snow. Sutherland felt panic, the imminence of failure: he went on, talking fast, not wanting to allow the little man time in which to refuse to help, 'I'd like to record your own feelings, your gut-reactions to whatever it is that's been going so wrong. I'm not here as some kind of investigator prying into other people's business, nor would I pre-judge any of the issues. For instance I'm well aware that if there was a bomb on that aircraft it could just as likely have been a non-Sami who planted it; I know perfectly well that such an action isn't in the Sami character at all. All I'm asking for, Isak, is – well, for you to as it were review the present situation, how things have changed socially and/or politically since I was last here, and how any identifiable problems might be resolved. And your view of the future, where we're likely to go from here. . . . Isak, I hope this may not be too much to ask of you?'

He sighed. Preliminary to refusal, Sutherland thought despairingly. But then: 'Maybe. Maybe in very general terms. But I'd need to think, to—'

'Isak, this is absolutely wonderful! I'm *deeply* appreciative of your willingness to help. You're the only person I can rely on absolutely, there's simply no one I could turn to with

76

such confidence. . . . Look, tell you what – come to the hotel this evening, have a meal? Just social, a nice relaxed evening?'

Isak threw him a sideways glance. His breath jetted like steam from a kettle. He said slyly, 'You're a party of four, I'm told.'

Sutherland explained, 'He'd checked with them here, because in my letter I wasn't able to say exactly when I'd be arriving. They told him I'd asked for four rooms. So, I had to come up with an instant explanation for this – er – *entourage*.'

Gus was to be himself, no lies were needed. Ollie had been hired as a general assistant; he was an expert skier and had been on two ski-trekking expeditions in the Arctic before this. Sophie was a freelance reader and translator based in Oslo, and the Norwegian publishers had engaged her, since she spoke Lappish well, to smooth the professor's path for him.

Ollie asked, 'Isak's definitely going to help you, is he?'

'As good as said he would, yeah. Wanted time to think, though. Think out what to say or not say, I guess. That's when I asked him to come for supper.' Carl looked at Sophie. 'Let's be nice to him, huh?'

The three men were on their second drinks when Isak arrived. The small bar was full, the crowd including Lapps as well as Norwegians, and there was no sign of the bad feeling that had been so plain in Kautokeino. Isak had stopped in the entrance: short-legged, wide-bodied, with lank black hair hanging over his ears and small, dark eyes shifting around, other Lapps spotting him and nudging each other – *Look who's here*. . . .

After he'd been given a glass of whisky and there'd been some exchanges in Lappish and Norwegian with the

77

Americans, he asked Ollie, 'You don't speak our languages?'

'I can say *I regret I do not speak Norwegian.*' He asked Stenberg, 'Would you apologise for me, please?'

Sophie had her dislike of their guest well hidden when she drifted in and joined them. The conversation washed over Ollie's head but he was given translations from time to time, and at first it was all about *yoik*. She'd complimented him on his artistry, apparently. Isak spoke bitterly of the long span of years during which *yoik* had been outlawed, banned by the priests, who'd declared it to be the voice of the devil speaking through the souls of men. The priests had also destroyed the Samis' most sacred objects of worship and of ritual significance. They'd burnt all the *shaman* drums that they'd been able to lay their hands on, for instance.

'What's *shaman*?'

'Sacred.' Gus added, 'As in witchdoctor.' He'd changed the subject: 'I was saying, Ollie, you never see a cop, do you? I mean in the streets. Not a single one this afternoon – right? And in Kauto yesterday, did you see any? Well, I did see one *politi* car in Alta—'

'Alta.' Isak had caught that word, and broke in to say there'd been a newsflash to the effect that the Sami whom Alta police had been holding had been released without having been charged. People were saying that the *politi* were floundering, could only arrest one innocent citizen after another, not giving a damn so long as it was a member of the Sami race. . . . And there was worse news now – *far* worse, profoundly disturbing. . . .

Translations came in snatches, Gus and Sophie sharing the chore. At this point Isak was admitting that it was more rumour than hard news; but it was all over town although nobody could tell where it had started. Of course, the long-haul Finnish buses passed through Karasjok, coming up from the border at Karigasniemi; there'd been one through today, and its driver or passengers might have sown the seed. . . . Small, sly eyes rested on Sophie. Sutherland frowning, fondling his ginger beard while he listened to the drone of Norwegian. Getting to the point at last, Isak told them that in southern Lappland three soldiers of the Finnish Army had been found stabbed to death on an ancient place of worship.

Sutherland asked what kind of lunatic could have done such a thing. And what for? To blacken the image of the Sami people?

Most of whatever Ollie missed during the course of the dinner-party was covered in a *post-mortem* review later, after Isak had shambled away into the snow. His answer to that question had been 'All one can say is there are dark forces at work – powerful, secret forces . . .' He'd muttered this, and added, 'But it's no time or place to speak of such things. Tomorrow, professor, we might meet alone and talk?' Sutherland really came alive at this: '*Right*, Isak! Where, and what time?'

They'd agreed to meet at eleven at the snowscooter shop. Sutherland was in great form from that moment on, and more generous with the wine.

Sophie had asked Isak, when they were getting up to move from the dining-room, 'Did you say the place where those murders were committed is in south Finland?'

'No. As it was told to me, well south of the border. Therefore perhaps not as much as halfway down the length of Finland, but in south Samiland.' His small eyes had glinted, seeing a chance to make a point. 'So it would be of little concern to Norwegian people. But to us whose home is Samiland – irrespective of foreigners who have settled here or there, in the various parts of our land – for us, this crime has been committed in *our* country.'

He'd been pleased with himself at having put that one over, especially as it had left the elegant, rather disdainful young woman stumped for an answer. Like Sutherland he'd been in a good mood thereafter, despite the worry of having a visitor of a very different kind in town, and a clear need to keep the two apart.

He slithered down the steep, rough shortcut to the lower road and hurried eastward. There shouldn't be any problem, he thought, neither the Yanks nor the other were likely to be here long. He had the fur flaps of his hat down over his ears and his coat-collar buttoned up around his jaw. Temperature about minus thirty, he guessed. Absolutely clear sky, stars dazzlingly bright in it. He had not brought his car to the hotel for the good reason that although one rarely met *politi* on the streets – the young American had been right, on that – they tended to materialise out of thin air if you'd had a few drinks and then got behind the wheel of a motorcar. One tot of whisky was enough to put you over the limit, and to be caught driving in that condition meant prison, no lesser sentence being available to the courts.

He turned right. Skirting the police station, as it happened. Then at the bottom of that road, left. Not a soul stirring anywhere, although there were still lights in many windows. The buildings weren't at all close together here in the centre of Karasjok; they were spread loosely, plenty of open space between them, so that you could sometimes take shortcuts from one road to another, if you had good boots on and didn't mind forging through virgin snow. Plodding on, thinking that in the morning he'd decide what sort of bullshit he was going to hand Carl Sutherland. It was as well to appear willing, he thought, and to seem to be as baffled and as worried as the Americans themselves. Although, what business they imagined it could be of *theirs*. . . .

He was walking up the path to his house when a voice spoke out of the dark, in Norwegian with a strong foreign accent: 'At last. . . . I'm coming inside with you, Isak, we have to talk.'

'Johan!'

'Come on, let's not hang around.'

'But my niece—'

'She's still up. She's been watching television most of the time. Send her to bed, tell her you've brought a customer home, talking business.'

'I was about to say, my niece would have let you in, you could have waited in the warm. If I'd known—'

'You'd have drunk less of the Americans' whisky, eh?'

The bastard knew every bloody thing that happened. Watching Inga through *this* window, another in the hotel watching *me*. . . . 'I'm sorry you had to wait, anyway.' He opened the door. 'Inga, are you awake?'

'Oh, uncle . . .'

Appearing from the living-room, she stopped when she saw another man behind him, in the dark outside the door. Big, twice Isak's size: his face wasn't visible. Isak told her, 'Go to bed, girl. My friend and I have business to discuss.'

'Wouldn't you like some soup, or—'

The big man said, 'No, thank you.'

'Up to bed with you, my pet.'

The visitor didn't come into the hallway until she'd gone. Then he muttered, kicking snow off his boots and pushing the door shut, 'Fond of her, aren't you?'

'She's – all I have.'

'All a red-blooded man might want, too. On a cold night, eh?'

In the living-room, he kicked that door shut too. Unzipping his padded coat and pulling it off. 'You said she'd have let me in. If you're so fond of her, you should tell her never to do any such thing. . . . Who are these Americans?'

Isak explained who, what and why. Describing Sutherland and his reasons for being here was easy, but accounting for the others' presence less so, rather lame-sounding when you put it into words. He hadn't taken note of this until now, he'd swallowed Sutherland's explanations without much thought. Now, the student, Stenberg, was the only one of the three one could easily accept. He saw a sneer on his visitor's face too: 'Ferreting around for the latest news, for a book of an academic nature that's already in circulation? Doesn't it strike you as peculiar? Is this a professor of anthropology or a newspaper reporter?'

'He's well known, his book was—'

'Or CIA?'

Isak shook his head. 'Professor Sutherland is widely respected. Why, I myself—'

'Be difficult to find a better cover, wouldn't it? I'm surprised you're so gullible, Isak.'

'I had no' – he corrected – '*have* no reason to doubt—'

'That was the professor who interrupted us on the bridge, I suppose.'

'Yes, but I'm quite *certain*—'

'I was about to say, this afternoon when we were interrupted, there's been a leakage of information. Somewhere, someone. Since you've been coordinating some aspects for us, indeed since you know more about the business than anyone else in Finnmark except me, naturally I come to you first. For your thoughts on the subject only, Isak. I'm sure you'll tell me you could not possibly have let a word slip out – even when you've had some drinks like tonight?'

'I'd be happy to declare on oath—'

'You're fond of whisky – right?'

'No more than the next man.'

'You mean no more than the next Sami?'

Isak scowled. 'I've heard your people swill vodka out of buckets. But I don't accuse *you*—'

'Better we should not become aggressive with each other, Isak. After all, this is as much in your own interests as anyone else's. Unless our security is guaranteed, I've told you, my people will withdraw, they won't touch it. Then your dreams vanish, don't they? Maybe even worse, instead of being installed as the first President of the Sami nation you could be left holding the baby. Huh?'

Isak sighed, and turned away. It was a scenario he didn't like to think about.

'Does your niece know anything about our movement?'

A shake of the head. 'Nothing.'

'Let's try another subject. I hear the Alta police have let Pelto go.'

'Yes.' Isak turned back to face him. 'I heard it on the radio. But he knows nothing, he did only what he was told, and he didn't know who told him. The only thing he could have done, *if* he'd opened his mouth at all, would be to incriminate *himself*.'

'But Aikko knows a thing or two, eh? And he was in the lock-up for several days. Maybe *he* talked?'

'It was weeks ago, they had Aikko. And others with him – who'd done nothing – so he was just one of a crowd they were holding, wasn't he. And look – if he'd told them it was Pelto who – well, wouldn't they have grabbed Pelto *then*, right away? And then not let Aikko go either?'

'They don't have to be idiots, Isak. It would make sense to wait so that nothing pointed at Aikko as an informer. They'd still keep tabs on both of them – to see who came to visit, that sort of thing?'

'What kind of leak was this?'

'An entry route. There were people waiting. Watching.'

'But Aikko had no such information, surely!'

A nod. 'Right. No more than you do. That's true. Six of one, half a dozen of the other. But suppose some very small piece of the business becomes known, Isak. An astute man might ask himself how might people come and go? Not via the Norwegian/Soviet part of the frontier; that's fenced and guarded. So it must be through Finland, right? Where there's no fence. Then – well, you could work it out, to some extent. Eliminate the unlikely sectors, and so on. Then you're on your way, eh?'

'These men who were – you say watching—'

'Hey, that's *my* next question. Their leader, of part Sami parentage, is a *vanrikki* in the Finnish Army.'

'*Is?*'

'That's what I just—'

'I thought maybe – some link with this and the story you told me on the bridge, about three Finns killed. That's going round like fire now, by the way.'

'No. No connection.' A shake of the head, and a smile. 'Your imagination, Isak, really. I suppose it's the artist in you. No, listen – this Finn. I heard he was here in Karasjok a few weeks ago, asking questions. A man named Clas Saarinen.'

'I never heard of him. Or of *any* Finn asking questions.'

'You go away on business quite often, don't you? On your snowscooter business.'

'Not recently, I haven't.'

83

'And on *our* business. Are you so sure your niece spends *all* her time watching television when you aren't around? You were in Alta, for instance, on a mission which you and I have forgotten about, at the time Saarinen was visiting here. And somebody did call at this house, a stranger. Did you hear of it?'

'Someone might call.' Isak frowned. 'Doesn't mean she'd open the door to him, not to a stranger. If you'd told her you were a friend – the same one she knows I went to meet this afternoon – that'd be different.'

'What if *he*'d said he was a friend? And if she was lonely? Or just liked the look of him?'

'Inga has a steady boyfriend. A mechanic, he works for me. But anyway, as I told you, she's – she knows *nothing*.'

'Let's ask her.'

'Ask – what, *now*?'

He was at the door. 'Come on.'

Upstairs, he stayed in the passage, pushed Isak into the girl's bedroom.

'Inga . . . Inga darling, are you awake?'

'What's – what—'

The light blinded her. She was up on one elbow, blinking at him, dazzled, the other hand moving to shield her eyes. Isak murmured, 'I'm sorry, darling. It's just a question my friend here needs to ask you – rather urgently, you see. No, don't worry' – she'd snatched at the bedclothes, pulling them up to her throat – 'he won't come in the room. Only wants to ask you this, then we'll leave you to go back to sleep – all right?'

The man standing back in the dark passage could see her scared, pale face above the blankets. He'd counted on her being scared, it always helped. He explained, 'I am from near Helsinki. I'm looking for a friend of mine – from Rovaniemi as it happens – who seems to have vanished. His name is Clas – Clas Saarinen. . . .' He saw the reaction clearly – in her eyes, and a parting of the lips to match that widening. Then the tip of her tongue, wetting the lips. . . . 'Clas is quite young, a good-looking fellow, most girls would remember him. Name doesn't ring any bells? Clas Saarinen?'

She stammered, 'No, I don't know – anyone that name or – why should *I*—'

84

'There was a chance he might have called here wanting to see your uncle, when he was away in Alta that time. Not so long ago, actually. Are you *sure* you don't remember such a person calling here?'

'No, I *told* you—'

'Well, that's it, then. I'm sorry. I'd hoped — but never mind. . . . Sorry I had to disturb you, Inga.'

Isak went to kiss her before he put the light out and followed the man down the stairs. His guest knowing for a fact now that Saarinen had been here. In all the circumstances it couldn't possibly be coincidental; the Sami world was a small one, numerically, but Clas Saarinen had come to the house of the one man in Norway — well, one of two — who could have told him anything at all, and that man's sexy little niece must have blurted out *something*. Not much — but for Saarinen, enough. There'd be no mileage to be gained from grilling Isak now, however: it was obvious that nothing would induce him to admit that either he or she could have let any cat out of the bag.

No matter. As with any other cat, there were more ways than one to skin it.

Isak muttered as they came into the living-room, 'Hope you're satisfied now.'

'Except that your neighbours say a stranger did come.'

Isak was taken aback, but only for a moment. . . . 'Well, someone knocks, asks directions maybe — would *you* remember, two months later?'

'If I lived in a place like this — yes.'

'A scatter-brained chick like her wouldn't. Even if my long-nosed bloody neighbours are telling the truth, which I'd doubt. Incidentally, which ones—'

'It doesn't matter, Isak.'

'To me, it does. . . . But listen, here's something else now. There wouldn't need to be a leak at all. If your people had left some tracks or something? When all these rumours are going round and the government's beginning to sweat a bit, then some hunter or frontier patrol finds a fresh trail?'

'It's not impossible.' The big man nodded. 'And obviously I've considered it. But I can't take a chance on this whole scare being no more than a fluke. If we see the least possibility of a leak, I have to take steps to stop it or we'll *all* be stopped. I must have told you about six times – well, if my superiors suspected even as much as I suspect now, they'd call it off.' He yawned. 'That's why I'm here. And the answer must be Aikko, I'm sure of it. On the other hand we now have these Americans of yours. When will you next be seeing them?'

'In the morning. Professor Sutherland wants my views on the present situation here. I'll hand him a load of shit, of course – which he'll probably record on tape. How the rumours of violence sicken me, how I'm certain no Sami could have placed that bomb. But I know nothing, nobody talks to anyone else, nobody knows where it starts or – oh, you know.'

Isak's visitor pulled out a chair and sat down with his elbows on the table. He was about the same height seated as the Lapp was on his booted feet. He said thoughtfully, 'I believe you can do better than that, my friend.'

Isak shrugged. 'So tell me what to say, I'll say it. Like coffee now?'

'How kind. . . .'

Waiting, the big man rested his stubbled jaw on his fists. Concentrating, shaping ideas and fitting them into existing plans, manpower. . . .

Markov, who was with Pereudin at an *overnatt*ing on the other side of town, could go by bus to Alta and silence Aikko, Belyak decided. This would eliminate one possible source of the leak – the least likely, admittedly, of the three which existed, one of whom was at this moment making coffee in the next room. Markov must be warned not to enlist help from, or even make contact with, either of the two Spetsnaz agents resident in Alta: this warning would have to be given because (a) he hadn't operated solo before, and (b) he did have, in his memory, the name and addresses of those agents, and might be tempted to make use of them.

(Agents there and at the other ports – at which there were to be landings by naval Spetsnaz teams from midget submarines, when the moment came – and others residing near airfields, communications centres, radar sites, etcetera, were all long-settled people, completely accepted in their own communities. Not all were active: some were elderly, had only to provide safe houses or transport, or communications facilities. In Russian they were classified as *zamorozhenniye*, or 'frozens', and their cover was sacrosanct, on no account to be compromised. This operation might be aborted, for instance, and since they wouldn't have lifted a finger before being activated they'd still be there for *next* time.)

Anyway, Markov could handle Aikko. And another reason to warn him not to rock the boat was the fact that this would be a doubly clandestine action, that no reports would be made of it. No reason for any, as long as the job was done. First Aikko, who'd served his purpose. Number two was the kid upstairs, and she'd be Pereudin's meat. In more ways than one – knowing Pereudin. He could do his bit a day after they'd all moved out. He'd come with a message: *Your uncle wants you to join him, there are reasons it's unsafe for you to stay here alone, I'm to take you to him now. . . .* Well, he'd take her *someplace*. It would be killing two birds with one stone, not only eliminating the girl as a possible leak but also buying insurance for Isak's continuing obedience – as long as he believed she was alive, and while he was having the last dregs of usefulness squeezed out of him.

Now there were these Americans. Which alone would have justified his coming up here, might conveniently become the official reason for having done so. V.V.Rosenko might be allowed to conclude that Belyak's intelligence net was so effective that he'd been able to arrange to be on the spot when the Yanks arrived.

In fact – he snapped his fingers, as the whole thing fell neatly into place – it was *perfect*. It would justify his sending an order back to Yuri Grintsov now, telling him to come up as far as the border, say, with reinforcements. And a small team, just in case of any slip-ups, on the road up to Kautokeino. Markov could come down by that route from Alta – it would be his best route, in fact – and R/V with that team at the *Statens fjellstue* near the border or the other one, close to the highway at Aiddejavrre. Gerasimov, maybe, for that job. . . .

'Here we are then. Coffee.'

'Good man. And now listen to me, and I'll tell you how I want you to handle your Yanky friends. You may find the task a bit strenuous physically, but it'll only be for a week or two and it certainly won't do you any harm. . . . To start with – thanks, no sugar – you'll have this meeting with the guy tomorrow, and you'll be enthusiastic, full of an idea you've spent the whole night thinking about. You'll make him a proposal which – well, if he wants to know what's going on, and obviously the arsehole *does*, he's come half across the world for it and you can be damn sure it's not for any fucking book he wants it, either – look, he's going to jump at this, I tell you. . . . You have comrades, Isak, in a *siida* down south. Near the border or maybe beyond, in Finland. They move around, according to weather, snow conditions, all that, so locating them may not be too easy. But you heard from one of them, when he passed through here in October – he told you he has all the answers, what's happening and about to happen, and the identities of those who're conspiring. You'll offer to take them to find this *siida*. Until now you've tried to stay clear of it, but you've woken to your sacred duty to the Sami people – well, Christ, you'll know how to ham *that* up!'

'And what happens after that?'

'You'll get them down into the wilds, that's all. Then I'll take over. But let's have a look at the maps now – over there, in my coat pocket. . . .'

Any day now, Rosenko's decision would be made known: whether to start now or wait for the spring. Either way, with the surprise appearance on the scene of these Americans, Belyak knew that quick and resolute action was precisely what Rosenko would expect of him.

5

The Volkswagen rumbled southward over the snow-packed Route 96, which ran down to the Finnish border at Karigasniemi. The distance was only nineteen kilometres and they weren't going even that far, not on this highway; there was a turn-off just before the border, a minor road leading south and keeping company with the river, as so many inland roads seemed to do. That particular river being also the frontier. To Finns it was the Teno, to Norwegians the Tana and then farther south the Anarjokka; whatever you called it, it was a famous breeding water for Arctic salmon, Sophie said, and in summer it was a Mecca for fishermen from all over.

'You fish, Ollie?'

'I've done a bit. Haven't had a chance at salmon, though.'

'Come back here in summer, we take a boat, I teach you?'

'You're on!'

He thought, *We might teach each other . . .*

The VW was getting along reasonably well, but after the turn-off it might not be so good. The map showed it as only one lane wide, and it obviously wouldn't rate the same maintenance and snow-clearance priority as this or any of the roads they'd used so far. Isak had warned it mightn't be negotiable at all, or anyway not for very far. They were hoping to get to where it became a cart-track, at a place called Jorgastak, near which there was said to be an *overnatt*ing. But if necessary they'd leave the van at some earlier point, trek on on skis. It wasn't any great distance but conditions could deteriorate suddenly; snow was expected, and the daylight hours were short.

At lunchtime the day before yesterday Sutherland had returned from his meeting with Isak in a state of excitement: he'd found them in the hotel lounge. 'I have a lot to tell you guys. Come down to my room while I wash up?'

Sophie had probed, on the way, '*Good* things to tell us?'

'I'd say so.' He'd nodded grimly. 'Isak made me a proposition which I personally am going along with, although I haven't committed you people, in case – well, I'll explain that.' He'd glanced round. 'Except you, Gus, I'm naturally counting *you* in.'

They'd trooped into his room, and while he was changing from boots to shoes he told them that Isak had offered to guide him south, by road and then on skis, to where the huge nature reserves spanned the Norwegian–Finnish border. Somewhere in that area was where he believed one particular *siida* would be wintering its herds, and a member of that *siida* had told him months ago that he knew what was being cooked up politically and the identities of the people behind it. Isak had no idea how this individual, who was a decent, honourable Sami and well respected in the community, could have such knowledge, and he hadn't done anything about it because he hadn't wanted to become involved himself. Now he realised he'd been wrong, that he'd shirked what he should have seen as his duty. The recent outrages had appalled him, and being convinced that no Sami people could have instigated such crimes he felt he was under an obligation to establish the truth, if that were possible. Right up to last night's dinner party he'd been undecided, but now he'd seen clearly where his duty lay.

'So he wants to make the trip anyway, and he'd be glad of some company and happy to help with what *I'm* after, since the two objectives coincide.'

Ollie had asked what a *siida* was, and Sutherland explained it was a sort of reindeer-farming commune. A number of families, each owning its own deer, got together to share the work of husbandry. They'd take it in turns for instance to watch one large herd, instead of each family unit having to spend many more hours watching one small group of beasts.

'Anyway,' Stenberg said, 'could be the breakthrough – right?'

'That's how I see it, sure.' Sutherland looked at Sophie. 'What's *your* reaction?'

'I suppose I feel the same.' She'd shrugged. 'Although he didn't mention any of this last night, he didn't *seem* to have any such – dilemma – in his mind.' She shrugged again. 'But as you said—'

'He needed to get his thoughts straight on it. He'd said yesterday he wanted time to think. . . . Sophie, I know you don't like him, but – well, he'll be *with* us, it can't be any spoof, can it?' He paused, looking at her. 'But there's one aspect of this thing I have to point out to you. The three Finns who were murdered – it happened down there, someplace, and they were investigating the same phenomena that we're interested in. I have to make this point, Sophie, and ask you to consider it.'

'To stop me going with you?'

'No, by no means, but—'

'We would not be going very far into Finland, from what you've said?'

Stenberg cut in: 'Last time we talked about it we agreed they could've been killed just about any place. So locality's of little consequence. The only relevance – this must be Carl's point – is what questions those guys may have been asking and what questions *we*'ll be asking.'

'So play safe.' Sophie smiled. 'Let Isak ask all the questions.'

'Ollie.' Sutherland glanced at him. 'You with us?'

'It's what I was hired for, surely.'

He realised Sutherland was only trying to scare Sophie out of coming; he was also fairly certain the professor was wasting his breath. He'd begun again now: 'Seriously, my dear – wouldn't you agree it may not be quite your scene?'

'You want to leave me behind.'

'No, you're wrong, I don't. We'd *all* like to have you along. But for your own sake – and OK, ours too, in a way – don't you see what you'd be getting into? Rough going and rough living, sleeping in tents, whole days on skis, maybe a *lot* of whole days?'

'I love skiing and ski-trekking and I have never minded sleeping in a tent. I will not take a silk nightdress, if this is the kind of problem that's bothering you.'

Stenberg muttered, 'I'll leave mine behind, too.'

She'd made it plain that she was coming, anyway, and there hadn't been time for argument, they'd needed every minute of the day and a half they had, for various kinds of preparation. Ollie had everything he'd need, but there were shortcomings in the others' gear. Luckily Karasjok boasted both a sportswear shop and one that rented ski equipment, so most deficiencies could be taken care of. Some items were bought, others hired – including three two-man tents, insulated mountaineers' tents. Sophie would have one to herself – despite Stenberg's attempts to persuade her that as she spoke Lappish she'd have to share with Isak. Then there were rations to get together. They made lists and bought most items from the two local foodstores, while Isak offered to provide both fresh and salted reindeer meat, getting it from Sami herdsmen. All the heavier gear – including tinned food, the tents, snowshoes, two shovels, one machete, a naptha-burning cooking stove, cooking pots and several half-gallon containers of fuel – would be carried on a light pulk which Isak produced from his scooter store.

Gus, questioning the value of the Volkswagen in deep-winter conditions, suggested that a heavy diesel truck might get them farther; wouldn't diesel be best anyway for long-range work? Ollie had to explain to him that diesel fuel had a certain water content, so that in excessively low temperatures it froze. Sutherland hadn't thought of this, either, and there seemed to be a lot of elementary cold-weather know-how they lacked, despite having completed some survival course before departure from the USA. Another fuel question, for instance, and again from Stenberg – why not hexamine tablets for the cooking, why naptha which was so much heavier and more cumbersome, when weight of stores was a crucial factor? It hadn't occurred to him that in a snow-hole or other weather-proofed bivouac either hexamine or ordinary petrol fumes would kill you, whereas naptha – lead-free petrol – was non-toxic. One way and another Ollie was satisfied long before departure from Karasjok that he'd begun to earn his pay.

Most of his own equipment was stuff he'd had and used in his SBS days. Special Boat ranks tended to invest in their own gear, mainly because Service-issue items were usually inferior – heavier, as often as not, and less efficient. His boots, for instance, which he'd bought in Exeter from Arktis, were ski-march boots handmade on wooden lasts by the Swedish firm Lundhags. They were something like para boots but made of rubber-covered leather with lace-up fronts and insulated felt insoles; they'd cost him some money, but your feet were the things you moved on, and as far as he knew there wasn't anything better you could put on them, for hard going. Then he had Helly Hansen 'Lifa' thermal underwear, which had the useful property of pushing sweat out into the next layer of clothing instead of leaving it to freeze on your skin. Over that went a Norwegian Army shirt – heavyweight cotton, polo neck with a zip-up front, elasticated cuffs. He'd got that from Arktis too – and Canadian heavyweight socks. For outer wear he had a Ventile suit – windproof and waterproof, as worn by Captain Scott at the South Pole in nineteen twelve. To go on top of it in really extreme conditions he had a Goretex jacket.

'And what the hell is *this*?'

He was packing stuff into his bergen, and Gus Stenberg was holding up a furry-looking object.

'Let me guess. . . . Dead monkey?'

'Fibre-pile suit. Extra insulation when needs must. Goes inside other gear, you don't even have to take your boots off.'

He demonstrated it. The suit was made of a lightweight fur fabric, and the pants had zips right up the sides so you had only to drop your outer trousers, wrap the fur legs round yourself and pull the zip up. The hip-length jacket zipped up in front, and with the fur inward against your body it provided a high degree of insulation. The fact it looked like the remains of some animal that had been in a road accident was accounted for by its having seen a lot of service, including a few weeks on wind- and sleet-swept hillsides in the Falklands a few years ago. The same applied to his sleeping-bag, also ex-SBS equipment and rather evocatively called a North Face Bigfoot.

'And this?'

'Bivvy-bag. Goretex, like that coat. The sleeping-bag goes inside it and stays dry no matter what. Don't you have something like it?'

He didn't, and Sutherland didn't either, which called for yet another visit to the shops, this time without success — no bivvy-bags, no material from which to make some. Checking Sophie's equipment then, and finding she didn't have one either, he told her he had a spare and lent his to her. It was all very well her telling everyone how often she'd slept in tents, you could be damn sure she'd never tried it in Finland in February.

'How are we doing, Miss Eriksen?'

She was beside him in the front of the VW, on this trip, leaving the others to converse with Isak at the back. Not that there was much conversing going on; Isak was morose and jumpy, locked into his own thoughts, apparently. Maybe scared by the responsibility he'd taken on. Sophie answered that last question: 'I think we are about halfway to the frontier.'

Not that they'd be crossing it, at that point. They'd be turning down, driving along the Norwegian side of it, when they got that far.

The river here, on the left and sometimes close to the road, was the Karasjokka. On the right, power-lines were strung between pylons that dwarfed the trees. It was well wooded country along this stretch of road and river, but above the tree-line, up on the right, nude hilltops gleamed dayglo-white against the grey, snow-threatening cloud. Isak had said they'd have snow by nightfall if not sooner. A very sudden change, after the recent sunshine and clear nights.

Sophie had telephoned her department in Oslo to tell them where she was and where she was going, but the colleague to

94

whom she'd given this information hadn't seemed very interested, she'd told Ollie. He'd muttered something about making a note that she was at the Karasjok *turisthotell*, in case anyone wanted to get in touch. She'd banged the 'phone down. . . .

'They are so *dum*!' A high note of exasperation. . . . 'The only intelligent man in that place is my boss – who happens to be a Sami.' She'd noticed Ollie's surprise. 'Oh, yes, there are Samis in good jobs now. They are fine people, you should not judge by a few who are like Isak. That is why all this business is so unbelievable to us, you know?'

He'd thought of putting a call through to COMNON, to let Grayling know where they were going and why, but he'd decided against it. Jarvis had only given him that contact so that he could pass on any urgent or important information, and as yet he had no information worth passing to anyone. That had been one good reason not to call in. The other was a long-held aversion to reporting to anyone about anything at all when you didn't have to.

What it came down to was that you were again, as in that previous existence, on your own. There was an objective: you had to get there, and come back with the information. The only insurance – life assurance – was packed in the Berghaus bergen in its three component parts, the longest of them being the 28-inch barrels.

He had a hundred cartridges now, having bought another fifty in the Karasjok sports shop.

Sophie broke into his thoughts, telling him, 'That was Muotkenjar'ga'.

'My God, *was* it?' He rolled his eyes. 'Now I can die content.'

'If you do not watch the road, we will *all* die.'

'OK. Although I'd much sooner watch you, Sophie. . . . How far to the turn?'

'About five kilometres. Soon this road will bend to the right, we do not then see the Karasjokka any more, we come instead to the Teno.' She added, 'Where if you are a good boy I may one day take you fishing.'

95

'I'm going to hold you to that, you know.'

The riverside road wasn't as bad as it might have been, but it was no highway either. There was a layer of loose snow over the hard underlay, and the tyres' studs didn't grip so well. With some danger of skidding it meant slow progress. On some stretches the surface improved – presumably where a more conscientious farmer had been doing his community service with a snow-blower – but after a few kilometres they'd be down to a crawl again.

'Must be glorious in summer.' Glancing to his left, at the wide river of ice. You could imagine it unfrozen, its water flowing between green banks, the wooded hillsides on the Finnish side reflected in its surface; and a boat drifting, himself and Sophie in it. . . .

'Here we go, road's a lot better suddenly.'

'Coming to a settlement, that's why.' Gus was where Sutherland had been, peering over at the map on Sophie's knees. 'Could be – whatever *that* says?'

'Iskuras.'

It wasn't, though. Iskuras might be a couple of houses and some sheds, three adults and a dog, but this was even smaller. Isak was saying something to Sutherland as they approached it, Ollie putting his foot down to take advantage of the improvement in the road's surface. Sutherland called, 'Isak wants to make a stop here, Ollie. Some kind of restaurant. Pull in, will you?'

Sophie and Isak were talking in Lappish while Ollie slowed the van; she said as they stopped, 'He knows these people, he says they will open for us.' Sutherland justifying the halt to Gus: 'He's our guide, after all. If he says we have time, we better go along with it.' Isak jumped out, hurried into the timber building over which a sign spelt out *GRILL-KOK*, and by the time the rest of them straggled in he'd ordered coffee and sandwiches and left the room by another door. They'd be reindeer meat sandwiches, Sutherland said after a conversation with the proprietor. He and his wife were Lapps, of course. He told Sutherland the road would be OK as far as Jorgastak, and that just beyond it the *overnatt*ing on the river bank would surely accommodate them. It was owned by his

wife's brother, used mainly in summer and by fishermen. . . .
Isak returned from a visit to the lavatory – which had probably
been the real reason for stopping here – and the proprietor
took him by the elbow, steered him out of the room. Stopping
in the passage outside, he asked him, 'Who are these foreigners? What do they want here, at this time of the year?'

'The one with the beard is a professor, and he wrote a book
about ourselves and our country, history, all of it. With my
own assistance, actually. But he was never here in the winter,
or visited a *siida* in our highlands; and since he and I are fellow
authors and historians – well, he'd heard of me in America, of
course, I'm famous there – I thought I might as well bring him
along. And the others are his assistants, they make recordings
and so on.'

'Are you taking them across the river?'

Isak shook his head. 'West. Into the *vidda*. West from
Jorgastak.'

It was what he'd been told to say. He'd been told to find
someone hereabouts and somehow create an opportunity to
say it; this fellow had made the opportunity *for* him, very
nicely. He added, 'The one with the beard is a friend of our
people, I'll take him wherever he likes.'

'You don't think there's danger to them out there?'

'What danger?'

A shrug. . . . 'All right, so you don't believe the stories. The
Finn soldiers murdered, for instance?' He saw Isak's grimace,
and raised his voice: 'Look, if you want *proof* – all right, you'll
tell me that in January we don't ever get many tourists. And
you'd be right, most have the sense to wait for warmer weather.
But haven't you noticed that this year there are *none*?'

'No ski parties from across the river even?'

'You're our first visitors since New Year. Why, we might as
well hibernate, like – you know what.' He'd jerked a thumb in
the direction of the river and the Finnish forests. 'Same that
side, we're told. Not a soul!'

There was so little of Jorgastak that if they hadn't been looking for it they could have passed it without knowing they'd come this far. Snow was falling, dimming out the last of the daylight, driving on the northerly wind from astern and sucking-in in front to plaster the screen and give the wipers all the work they could handle. Tyres hissed in the new, soft overlay: a few hundred yards behind the van its tracks would already have been covered. A road led off to the right, a curve west into the Finnmark interior, marked by fence-posts and felled trees; despite the divergence it looked more like a continuance of this route than did the narrowing, near-invisible track southward, parallel to the river. But this was the approach to the fishermen's pub. The woman in the *grill-kok* had described its location, and Isak had told them he'd been here himself, years ago, would know it when he saw it.

Yellow light gleaming from an upper window provided a beacon, made the last few hundred metres easy. Oil lamp – unless they had a generator. Snow was banked high where space had been cleared around the timber building. Stenberg said as he backed the Volkswagen up close to its shelter, 'May be hard work tomorrow, skiing in this stuff.'

It would be less cold, though, in fact the difference was already noticeable. It was always warmer when snow was falling; usually you'd reckon on temperatures of between plus one and minus five. Plus wind-chill factor, if any. He made a mental note that first thing in the morning he'd check on the feel and consistency of the snow, and check the temperature, so as to choose the best wax for their skis. Also to ask the people here to run the VW's engine every day.

Inside, the first impression was of warmth and the odours of heating-oil and cooking. Stewpot kept permanently simmering, no doubt. Or soup pot. If it was stew you could bet the meat in it would be reindeer. The house was kept warm by one big, wood-burning stove. Reindeer hides, virtually hairless from age and wear, covered the wood-plank floors. The woman came lurching down the stairs, having shown Sophie up to a room; a lot of Lappish and Norwegian was being yelled to and fro as the men carried the gear in – Arctic gear only, of course, their other stuff having been left in the hotel in

Karasjok. Ollie hauled his bergen up the rickety stairs and into a fair-sized room with four bunk-beds in it. Fishermen's dormitory; and a night's lodging here for the five of them wouldn't much deplete the US budget this year, he guessed.

Supper was served within minutes. Reindeer stew: and it wasn't bad, but he had a suspicion that after this trip he wouldn't ever think of venison as a luxury food again. At Sutherland's request they'd unearthed a bottle of red wine, and then a second one appeared as the meal wore on rather slowly, but Isak had his own liquor, a colourless liquid from an unlabelled bottle which the proprietor had brought in. It smelt like methylated spirit, but Sophie said they called it brandy – *brennevin*. Ollie tried some, and decided it *was* meths.

'I'll stick to the plonk, thanks.' Stenberg reacted similarly, after he'd tasted it. Isak, waving his mug, shouted what sounded like some sort of challenge at them, in Lappish; Sophie murmured, 'He is becoming drunk.'

Hardly surprising. And maybe slightly more advanced in the process, Ollie thought, than the word 'becoming' suggested. But he seemed to be waiting for an answer – peering at them, his face looking squashed as if it had been trodden on. Sutherland said, 'He was quoting a sort of proverb – "In Lappland one does not get a wife without spirits".'

Ollie looked at Sophie. 'He's after you. He can sense how fond you are of him.'

'Comes from their courting routine.' The professor explained, 'Traditionally the suitor appoints some prominent member of the community to be what they call "Chief of the Wooing". This guy leads a deputation to visit the bride's parents and argue the suitability of the match, what a marvellous deal the girl's getting, and so forth, and they have to bring presents with them, amongst which quantities of hard liquor is an essential. Hence "no wife without spirits".'

Isak was giving himself a refill, the neck of the bottle rattling on the edge of the mug as he poured with shaking hands.

'Will he be fit for skiing tomorrow?'

Gus was swilling wine as a mouthwash, trying to get rid of

the taste of that gut-rot. He suggested, 'Could be what he needs for it, like anti-freeze.'

'I'd guess he can take it.' Sutherland asked Sophie, 'Your room OK?'

'Oh, it's — all right.'

'Is there a lock on the door?'

'No.' She'd glanced fleetingly at Isak. 'If I scream, please come quickly.'

Stenberg said, 'Ollie's liable to do that even if you *don't* scream.'

'Is *he* in our room?' Changing the subject, primarily, since Sophie had seemed embarrassed by Gus's silly comment. Sutherland said, sure, he thought Isak would have to be sharing with them, there were only the two dormitory rooms up there. Which made it seem unlikely that they'd be getting the early night they all felt they should have, in preparation for tomorrow's trek.

But Isak was getting more boisterous and noisy at this stage. He'd eaten only about half the food he'd been given, although everyone else had finished; the Lapp woman had collected the empty dishes, and it was her idea now that Isak should entertain them all with a performance of *yoik*. She'd been leaning behind his chair with her short, thick arms round his neck, talking loudly into his ear; Ollie had been talking to Sutherland — telling him he'd had to leave the professor's book, the copy he'd lent him, at the hotel, but that he was looking forward to finishing it when they got back. And as he said it — he was to remember this later, although at the time he dismissed it as part of the peculiar atmosphere of the evening and the environment and Isak's outlandish behaviour — he became aware, surprisingly, of a doubt, presentiment, a shadow of uncertainty in connection with that phrase '*when* we get back'.

As far as the professor's book was concerned, the truth was he hadn't got into the second chapter yet, and rather doubted if he ever would. But then he'd lost Sutherland's attention anyway: there was an upheaval at the end of the table, Isak struggling to rise and the woman hanging on to him. It looked as if they might be going to dance, but in fact Isak slumped down near the stove; he was helped into a squatting position, one hand grasping the leg of a chair for support, and his face began to darken, suffusing with blood before his mouth opened to emit the first strangulated moans of what Ollie realised had to be a *yoik*. He felt slightly under the weather himself, having drunk a certain amount of wine and the taste of meths still lingering; the weird sounds deadened his awareness of the surroundings, gave him a sense of detachment, unreality, and Sophie was on her way out of the room before he'd realised that she was leaving them. She'd muttered as she left the table, 'I would like so much to hear this, but I cannot remain awake another minute. Good night, please excuse me.' She'd rattled it off, then disappeared, getting away before anyone could try to detain her, and he hadn't had a chance to say good night. Then he was wondering how Gus Stenberg had the bloody gall to be following her up the stairs, until he heard him calling to her, 'Don't worry, Sophie dear, I'll get it on tape and you can hear it some other time.'

He came back with the recorder, cleared a space for it on the rough-surfaced table and switched it on. It was battery-powered, had to be so he could use it outside and in the wilds of nowhere, which was where they'd be as from tomorrow.

The *yoik*ing noise was continuing spasmodically, indescribable except that no one could be surprised at this art-form never having caught on anywhere except in the remoter areas of Lappland, the Lapp woman was rocking to and fro like a trained bear, and Sutherland had his eyes shut. Ollie had to leave them, temporarily; the loo was on the ground floor and was really an outside one which had been linked to the back of the house so you didn't have to wade through snow to get to it. An iron bar was provided though, obviously for the essential purpose of smashing ice.

When he got back the *yoik* was finished, and at first glance he thought the reason for this was Isak having passed out. In fact he hadn't, technically, but he was slumped against the side of the stove and he looked ill. Drunken euphoria had evaporated and his complexion had changed from mahogany to the colour of dirty snow. His eyes were slitted, weepy, moisture glistening in sparse stubble on his cheeks. Gus was re-winding his tape; he murmured to Ollie, 'The artiste is distinctly stoned. . . . Oh, God, *no*. . . .' Because the Lapp woman was pressing the refilled mug into one of Isak's hands. The fingers closed round it slowly: then he'd opened his eyes wider and he was lifting the mug, trying to focus on it and not finding that too easy, slopping liquor everywhere. Sutherland stirred, getting to his feet and muttering that this had gone far enough; generally speaking it wasn't a good idea to mess around with Sami when they were smashed but he couldn't be allowed to poison himself, best get him upstairs. . . . Isak spoke then, a kind of moaning cry in Lappish, and squinting up at the professor.

Stenberg asked, 'What'd he say?'

He'd said – Sutherland interpreted – *Please God, help me*!

More mumbling. He was drunk all right, but it was more than that too, Ollie thought, more like some emotional crisis. His voice rose again: slurry Lappish, loud then dying into a sort of growling, dribble running down his chin. The words Sutherland had been able to hear had been a quote from the New Testament: *Take this cup from me.* . . . Sutherland had been going to him, but the proprietor was already there, crouching beside him and prising the mug out of his fingers, taking that request literally. Sutherland looked round at Gus and Ollie, told them, 'He wasn't talking about the booze, then. He's in a blue funk, if you ask me.'

'Scared of taking us down there. . . .'

'Maybe. *Something* like that.'

In the morning Isak was pale and shaky, but told Sutherland he was OK. He'd only drunk that much *brennevin*, he said, because it was the best cure for stomach trouble, from which he'd suffered on the way down here.

He'd slept on the floor beside the stove. It wouldn't have been easy to haul him up the stairs, and nobody had had any burning desire to have him up there, so they'd just covered him with a reindeer hide. He ate a large breakfast – pickled fish and cold reindeer meat – not, as Gus commented, every lush's idea of a good start to the day – his only problem being the difficulty of lifting a coffee-cup to his mouth without shaking all the coffee out of it on the way up.

Sophie questioned whether they should start today. Stenberg pointed out that if they hung around he'd only tie on another one, and the other two agreed.

Snow showers were intermittent, and there was a lot of new snow on the ground. Wind still northwest, ground temperature minus two. Ollie looked through his set of ski waxes and decided to use purple, which was prescribed for fresh snow at temperatures around zero. Sophie said she'd take a chance on that – they had a long discussion about the various waxes and their use in different combinations, a subject on which cross-country skiers tend to have conflicting views – and he offered to wax her planks for her. The Americans had their own waxes.

Sutherland and Sophie were with Isak when the proprietor asked him casually, 'Will you be going on south along the river now?'

Isak pointed west. 'That way.'

Sutherland thought he'd got his sense of direction confused. 'You surely don't mean west – into Finnmark – do you?'

'West.' Isak nodded, without meeting his eyes. 'It's where the *siida* was last seen.'

Isak wasn't only hungover, Ollie thought, he was withdrawn, locked into thoughts that weren't for sharing. It seemed strange, too, that he hadn't mentioned the change of route until he'd actually been asked about it. Ollie got the news from Sophie when he was applying wax to her skis. She said, 'The only person who could have told him was where we stopped yesterday, the man there. They were talking together outside, you know.'

'So why did he have to keep it secret until now?'

She shrugged. 'He says he was ill yesterday. *Something* was wrong with him.'

103

'You'd think he'd have mentioned it.' He'd nearly finished the waxing. 'Even that road doesn't go far, though. It stops dead, having got nowhere.'

'Then we will be on the *vidda*. You will see how *wonderful*—'

'You're quite a girl, Sophie.'

'What else should I be?'

'It was a way of saying you're fantastic.'

'I think we should – save it, Ollie.'

'Yes.' He'd straightened and his arms were round her, waxy hands carefully out of contact. 'Yes, I know. But – when this trip's finished?'

'Do you think I would just let you say goodbye?'

Kissing. *Look, no hands*. . . . None the worse for that, however, or for being the first time; except it was so hard to stop he didn't know afterwards how he'd managed it.

Half an hour later they were set to go. Ollie pulled on his headover – a wool tube worn round the neck like a bulky collar, but there to be pulled up over the lower part of the face when you needed it – and zipped up his jacket. Oiled-wool ski hat, Dachstein mittens. Seeing Gus adjusting the position of Sophie's back-pack for her, he wondered how on earth the young American – who appeared to be entirely normal, male, virile, etcetera – could stand back as he was doing, not at least *try* to compete for her interest.

There were three tow-lines on the pulk, as was necessary to control it on gradients. Isak took the centre, leading, with Ollie and Gus right and left; on downhill slopes they'd drop back to restrain it, and so on. Sophie followed behind the pulk, with Carl behind her at some distance. The snow was deep, on top of a hard underlay, and more of it was driving intermittently on the northerly wind, straight into their faces as they started back to the place where the road curved westward.

They'd been on the move for nearly three hours, making

steady progress, Isak seemingly having no health problems. By the end of the first hour the snow had stopped falling, and also they'd come to where the road ended. The only difference this made, effectively, was that they didn't have the lines of cleared trees to steer by now. Ollie was wearing a wrist compass – he also had a Silva compass for map work, in a zipped pocket – and he was keeping an eye on where Isak was leading them. Slightly south of due west, so far, following the general line of a river. Other frozen streams led into it, coming down steeply from high ground to the north; they'd crossed four, clambering over ice, and now as they came to a fifth their own river was bending away southward. Ahead, in a depression which in summer would surely be a bog, lay a frozen lake, with the land rising again beyond it.

Isak stopped, staring southward where the river lay fairly level, curving back a little to the right after that bend and with unbroken snowfields rising on both sides above a scattering of small trees. Ollie and Sutherland stopped too: then Sophie, as the pulk came to a halt in front of her. Stenberg was rearguard at this stage: he, Ollie and the professor were changing positions at each hour.

Sutherland shouted, 'Snowscooter!'

Ollie had just heard it too. The sound was getting louder rapidly and it was a harsh intrusion, seemed not to have any rightful place in these surroundings, the silence and emptiness of the snowbound land. Sophie was right, he thought, it was an 'out-of-this-world' sensation that hit you. He'd experienced it before, here in Norway on long-range ski patrols years ago; it was akin to the kind of thrill men sought when they climbed mountains or travelled to the Poles. He'd forgotten, hadn't linked this to her enthusiasm for the high plains, this sense of removal, timelessness. Glancing back, he saw her and Gus coming towards him. Sutherland and Isak were both looking around at the apparently empty snowscape out of which the noise was rising – a jarring, unpleasant racket.... Sophie called, 'There it is!' Pointing with one ski-pole: her poles had unusually long tips to them, he noticed. The scooter was up beyond the lake, had just lifted into view over the rounded

105

skyline. Sound dropping as it slowed, then stopped, a swirl of snow settling around it, engine only muttering now and the rider just sitting there, staring down in this direction. Isak shouted to Sutherland in Lappish. Sophie said, 'He's going over to talk with him. I suppose to ask if he knows where are these people.'

Isak had a downhill run, then some flat and a stream to cross. After that he'd be climbing. Gus said, 'That'll sweat some of the poison out of his flab.'

Kill or cure. . . . But Isak had to be tougher than he looked. Heavy bones, and probably more muscle on that short, thick body than flab, Ollie guessed. Plus a remarkable tolerance for strong drink. . . . The scooter rider still sat and watched him struggling over. Ollie muttered, 'Why doesn't the lazy sod go down to him?'

'Has his own work to do, maybe.' Stenberg suggested, 'Rounding up stray deer, or whatever. . . . Hey, wouldn't it be nice if he's from the crowd we're looking for?'

'It's not impossible.' Sutherland had ski'd over to them. He was all right on the level, trekking, but downhill he was no skier. In any case these skis and the loose-heeled bindings, ideal for cross-country work, weren't suited to downhill running. Sutherland added, 'Let's all cross fingers, now.'

Isak had given up. He'd stopped – arms spread, his ski-poles dangling from their extremities. They heard fragments of an exchange of shouts; then the scooter engine snarled, shattering the surrounding peace again as the stranger began to glide down towards him.

'Mahommed's coming to the mountain. . . .'

The scooter rider could have been Mahommed, as far as Isak knew; he'd expected to be met by the man he'd last seen in his house in Karasjok, but he'd never set eyes on this one before.

'You're Isak, huh?'

This was a Sami, but from the east. He spoke North

Lappish, not East Lappish or the Anar dialect; he was talking the language that was spoken by three-quarters of all Sami people, but he spoke it with an outlandish accent.

Similar accent to Johan's.

He was looking over Isak's head. 'So those are your Americans. . . .'

As if he'd never seen any before. Maybe he hadn't. Isak asked curtly, 'D'you have a message?'

'Wouldn't be here if I hadn't. Here it is. . . . Turn southeast here, cross into Finland and continue southward, looking for your friends. I'm telling you now, they'll be in the mountains beyond the Lemmenjoki. Maybe in the Viipustunturit. So you take them south, past the west flank of the Maarestunturit, and on through the High Gap. D'you know it?' Isak nodded, scowling, and the stranger went on, 'Right *through* it. That way we can't lose you, or we can pick you up there again if we *have* lost you. Got it?'

'For how long should I search?'

'How long is a piece of string?'

Isak glared at him, waiting. . . .

A shrug. 'You'd search until you found them, wouldn't you?'

'One cannot find what isn't there.'

'Well, say a few days.'

Four hundred metres away, Sutherland said, 'Can't be one of our guys. Wouldn't need such a long conversation, would he, he'd have let us know.'

Gus shrugged. 'He'd have to explain what he's after. Maybe have to persuade him the other one did make certain promises. I mean that he'd tell him, whatever. . . .'

Isak asked the scooter rider, 'And then what?'

'Eventually you will return to Karasjok alone. But don't worry about that, you'll be told what to say, and your story will hold water, you'll be in the clear.'

'What kind of story?'

'Maybe an avalanche.' A shrug. '*Some* such—'

'No!'

'*What?*'

'I am – not a murderer! I can't *do* such a thing, I'm—'

Sutherland said, 'Hell of a long confab, isn't it?'

'We might be in luck.' Sophie was the optimist now. 'He must either be from the *siida* or he knows where it is. Otherwise they would not have so much to talk about.'

Stenberg agreed: 'I think you're right. . . .'

The snowscooter rider said, 'Johan does not ask you to kill anyone. Only to do as I have said.'

'I would have a hand in it, though! An accomplice!' Isak panted, 'Johan and I have agreements, he knows I could not *possibly* be tainted with—'

'Oh, listen – I almost forgot to mention – I was to tell you that your niece, Inga, is with us. Pretty little thing, eh? No harm will come to her, Johan says, as long as you see this through. *Then* you'll have her back – unharmed. All Johan wants is for you to lead these Americans into Finland, into the mountains down there in the reserve. That's not asking so much, you know. Especially if you don't want Inga to be – well, there are nine of us, nobody'd be in any rush to cut her throat. . . .'

It had sunk in. These things were actually being said, presented in that nasally-accented monotone. It was like something in a nightmare – unreal, incredible – but the words *had* been spoken, echoed and re-echoed now in Isak's brain while he faced the scooter-rider's contemptuous smile.

'Jesus, see *that*?'

Sophie squawked, 'They're *fighting*!'

'Oh, no, surely—'

Revving, picking up speed, showering snow as the belts gripped. . . .

Isak had aimed a swipe at him with one ski-pole, and almost fallen. The rider had been laughing as he'd opened the throttle. Isak leaning heavily on both poles now, staring after the machine as it swept away – up over the rise, a scream of sound that hit its peak as scooter and rider topped the skyline and tipped out of sight.

'Just waved that pole, didn't he?'

'The hell he did.' Gus, glancing at Sutherland, allowed amused contempt to show in his expression. Maybe for the way the older man always wanted everything to be nice, right, happy – as if by pretending everything was OK he'd make it so. . . . 'Ollie, you saw him hit out at the guy – right?'

Ollie nodded. Isak was on his way back. This side of the stream he had to climb, and when he got to them he was breathing in short gasps. But also, you could see the same kind of desperation in him that there'd been last night. He said in jerky Norwegian, 'The *siida* has gone into Finland.' Pointing southeast. 'That way, now.'

'Was he sure of it?' Stenberg asked, 'Does he actually know the people?'

Isak was still out of breath. Ollie, hearing Sophie tell Gus the man *would* know them, they all knew each other, was thinking, *He's got the frights again.* . . . Isak panted in Lappish, 'Yes. Yes, he was sure. . . .'

'But—' Sophie asked him, 'You *hit* at him?'

A nod: breathing speeding up again. . . . 'He spoke of – my niece.' Mud-coloured eyes pleaded with Sutherland's pale

109

ones. 'Inga. You saw her, spoke with her at my house?'

'Sure.' Carl nodded. 'Pretty kid, very nice manner, I was impressed. But why, what—'

'He spoke of her—' Isak looked sick, and it had nothing to do with drink, this had hit him in the last few minutes – 'disrespectfully – *insultingly*—'

'Then you did right to take a swing at the bastard!'

Stenberg cut in, 'So you knew that guy, he knows your—'

'Christ's *sake*.' Sutherland threw him an angry glance; he put one arm round Isak's shoulders. 'Lousy thing to happen. Try not to let it get to you, old pal. . . .'

Ollie was given the translation a minute or two later, by Gus, to whom Sutherland had muttered, 'They *all* know each other, damn it. Sophie just made that point, didn't she. Any case, this was obviously very private business, family business.' But the scene was fixed in Ollie's mind for a long time afterwards, like a film stopped at a single frame. Isak's look of anguish, Carl's arm round the little man's heavy shoulders, compassion in Carl's face and – in total contrast – only sharp curiosity in Sophie's.

6

The snow was coming down like a wall travelling horizontally on a wind of about force four. When you struggled round to look back into it, it was blinding after a couple of seconds; you'd see an upright figure at maybe forty feet – having cleared your goggles – but not much farther. Southward or southeast, the way they were going when Isak happened to be on course, you could see a couple of hundred yards most of the time, better than that when there was a lull. For the sake of maintaining contact they'd closed their distances apart by shortening the tow-lines, and Sophie was right in behind the pulk now, the rearguard not far back in her tracks. Ollie was leaving that station, passing her and the pulk, poling hard to catch up with Sutherland who was on the left; he called to Sophie as he passed her, 'You OK?'

Her masked face turned his way: the red cap was white now, her green windproof smock also whitened. She'd ceased to be a girl, to an uninformed outsider's eye she'd become a *yeti* lunging through soft snow in company with four others. His own eye, of course, was not an outsider's, not any more, he saw through all that disguise. She'd raised a hand in answer, telling him 'OK': he yelled 'Keep closed up!' then had his head down again, pushing on hard to get up beside the professor. He was there, within a pole's length, before Sutherland discovered he had company; then the snow-covered head and shoulders swung round. . . .

'So what's new?'

'Time to find somewhere to bivvy-up, get settled before dark – shelter, trees, forest. Tell Isak?'

He wanted to find a good place to bed down, before Isak wasted more time and energy wandering off at tangents. . . . Taking over the tow-line meanwhile from Sutherland – who had to pass the message because he himself wasn't able to communicate with the Lapp. Sutherland let him take this side's share of the pulk's weight, then disengaged himself and veered clumsily away. Ollie looked back to check that Sophie was in station. Not that she needed any help, she was at least as competent on skis as he was, and a lot more so than either of the Americans, but there was always the worry – in his own head, anyway – that a few moments' inattention would be enough to cause her to lose contact, and when there was nobody in the rearmost position – as now – it was a real danger. If she'd had to stop for some reason – adjusting a binding or her back-pack, for instance, if she'd stopped for half a minute too long nobody would have known and within another minute she could be lost, the ski and pulk tracks ahead of her filled with new snow. Sutherland was closing in on Isak, he saw. Close to the river, the Finnish border, there might be a place suitable for a camp, in the valley where the trees grew thickly. The lee side of a dense birch grove would provide shelter from the storm, for instance, and also protection against avalanches – if there happened to be any such danger.

There was no question of bivvying anywhere around here, in present conditions. This was still high fell country – Sophie's dreamland, for God's sake – treeless and windswept. It was a wind, incidentally, which would be converting a static temperature of just below freezing point to something more like minus fifteen. And avalanche hazards did exist, had to be looked out for. Even the slope they were on now – slight

112

downhill gradient, no apparent threat – steepened sharply higher up where the visibility cut out any view of the summit, or ridge, or whatever it rose to. . . .

A few days of this, and they'd all be in better shape than they were now. But there'd be some aches and pains tonight, he guessed.

Isak was slanting left, slightly upslope. Carl still with him: both hunched, leaning into the work. Aiming to skirt more closely round the high ground on this side, then – Ollie hoped – to get down to the tree-line. Carl was separating from him, side-stepping up to his left, putting himself where Ollie would be when he'd climbed that shoulder. Out to the right, Gus had just noticed that they were changing course.

Carl shouted, 'Round this hill, then we run down into the forest. OK?'

Ollie pulled the ice-crusted headover down clear of his mouth. 'How's your friend?'

'I don't know what's been into him. Seems OK now but – Christ, I don't know. . . . I'll take this tow again now, right?'

'Fine, I'll join Isak. Keep an eye on Sophie, will you?'

Verbal communication, having got that basic requirement across to Isak, would not be necessary. A word or two of Norwegian, supplementing gestures, would get them to some suitable location. Isak shouldn't have needed direction, of course, this should have been second nature to him – this was his kind of country, he'd been born in it, as likely as not in a tent, taken his first toddler's steps on skis. . . .

He'd laid a false trail, though.

There'd been time to think about this, and it was a solid fact, inescapable. It could have happened by chance, just turned out this way, but the plain truth was that by starting westward and then making this sharp change of direction he'd seen to it that they did a disappearing trick. The Lapp couple in that fishermen's pub, who'd been the last people to see them before they'd left what might at a pinch be described as civilisation, had been told the party was heading west into the middle of Finnmark, and if for any reason anyone came looking for them that was the direction in which they'd been pointed.

Making camp. . . .

Bulky in arctic gear, they lumbered around like divers on a seabed – clumsy, slow-moving, cocooned against the oppressive cold. Getting the gear off the pulk and the tents up was the first essential; skis and poles were dug into the snow like fenceposts marking the camp's perimeter, inside which their boots had soon flattened the snow into a hard floor. Back-packs slung meanwhile from branches. A short distance inside the wood Sophie had the naptha stove going, with the pulk's tarpaulin cover rigged to provide temporary shelter while she boiled water to make tea. She was handing out steaming mugs of it by the time the tents were up. They were hemispherical and well insulated, expensive items to hire. Set close together on the edge of the birch forest – which itelf was in the lee of a hillside too steep to hold much snow, so there was no avalanche danger – they formed a camp that was about as well sheltered as it could have been, in present circumstances. But it was going to be better soon: Gus had said, standing back with his mug between mittened hands, and looking at the little semi-circle of rounded tents, 'That's about it, eh?' and Ollie had told him, 'Not yet, it isn't. If you'd lend a hand, we'll make a shelter to cook in.'

Because the tents were small and had integral groundsheet floors in which you wouldn't want to burn holes. Also, it was going to be necessary to boil water and if you did that in a tent you'd have condensation to make everything soaking wet, then ice on the inside of the fabric.

He put them to work cutting and stacking wood. Posts for driving into the snow as uprights, and branches to lash horizontally, forming a back wall, two end walls and a sloping roof. The cover from the pulk dictated the shelter's size, covering the roof to make it watertight; you ended up with a cookhouse shack that had its open side facing the tents, and it contributed to the shelter from that windward direction. Then in the space between it and the tents you could build a camp fire to help raise morale as well as temperature a little, give some light and keep a kettle simmering without using up reserves of naptha. Despite the falling snow it would burn all right, once it had a good heart to it; most of the snow was passing overhead anyway, and the bivvy gave shelter to that patch of ground. Meanwhile, getting these jobs done – and more to come yet, you'd need a lot of firewood – had served the secondary purpose of keeping them on the go while the sweat dried on their bodies; it had been hard work getting here, and that was an essential preliminary to relaxing.

Sophie said, 'I think you are a genius, Ollie.'

'Someone's noticed, finally.' He was building a firescreen, half a dozen logs on top of each other horizontally with uprights pushed into the snow at both ends to hold them, on the lee side of where the fire would be. This was what had provoked that expression of admiration, but it was only so sparks wouldn't blow on to the tents. He said, 'No problem, as long as the materials are handy. As they usually are. . . . But the next thing, lady and gents – while Gus starts collecting firewood for us – is to decide what we want to eat. Any preferences – Sophie?'

She turned to Sutherland. One hunched *yeti* inviting comment from a shorter, thicker one. Sutherland proposed, 'Fresh meat ought to be used first, I'd say.'

'All right. It's deep-frozen now, but it'll thaw in the pot. First task therefore is to heat a lot more water. How about baked beans with our venison?'

Sophie had a tent to herself, Ollie was sharing with Stenberg, Sutherland was to have the pleasure of Isak's company in the third. Sutherland said he'd do the cooking; he asked Sophie, 'Unless you'd like to?'

'You think I'm crazy?'

'OK, fine. . . .'

He did most of the cooking for his family, he'd told them at some stage. His wife ran an art gallery and was on committees, she was happy to leave it to him and it happened to be one of his hobbies. He probably hadn't done it quite this way before though – he had the largest of the pots on the naptha stove, and had to feed shovelfuls of clean snow into it until there was enough water to cook in. The meat would be boiled after it had thawed. The rest of them were coming and going, collecting and stacking birchwood and fir-cones, and Ollie stashed all the meat, fresh and salted, on the roof of the bivvy, out of reach of animals.

'Especially wolverines. They're greedy buggers.'

'Maybe wolves too?'

'I don't know. Not so many around now. I'm told people hunt them from helicopters with automatic weapons. Still—' he nodded to Gus '—I'll put my cannon together, just in case.'

If there were wolverines around they might be attracted by the smell of the meat. The fire would be a deterrent, if it could be kept going all night. Isak joined Sutherland, selecting the meat to be used now, and Sutherland left him to it, admitting that where reindeer were concerned a Sami had to be the expert. Only Sami men cooked meat anyway – in families or groups where the old traditions were observed – Carl said.

Isak wasn't talking, wasn't joining in at all. He'd been helping out with the chores but doing it as if he was one man alone, never part of a team. He might be ill, Ollie thought; having started the day with at least some degree of alcoholic poisoning, even if he'd sweated it out during the day's trek it was bound to have some lingering effect.

Carl told them later – four of them crowded into one tent with fresh mugs of tea, Isak squatting in the bivvy tending the stove and also nursing the fire into a blaze – 'The Sami people have their own views on which parts of the deer are best, and how to cook them. Here I expect he'll just boil it, as I would have, but he might boil it first then just sizzle it in a pan. The tongue, tail and marrow-bones are their particular delicacies.'

'I'll tell you one thing.' Stenberg had had his head out through the tent's opening. 'He has a pint bottle of that poison, and he's taking swigs out of it.'

'Hair of the dog.' Sutherland had an excuse for anything his Lapp friend did. 'I dare say he needs it.'

Ollie agreed. It could be hangover that was making the little man so morose. 'But I'd like to point out something else that's been bothering me. . . .' He gave them his thoughts on the false trail Isak had left, the fact no one could have any way of knowing where they were now or that they'd be even farther south by this time tomorrow.

'Does it matter?' Sutherland spoke from the back of the tent. 'Who's likely to come looking for us?'

Scalding tea burnt Ollie's throat.

'Only happens to be a fact that—' he paused; he'd been about to say that if anything drastic happened to them now, no one would know *where* it had happened, any more than it was known where those three Finns had been murdered. He'd stopped himself saying it because he didn't want to worry Sophie. Although she probably wouldn't be any more easily frightened than anyone else. . . . He finished '—that if anyone did want to know where we are, they'd find they'd been misled – to the extent that there's no way they *could*, now.'

'Except Sophie's people.' Stenberg reminded her, 'You called them, didn't you, before we left Karasjok?'

'Not exactly.' She moved, drawing her legs in under her. They were sitting on foam sleeping-mats on top of the ground-sheet. 'I did call, sure, but I spoke to one of the department's halfwits and he said he would write down that I was at the *turisthotell*. It made me angry and I did not bother more with him.'

'Carl's probably right, anyway.' Ollie shrugged. 'Probably nothing to lose sleep over.'

Starting out westward from Jorgastak had certainly been a surprise decision of Isak's. There didn't have to be anything sinister in it; it could have been just his dithering, not knowing where to start looking, not trusting his own judgement that the *siida* would be down in Finland. You didn't have to be paranoiac about it.

The tent rocked to a gust of wind, the wood fire flaring then dying down again. Have to keep it fairly low, he thought, when we turn in. And one man on watch: he, Stenberg, Sutherland, sharing the dark hours, maybe – for the care of the fire and the chance of wolverines or wolves, whatever, stealing that food. . . . The point about nobody knowing where they were really did *not* matter, as long as he kept doing the job they'd hired him for – keeping them from frostbite, exposure, avalanches, made sure they only crossed rivers where the ice was thick, and had plenty to eat and drink, didn't stray and get lost – and about fifty other things most of which he'd forgotten in more recent years of acquiring quite different skills.

It was dark now. Firelight flickered outside the tent, lit the interior of the cooking shack where Isak squatted close to the naptha ring, yellow fingers of heat licking up around the pot. It had to be at least thirty below, out there, but the firelight was cheerful and in this tent the warmth of four bodies in a confined space contributed to some degree of comfort. A hot meal would be even more warming, and then there'd be comfort in the sleeping-bags. He'd annoy them with a lecture, shortly – even if they protested that they knew it all now – about drying damp clothes inside sleeping-bags, boots inside them too in plastic bags, and wet socks and gloves, hats, whatever, inside your clothing – in the armpits was a good place – to dry from the body's warmth. Every item of clothing had to be dried out, one way or another, every night; if you went out in the morning in a damp shirt it would freeze on you as you crawled out of the tent.

The fire was well established and radiating plenty of warmth, melting the snow around it and creating slush farther out. Ollie had given them his talk about drying their gear, and avoiding frostbite, watching each other for the signs of it and how you'd treat it if it occurred. One of the points under the heading of treatment being *not* to expose it to direct heat like this fire's.

Stenberg had remarked, dismissively, 'Common sense is all that is, really.' He asked Isak in Norwegian, 'How about a *yoik* before bed-time?'

Sophie's eyes flashed in the firelight: 'Gus, I warn you—'

'So do I. Back off the fire a bit, Gus. You're going into an ice-cold tent from here, and that's common sense too, OK?'

'Isak.'

The eyelids lifted slightly: small features mole-like in surrounding fur. Fur hat, fur ear-flaps dangling, stubble blue-black on the little pointed face.

'*Yoik* for us, would you?' Gus made the request in Norwegian; Sophie murmured in English, 'That is what I am warning him about. I will *kill* him . . .' Isak was blinking, considering the request perhaps, but with his thought-processes somewhat slowed. Gus urged, 'We were very impressed with the *yoik* you allowed us to hear last night.'

The dark eyes shifted to Sutherland. 'I *yoik*ed last night? Of what did I *yoik*?'

'To be truthful, I couldn't say.' Sutherland admitted apologetically, 'As you know, my knowledge of the Sami language is sadly limited. I enjoyed the melody, the whole sound, but the actual meaning – well, a word or two here and there, maybe—'

'What *yoik* was it I sang?'

He was asking Sophie. His mind would be a blank, of course, he'd have no memory of having sung at all. . . . Gus was telling Ollie, 'Wants to know what he sang about. If you could call that singing, and as if anyone could have the faintest notion.'

Sophie told Isak regretfully that she'd gone up to bed before the *yoik*ing started. If only she'd known such a treat was likely to be offered, she'd have stayed, of course.

'Was it the song of Nilas?'

'May have been.' Sutherland nodded. 'May well have been.'

'This one. . . .'

Isak's neck began to swell like a bullfrog's. In the flickering half-light and under the stubble his deepening colour wasn't noticeable, but the sound as he began to squeeze it out was similar to last night's.

> Voia voia, nana nana, very gentle, very loving, very clever/ Voia voia, nana nana, big and lovely, best girl in the country . . .

'That one, was it?'

Sutherland shook his head. 'I don't think so.'

He began another verse . . .

> Voia voia, nana nana, Birru Baergalak, now I'll kill all
> Nilas' reindeer/ Satan's false Elle's rotten trousers; still
> are many, many like her . . .

He'd stopped again. 'Uh?'

'No, I'm sure that wasn't it.'

Gus asked Sophie, 'Are *you* sure you translated it right?'

'Certain. Of course, you need some understanding—'

'I'd *say* so. . . . But incidentally, what does *voia voia nana nana* mean?'

'Nothing at all.'

A nod: 'That's what I figured.'

Isak said, 'The reindeer *yoik*, it may have been. This one again is very old.'

> Splendid reindeer, springing, springing,/ Voia voia voia,
> nana nana nana/ Reindeer springing like the windstorm/
> Voia voia voia, nana nana nana/ Finest horns among all
> reindeer . . .

Sutherland said into the sudden, hard-breathing silence, 'No, it wasn't that one either. Quite different sound, I'd say.'

A strong gust of wind, with snow in it, made the fire roar up, flames licking at the screen of logs. Ollie moved the kettle back slightly with his boot; they were feeding the kettle periodically with clean snow. Isak, after a few moments' frowning concentration, told Sutherland, 'There is another old reindeer song. If I'd thought of it I might have sung this one to you.' He began to swell again, hit the note he wanted and then the harsh gutturals came again:

> Silken coated, silken coated, voia voia voia, nana nana
> nana/ Running like the sunbeams, voia voia voia, nana

nana nana/ Small calves lowing, voia voia voia, nana nana nana/ Rushing . . . Rushing . . .

His voice tailed away as if the pressure in his lungs had failed. Carl was shaking his head. Sophie translated the lyrics and added, 'Gus, say *yes*, this is it – or the next one, *please*, so we don't have to be tortured all night?' Gus murmured, 'Doubt if it'd stop him now. He's beginning to enjoy himself.'

'If he is, he is the *only* one who—'

'Hey, look here!' Sutherland slapped his knee. 'Just remembered – Gus put last night's show on tape!' He turned to Isak. 'Want to hear yourself, Isak – the way Gus here taped it?'

'You recorded my *yoik*?'

Ollie broke in: 'Sorry to interrupt, Carl, but I suggest it's time we all hit the sack. To stay fit we need sleep, and we *must* all stay fit – OK?'

Sophie murmured, 'Heavens, yes, look at the time. . . .'

Gus was joining in, supporting the proposal in Norwegian. Isak said flatly, ignoring him, 'I should like to hear it.'

'Oh, *please* not. . . .'

'Actually I wiped the tape,' Gus said in Norwegian. 'Sorry. Just remembered. The acoustics in that room were hopeless, really. . . . Maybe you'd let me record you some other time, Isak. I'd like that reindeer song, for instance – well, both of them.'

He told Ollie afterwards in their tent, sipping hot cocoa, 'Difficult to imagine anyone wanting that sound on tape or any other way. Jesus. . . . But last night's performance wasn't entirely without interest, huh?'

'It had its moments.'

'Would anyone believe it, if you told it straight?'

'If they'd been here, seen the people, they might. . . . But thinking about it, I'd say Isak was as pissed last night as I've ever seen anyone. So it's not surprising he's been acting strangely today, when you think about it.'

'I don't know.' Stenberg blew on his cocoa. 'Carl's worried too. Actually admitted it – and he's not a man to admit anything's wrong until his nose is really *in* it.' He drank some,

121

noisily. Then: 'D'you get this feeling we might be on one of those wild goose chases, Ollie?'

He'd opened his bergen and was pulling out the shotgun's barrels. Then the stock; hooking them together, then delving in the bag for the fore-end and snapping it on. He opened the gun, jerked it shut again. He'd wiped it dry of oil before they'd left Karasjok; he'd have acquired some non-freeze lubricant from his hosts at Elvegardsmoen if he'd thought of it when he was there, but he hadn't, and ordinary light oil would have frozen, locked it solid, so the answer had to be no oil at all. He said – about Isak – 'Could be something to do with his niece, some family problem that's driving him to drink, I mean it doesn't have to be anything that need bother us in terms of our own objective. He wouldn't have dragged us down here just for the hell of it, after all.'

Two cartridges went into the pocket, two others into the gun's chambers.

'I'll wake you in two hours, Gus.'

'Preferably not by letting that thing go off.'

He was taking the first two-hour watch, then he'd get four hours' sleep while Gus and then Sutherland took their turns. Logic told him there wasn't any need to have a man on watch, but instinct contradicted logic; he knew that if he'd forced himself to turn in now he wouldn't have slept, he'd have lain awake in his sleeping-bag and kept a listening watch all night.

He threw some birch branches on the fire. It was green wood and soaking wet, but the fire was well enough established, you could just about have burnt water on it. He'd backed into the cooking shelter, with a folded sleeping-mat to serve as a cushion on top of the pulk; he was sitting with the mug of cocoa on the pulk beside him and the gun across his knees when Isak slouched into the firelight, back from relieving himself out there in the dark.

Isak saw the gun, and stopped. Motionless on his short legs in their reindeer-hide gaiters: staring at the weapon as if it threatened him. Ollie pointed at the store of meat above his head, then out at the darkness, making a pantomime of shooting at some animal. Isak didn't get the message, still stood there staring, so Ollie called, 'Carl? Tell Isak I have this gun only in case animals come to steal our rations, would you?'

Sutherland made the required statement in Norwegian, and Isak relaxed, turning towards Carl's tent. Ollie added, 'Better remind him to shake the snow off before he joins you in there.'

'You're like a dog with a bone, Ollie.'

That comment had come from Gus, in the end tent. Isak was beating snow off his furs; then he'd ducked in. Probably would have done that anyway, Ollie guessed; and his final glance had been just as hostile, taking in both the gun and Ollie. Maybe one shouldn't tell a Lapp how to handle conditions in which his people had survived well enough for several thousand years.

Sophie, he thought, *Sophie. . . .* Hearing her ask him again, *Do you think I would just let you say goodbye?*

Carl was stirring a saucepan of porridge over the wood fire while water heated for coffee and eggs on the naptha ring behind him. The eggs would be hard-boiled, for ease of handling. By the time they'd eaten breakfast, packed the gear and completed a few other tasks such as refilling water-bottles with melted snow, it would probably be light enough to get on the move. Ollie was impatient for it; they'd all been complaining of stiffness, muscles aching from yesterday's hard work, and he'd been ashamed to discover how unfit he was after the recent months of inaction.

Sophie caught him doing some loosening-up exercises, outside the radius of firelight. She'd come from the blind side, having been out there for her own purposes.

'Is your back all right, Ollie?'

'Perfect. When a fracture mends, it's mended.'

'So why did you have to leave your Royal Marines?'

'I didn't have to, I chose to. It's a long story, though.' A connecting thought hit him then for the first time, and surpris-

123

ingly. He told her, 'Until a few days ago I was wishing I hadn't left them. But you know, now I'm glad I did?'

'Then I am glad for you.'

He put an arm round her shoulders, round a lot of bulky clothing. 'Don't you want to ask *why* I'm glad about it?'

'No. I don't have to.'

Near the fire, Isak was using his sheathknife to cut strips of hard, salted meat for chewing along the way. Ollie joined Sutherland. He asked him, 'Have you thought any more what the trouble might have been between Isak and his pal on the scooter?'

'I can't say I have, Ollie.'

'Well, *I* have, and none of it adds up. For instance – well, look at what we're supposed to accept. . . . These two Lapps meet – by chance, right? – about a hundred k's from anywhere except the nearest snowdrift. The one on the scooter says, "Your friends aren't in this area, they moved down into Finland. And by the way, half Karasjok's screwing your niece blind." So Isak takes a swipe at him and then comes back and tells us "Now we go thataway. . .".'

Sutherland wasn't amused. 'We haven't the least idea what might have been said about the girl, do we?'

Stenberg, who'd joined them, put in, 'Don't even know she was mentioned.'

'So, Ollie,' Sutherland, crouching, waxing his skis, sounded irritable, 'whatever trouble there was between those two doesn't necessarily bear on our business at all. Why don't we simply accept that Isak has some personal problems – OK, very likely concerning his niece, after all that's what he *said* – which don't happen to be any of our business – and just fucking well forget it?'

'Except,' Stenberg murmured, 'that if Ollie's saying he wouldn't trust our little friend further than he could piss against a storm-force wind, I don't believe I'd disagree with him.'

'So what options do we have?' Sutherland stood up. 'Except we either take advantage of what he's offering us, or we pack up and go home without a damn thing to show for a hell of a lot of effort and expense?'

'Carl, I don't think we're actually in dispute.' Stenberg rested one hand on his professor's shoulder. 'We considered the options before we started, didn't we? We took the decision, and I don't think anyone's arguing against it – only saying Isak needs watching, maybe – but clearly we *have* to see this through.'

'Why?'

They both looked at Ollie. Daylight growing overhead, throwing the wooded hill behind them into silhouette. It had seemed a moment ago as if Sutherland had been inviting his assistant to make a decision for him, whether to go on or turn back. Stenberg demanded, 'What d'you mean, *why*?'

'I'm interested in your motivation. O K – the book, research, I know. . . . But Gus just said, *We have to see this through*. You're the writer, Carl, he's not, he's only your assistant – right?'

Isak had called out in Lappish, and Sophie was answering him. Sutherland, who'd finished the waxing job, turned towards them, in profile against the dawn. Stenberg answered Ollie's question: 'We undertook to get to the basics of this business. Carl being known to the Sami, we felt confident we would. And nobody likes to promise and not deliver, do they?'

Stenberg had told him in Kautokeino that Washington was footing all the bills, but he hadn't admitted that the Pentagon's or the CIA's or NATO's thirst for intelligence from this Northern flank had been the reason for mounting the expedition. The impression until now had been that Sutherland had planned a research trip, and they'd decided to buy a stake in it, but from what Gus had just said it seemed likely they'd actually recruited Sutherland for this reconnaissance.

125

7

They crossed the Anarjokka about an hour and a half after starting out. Then in Finland, leaving the river behind them, they were traversing what the map showed as a swamp. Except for knowing that in this region the river marked the Norway/Finland border there'd have been no way of telling you'd left NATO territory.

Circling around the base of a hill – half an hour later, beyond the swamp – then turning the curve into an S-bend to pass around another, its twin. . . . Ollie checked the route by compass as they went along, identifying landmarks against features shown on his map – rivers, peaks, and the slopes as indicated by contours. Isak was leading again, Carl on the right, Gus left, Ollie tailing Sophie. Hills around them were of moderate size, but farther away were mountains, one range in particular looming ahead – massive and towering, hunched against dirty-looking sky like an advertisement for some product that washed whiter.

A lowering sky, and darkening. More snow coming, maybe. There'd been a drop in temperature since about dawn, but it had been rising again since then.

About ten kilometres from the border there was another

frozen river to be crossed. Then a long uphill stretch. . . . Ollie thinking about Carl Sutherland in this new image – the professor as a hireling like himself, here not to revise his famous book but as a paid agent sent with his paid student-assistant to snout out intelligence for – well, for the CIA, presumably. No matter what Jarvis had said or even what he'd believed, it wasn't easy to think of any other organisation – except maybe the KGB – who'd recruit a distinguished academic as a field agent.

It was annoying to have been told so little – in fact to have been misled – when one's own background had been made public knowledge.

He'd been looking up, ahead and to his left, at that moment, up at a shoulder of the mountain, and he was seeing a human figure. . . .

A man – standing, leaning on ski-poles, looking down at them as they passed below him. A skier – alone, and as immobile as a statue. The others had seen him too – in that empty waste of snow, the high, bare hillside it would have been hard not to – and they were stopping. Ollie kept on, closing up to Sophie, who'd reached the pulk and swung its end round so that it was broadside-on to the slope. Gus came down to them, snow lifting in a sort of bow-wave round his ankles as he demonstrated his own rather eccentric telemark-style stopping technique. Not bad either, considering how little control one had, with the loose-heeled cross-country bindings; he was a better skier than Sutherland, anyway. Sutherland was with Isak, and waving up at the watcher on the hillside, shouting to him in Norwegian, Isak meanwhile standing like a dummy as if he knew it was pointless, that there'd be no reaction from the stranger. Sutherland gave up too now, and he and Isak came over to join the others.

'Isak says' – Carl spoke jerkily, short of breath – 'says it can't be one of the people we're looking for. Not out here on his own and with no reindeer. He says we ought to keep going, the *siida* could be on the move and we shouldn't hang around.'

'That's a new one, isn't it? That they'd be on the move, we'd have to chase after them?'

The professor shrugged. 'I don't know. I suppose if they'd found the grazing grounds already occupied they'd have to find some other place. There's another big range beyond the Lemmenjoki, right?'

Sophie pointed up at the hillside. 'He's gone.'

The shoulder of the mountain gleamed white, bare and empty. From this distance and angle no ski-tracks were visible, you'd think there'd never been a living soul on that glistening expanse.

Gus said, 'Could at least have waved back at you, couldn't ne?'

'Oh, I don't know.' Sutherland shrugged. 'In Kautokeino they weren't exactly friendly, were they? And that guy's most likely a Sami, and we're tourists, *non*-Samis – so what the hell, he wasn't blowing kisses. . . . Move on now, shall we?'

It was a convenient time to swap places with Sutherland, taking over the right-hand tow-line. Ollie pulled the headover up over his mouth and pushed off, traversing down to that position. Picking up the rope: getting on with the routine of this trek, but inside his skull grappling with a new and disturbing idea, a feeling that they were being led, directed, by some external agency. It had been started by the sight of that skier just standing, watching them: a herdsman herding. . . .

The way to get rid of this unpleasant impression was to think it out, translate what was no more than a *feeling* into logic, measure it against logic. If they were being led into a trap, for instance – well, the *siida* would be the bait. *Would have been* – and they'd jumped at it, swallowed the hook. Isak would have baited the trap with this *siida* story in his meeting with Sutherland after the dinner party in Karasjok. Having established what the Americans wanted to know about, what they'd come all the way to the Arctic for, he'd have dreamt up this fictional source of information, maybe after first discussing the project with others, late that night or in the morning.

(Moving on now. The gradient was still upward but it wouldn't be for much longer, there'd be a downhill section before the really hard work began.)

129

Examining the new scenario, hoping to find items that wouldn't fit. . . . Basic premise being the false trail laid by Isak yesterday. *That* made sense only too well, in the context of this scenario: if someone was thought to have disappeared in Norway, why would a search or investigation be mounted in Finland?

Connection here – and a close one – with the three Finns. They'd been looking for the same kind of information, and their corpses had been found somewhere down south. Down *there*, beyond those mountains.

They made one more stop before starting the climb into the mountain pass, the High Gap as Carl had said Isak called it, for a snack of biscuits and raisins, chocolate and hot tea. The wind was rising, from the northwest again, and the clouds looked pregnant with snow. He knew that within the next two hours he'd have to find a camp-site, and the best plan seemed to be to get through this pass – which might take about an hour – then ski down to the tree-line on its other side to get into shelter. The others concurred; and in fact he'd assumed command, to all intents and purposes, and subject – with reservations – to Isak's guidance. Strong reservations, actually, tempered only by the fact that nothing was yet provable. . . . But this was to be only a short rest, just long enough to eat and to gulp down the tea, which had been made early this morning and was contained in their Thermos flasks. They were in shelter here, a tongue of the forest pushing up across the saddle; they'd had a run downhill into this dip, and it was the last down-gradient they'd enjoy until they were through the pass.

Once they were through it, Isak had told Sutherland, they'd be on the grazing slopes where he hoped to find the *siida*, if it hadn't moved on southward.

And if it existed, Ollie thought.

Ahead, as they left the trees' shelter, their route was an uphill struggle between two mountain massifs and with a westward turn just short of another which from this angle and distance seemed to stand directly across the gap, blocking it and towering over it.

Isak stopped twice on the way up, and then again for a third time when they were actually inside the pass. Each time he had to be urged on – Ollie yelling, Sutherland interpreting in milder tones and his Lapp friend reluctantly complying. Climbing on, then, and it was hard work – not particularly steep, but seeming to be going on for ever, a long, hard plod with a deadline to it, a need to hurry. Snowstorm threatening, darkness in an hour or not much more – hour and a half, maybe – and he'd want to set up camp before that. Even without Isak's delaying tactics the timing would have been tight.

It began to snow when they were about halfway to the bend, and within a minute the tops and upper slopes were hidden. A few minutes later – when Isak stopped again – it was like being in a tunnel roofed with the horizontally-driven snow which the wind was blasting directly into the funnel of the pass. Visibility overhead was nil, wasn't a lot better any other way; to look back was to be blinded. Isak, his deerskin outer clothing already plastered white, was staring up, and all around: like a man lost, wondering where he was, what he was supposed to do next. . . . Then he'd started forward again, hunched and hurrying, and they were all plodding on – heads down, a too-slow, slogging progress up the soft incline, the pulk heavy on its nylon ropes, snow accumulating on it and adding to its weight.

They were close to the bend westward – where he'd been hoping conditions might be easier, with some partial shelter – when there was the crash of the first explosion overhead. He didn't think of it as that, to start with; his first thought was of a snow-boom preceding an avalanche. Then he saw Isak drop the tow-line, clamber clumsily around and start back, back the

131

way they'd come. Knees bent, skis apart, a crouched, ape-like figure passing within a yard of Stenberg, ignoring his shout: he was skiing directly into the direction of the storm. There was a second *boom* then: and that was no snow-slope breaking up, it had clearly been a detonation, explosive, with that distinctive *crack* to it. . . . All this had happened in the space of five or six seconds, and by this time he'd guessed at explosive charges intended to start an avalanche, trapping and drowning them here. And Isak had been expecting it. He shouted at the others, 'Back! Come *on*!' and heard a third explosion somewhere high above their heads in that white vagueness where the driving snow completely hid the mountain's overhang. Isak had vanished – not difficult, visibility that way being only a few yards – but he'd been waiting for this to start, ready to cut and run, save his own life. Sutherland had snatched up the tow-line that he'd dropped; there was a deep rumbling sound overhead, louder than the wind's racket now, the growing thunder of an avalanche. They'd heard that shout and they were moving the right way, but not fast enough. He shouted, 'Follow Isak's tracks!' Then to Sophie, who was suddenly beside him, to take the lead: 'Keep to the left of Isak's track and we'll use you as marker!' And it would give her a better chance. . . . He *hoped*. The noise was still growing, a mounting roar; and maybe it was behind, more than overhead. It was hard to know, the snow was enclosing, disorientating. All moving now, quite fast and in the right direction, Sophie well ahead skiing straight into the wind and blizzard. But she'd have her hands free for keeping her goggles clear and she'd give the rest of them – or anyway Sutherland, in the lead position – a mark to follow. From behind it sounded as if the whole mountain was breaking up, crumbling down to fill the pass, rock maybe as well as snow. Please God, behind. . . . Whoever it was up there, they might have misjudged the timing; and they still couldn't see into the pass, couldn't know they hadn't been successful – hadn't *yet* . . . Sophie was a phantom slaloming to and fro across their front, which was clever of her. Noise deafening, a full-blooded roaring as the fall gathered speed and weight. Ollie was on this closer side to it and Gus was out to his left,

Sutherland having wisely moved up ahead of the pulk since it was slower on its thin runners, in this soft stuff, than they were on skis. If the avalanche was going to hit them it would come from behind, he thought, it would fill the section of pass immediately below the main fall, then spread both ways, spilling through; and the main fall would be where they most likely would have been if Isak hadn't delayed them as he had. But if it was coming, Ollie knew he'd be the first it would over-run. He pulled the headover up higher, remembering an avalanche-survival lecture and something about covering your mouth and nose. When you were in it you were supposed to make swimming motions, to clear an air-space in which you might be able to breathe for long enough to fight your way out; also, before it had you submerged, you were supposed to get rid of your skis and poles which otherwise would lever your body around, breaking limbs. . . .

Crouched into the whipping snow, head down because if you faced right into it you couldn't see anything at all, head down like that and squinting up through crusted goggles – having to wipe them every few seconds – he had Gus in sight on his left at about maximum visibility range, and glimpses of Sutherland stooped almost double, skis wide. . . . He'd have Sophie in sight as she wove to and fro across Isak's track. The pulk's weight was a jerky tugging as it tried to veer this way and that, he and Gus alternatively checking it: and then a truly weird sensation was possessing him, a feeling that despite his forward motion, the battering of wind and snow from the front, he was skiing backwards.

Surface snow from behind, overtaking him. . . .

Rising round him as it overtook, deepening, piling on itself – the spill from the avalanche, as he'd anticipated. But the noise back there was lessening, had begun to drop just in the last few seconds. He let the nylon rope pay out, because the onrush of snow from behind was slowing him – although he was still moving forward. . . . Coming *out* of it! He'd been expecting to be hit from behind by a solid wall of snow six or ten feet high, travelling fast enough to knock him down, bury him as he turned over and over in it – you were supposed to spit, when you came to rest, as a way of finding which way up you'd ended – but this had been just a small residue, the *end* of the spill from the main fall, which must now have finished, because the noise had stopped completely, the wind had taken over again, its howl having been drowned out for a while; and he was picking up speed, coiling in some lost metres of tow-rope as he caught up on the pulk. He had a glimpse of Stenberg – his first sight of any of the others for several minutes – but he couldn't see the pulk yet. Thinking about those explosions – the probability that whoever set them off would still be up there, but blinded in the blizzard, not knowing he'd failed. . . . Feeling the weight of the pulk like a big fish fighting on a line – and a figure suddenly in sight and rushing closer, swerving across his own front to the left, Ollie swerving the other way because of the pulk, the line. Two other figures then. Stemming hard to slow himself, passing the pulk which was slewing around all over the place, nobody controlling it now, seeing that that shape was Sutherland and the reason he'd swung across had been to avoid crashing into Sophie – who was stopped, had Isak in front of her – on his knees with his arms above his head. Scraping to a stop beside them he caught the end of her shout, '—tried to *knife* me!'

She was gripping one ski-pole in both hands with its tip resting on Isak's chest, roughly where his heart would be. The pole's tip was actually *in* the leather of his coat. Sutherland came panting up, gasping for breath, having finally managed to stop himself – by the look of him, probably by falling – and Gus skidded in wildly from the left. Sophie shouted above the wind's noise, 'He was stopping – maybe thinking we were dead. If he had his way we *would* be!' She jabbed with the pole, and Isak jerked backward. She went on, screeching, 'I call stop, wait, but he – I catch him, his arm, and he turn with *this*!' Her left hand came away from the pole with Isak's sheathknife in it. Taking it from her, Ollie saw that the ski-pole had a sharp, spear-like tip. And from what she'd just said, she'd disarmed him, for God's sake. . . . She yelled, 'He was bringing us here so they could kill us, you know?'

Sutherland began – high-voiced, very shaken – 'I think we should hear what *he* has to—'

134

'For all they know' – Ollie shouted him down, taking over, because there was no time to waste – 'we *are* dead, and while this storm lasts they're blind. So now *fast*, back where we came from – out of the pass – then sharp left, down into the trees. I'll lead – OK?'

'Check.' Stenberg showed up as coolly authoritative now too. 'I'll take care of Isak, Sophie.' He had an automatic pistol in his hand; he was giving Isak a close-up of it, under his nose. He told him in Norwegian, 'Ski two metres in front of me. Get as far away as three, I'll kill you. . . . Sophie, lend a hand with the pulk?'

About two kilometres inside the fir-wood he found a place that would do. A big tree had fallen, raising a mound of earth in its roots. The mound would provide a back wall for the bivvy and the slanting trunk could serve as a ridge-pole for the roof. He checked in case a bear might have established a prior claim; there were said to be only three hundred bears left in these parts, but it was the sort of place one of them might have picked in which to make a den for winter hibernation – in which case there'd be an entrance tunnel and also a ventilation hole in the top. Which there was not: so OK. . . .

There was a lot of work to do now, including timber to be cut, but also he wanted to check that they hadn't been trailed down to this wood. He told the others what he wanted, while he put his shotgun together, loaded it and filled a pocket with cartridges. 'You might fix a hot drink, Sophie?' Isak could be put to work, with supervision. He told Sophie, who was already unlashing the pulk's cover, 'When the bivvy's built we'll cook inside, but for now you could pick any sheltered spot a bit out of the way, and get the stove going. I'll be back in about half an hour.'

He went back, on skis, not over the tracks they'd made coming through but off to the side of them; taking his time, watching and listening. Then from the edge of the wood, where they'd ski'd down into it, he was looking for tracks other than their own. Or movement out there in the blizzard. The tracks were filling fast, would have disappeared in an hour, and by that time it'd be dark anyway.

Out there, somewhere, were people who'd tried to murder them and might be under the impression that they'd succeeded. They'd get down into the snow-filled pass when they could – now, or at first light tomorrow – to probe for bodies, he guessed. . . . Could be 'they', or just one individual: one pair of hands would have been enough to detonate three charges. This was the sort of question Isak was going to answer before long: how many men, what kind, who gave orders? One thing for sure was that they weren't to be under-rated: they'd made a mess of their ambush, but they'd have been blinded by the snowstorm, which would have been a lot worse up on the top than it had been down in the pass, and it was a reasonably safe bet that they were the same people – or the same *kind* of people – who'd murdered three well-armed Finnish soldiers.

Which made statements about Lapps not being a martial people look pretty silly.

He waited for five or ten minutes, thinking it out, and deciding that they *might* have got down from the top quickly enough to pick up the tracks leaving the pass, but that the odds were strongly against it; and, more importantly, that if they'd been coming, they'd have been here *now*.

They'd come eventually. There'd be no tracks to follow, but common sense would tell them that anyone in this situation would have got away downhill and to the nearest cover. Once they'd realised there were no bodies in the snow or the rubble in the pass, that would be their conclusion.

By then, we'll be gone.

When he got back, materials were piling up and he got down to work. Larger branches made for roof-timbers sloping from the tree-trunk, smaller ones went on top of them at right-angles, and two of the tents were spread flat on that framework, with dirt and snow then shovelled over to hold the structure down and also camouflage it. The third tent served as a curtain over the entrance. The job was nearly done before he told them he wanted a smaller hide as well – a dozen yards away and higher up, where it would overlook the approaches to the main one. One pulk-rope slung between two trees and the pulk's tarpaulin draped over it covered the basics, with the addition of brushwood, forest litter and snow to make it a lot less visible. Both shelters were floored with branches, with sleeping-mats on top. Gus had been cutting most of the wood, with the machete, and he and Isak bringing them along; he'd put his pistol away, as the machete was a fearsome enough weapon and Isak was clearly aware of it.

With both bivvies made and floored, the pulk was lifted into the big one and unpacked. There was some clearing up to do around the site, and camouflage to be checked from all angles. Then they crowded into the larger bivvy – where Sophie had now set up the stove – and she handed out mugs of tea. Ollie had checked that no light from the stove showed outside, as long as the curtain was covering the entrance.

'Does Isak get any tea?'

They'd pushed him to the back, against the earth wall. Chin down on his chest, not meeting anyone's eyes. Ollie was in the entrance with the shotgun. Having thought about it, he nodded. 'Yes, give him some.' Emerging from other thoughts, and looking round at them all. 'Well done, folks.'

Sophie smiled at him. 'The same to you, Ollie.'

'I second that.' Gus nodded. 'We going to ask this revolting little fink some questions now?'

'Well. Let's get some priorities settled first. Essentials such as – well, yes, we'll keep him alive, because (a) he's got some answers for us, I hope, (b) if we can take him out with us, on the hoof, he may be useful as a witness to all this business, when the dust settles. Right?'

Gus nodded.

'Second – well, obviously we've got to find a way out of this. To Karasjok or Kautokeino, or to a telephone or radio-telephone if either's closer. Which I suppose it would be. But we'll decide tomorrow on tactics for our withdrawal. The basic question's whether we can move in daylight or have to wait for darkness tomorrow. Weather conditions – and recon-naissance by me at first light – will give us that answer. So the

137

next thing – arrangements for tonight. Incidentally, whatever we decide tomorrow, we can only spend one night *here*. I don't think there's a chance they could find us tonight, but tomorrow's another matter. . . . Anyway – Gus and I will take alternate watches, two hours on and two off. No disrespect to you, Carl, but we're on a war footing now – which is my racket, more or less, and I suspect it may be more up Gus's street than yours. OK?'

'If that's how you want it.'

Ollie had already jumped to certain obvious conclusions, about Gus Stenberg. He went on, 'The guy on watch will occupy the smaller bivvy, and Isak can doss down in there. It covers the approaches to this one, and as we can't trust this little sod now it kills two birds with one stone. Does this make sense to the CIA?'

Stenberg looked surprised. 'I guess it'd make sense to anyone.'

'Any questions or ideas?'

Sophie said, 'If we have to get away by night, taking Isak will not be easy. Even in daylight, really.'

'True. But when we've de-briefed him he may decide he's better off with us than with his friends. They weren't concerned for him when they fired those charges, were they.'

'I don't know. He was quick enough. The intention may have been for him to get away.'

Sutherland sighed, shaking his head as he glanced at Isak. His old pal. . . . Ollie looked from him to his 'assistant'. . . . 'How about some enlightenment from you, Gus. For starters, what about that gun you're carrying?'

'Beretta, nine-millimetre.'

'Shorter-barrelled than that, I'd have sworn.'

'You'd've sworn right. In a sense.' Stenberg pulled it out and handed it to him. 'Watch out, it's loaded. . . . No, you're thinking of the parabellum, aren't you? This is the Model 84, nine-millimetre short. Easier to tuck in an armpit.'

He passed it back. 'Why would a student of anthropology need such an item in his armpit?'

Sophie laughed. 'Student of Central Intelligence, you mean.'

'People seem to have this fixation.' Stenberg shook his head. 'And while I don't like to contradict a lady—'

'Married man, too. How many children, Gus?'

'As it happens, two.' Frowning at her. . . . 'Where did you do your homework, Miss Eriksen?'

'I did not have to do homework, Daddy. It is just obvious.'

'Hah.' He smiled crookedly, with a side glance at Ollie. 'Just on account *I* never took a pass at her.'

'Did you recruit the professor?'

He hesitated. Then shrugged. 'OK. Between friends. . . . Sure, I dug him out. I was tasked with this enquiry only because I happen to speak Norwegian. Norwegian mother, see. But I'd hardly heard of Lappland, so I had a whole lot of research to do, and one basic source of information was Carl's book. Then someone said, hey, what about this guy Sutherland, if he'd agree to help what better licence could anyone have to go in there and ask questions?'

Sutherland admitted, 'My first reaction was to tell them to go to hell. But they offered me a *very* substantial fee, Ollie.'

'I imagine they'd have to.' He shifted his position. After the hiatus in the pass and the rush of subsequent activity he'd been soaking wet, but he seemed to have dried out now. He looked at Stenberg, 'So the Lapp-lore, reindeer bullshit – clicking toes, blood pancakes, drinking piss—'

'It's known in the trade as "pure research". I admit, until recently the only reindeer I ever heard of had a red nose and answered to the name of Rudolf. But I should tell you one thing – Carl's motive, taking this on, was not only money. He was at least as concerned to prove his Sami friends are not terrorists.'

'Shows how wrong a man can be.' Sutherland threw Isak another glance. 'Except that's unfair on Samis generally.' He nodded. 'I take it back. One rotten apple, and *I* had to pick him out, from the entire barrel.' He switched into Lappish: 'I would never have believed this, Isak. I trusted you.'

Isak mumbled some answer, without looking up. Carl was asking a question, then. . . . Sophie translated, 'He said they have kidnapped his niece, as hostage to make him do this.'

She added a moment later: 'They said they would kill her, if he did not—'

'Well, my God!' Sutherland was craning round, in the confined space. 'You get that bit? *That*'s what—'

'Ask him' – Ollie cut in – 'Sophie, ask him who he means when he says *they* kidnapped her.'

She put the question in Lappish. Isak's head sank lower. As if trying to pull it in tortoise-fashion. . . . She tried again, won another short reply.

'He says they would kill her, if he named them.'

'Tell him we'll try to get her back, that we're the best chance he has, but we can't do it without his information.'

Isak had shut his eyes. His mouth stayed shut too. Stenberg growled, 'He tried to get us killed, damn it, why do we have to be so fucking *kind* to him?'

Sophie pointed at her ski-poles. 'This frightened him, before.'

Sutherland came to life as she picked one up. 'No – *Jesus*, you can't—'

'Carl, she only has to let him think she might.' Stenberg wasn't deferring to his professor now, their roles had changed completely. He said, 'I'll have the tape-recorder ready to catch this. It's on the pulk there, Carl, would you pass it over?'

Ollie murmured, 'Just scare him, Sophie.'

'What d'you think I *am*?'

'Interesting question.' Stenberg reached out, taking the recorder from Sutherland. 'I never heard of anyone going around with spears instead of ski-poles.'

'Then you should have done your research better, Gus.' She told him, 'In old books are many drawings of Sami on skis long, long ago, and they have ski-poles different, left and right. They were both poles for skiing but one was a spear and the other a long-bow. . . .' She showed him. 'This one is an ordinary pole with a special tip. A woman alone needs *some* protection.'

'She ever threaten you with one of those, Ollie?' Stenberg added, busy with his recorder, 'Hey, we still have the famous *yoik* here. The lost chords, you might say. . . .' The humour was brittle, surface humour, nobody even with a thought of smiling, none of them happy with the moment, minute, hour. . . . Sophie least of all. Resting the point just below Isak's chin, then pressing so that it buried itself in his sweater. He muttered in Lappish, 'Kill me, if you like.'

'Wouldn't help *her*, Isak.'

The niece, she'd meant. The little eyes were open, like brown marbles staring back at hers. Light from the naptha ring played on the pole's metal shaft. Gus muttered, 'Let him feel it.' She pressed forward fractionally: the eyes closed, and he was trying to press himself backward into the earth wall. Beginning to moan – a thin, keening sound, expressive more of despair than pain. Or fear of pain to come. Sophie spoke fast and shakily in Lappish: it was probably a plea to Isak to give in and talk to them but from its tone and urgency it could as easily have been a prayer to God. She was chalk-white and her hands were trembling, her whole body trembling. Ollie said abruptly, 'Give me that thing.' Then as an excuse – it had burst out of him, an erupting need to spare *her* – 'He doesn't believe you'd go through with it.'

'He's so right. . . .'

'He'll believe me, though.'

He took the pole carefully, sliding up against her, and as soon as she'd let go her hands whipped up to cover her ears, to shut out that sound – which was on a raised note suddenly like a change of gear. . . . But she'd changed her mind, she flopped sideways across Sutherland's legs, reaching to the tape-recorder, pushing Stenberg's hands out of the way and pressing the 'on' switch and then 'rewind'. Wanting *anything* that would drown Isak's misery. . . . Ollie said, 'Carl, tell him I'm a ruthless sod, I'll stop at nothing. Beg him – as his friend, *beg* him to give us the facts, promise on your personal word we'll try to save his niece.' Sutherland began at once in Norwegian, in an imploring tone; he looked as sick as Sophie had. She had her back this way now, and anyway Ollie was keeping his eyes on Isak's closed ones, muttering under his breath, *Come on, you little creep, come on, talk*. . . . There was a click from the recorder, humming, then bursting into the tense, dark circle and drowning out Isak's whine came his own harsh, glottal, drunken slurring of the *yoik*.

> See them come, the nameless, voia voia!/ Stealing from the haunts of Rota, woolly ones padding, padding/ Then over the high vidda like Spring's white torrents rushing!/ Horde of the nameless flooding to Kautokeino bloody knife!

Sophie had stopped the tape, eyes wide on Isak, who was staring back at her. Her lips moved, as she thought back over the lyrics, working out their meaning. Then she'd whispered, 'My God . . .' and touched the switch again.

> Swiftly from the day-side, warriors rushing, rushing/ Through the kvener's forests burning wolf-like, voia voia!/ Others floating through merons' secret ways, voia, nana nana!/ While swooping low come eagles, bearing in blood-red talons freedom for Sameätnam!

Now there was a blur of *voia-voia*s, *nana-nana*s; hoarse muttering, drunken laughter, heavy boots scraping on bare boards. Sophie switched off the tape. She asked Isak, 'When?'
'When the NATO soldiers leave.'
She still stared at him. She looked stunned. She said to Ollie without looking round, 'You can put the pole down.'

8

After that one straight answer Isak came out of shock enough to clam up again. Her second question, which he declined to answer, had been who was behind the conspiracy inside Norway; he'd stared at her blankly, as if he hadn't heard. She asked, 'Who told you to bring us here to be killed?' and he answered without any hesitation, 'Those who have Inga.' And that was it, he wouldn't elaborate on it or speak again. Ollie had been waiting with a much more urgent and immediate question: who was out there *now* – what kind, how many?

Because they'd still have the same murderous intentions. If anything, more so, having shown their hand.

Sophie had explained the *yoik* – first what it meant, the allegorical interpretation in general import, then some of the detail of its phraseology. She'd played it through a second time, and recorded translations of it in both English and Norwegian. Explaining that 'the nameless' and 'woolly ones' meant bears and by implication Russians; so Russians were to invade in the spring through Finland – *kvener* meaning Finn, in Lappish – and there'd be simultaneous air and sea assaults or insertions. *Merons* were Lapps who earned their living from the sea, in old Sami tales wolves were said to 'burn' when they

143

were killing — 'burning' through a herd of reindeer, for instance — and the reference to 'spring's white torrents' supported the one answer Isak had let slip, that the invasion was to be launched after the Commando brigade and other NATO forces left Norway.

Early April, or even the end of March.

Getting this to Grayling was the first essential. A secondary problem might be to convince him and his NATO seniors that the *yoik* meant anything at all or was to be taken seriously. Even here and now, to people who'd only by sheer luck survived an attempt to murder them, it took some effort to accept it.

Sophie gave up her efforts with Isak. She said, 'We have what we came for, don't we? A thousand times bigger than we thought?'

Meaning that she and whoever she worked for in Oslo had expected nothing more than domestic troubles, localised Sami agitation — by Sami individuals of the Isak type — that could have been dealt with politically or at worst in the courts.

'Only thing is' — Stenberg stated the obvious — 'the knowledge is useless until we can get it back.'

It might have been nearer the mark, Ollie thought, to have said *unless* we can get it back. Those three Finns had surely been slaughtered to safeguard the same secrets — and they'd been professionals. You could bet, too, they'd have had more than a shotgun, a pistol and a pair of sharpened ski-poles.

Make a break for it alone?

Leave these people bivvied up somewhere, come back for them later, preferably with strong support?

It would have to be Finnish support. You couldn't think of bringing NATO personnel across the border.

He was looking at Sophie while these ideas were running through his mind; she returned his stare enquiringly, as if she thought he had something he was about to say to her and was waiting for it. Her eyes — greyish, and so expressive he thought with practice he'd be able to read her thoughts through them — held his almost mesmerically, until he looked away: thinking that those people out there — who'd be holed-up like this, he guessed, waiting for daylight just like this – were probably Soviets, and if they were you could guess they'd be Spetsnazi, since those were their behind-the-lines specialists.

And come to think of it, the killing of the three Finns might well have been a Spetsnaz job. Set up to look like some ancient Sami ritual.

So forget about leaving *her* here.

'Let's decide what's our best route out.' He unfolded his map, and the others shifted closer, crowding in so they could see it too, by the light of his pencil torch. The map was captioned JOINT OPERATIONS GRAPHIC (GROUND), with the note *Users are urged to refer corrections of this graphic to Commanding General, US Army Topographic Command, Washington, DC 20315*. He'd bought this one, also some sheets covering the adjoining areas, in a shop in Alta, and it occurred to him that a Spetsnaz team in a bivvy or snow-hole not far away might at this moment be studying an identical 'graphic'. . . . He said, 'We're here, look. And here's Jorgastak, where we left the Volkswagen. Not all that far, straight up the river instead of the circular route Isak led us.'

Stenberg rubbed the bridge of his thin nose. 'Won't they have Jorgastak staked out?'

'I would, in their shoes. I'd aim to stop us long before we got anything like that far, in fact, but for a longstop' – he nodded – 'sure. . . . But what we really need is a telephone or radio-telephone, the VW's not important. We could make for this place – here, Angeli.' He pointed it out, a dot labelled with that name on the Finnish side of the Anarjokka, not far north of where they'd crossed the river when they'd come south out of Norway. There were several other settlements marked, to the east of Angeli, along a dotted line which according to the map's legend indicated a cart-track. Obviously, the enemy might have the approaches to all those places covered too, if their manpower allowed it; but he didn't mention this possi-bility. He said, 'One place or another there'll be either R/T or a landline, *must* be. Then we might be lucky and get transport up the Finnish side – this is a road, of sorts – so we'd stay clear of Jorgastak.'

Stenberg said, 'Or get them to send a chopper for us.'

Ollie asked Sutherland, 'What d'you think, Carl?'

The professor's beard wagged, and the light of the naptha flame glittered in his pale eyes. 'Your department. I'll go along with whatever you decide.'

'Right. So we'll make for Angeli. They may try to stop us — *will* do, if they guess we're on the loose — but if we're lucky they just *might* be digging for our bodies in that pass. If we get a clear run through we'll do it in a day, easily. Or in a night if we find we can't move by day. Nights being three times as long as days we could take our time and make sure no one breaks his neck.'

Thinking mostly of Sutherland, who'd be as likely to break his neck in daylight as in the dark. But the risks involved in night travel would be more than the obvious ones of skiing into unseen hazards. The weaker force's best hope lay in avoiding contact, which was a lot easier if you could see where you were going.

'Will we take Isak?'

'I don't know what else we'd do with him, Sophie. Besides, if we can get him back into Norway he may open up, start divulging. There's a charge of accessory to murder to hang over him, isn't there?'

And treason, presumably. Also, if 'they' had murdered the niece by then, and Isak knew it, there'd be nothing to stop him talking. Meanwhile the only existing evidence was the *yoik* tape and Sophie's interpretation of it; if Isak could be pressured into talking, delays might be short-circuited.

Although taking him along wasn't likely to make the withdrawal any easier.

Ollie took the first watch, and let Stenberg sleep for longer than his ration of two hours. He had a lot to think about and if he'd turned in too soon he wouldn't have slept anyway. Unlike Isak, snoring steadily at the back of the small bivvy.... Getting out — getting the intelligence and these people out — was the problem he had to work on. Thinking around it time and time again, coming up against the same walls: there were too many imponderables, such as who the enemy were, where

146

they'd be in the morning's first light and later, how many of them and what equipment they had.... The only answer seemed to be that having decided which way to go you'd play it off the cuff.

After about three hours the thought of stretching his spine out horizontally began to have strong appeal. He jerked on the string that had its other end looped to Stenberg's wrist inside his sleeping-bag, and finally got a response, a double tug of acknowledgement.

A minute later the other bivvy's tent-flap opened long enough for a gleam of candlelight to show, soft yellow glow with falling snowflakes slanting across it and the blackness of Stenberg's bulk emerging, blocking it out, leaving the surroundings blacker than they'd been before. He heard the American blunder away into the trees, then the sounds of natural functions before he re-appeared.

'Any wolves around, Ollie?'

'None I've heard. But *your* toes don't have to click, do they? They'll have heard that lot in Kautokeino.'

'Remind me to get fitted with a silencer.... Snow eased a bit, has it?'

'Not really. We don't want it to, either, we want it heavy and continuous. Good sleep?'

'While it lasted, sure.... How about Isak?'

'Like a dog. Hasn't stirred or once stopped snoring.'

'Incredible.'

It was, in the circumstances. And 'like a dog' was not inapposite, there was something close to the animal in that ability to flop down and pass out, with the situation as it was. Ollie envied him. Except if you were either on the go or dead to the world, when would you do your thinking?

Maybe a Lapp didn't. Maybe he just followed instinct. Stenberg asked, 'Take over the shotgun, shall I?'

'By all means. I'll leave it with you. But tell me about your CIA background, Gus. I'm not asking out of idle curiosity, more because we're liable to face some crises in the next day or two. You can handle yourself, can you?'

'Well, I have this Beretta and I can shoot straight.' He'd

paused. . . . 'Look, I'm a desk man, Ollie.'

'Desk—'

'That's the plain truth of it. No point pretending otherwise, I'm sorry. Like I said, they gave me the brief because I speak the language, that's the only reason. . . . Jesus, we weren't expecting to be up against the fucking KGB, were we?'

'No, we weren't. And anyway it's no fault of yours. They did at least give you some kind of survival course, I was told.'

'Two lectures and a piece of film.'

'Oh. . . .'

'But Carl and I have both ski'd most of our lives when we've had the chance. Recreationally, of course.' He added, 'There again, we weren't trekking to the Pole, were we? Little visits out of Kautokeino and Karasjok, day trips with a packed lunch from a hotel, was all Carl had in mind.'

On that basis it was surprising they'd wanted a 'minder' along. But then, *they* probably hadn't. Someone in London, behind or above Jarvis, had decided that London's eyes and ears should be out here with them.

He said, 'I dare say we'll make it without even seeing the bastards.'

And pigs can fly. . . .

'Have you thought about how we proceed from here on?'

He nodded into the darkness. Hearing distantly the voice of what might have been a wolf, over the lower note of wind in the trees. . . . 'We'll move out before it's light. Leaving the pulk; we'll have to share some extra load between us, cache the rest here. I'll scout ahead and we'll keep in cover – trees – and move in stages, a few hundred metres at a time. Remember the place we stopped at yesterday – the trees in that dip, on the ridge? We'll head for that same place. That far, we'll have cover all the way, but at some point we've got to get over to the other side of the ridge, into the forest that side – to get to Angeli or one of those places – northeastward, right?'

'Right.'

'So we'll have to cross open snowfields somewhere, and where the trees grow up on to the ridge is where exposure will be shortest. Maybe a couple of kilometres out in the open –

with luck it'll still be snowing. Otherwise if they had men on the high points with binoculars they'll see us no matter where we try to cross.'

'Say some prayers for snow, then.'

'But there's no way to guess where they'll be. Could be busy in the pass, looking for our bodies. Touch wood. . . .' He rapped the stock of the AYA. 'Or they could be out looking for us, here in these woods. OK as long as we've cleared out ahead of them – especially if it's snowing to fill our tracks.'

'Night movement wouldn't be better?'

'No. It'd mean waiting for dark tomorrow afternoon – giving them time to find out we weren't under their avalanche, so they'd have deployed accordingly, to cover the routes out of here. . . . Incidentally, I don't know if you'd thought of this, there was quite likely a rock-fall amongst the avalanche, we wouldn't have stood a fucking chance if we'd been in it. . . . Anyway – if we can get away fast, we're ahead of the game, if we can't we'd be handing *them* the advantage. Another thing is that night skiing isn't so easy when you've no experience of it. You said you and Carl have done plenty of skiing, but I wouldn't say he was all that good at it. . . . But third, if those are Soviets we're up against, they may have night vision gear with them, thermal viewers or IR nightscopes, in which case we'd be worse off than we'd be in daylight.'

The wind was down by morning, and although snow was still falling it wasn't quite as heavy as it had been. Ground temperature minus five. Sutherland made breakfast, a big one to allow for a day in which there mightn't be much chance of any pauses for snacks, while Ollie saw to the pulk stores, which items should be taken on their backs and what should be abandoned. The tents were too bulky, would have to be left here; nights in the open henceforth would be in bivvies or snow-holes. He took the tarpaulin, though, the pulk cover.

149

Both shovels would be needed – but not the tape-recorder. With luck there might not be many more nights out, or even *any*, but one had to take along enough rations to allow for all contingencies – in other words, all the food there was. . . . An irritant in his thinking – he'd woken with it – was recognition that his earlier thought of making a solo exit, leaving the rest of them in some secure hide, would have been the most pragmatic solution to current problems. Both for getting the intelligence to Grayling – the number one priority – and for the whole party's survival hopes. He'd shied away from it for personal, subjective, psychological reasons, and he should have known better, should have remembered the SBS motto *By Stealth, by Guile* and acted on it, ignored the natural reluctance to seem to be running out on them. Sophie wouldn't be any better off now, if they ran into Soviets on the way out, than she would have been if he'd left her tucked up in a snow-hole.

'Better re-wax skis, folks. It'll be wearing thin and I hope we'll be covering a lot of ground today. Swix Blue looks about the best choice. . . . Gus, will you take charge of Isak? If he gets tricky, shoot him. I mean it – better him than *us* dead. . . . Carl, would you interpret what I said, so he knows it?'

As an encouragement to him to stay in line. But also Ollie wanted to encourage Sutherland, drag him out of his glum silence. Saddened by his own misjudgement of Isak. And having no part to play now the charade of book research was blown. Leaving him out of the night watchkeeping roster mightn't have helped either.

Stores were repacked and skis waxed inside the bivvy by candlelight. They were taking quite a lot of extra weight, things from the pulk – such as the naptha stove and containers of fuel, the machete, all the reserves of rations, and so forth. Isak, who'd been travelling light and now had no pulk to tow, was allocated a lion's share of it.

The final task was to collapse the larger bivvy. The small one had already been dismantled, and now the main shelter became a heap of snow-covered debris with the pulk buried under it. It was still dark; Ollie hoped to have the party up on the ridge by the time the light came, although he knew this might be optimistic. He arranged the shotgun so that its stock protruded from the open top end of his bergen, where he could grab for it quickly if he had to.

'Ready, Sophie?'

He'd be leading and she'd be the link between him and the others. She was the best choice for it, being a better skier than any of them, including himself. She asked him as they started off together through the trees, 'How good are our chances, Ollie?'

'Well. Given reasonable luck, they're *very* good.'

'But we don't know how many of them there may be. Also, this isn't a small thing now, it's *huge*, a threat to the whole world. . . . I was awake in the night, Ollie, it was like a nightmare but a real one – I mean that they cannot *possibly* allow us to get away!'

'Not if they can help it – no, they can't. But look – at first light, in say about one hour, either they'll be looking for our bodies in the pass – which is what I'm betting on, and incidentally it'd take them quite a few hours – or they know they made a ballsup of it, in which case they'll guess we came down this way. So they'll come down here to look for us. But by that time we'll be miles away – d'you see?'

'Maybe they wouldn't all be looking for bodies. They can't be stupid.'

She was right. Probably. . . .

He stopped. 'This'll be about right for you. You'll have Gus in calling distance behind, me about the same distance ahead. I'll stop at intervals and wait for you to catch up with me. And so on. But listen, Sophie – on the subject of what chances we have, etcetera. There'll be one tricky stage, soon after it's light, a couple of kilometres of open snowfield to cover. High ground, no trees on it. Can't be helped, we have to get over in that direction and that's the only way, unless we wasted hours by going right down into the valley and then climbing up again, and we haven't any time to waste. . . . But here's my point. If we run into trouble, there or any other place, if you see we're in real trouble and you have a chance to get away on your own – well, for Christ's sake *do* it, just take off. I'd do the same if that was the situation. You and I are the only ones with any chance of making it on our own, and it's vital that *someone* does – OK?'

She nodded. 'OK. But otherwise, Ollie – make it together? Please?'

He reached over, squeezed her arm. 'That's exactly what we *will* do. And *please* to you, too.'

Seven kilometres, he'd reckoned from the map, mainly northward but in a curve following the contour they were on now, and in tree cover all the way. Then he'd turn northeast up to the tree-line and get himself orientated, locate the dip in the long ridge where the firs spilled over across that saddle. He'd go up through that extension of the forest: from there on, you'd need some luck.

Progress wasn't as good as he'd hoped it might be. It was slowed by the three in the rear, by Isak mostly, it seemed. Advancing in stages, five or six hundred metres at a time, each time re-establishing contact. One change for the better was that the snow was falling more heavily again after the first half-hour, and the wind had risen with it; it didn't make for comfort, but it would improve their prospects when the time came to cross that open ground.

It took an hour and a half to cover the seven kilometres. By that time there was enough light overhead to pick out the silhouette of one of the peaks flanking the pass, and get a compass bearing on it. No cross-bearing, and he knew magnetic compasses tended to go mad in these parts, but it looked about right. He waited again for Sophie, and told her 'Ninety-degree right turn here. Then best close up a bit.' She'd wait for the others, and warn them about the turn.

Heading east then, uphill.

The trees thinned. Twenty metres from where they finished in a ragged edge he could feel the wind through the headover on that side. At this height, of course, when you lost the woods' shelter you'd get all the wind there was, and with a ground temperature of five below zero you noticed it. Wind about force three, roughly nine miles per hour, combining with that static temperature would work out as about minus fifteen, sixteen. Snow plastered down, driving from the left, blinding but also camouflaging, blending human figures into the background patchwork of whitened land and dark trees, through a veil of snow, dim but gradually increasing light. He stopped, waiting again, watching for any movement or object that might not be natural to its surroundings. Then hearing the scrunch of her skis.

'Take a rest, and keep the others here with you. I'll be back.'

He went on alone again.

The firs ran up to the skyline on his right. That was the bit he'd been aiming for, and he'd overshot it by a few hundred metres. In front of him where he was crouching in a clump of ragged, wind-stunted trees, a slope of unmarked snow led up to the ridge. It was overlooked – would be, if they'd posted a watcher there – from that belt of trees beyond. . . . He slid back to the others. Unless they had a whole regiment of Spetsnazi in these mountains, he thought, they couldn't have *every* open area under surveillance. Except that in full daylight a few O/Ps on selected high points might cover a lot of ground. But by the time it was fully light he'd have his lot in cover again, would certainly have got over this next bit.

'This way, lady and gents. Couple of hundred metres, then right up on the ridge. Trees all the way for cover. OK, Carl?'

'Sure, I'm fine, don't worry about *me*. . . .' Breathing hard, trying not to let it show. Isak silent, stooped under his heavy load. Those two were the liabilities, the drag on this party's chances. . . . Ollie led them back, then slanted up so their track became a curve and they were climbing, in file and a few yards apart. It took about a quarter of an hour's hard plodding before they were on the ridge where yesterday they'd stopped for refreshment.

In the pass, they'd be prodding with poles now, poking around for bodies as the light hardened. He wondered how long they'd persist, how long before they'd decide there weren't any.

But maybe they knew already. Might have known at the time, cursing whoever had fired the charges too soon. In that case they'd be deploying now to cover the exit routes. It was more than just a possibility; he knew that if he'd been running their end of it that was what would have been happening – would already have happened, before dawn. You might leave one man to search for corpses if you had some reason to believe the trap might have worked, but you surely wouldn't have left the rest to chance. You wouldn't know anything about any *yoik*, but nor would you know Isak hadn't shot his mouth off.

He'd climbed the slope on the other side of the saddle and was looking out over the wide expanse of open snow, down-sloping from south to north, which they had now to cross in this milky dawn light. A vagueness of shadow beyond it *might* turn out to be the tree-line on the other side which he had hopes of reaching. Alternatively it might be simply distance, space, an extension of the gauntlet they were about to run. But one thing you could be sure of was you wouldn't get there at all if you hung around here while the light increased and the enemy got their act together.

'Now. If we're all fit.' He pointed. 'Long traverse, over into woods on the far side. Traverse just steeply enough to make it a mildly downhill run, but we don't want to end up lower down than we have to, at this stage.'

Up to the right was an emptiness of falling snow, behind them the darkness of the wood they'd come through, and downhill you were peering into snow that swirled straight at you on the wind. The shortest way to cover – safety, if that word applied – was the way he was now pointing them. Telling Sophie, 'You stay downslope of us, on the left flank. I'll be up on the right. I'll ski down to help anyone who may need help, but the rest of you do *not* stop, not until you're well into the wood.' He glanced at Sutherland: 'Take it easy now Carl, we aren't racing.'

He side-stepped uphill, allowing the others to get going first, and then kept his traverse shallower to start with so as to stay well above them, on what he saw as the danger side, if there was such a thing. *If* there was – enemies higher up, who might come down to cut them off? – Sophie would be well placed to turn her planks straight down the hill, and go.

154

If she'd do it, as he'd told her. He thought she would. He thought he knew her well enough, despite the very short time he'd known her. He hadn't dreamt of the world containing anyone quite like her.

Make it together? Please?

No shots, shouts, whistles. Yet. . . . They could have been the only human beings in these mountains. Five lots of ski-tracks being laid parallel to each other across several hundred acres of soft-topped snow, scarring the unblemished surface like smoke-trails fouling a clear sky. With so much new snow falling the tracks wouldn't last much longer than the wind would take to wipe such a sky clean again. But the soft, fresh surface was a retardant, clinging to the waxed skis. To have described it as being like skiing in treacle would have been an exaggeration, but with this sharp awareness of being exposed, vulnerable, that was how it felt. Even though he could see the forest ahead now, the darkness having resolved itself into a finite mass of trees – safety, beckoning. . . . With about half the distance covered, he guessed, glancing back to compare one distance with the other. The higher slopes were still not visible, still hazed-out in falling snow, so no O/P up there would be of use to them at present. In fact it might not be as easy as he'd envisaged to site O/Ps to maximum advantage when you couldn't be sure how visibility might vary from hour to hour. Whistling in the dark. . . . Sutherland was doing all right – in his stiff, awkward posture, concentrating hard on not falling. Which in present circumstances was about the best contribution he could make. Isak was on Carl's left, skiing with no style but with total ease, an ease bequeathed to him by ancestors who'd lived on skis through all the dark winters of the past three thousand years. Gus was below and slightly behind him, and below Gus was Sophie, relaxed and stylish despite the burden of a back-pack.

Trees looming close now, a solid-looking barrier through the snow's white swirl. Less than a minute, you'd be—

Sutherland faltering: arms flailing for balance as he struggled to stay up. . . .

Made it!

Ollie yelled, 'Well done, Carl!'

Then they were in the trees. Sutherland breathless, sagging: for him it really *had* been an ordeal. They drew together around Isak, who wasn't moving an inch to join anyone, only standing hunched under his load, donkey-like, coated in wet snow as they all were; and he couldn't be left on his own. . . . Ollie was moving that way when he saw, with disappointment amounting to shock, that this was only a belt of trees they'd come to, a strip of woodland lying like a runner of carpet up and down the mountainside and with more open snow beyond it. He could see light and whiteness through from that side, from only about thirty metres' distance. Not only were they going to have to do it again, it could be that this was to be the pattern for some distance yet, belts of trees with open areas intervening.

Breaking the news to them, he tried to make light of it: 'One more bit of open ground, unfortunately. Never mind. . . .' Feeling sympathy for Sutherland, who'd have been thinking he'd made it, got the worst over. But then from that other side, standing well back in cover, he saw the river – a mountain stream that was now a solid mass of ice down the middle of this narrow parting of the wood. *Spring's white torrents rushing* . . . He could imagine it, as it would be when the great thaw came. But also it gave one some hope, explained the existence of this open strip, and one might assume the pattern might *not* be repeated.

'Ollie, see that? It's a tourist *fjellstue*.'

Fjellstue meaning 'mountain hut'. It was below them, about three hundred metres down and close to the stream, a log cabin under a heavy roofing of snow. They'd built it on a flat piece of ground where the stream curved and then fell away into what at other times of the year would be a waterfall below that small plateau. You could see why the foresters had chosen that site for their tourist rest-house; in spring and summer it would be an idyllic spot.

Stenberg screamed, '*Isak!*'

Turning – too late – he caught the blur of movement as Isak flung himself out into the open. Crouching, launching himself out and downward. He'd dumped his two packs and thrust out poling between the trees, and he was away, *gone*, over steeply falling, uneven ground, closer to the wood than to the hut or the stream. A first reaction was to go after him, but caution held Ollie back. Then, turning to stop anyone else who might have been thinking of giving chase, he saw Gus fling out a pointing arm: 'Hey. . . .'

Not so loud, that shout: and just as well. Just as well one hadn't tried to go chasing out there, too. A man had come out of the shack, or from the far side of it. A heavy figure, dark bulk indistinct through the driving snow but levelling a gun – a submachine gun – waist high, swinging with it to cover Isak's downhill rush. Isak, swerving in a sheet of pluming white – to his left, away from the gunman and towards the trees, was hit by the first burst, his short arms flying loose like a shot bird's wings, poles trailing, still more or less upright and travelling fast but out of control, the gun blaring again briefly as a squeeze on the trigger sent a short burst after the first longer one. Isak hit a tree, a ski flew off, was still in the air when the body crashed to rest against another tree lower down, the ski flopping soundlessly into soft snow halfway between Isak's body and the man who'd killed him. From the time of Stenberg's shout, to this sudden stillness – Carl Sutherland with his back to the scene, face against a tree-trunk, head on his forearms – the whole of the action had lasted about twelve seconds.

The gunman had been crouching, facing up the mountain-side, the direction from which Isak had come rushing towards him out of the screen of falling snow. Watching from the trees' cover Ollie saw him straighten, turn to stare at the body, maybe watching to see if it was going to move again. He'd cross over there to inspect it, presently. Reaction to that thought was immediate: the circumstances were so clear and so inviting that he didn't have to think it out, he saw the whole thing in one clear picture, was already moving to implement his part in it. The gunman was looking uphill again, satisfying himself that the man he'd killed had been a loner, as *he* was. It was obvious that he was because if there'd been anyone else in the cabin they'd have come out by now, there'd have been reaction from any colleague in visual or audible range, too. Ollie muttered, 'Wait here, keep quiet and out of sight.' He'd backed into the trees, well in, dumping his bergen; now he unclipped the bindings of his skis, kicked free of them. He crouched over the bergen, pulled out the shotgun.

'Ollie—'

He shook his head. 'Remember what I told you.' Then: 'Gus, see what we need to take from Isak's packs. Essentials only.' He began slipping and sliding down through the wood, using his free arm to catch hold of trunks here and there to control a rapid downhill slither, slowing it a lot more about halfway down. Very slow and stealthy, then, stalking, and shedding the mitten from his right hand, his brain clear as ice-water. In that moment of hesitation when he'd thought of chasing after Isak he'd assessed the Lapp's intentions as being simply to get away, seizing a chance to put distance between them when they'd been preoccupied, peering at the log cabin, and judging that they'd be disinclined to follow when it would have meant a long descent into the valley. Then he would have made his own way to – well, Karasjok, maybe, looking for his niece. But there'd been no one visible down there, until this character had appeared beside the hut, Isak clearly hadn't been joining *him*. So, this was one man alone, here as a lookout or to maintain the cabin as a base that might be used by others at other times – might be the base for their present operations, the avalanche stunt, and they'd left one man to guard it while the rest were busy. One guy alone, and he'd be taking a close look at his victim's body, was certain to, as soon as he felt sure no other skiers were about to come bombing down as that one had. The body was piled against a tree and bent in a way that suggested broken bones. There was a live, intact body within a dozen feet of it now: in the wood's edge, the mixture of white and black, snow-camouflaged and motionless. If you hadn't seen Isak fall you probably wouldn't notice his remains now, or at any rate you wouldn't have identified them as what they were; in its similar coating of snow it blended with the natural forest debris. Only churned snow around it, the track it had scored in the last few metres of its travel, would draw an eye to it. And there were no such signs *here*, a few metres deeper into the wood.

The shootist was coming. Drawn, predictably, to inspect his prey. He'd been difficult to locate from this position until now, with the cabin's log wall behind him and through scraps of undergrowth and the snow still blanketing, but he was in the open now, glancing frequently uphill as he made his way across. He was wearing snowshoes, which accounted for the clumsy way he moved. Also a fur cap with earflaps, goggles pushed up on to the upper part of a balaclava, and a white snow-smock as outer garment – unnecessary, since any outer garment was mostly white, in the present state of things. Still grasping his gun – submachine gun – two-handed, alert for a second target. *Right here, looking at you.* . . . The left side of Ollie's face was pressed into snow at the base of a fir-tree, the AYA projecting on the right, most of the gun snow-covered, lined on the heap that was Isak's body and slanted upward. He'd barely have to move it, when the moment came. He was counting, also, on Isak's body being the focus of the man's attention. Why should he look elsewhere in this wood; he'd have been here hours, maybe days, knew only too well what a fir-wood looked like, that the only movements would be branches bending to the weight of snow, releasing when it slid off. . . . He'd stopped. Facing up the mountain again, the gun ready – like a man waiting for driven game. Then relaxing, turning this way again – at least, the lowering of the weapon's slant suggested a degree of relaxation, lowering of the guard. Lifting his feet comically high to place the snowshoes flatly: on Isak's tracks now, *that* close. . . .

Stopped. Staring at the body. Maybe deciding which bit of the contorted heap was what.

Raising the gun slowly, and sighting. . . .

A single shot into the head. The *crack* of it echoed up the mountain slopes and was lost in the depth of firs. Ollie hoping it wouldn't start some rash movement from above, that they'd stay put and silent. The Russian – if that was what he was – was now slinging his gun, pushing the strap over his left

159

shoulder. It made a difference, made any further loud sounds avoidable, and reaction to this change of circumstance was so instant as to be virtually a reflex. His right hand relaxed its grip on the AYA, shifted very cautiously to his belt, the sheathed knife. The Russian had both hands free now, having slung his weapon, and he was crouching to straighten Isak's body, see what it was he'd shot. Ollie's weight hit him before he could have known there was another human within a mile. Going down under the impact, his head simultaneously wrenched backward, he had about one second more of life before the carbon-steel blade stabbed into his throat, up to the knife's hilt.

He was an Asiatic. Farther into the trees where he dragged him, removal of the fur cap and balaclava revealed lank black hair which gave a first impression that this was – had been – a Lapp, but the features told a different story. Mongolian, maybe. A fair proportion of Spetsnaz ranks were non-Russian Soviets, one had heard. A feeling of relief – not surprise, since this had been almost a certainty – because initially, before he'd started this move, the possibility of it being a Finn, some kind of special force man like the three who'd been murdered, had occurred, then been dismissed, but must have lingered. . . . There'd be no papers, so there was no point looking for any. The gun was Swedish, an MKS 5.56-mm short-barrelled assault rifle with stock folded, and he found two spare clips for it, twenty rounds in each, in a pocket inside the zipped outer covering. The clip in the gun was still about half full. Another pocket contained a clip of 9-mm parabellum ammunition and some loose shells of the same type: so, treasure still to come. . . . He had the body lying with its head downslope, so blood pumping from the severed jugular flowed clear. He'd got comparatively little of it on himself. Searching for a weapon that would take this 9-mm ammo, some kind of automatic pistol to take that short clip, he found a sheathknife and a German-made Silva-type compass. Then, strapped to the ribs inside other layers of clothing, a soft leather holster containing a SIG-Sauer parabellum automatic.

On his way back to rejoin the others he picked up the discarded mitten.

'All right, you people?'

Calling ahead, in case his arrival scared them. Sophie staring at him: wide-eyed, speechless. . . . Sutherland asked, 'Was that your shot we heard?' Ollie straightening, checking the MKS magazine to count exactly how many rounds were left. Stenberg muttered, 'Told you, Carl, it was a rifle shot.'

'Submachine gun, actually. This one. Mine, now. Carl, d'you want the shotgun?'

'Well, no, I doubt I'd be—'

'Sorry about Isak.'

'Yeah.' Sutherland spread his hands, let them drop back against his sides, as if words failed him. Ollie passed the shotgun to Stenberg, flipping it open so the cartridges were visible. Sophie found *her* voice: 'We thought he'd shot you. But you – you killed *him*. . . . Ollie, for God's *sake* – I mean, just like *that*, you—'

'He was making sure of Isak. . . . Gus, I'll give you the rest of the cartridges. Have his knife too, if you want it.'

'Ollie, tell me what – *how* you—'

He nodded to her. 'I'll tell you as we go. Anything you like, but I want to get over that bloody river. What's out of Isak's packs?'

But he had to tell them about it, and it made a difference. The way they looked at him, spoke to him – especially Sophie. It isolated him: as if he and they had separated into different species.

They crossed the frozen waterfall and entered the wood on the other side, stopping again when they were back in cover, at Sutherland's request.

'You can have this, Sophie. You might need it.' The SIG-Sauer pistol. 'I'll show you how it works, if—'

'I don't want it.'

'He killed Isak, Sophie.' He held her upper arms so that she had to face him and hear this. 'Shot Isak down without a moment's hesitation. He was a Soviet, incidentally, Mongolian or something like it. It would almost surely have been his lot who murdered those Finns. What *should* I have done?'

'I made no criticism.'

'Oh yes, you did. You're making one *now*, that tone of voice. . . . Listen to me, Sophie. Those Finns – then Isak. Just *bang*, like knocking off a rabbit. Because he knew anything that moved here had to be his enemy – except his pals, he'd know them, but anything else that moved. It could as easily have been you, *would*'ve been if you'd been first out of the trees, next time it *might* be. Also, remembering what I said earlier, you *could* find yourself on your own, suddenly. . . . Will you take this, please?'

'All right. Show me how—'

'Yes. Look. . . .'

Sutherland came back to them. 'Sorry to hold us up.'

This part of the fir-forest seemed to last for ever, after they got going again. But in fact it didn't, it had only been his anxiety, whether to turn downhill here or farther along, that made each minute seem like ten. The trees ended finally about three kilometres from the river, where the mountainside ahead as well as on their right rose too steeply for trees to grow on it. So now they *had* to turn downhill. He was glad to have his mind made up for him, and to make some progress northward at last. Whether or not they'd be in the cover of woods all the way now was a moot point, and the map didn't show it clearly. The scale wasn't large enough, for instance where it showed a river, to indicate whether its valley was wooded or not, and in the present situation just a few metres of open ground could be crucial. The map showed trees everywhere except on the mountain heights, which obviously would be bare, and lower down you'd just have to take it as you found it.

He'd been thinking about strategic factors too, for instance the size of the back-up there must be to these front-runners. Spetsnazi would be making the recces, handling contacts like Isak and feeding back intelligence, but when the time came they'd be ahead of invading forces and doing their own things such as assassinations, sabotage of communications and so on. The forces to follow them in would be in training now – or even trained, ready for the whistle. And if so, if tomorrow the Spetsnazi reported that the operation's security was looking shaky, wouldn't they attack at once?

Isak had said the move was planned for after NATO forces withdrew. But Isak wouldn't have been told everything; nor would he necessarily have been telling the whole truth when he'd blurted that out. A disadvantage in holding off until the end of March would be that with the thaw well advanced, all the 'white torrents rushing', they'd have to bridge rivers instead of driving straight over them, divert around huge areas of swamp instead of rushing straight across. You'd gain on the roundabouts, lose on the swings.

Conclusion: it could be a mistake to rely on having eight weeks in hand, and Grayling should be advised accordingly. They *might* attack next week, or the week after. After all, only 3 Commando Brigade Royal Marines, comprising about four thousand of those twenty thousand NATO troops, had actually deployed in Norway yet.

Another thought then, on the river-bridging subject: fast-moving incursion forces would be hampered and slowed down if they had to bring all their bridging materials up with them. If the clandestine operation in progress now was to be followed by a lightning strike, as it would have to be, and as indicated by the words of that *yoik*, they'd surely want to find bridging materials already there, at crossing points. So, putting oneself in the Soviet planners' boots, wouldn't you have dumps set up where you needed them? With such an enormous area of wilderness, there'd be no problem finding forested areas in which to hide them, given time, and Spetsnaz infiltrators, and a few Isaks here and there. . . .

'How did you kill him, Ollie?'

He glanced at her, wondering if she'd caught him up just to ask that question. 'Does it matter?'

'I thought you were a — canoeist?'

'Also a commando. *Was*. . . . Look out where you're going. . . .'

Instead of looking at him. The ground was uneven as well as steep. Where the trees grew really densely it was easier to take skis off and carry them. She persisted: 'I suppose you did it with your knife.'

'Whereas you—' gesturing towards her ski-poles '—would have skewered him.'

163

'I wanted to say, really, I was not criticising, *blaming*—'

'I know.' She had been, in the shock of the moment, but she'd have needed to be unattractively hard-boiled *not* to have reacted in some such way. He began, 'Don't think about it. The fact is, it was him or me. Or *us*. And it could happen again, so—'

'Trees end here!'

Stenberg—higher, out to the left. Ollie slanted left too, to the same edge but lower, and the others joined him. Crouching, facing out northwards, with an open slope falling away in front, a steepish drop to yet another frozen stream. Or the same one, if there was a bend in it below the cabin. Looking down to his right, his eyes followed the streak of ice down to a confluence, another stream joining from the wood's other side. So you had one each side, enclosing this lower apex of the wood like the arms of an inverted 'Y', and combining there to form a river which continued northward through a widening valley.

Too wide. You might cross it in the dark, but he knew he'd be crazy to try it now. Trees were dotted around, but much too sparsely to be any use as cover.

The only way out, therefore, would be eastward. Far enough east, then turn north along the far side of that valley. Considering it, visualising the map in his memory, concluding *OK*. . . . So immediately, begging a few questions such as whether the east side of this wood might be under surveillance, cross over there, out that way. . . . He glanced round, told Sophie, '*That* way. . .'. Then turning back, with a lull in the blizzard in that moment so that visibility cleared, he saw with a shock of alarm, a solid bang in place of a heartbeat, just how right that decision had been – *if* it could be acted on.

He was staring across this steep, narrow gulch at a tent – at the top of the opposite slope, up against the facing wall of trees. Then a movement had attracted his eyes to the left where a man was standing fifteen or twenty metres from the tent with binoculars at his eyes, watching up the line of ice towards whatever he could see of the higher slopes.

164

Watching for anyone who might try to cross. Maybe with binos he could see to where the stream must have made a dogleg change of direction. While the other guy – who was now deceased – would have been watching the upper part.

This one might have heard the shooting, would be taking an interest in the scenery for that reason?

Not unlikely. But extremely lucky one hadn't fired the AYA. He'd know the difference between submachine gun fire and a shotgun blast, all right. That could be another Swedish MKS on his back, incidentally.

The snow-curtain thickened again, and the tent and man were almost invisible. If one hadn't known now where to look. He muttered, backing into the trees, 'Out the other side. . . .' If there wasn't a lookout there too. They'd pitched their tent where it had shelter, there might well be more than one of them using it, like another watching the other side. If so, you'd be stuck here. . . .

But from the other edge, ten minutes later, he couldn't see anyone. . . . The thought that he hadn't seen a bloody great tent either, at first glance, made him spend more time on it, try harder.

'Can't see any. . . .'

He wished *he* had binoculars.

Snow, ice, trees. Below, to the left, it was a shifting, impenetrable whiteness, he couldn't see the bottom of the stream.

'Hang on a minute. Well – *few* minutes.' Genius being an infinite capacity for taking pains, the price being survival or non-survival, and a possibility there could be a watcher on this side, in *these* trees. . . . With the gun slung on his back he ski-crawled – moving on his hands and knees, with one hand and one knee to each ski. Three-quarters buried in snow by the time he was far enough out to squirm around – bedded in its deep, wet softness, unslinging the submachine gun as he faced back towards the trees he'd just left, to examine them yard by yard, uphill and downhill, watching for movement or for shapes that might *not* be rooted in the shallow soil. He could see Gus – then Sophie – just as a Soviet would have if there'd been one here. Otherwise Mother Nature seemed to have the place to herself.

He crawled back, a mound of snow travelling slowly on two planks.

'Looks good.' Standing, beating snow off himself, then taking his ski-poles from Sutherland. 'Let's get over there now, while we have a chance.' And luck, sheer luck, to have it, just when they needed it and the whole area obviously staked out by Spetsnazi. He'd suppressed an urge to say *Let's get over there double-quick, for Christ's sake. . . .* Because he didn't want Sutherland to feel there was pressure on him and consequently mess it up. Another instant thought as he contemplated this new appearance in the open was that the first one out was the person most likely to get shot. As had been shown with Isak, whose escape attempt had saved at least one other life: someone would have started over, before that guy showed himself. So he didn't want Sophie taking the lead now. 'Gus, you first. Then you, Carl. Take it easy. . . . Then Sophie. And last but not least, yours truly.'

The iced-up stream was an awkward thing to cross, but Stenberg made a good job of it. Sutherland was clumsier but he got over all right. Then as he set off on the other side in Stenberg's tracks he made the mistake of trying to look back to see Sophie following. Ollie saw him in trouble – about to fall backward, then wild, all over the place, struggling to recover but finally over-balancing forward, slamming down in a forward dive. Muffled cry as he hit the snow. Sophie was across the stream and heading for him, Ollie still this side. When he got to them she said, 'His right leg. . . .'

Sutherland tried to get up, with help, but folded again on that leg. Swearing through clenched teeth, desperate. The safety binding on the right ski hadn't released, although in a forward fall it should have. Ollie was already guessing what might have happened to the leg. He hoped he was wrong, that the tendons had *not* been torn. . . . But out here in the open was no place to hang around, with at least one Spetsnaz within a few hundred metres and by the looks of it this whole area infested by them. . . . 'Get his pack off, would you.' He dumped his own bergen, released Sutherland's other ski and slung him up in a fireman's lift. He told Sophie to bring what she could carry, he'd come back for the rest. Sutherland stifling groans and muttering apologies as he ski'd with him across his shoulders to the trees, well into cover. Stenberg helped lower him to the ground. But in a matter of seconds the picture had changed enormously for the worse. You could forget any idea of getting to Angeli or any of those other Finnish settlements now. In fact as a group, there wasn't a hope of getting *anywhere*.

9

South, he'd decided, was the best bet. Then hole up. He hadn't told the others yet. But it was a reasonable guess that the Spetsnazi would concentrate on barring the way back into Norway and to the nearer Finnish settlements – in which, guessing at the way they'd have set this thing up, they'd very likely have agents in residence, anyway. Small Finnish settlements in this area were therefore places to steer clear of. By now, he reckoned, they'd have a good idea that there were no corpses in the pass: they might also have found a couple near that cabin. And when they found those, it really would hit the fan.

Sutherland murmured, 'You're doing me proud, Ollie.' He was obviously in pain. Ollie crouching, making a ski-stretcher. He promised, 'When we stop for the night I'll strap that leg up for you. Meanwhile I'm afraid you won't find it's exactly first-class travel.'

He hadn't any morphine in the field-dressing pack he'd put together at the *apotek* shop in Karasjok. Stenberg had some painkiller tablets of US origin though, and Carl had taken some. For now, the only other thing you could do was move on as fast as possible.

When the stretcher was as sound as it ever would be, Stenberg helped him lift the patient into place and strap him there. In AW training, making emergency ski-stretchers for evacuating casualties had been routine, but you'd had a canvas kit which he did not have here, so this was improvisation, very rough-and-ready. The runners were Sutherland's skis, with the poles and some straight branches lashed across them for a basic framework, and brushwood on that, topped with a sleeping-mat. He'd used string to bind all the joints, and now a minimal length of nylon tow-rope to hold Carl in place on top of the contraption.

'Still going to make Angeli, are we?'

'Afraid not.' He explained, 'They'll be expecting us to go that way, Carl. Or back into Norway. If we could have got through quickly we'd have had a good chance of making it, but – well, apart from anything else – I should think they'll be deploying more guys from the pass by this time.'

Also, rapid movement or fast reaction had become less easy.

'So where now?'

'That way.' A movement of the head, southward. 'As far as we can travel in roughly two hours – because we'll have to stop in time to dig-in, and we'll need some daylight in hand for that.'

'But – going *south*?'

'That's it, Sophie.' He snapped his skis' bindings shut. 'To get clear of this area and in a direction I hope they won't think we *would* have taken. Just as it doesn't make a lot of sense to you, right? Then tomorrow west and northwest, through the nature reserves and into Norway, towards Kautokeino.'

She was frowning. 'That is a long way, you realise how far?'

She hadn't asked him who'd be making the trip. It obviously hadn't occurred to her yet that Sutherland wouldn't be able to, so that some division of forces was going to be unavoidable. He told her, 'With any luck we won't have to trek as far as Kauto.'

'You mean get to a telephone before. But Ollie, I know the *vidda*, I do not believe on that route there can be *any* place—'

'Let's talk about it tonight? I do have some ideas, but right

170

now there isn't time, and *that*—' he pointed '—is the only way to go that isn't suicidal. OK?' He looked down at Sutherland. 'It'll be bumpy, Carl. Just have to grin and bear it.'

'Why grin?'

'OK. Just fucking bear it.'

Cheap laughs, from people with taut nerves. . . .

He thought he was going to have to send Sophie through on her own. From the skiing point of view she'd have no problems, and she knew the country – at least, once she got over into Finnmark she'd know it, to *some* extent. The idea didn't exactly fill him with joy or enthusiasm, but he didn't see how he could leave the other two on their own.

'Right then, we're off. I'll lead, you two right and left, same routine as with the pulk.'

Stenberg bent to pat the sleeping-bag. 'Good luck, pulk.'

Sutherland had been calling himself a Jonah, blaming himself for everything. Which was silly, Ollie had pointed out, while he'd been making the stretcher. OK, so Isak had stabbed them in the back, or tried to, but without him they wouldn't have known anything, they'd have drawn blank and gone home, and in eight weeks' time – cataclysm. . . . But also, Isak had saved their lives, as it had turned out, if he hadn't made his escape attempt *they*'d have been caught in that blast of automatic fire. Ollie had assured Carl he had no reason to blame himself. 'Thanks to you we have this knowledge, and what's more we'll get it out – *and* get ourselves out – no matter how things look at this moment. And, incidentally, anyone can take a fall, you didn't *try* to, did you? You take it easy now, OK?'

'You're a good guy, Ollie.'

The damage was to the tendons at the back of the leg. It was an injury of a kind he'd seen before, not in the Marines but in Alpine skiing, a similar forward fall in soft snow and a so-called 'safety' binding failing to release. Sutherland should have been getting expert medical attention, and the leg should have been in plaster now and for several weeks: he'd know it, too, Ollie guessed. When they stopped for the night, he'd improvise some kind of splint. Sutherland, of course, would be

171

under the impression that he'd be out of this wilderness in a day or two, so he wouldn't be worrying as much as he might have otherwise.

Fat chance of *that*, though.

Trekking south, the forest around them was sometimes sparse but always good enough for cover, with slight detours here and there. One major one – skirting a high valley that was full of reindeer. He led them round it widely, not wanting to meet or be seen by Sami herdsmen. The reindeer grazed mostly in small groups – like family parties – bunched together and preoccupied in feeding, their faces thrust deep in snow to reach the moss they lived on all winter.

It had stopped snowing twice, but the third time it didn't start again. Visibility expanded quickly, alarmingly; he guessed that back where they'd come from the Spetsnazi would be making the most of it, knowing there wasn't much daylight left now, scouring open areas and scanning distances from high vantage points. Ski-tracks from earlier in the day would have been filled by this time, but from where they'd started most recently, where Sutherland had had his accident, they'd still be visible.

You could only hope and pray there'd be no one there to spot them before it snowed again.

Snow tonight, please? Before they start searching on this side?

Not much to ask for – considering it could make the difference between life and death, also the difference between getting the news out via Grayling and the sneak invasion achieving complete surprise. In which case Finnmark would fall into Soviet hands before anyone in the West knew such a move was even being contemplated.

For all *that*, just a few hours of snowfall?

But in about one hour, now, it would be dark. While anxious to get as far south as possible, he'd also been keeping a look out for suitable locations for bedding down, and this place looked about as good as you could hope for. They were high up, close to the tree-line – birch here, straggling weakly upward as if individual trees had dared to face the mountainside alone, then found they couldn't make it, stuck there in isolation to be ravaged by the wind. Above them a great dome of white glistened, bleakly empty.

He called to the others to slow down, stop – Sophie and Gus having to drop back to slow the stretcher gradually and together, not put a sudden brake on that might tip it over. He'd seen a ridge down on the left, inside the wood, a spine that would be bare rock in summer, he guessed, slanting up through the trees and continuing above them. Snow had banked deeply all along it, would be metres deep and by now tight-packed, and there was surrounding cover from the trees. Also the approach to it from above was from the windward side, so that if more snow did fall it would drive in from this direction to fill the tracks they were making now and would make in the approach. Third, you could leave in the morning before daylight – through trees all the way down into the valley, then northwest through forest with no more open ground to cross.

He led them down to it on a dogleg track, traversing down into denser cover and then doubling back, a reverse traverse down to the ridge. Thinking of the early-morning departure: he'd made up his mind during the past hour or so, the decision forming more or less of its own accord, just growing in his general thinking, that he could *not* send Sophie off on her own. . . . Stopping again. Puzzling them – Stenberg making a gesture of exasperation – but needing to make certain of picking the best spot. It was going to be home for the Americans for several days, not just a hole-up for the night.

He was gazing back over their higher ski-tracks, back into hazy distance, mountainside with a dark stubble of fir and birch, a smearing of black and grey with more open areas here and there and the great rolling emptiness of the tops above. No movement, no indication of anyone following, yet. But he'd send one of the others – it would have to be Sophie – up to this position, in a minute, to keep a watch until darkness came.

'Right. Snow-hole for four. . . . Look here, Gus.'

He sketched it in the snow with the point of a ski-pole. Gus was going to help build it – or rather excavate it – so he might as well understand what was wanted.

'Entrance – actually a crawl-hole, tunnel. Just wide enough for one at a time to wriggle in. Like a big rabbit-hole, OK? We'll haul Carl in, in his sleeping bag, but we'll collapse the stretcher, we don't want the tunnel to be that wide. We bring all gear inside, you see. . . . So – entrance hole and tunnel, and the tunnel has to be lower than the chamber – the bed-sitter, you might call it. We'll dig in here, downward-sloping entrance, tunnel levels out after about two metres and slopes up again, and we make the floor of the chamber at a higher level than the entrance. Follow?'

'I can see it's a lot of labour.'

He nodded. 'Tunnel rises to this point, entering the chamber, which will be about fifteen feet by ten. It'll have platforms of hard snow to sleep on, and alcoves cut into the sides for (a) storing our gear and (b) the stove. . . . Reason the tunnel has to be lower than the chamber is that air rises as it warms – getting warmed by our body-heat, the stove when we're cooking, and minutely from a candle which has to be kept burning all the time. That's why we had to lump so many candles along, it's to ensure there's enough oxygen inside. If the flame goes out, there isn't – so you do something before you suffocate. Like clearing the vent-hole – hole in the roof, we keep a ski-pole in it. We'll have to watch the ventilation problem while we're digging, too – making the tunnel, for instance, when it's a dead-end with no throughput of air. We'll work in shifts, you and I, changing places, one digging and the other shifting snow out. Use a sleeping-mat for that, shovel the stuff on to it and the other guy drags it out – banking it out here. *There*, say.' He added, 'Maybe we'll get some help later from Sophie. It's a good four hours' work, usually, for guys who know what they're doing. But we might make it a little smaller than standard, this one.' He saw that Sophie had the stove going and a kettle of snow on it, close to Carl's stretcher so he could tend it. Someone would have to feed the snow in, but he'd do the rest. . . . 'Sophie, that's great. Now I'd like you to go back

174

up there – where we last stopped, right? To keep a look-out, just while the light lasts. Then you could help us with the hole, if you wouldn't mind.'

He wanted a look-out kept until dark in case the opposition had been very quick off the mark. It wasn't likely, but it was possible.

'Sophie. If they did come, we'd be stuck here, we'd fight it out. So if you see them coming – well, let us know, then take off. Don't say goodbye, just go like the wind.'

'Go where?'

'I'd suggest Route 93 where it runs up from the frontier to Kauto. Shortest way would be roughly along the line of the frontier. Then stop a car or something, hitch a ride into town and start raising the alarm.'

'That would be a very long trek. As much as – two days, *good* days?'

'Better than trying a shorter trip and walking into their arms.'

'All right.' She nodded. 'But it won't happen.'

'I know. Just so we know. In case.'

What they were both saying, really, was, *Please God may it not happen.*

'You said you would fight it out?'

'We're reasonably well armed now, after all. And once they were close, we obviously couldn't move fast enough to make it worth running for it.'

He heard Sutherland mutter, 'Just because I'm fucked up, to say the rest of you have to stick around and get killed – Christ Almighty—'

'Nobody said anything about getting killed, Carl. . . . But look, we don't want you getting frostbite either. Sit up, swing your arms, move as much as you can, move *all* your muscles – even if it makes the leg hurt – and rub it, it's better than bloody well losing it—'

'I don't have to *make* it hurt, for Christ's sake!'

'I'm sure. . . . Look, take a couple more of Gus's pills. But do what I said, please. . . . Once we're inside we'll make you more comfortable, but—'

'What are you doing now?'

'Stripping off.' He'd pulled a lightweight waterproof suit out of his bergen. 'I'm going to work in this. You have one, Gus, don't you? Digging's hard work, so you sweat, your clothes'd soak through and if you can't get 'em dry quickly they'd freeze. So it's best to strip, dry yourself afterwards and dress again – clothes in the rucksack meanwhile. . . .'

It was dark long before they finished, but it would have been dark inside anyway without candlelight. He and Gus manoeuvred Sutherland in, pulling him in through the tunnel in his sleeping-bag then getting him up on to one of the platforms, on a mat, and opening the bag so Ollie could splint the injured leg in a cage made of the brushwood from the stretcher, parcelling it with nylon rope. It was as close as you'd get to a plaster cast. Meanwhile Sophie had the meal heating up, a recipe devised by Sutherland – 'Reindeer Chowder' – consisting of sweetcorn with lumps of reindeer meat in it.

Ollie explained some basic rules of snow-hole living. Keeping the vent open in the roof, and a candle burning, and not to have water simmering or boiling for longer than necessary – because of condensation making clothes damp. Drying all clothing and boots, mainly inside sleeping-bags from body-heat. Keeping the shovels where they could be got at quickly in case of a cave-in. A line running through the tunnel, and a marker outside in case when you'd gone out there at night you couldn't find your way back.

Ordinarily you'd have a candle watch inside and also a sentry outside, but he couldn't imagine there was any prospect of enemies showing up during the dark hours. The danger period would start with daylight – tomorrow, the day after, day after that. They wouldn't give up, he thought, they'd surely be as desperate to stop the information getting out as he was to see it *did* get out.

'About ready, this chowder.' She looked round at Suther-

176

land. 'Shall I put it in mugs, d'you think, to eat with spoons?'

'How else?' The professor winced, shifting his position. 'No connoisseur would dream of having it served any other way.'

He was doing his best. But he was obviously in pain, despite the pills he'd taken. Ollie's respect for him had grown since the accident. He hoped he'd done the right thing for that leg, strapping it up as he had. . . . He put the submachine gun down on the snow-platform beside him; he'd dismantled and cleaned it and had now re-assembled it, having in the process re-familiarised himself with its rotary-bolt, gas-operated action. Stenberg asked him, 'What's that thing's rate of fire?'

'Around a thousand rounds a minute. But it's adjustable.'

'Did you ever handle one before?'

'Oh, yes.'

He waited, expecting to hear when, where and how, but soon realised there was no explanation coming. Sutherland broke the silence.

'Will you leave the shotgun here, with us? So we'd have that as well as Gus's pistol?'

Stenberg glanced at Ollie, frowning. . . . '*Leave*?'

Ollie nodded. 'You're not just a pretty face, Carl, are you?'

'Well.' Sutherland accepted his mug of chowder from Sophie. 'Thanks.' He looked at Gus. 'What else can he do? Think about it, old buddy. Someone has to take the word out — right? Well, he could go himself, alone, but he'd be disinclined to leave Sophie here. Alternatively he could send *her*, but on her own she'd be – well, vulnerable, wouldn't she? In spite of those secret weapons she carries. And think of this, now – if something went awry – I mean either of them alone, if they got stopped – well, back here we wouldn't know about it, we'd imagine the message was getting through and it would *not* be. And those guys out there won't be inactive meanwhile, we could finish up with *all* our chances shot. . . . My logic about right, Ollie?'

He nodded. 'I'd say so.'

'So they push off.' Stenberg folded his hands round the mug which Sophie had passed to him. He looked at Ollie. 'You and Sophie, while we two hold the fort, as it were.'

177

'While you sit tight, keep your heads down and wait for me to get back here. They'll be out there hunting around for us, you can bet on it, you *will* have to lie very low indeed. . . . OK, so there's an alternative, if Sophie went solo and at the same time I took you two out. The trouble with that is it'd be slow going, with Carl lamed, and I think we'll have a better chance of making it when the heat's worn off a bit. And meanwhile the absolutely vital thing is to get the message out, and I think this is the best way to do it. But if anyone has any better ideas, let's hear them.'

'Uh-huh.' Sutherland shook his head. 'As I just said, there's no other way to do it that's as sure. You two good skiers in tandem, that's the answer, *has* to be. And we'll be snug enough here – plenty to eat, well hidden – long as we *do* keep out of sight. . . . Will you leave us the stove?'

'Are you joking?'

'Well, we'd manage, I guess—'

'Of course we'll leave it.' He told Sophie, 'We'll travel as light as we possibly can. And I won't go the full distance with you, only as far as Route 93, see you safe aboard some kind of transport, then straight back here to evacuate these two. You'll have your tapes, the *yoik* and your own translations, and you can telephone your people and mine from Kautokeino.'

'Notify our guys too, Sophie?'

'Of course.' She nodded, sitting down to start eating. 'In any case my government would be very quick to tell all NATO countries.'

'But your department wasn't exactly on the ball, you said, when you called them from Karasjok.'

She shook her head. 'That is not whom I would call in this connection.'

Stenberg cocked an eyebrow. 'Defence Ministry?'

She shrugged, looking as if she didn't much like this line of interrogation. Ollie asked her, 'Might one assume that your own department wasn't primarily instrumental in giving us the pleasure of your company on this joy-ride?'

Sutherland chuckled. Sophie said, rather primly, 'If it was a

178

Sami problem, it would concern those who are responsible for Sami affairs. Obviously. But since it is not – well, you must be familiar with the Biblical quotation "Render unto Caesar"?'

Stenberg looked impressed. 'How's *that* for double talk?'

'Your English, Sophie,' Ollie told her, 'has come on wonderfully in the last week.'

Sutherland had been waiting with another question. 'Sophie. You said your government *would* be very quick to tell their allies, then "whom I *would* call" – as if some doubt existed?'

'I'm sorry. Perhaps my English is *not* so good, I should have said *will*.' She shut her eyes: in what Ollie guessed might be a quick burst-transmission of a prayer. Then her eyes were open, wide, and on *him*. . . . 'We *will* make it – won't we, Ollie?'

'Yes.' He assured her, 'We will. We have to. Absolutely have to, we'll make sure of it.' He'd have liked to have taken her in his arms, hugged her, *made* her believe it. Instead, he changed the subject. 'But if you've finished eating, if I were you I'd climb up on that nice bouncy bed we made for you.'

'I never heard a block of snow called a bed before.'

'You'll find it's slightly warmer up there. Because warmed air rises. Best of all, get up there and into your sleeping-bag.'

'So why don't you practise what you preach?'

'Because as soon as I finish this repast I want to take a look outside.'

'Doesn't he have all the answers?'

'Seems to, Sophie.' Sutherland nodded. 'And I can tell you one thing, I'm damn glad we had him along.' He looked at Ollie. 'But while you're at it you might answer this. If it doesn't embarrass anyone. How am I going to – hell, how shall I put it – how do I set about answering nature's calls?'

Stenberg rolled his eyes. 'Diaper lessons now.'

'Usual way, I'd imagine.' Ollie suggested, 'Crawl out – helped by this pal of yours – and dig a shovel into the snow to lean on. Or your ski-poles, but you'll need to have a shovel with you anyway. Before you go outside, have Gus check it's all clear out there. And don't go farther than you have to, making tracks. . . . On this subject, incidentally, it's very important that neither of you should leave any – er – personal waste around, where it could be seen. Including teabags, anything at all. Dig a hole, Carl – deep. When you've filled it in, take a shovelful of snow and throw it so it falls – it looks natural then, but not when it's raked over.' He paused. 'I want to tell you, for the record, I don't like leaving you here. But you're right, Carl, in the circumstances I'm sure it's the best solution.'

Stenberg asked him, 'How long would you expect to be gone?'

'Well, we'll start early, when it's still dark.' He looked at Sophie. 'I'd estimate the distance as about eighty k's, if we can cover it more or less as the crow flies. Fifty k's is about maximum as a day's run for a good skier with a full pack – maybe a hundred pounds of gear, say. We're both good enough, and we'll travel light, as I said, so if we really push it I'd reckon to do it in about a day and a half. With a short night-stop in between, bivvied-up in some wood. But if we get away really early in the morning we'll make the first day a long one, too. If that's all right with you?' She nodded, and he went on, 'Second night I'll be on my way back, so I'd be back here late on day three – with luck. But listen – (a) that'll be really pushing it, (b) the main reason for the two of us going together is we *could* run into trouble, they may have the whole border area staked out. If so, the plan will be for one of us to stay clear and sneak on through, and for my own preference that'd be Sophie. So then my return could be delayed somewhat.'

Sutherland shook his head, muttered, 'Jesus . . .'

'I thought of one thing, Ollie.' Sophie still hadn't got up on her snow-bed. 'We'll be going along close to the frontier nearly all the way, won't we. Well, I can show you where there is a tourist cabin like that one today. *Statens fjellstue*, in Norwegian, a State mountain hut. It's near the border – more than half the distance, I suppose, but if we could get that far maybe we might make use of it?'

He nodded. 'Save bivvy-making, wouldn't it. . . . How about some chocolate now?'

Sutherland handed his mug to her. 'That was great, Sophie.'

He lay back, put his hands behind his head. 'Seems so damn strange, this. When you stop to think about it. I mean – sitting here feeding our faces, chewing the fat, when just hours ago we saw two guys *killed*? And more guys out there aiming to kill *us* now?' He'd turned his head, staring at Ollie, finding it hard to express his feelings. . . . 'I have to convince myself this is *me* here, just sort of *accepting* all this stuff!'

'Yeah, well.' Stenberg shrugged. 'We mostly lead easy, comfortable lives, don't we, we forget how rough life can be – I mean, until you get fire, flood, earthquake, air-crash, whatever. Then – well, it's like if you throw a guy in the sea he starts swimming, right?'

Sophie nodded. 'Exactly.'

'But—' Sutherland stared around him. The snow-hole's curved walls and ceiling were glazed now, condensation from the cooking had frozen into a glassy coating of ice which dazzlingly reflected the single candle's light, a startlingly white brilliance from so small a source. Sutherland stared at Ollie again: 'But you – well, *Jesus* . . .' He wasn't saying it – whatever it was that was baffling him, that he couldn't grasp. The killing of the Russian, maybe. . . . He muttered, looking away again, 'You've been there before, I guess. Must have been. . . .' Then, after a few seconds' silence, 'Isak was a good-hearted little guy, you know?'

'Could've fooled *me*.'

'But he *was*, Gus. Didn't I tell you how helpful he was to me, when I was here before? Really welcoming, nothing too much trouble – for a complete stranger, foreigner. . . .'

Sophie said, 'That's how they are, the Samis, ordinarily. Foreign visitors have said they can be more outgoing than the non-Sami Norwegians.'

'Something surely changed *that*, with Isak.'

'The business with his niece, Gus. They had him over a barrel, didn't they.'

'But he must have been involved a long time before that.' Stenberg broke off some chocolate and handed the bar to Ollie. 'He'd have made his blunder when he joined in this thing, long before we came on the scene. Then we show up and whoever's calling the shots decides we have to be taken out, so they put the screws on him. That simple, isn't it?'

'On those lines, sure.' Sutherland winced: both hands on his leg on the outside of the sleeping-bag, shifting it. . . . 'What beats me is why the Soviets should've brought him or other Samis into it at all. If he hadn't been involved, pressured or not, we'd be as ignorant now as we were a week ago. Why wouldn't they have played their own hand, with no such contacts and therefore none of the attendant risks?'

'I think this is in the *yoik*.' Sophie pushed back her short, dark hair. 'The last line of the second verse – *Bearing in blood-red talons freedom for Sameätnam*. Sameätnam in Lappish means Samiland, Ollie, Lappland. So it's to be made to look like a Sami "freedom" movement.'

Sutherland nodded. 'Makes sense. They'd have used Isak and others like him as their front men. With those books he wrote, he'd be a natural.'

When Ollie took his look outside, he found to his satisfaction that it had begun to snow again. If it kept up for a few hours, all today's tracks might be covered. Nothing better could have happened, and he went back in to give them the good news. But he'd had another thought too while he'd been outside.

'Gus – a little more exercise now. It won't take long, just a little job out there, but we'd better strip off again.'

Stenberg said, 'Face the wall please, Sophie.'

'*Dum* . . . What's this now, Ollie?'

'I'm going to build a wall. We've a mass of excavated snow lying around, and if we make it into a wall screening the entrance Carl and Gus can go out when they need to and still be in cover.'

There was another dimension to it as well, which he explained to Gus while they were shaping the wall, piling the snow and compressing it. In pitch darkness, with snow swirling down, weighting the trees' branches. Goggles were useless, constantly snowing-up, he'd pushed them up on his forehead. Ice forming on the outside of the suit, sweat inside that would have turned into a sheathing of ice if you'd stopped work for

182

half a minute. . . . He explained – the wall would serve not only as a visual screen, but if they were attacked here it would be a defence too. He had the figures in his memory: to stop a rifle bullet required four metres of fresh snow, but only two if it was packed tight, and there was plenty here to make a barrier two metres thick, one and a half high. He told Gus, 'Ice is better than snow, of course, one metre's enough to stop any small-arms fire. Better still is ice-crete – ice with gravel mixed in it. You're safe behind twelve inches of ice-crete.'

'Where d'you get the statistics?'

People asked silly questions, sometimes. He gave him a silly answer as he swung up another load of snow. 'Learnt them at my mother's knee.'

'Yeah?' Pounding with his shovel. . . . 'She a commando too?'

'Pianist. At least, she was. . . . I want to put a curve in it, Gus, sort of curve it around the entrance hole, OK?'

During his first two-hour candle watch he sorted out rations for himself and Sophie to take with them. Only light stuff – biscuits, chocolate and raisins, and strips of the salted reindeer meat. Then he added two cans of baked beans: they could go in his own pack. Thermos flasks – to be filled with boiling-hot tea just before setting out – and teabags, sugar and milk powder. It might not be safe to make a fire, but if they made it to the tourist cabin there'd be a stove in it, she'd said.

They'd be travelling about due west. Several hours' trek to the border, then about forty kilometres through Norway before crossing back into Finland for another fifteen; back over the border again, and a few more hours' yomp to the highway. It was the frontier's zigzag course all along that stretch which made it necessary to pass to and fro across it while actually holding to a more or less straight line.

As Sutherland had suggested, he was leaving the shotgun

here. For their purposes it was really an ideal weapon. Ollie had told Carl, 'All you need do is point it at the tunnel, and if anything except Gus shows in it, pull a trigger.'

And *then* what?

He was glad neither of them had asked that question. Maybe they hadn't because they could guess as easily as he could that if the Spetsnazi did find the snow-hole they wouldn't last five minutes.

Everyone had turned in at about eight p.m., because he wanted to leave by 0400, to get six hours of travelling behind them before dawn. Then they'd have a good chance of reaching the log-cabin for the night's rest. While it was dark they'd keep close together, but in daylight they'd ski well apart, so that if one of them was spotted the other might not be, might have a chance of getting away. He'd reminded her an hour ago, 'I'm holding you to that agreement, Sophie. As far as I'm concerned it'd be – well, as near impossible as anything I can imagine – I mean to leave you and make a run for it – but I'll make myself do it if I have to. You mustn't hesitate either. No matter what either of us feels, the vital thing is for *one* of us to get through.'

She'd agreed. But he'd seen the nightmare in *her* eyes too.

She was asleep now. There was something to be said for physical exhaustion. The candle flickered slightly from the draught that came in through the tunnel, rose with a degree or two of warmth in it and was trapped for a time under the vaulted, gleaming roof. Sutherland, with one forearm across his eyes to shield them from the dazzling, mirror-bright ice walls, slept on his back and snored continuously, a rhythmic droning. Ollie went on thinking about Sophie. A mental picture of her as she'd been in the bivvy with her ski-pole at Isak's throat, the horror at what she was being called upon to do so stark in her expression that he'd *had* to take over, release her, and known as he did it that he was in love with her. Even if he hadn't known it before that moment. But now, there was a quality of desperation in his feeling for her, arising from the clear possibility that they'd never be able to do anything about it.

184

He could hear her asking him, *D'you think I'd let you just say goodbye?*

Imagining it – or trying to: having to ski away, turn down some forest slope and leave her, if *she'd* run into a Spetsnaz trap. . . .

Hell of a lot easier to be the one who stayed put. If it had to happen at all, pray to be allowed that privilege. Because it was an entirely realistic scenario. For example – and putting oneself in the mind of the Spetsnaz commander – no trace of the American party in those woods, except for their leavings, two men dead and one of them your own guy. You'd order a search for ski-tracks or other signs. Tracks would have been snowed over, but to a really expert eye there might still be traces, clues here and there. Then if the one who'd been near that tent with binos trained up the mountain, and maybe others whom one hadn't spotted – if they swore blind that no one had passed north or east of that river confluence – well, wouldn't the Spetsnaz leader be well able to put himself in *your* mind?

10

He told them as he wormed up out of the tunnel into the brilliant light, 'It's not snowing now.'

Quarter to four, pitch-black night, a wind with ice in it and fresh snow all over freezing into a hard crust but having nicely camouflaged this snow-hole and its front wall. He added, 'For the moment, it's stopped. Might start again, if we're lucky.'

Stenberg grunted – about the maximum response you could expect at this time of night and from a man not long out of sleep. He was crouching at the stove, stirring breakfast porridge – having already made tea, enough of it to fill their Thermos flasks as well. Sophie had glanced up from waxing her skis, but didn't comment. The fact that no snow was now falling meant their tracks would last, would be there to be seen and followed – in both directions. He doubted if there'd be any new falls in the near future either: it was too cold for it, and getting colder.

'You guys ready to eat your porridge?'

'Dish it out, Gus, would you?'

He'd had the last watch, and roused the others at three-thirty. He'd tried not to wake Sutherland, but the professor had stirred into life anyway when they began to move around.

His leg was aching. He was sitting up now, massaging that foot with the other one inside his sleeping-bag, and had declined an offer of more painkillers, saying he'd keep them in case the leg really began to hurt, as distinct from aching, and in any case the pills were going to have to last three days.

With luck, Ollie thought, he'd be back here in three days. But then it would take another two for him and Stenberg to move the injured Sutherland to and over the border, where he hoped a helicopter pickup might be arranged. But on the other hand the opposition would most likely be still around; you couldn't take anything at all for granted.

But there was no point worrying on and on about it, either. You couldn't make plans in detail, you just had to start, push it along as hard as it would go, cope with whatever hit you.

Leaving tracks all the way, though, for anyone with eyes to follow, and/or to track back to this hole. Like finding rabbits in a burrow: put in a ferret, flush them out. Easier still, collapse the snow-hole and kill whatever wriggled to the surface.

Christ, imagination. . . .

But they did look so helpless. They probably didn't realise just how vulnerable they were. Leaving them now felt like leaving a sort of decoy that might delay pursuit of himself and Sophie. It certainly was not a tactic, it was simply the way things had to be, the plain facts of a brutal situation.

The porridge was so thick he had to use a knife to get it off the spoon.

'If you made enough of this, Gus, you could use it as plaster on Carl's leg.'

Smiles. . . . But smiling was an effort. They were awkward, self-conscious in a peculiar way, sharply aware of the imminence of a separation that might – Ollie guessed – feel to the two Yanks as if they were being deserted.

And they *were*, of course. It certainly felt like it to him, in these final minutes.

'Carl, listen. Remember that although I'll aim to be back in three days, all sorts of things could delay us, or delay me after I've seen Sophie on her way. Try not to get over-anxious. I'll be as quick as I can – I want to get you to a doctor, get that leg fixed properly for one thing. Be patient, though. And for Christ's sake—' he gestured towards the tunnel '—don't put your noses out there when you don't have to.'

'We'll be here waiting.' Stenberg nodded. 'As long as it takes.'

Sutherland said, 'Sure, Ollie.' He was in his forties but from the look of him in this viciously hard light he could have been sixty. 'Just you two watch yourselves, hear?'

Ten minutes later they were shaking hands. Sophie kissed both of them. Stenberg said, 'Now I *know* it's a big moment.'

'Oh, no. The big one will be when we get together again.' She stooped to hug Sutherland again: 'What a celebration, huh?'

'You won't keep me from *that* party.'

'Good luck, Ollie. Take good care of our girl.'

'You two take care of yourselves.'

It wasn't a 'big' moment, it was a bloody awful one, and the only way to end it was to turn away and slide out through the tunnel, dragging skis and poles. Sophie came close behind him. He put a hand down to help her up, held her tight for about ten seconds. . . . 'Let's try to walk it, down through the wood, put skis on later.'

'OK.'

'Meanwhile, stay close together.'

'Tell you a secret, Ollie, I don't mind *how* close.'

'Tell *you* one – I love you.'

'Tell me tonight in the *fjellstue*.'

'It's a date.' And for the hundredth time, *Please God*. . . . 'But listen. It's a hell of a long trek, and time's vital, we've got to really stretch ourselves, OK?'

Downhill then, through dense but leafless birch, close together, leaving a track a drunken elk might have made.

By dawn they were in Norway. There'd been no border signs where they'd crossed, but there was a river – if it was the right one, which he was fairly sure it was because in the last ten kilometres on the Finnish side they'd crossed a configuration of rivers, lakes and then a mountain ridge all of which matched features shown on the map. This despite the fact that his map of this section was a Joint Operations Graphic (air), the shop in Alta not having had a 'ground' graphic of this part.

An upward plod from the river, with higher ground to the right and another string of small lakes to the south, took them into a growth of scrubby willow, birch and ash. From here with the light increasing there'd be a clear view back to that last bare ridge in Finland, he thought. The highest part of it was shown on the map as eighteen hundred feet, fields of virgin snow falling steeply northward and more gently south, which was where they'd crossed it. The object of pausing here was to look back at that high vista; if anyone was following, you'd see them.

It had been time for a breather anyway. In six hours they'd taken only two ten-minute breaks.

'Might have a snack, while we're at it.' Then he saw she was already eating; preoccupied, he hadn't noticed. She said, 'They'll be all right, Ollie.' Misinterpreting his reason for looking back; so he explained it to her.

'But they will be, anyway. They are very well hidden, aren't they?' Her eyes shifted: 'Except I suppose our tracks—'

'Right. That's the problem. Or most of it.' The light was growing from back there where he was looking; the wind, coming over that ridge, had stung like a whip, and they'd been glad to get down to the river. He said, 'It's a matter of luck. But I don't believe we had any alternative.'

If a skier or skiers appeared on that high ground now, you'd know for sure you'd lucked out. As would Messrs Sutherland and Stenberg. *They'd* have discovered it already, he guessed.

'Do you think they *would* be so close behind?'

'No.' He turned to face her. Chewing – raisins and biscuit. . . . He swallowed. 'No, but if they were there I'd like to see them before they see us. . . . You fit for the next six hours now?'

'Have to be, I think.'

'How d'you keep in such good training? Squash, gym?'

'Also swimming. Skiing, of course, weekends out of Oslo. And the last two days have been good training. Should we go on?'

'Just like to make sure of this. The light's better every minute.'

'If they were coming, what would we do?'

'Depends.' He shrugged. 'Most likely pick a spot where I could send you on while I ambushed our trail.'

Which of course they'd expect, be watching out for.

There was nothing in sight, nothing moving on that milky haze of snowfield. On the other side, dead ground from here, it would be fully light by now; this was the shade side.

'If they had found our tracks, they would also find the snow-hole?'

'It's – probable.'

Finding where the tracks started, they'd back-track up through the trees. They'd have found the tracks of two skiers and they'd know there'd been four in the party the day before, so they'd know there had to be two holed-up nearby.

Sophie caught her breath. Pointing. . . .

He'd seen it too. A movement – something dark against the white crest of that far-off shoulder. Focusing hard on it, mittens curved to shut out peripheral light, wishing again he'd brought binoculars. . . . Two others, now. Then a fourth. . . .

'Reindeer!'

She was right. It wasn't so much the creatures' shapes, at that distance, as the drifting movement of deer grazing, slowly shifting their ground, a movement that had nothing in common with that of men on skis following a trail.

There was nothing slow about the way they shifted *their* ground in the next two hours – on a weaving course, following contours and using ground where trees gave cover. Climbing slowed you down and used up energy best utilised in covering distance. No breath to spare for talking – not even in the pauses, brief stops when there was a good view back eastward. Then reassured, plugging on again, running out of trees, crossing the high, naked *vidda*, the rolling emptiness Sophie had previously found so compelling. For compulsion, he thought, read acute anxiety: the map showed there'd be at least twenty kilometres of this open land to cross, and if Spetsnazi showed up it would amount to a race – chase – no cover, no place to hide or ambush.

Another hour. By any standards this was a fast and gruelling yomp. He didn't know how hard Sophie might be finding it, but she hadn't once slowed or asked for a rest – and except for those few short pauses they'd been trekking for more than nine hours. He knew *he* was feeling it. . . . Running downhill now, though – and dreading the end of it, the inevitable climb that would follow – but for the moment quite a fast descent on snow that had been crusted hard by the blast-freeze action of the wind. Sophie was leading, three to four hundred metres ahead of him, slanting down parallel to the course of a frozen stream to where the land flattened into an expanse of bog blessed with a scattering of trees.

Mountains ahead. . . .

This had to be getting close to the Finnish border again, Ollie guessed. They'd be in and out of Finland for a while, following a reindeer fence that was shown on the map, presumably therefore was permanent, not one of those strands of old wire or string with bits of plastic flapping. . . . Running downhill had already become a *past* pleasure, a long plod now first across the bog and then up towards an opening in the range of hills, or mountains. You came to it, you crossed it, looked ahead, saw what came next.

Another hour. Snow's crust scrunching as the waxed skis bit into it and gripped. Legs and arms driving like pistons.

More deer ahead there. The shallow pass was full of them. There must have been several hundred, he guessed, without bothering to count the scattering of brownish, greyish animals. Lapps prized white reindeer above all others, Suther-

192

land had told him. And the wild deer tended to have more white in their coats than the husbanded animals did. In some herds the owners had used captured wild deer at stud, and within a few generations – a few years – you saw the increase in whiteness. *Silken coated, running like the sunbeams, reindeer springing like the windstorm....* Not that this lot – or three or four other herds they'd seen during the transit of the high *fjells* – were doing any springing or resembled sunbeams. More like antlered donkeys.... Looking ahead then, remembering Isak's other *yoik* which she'd translated that night in camp as *Big and lovely, best girl in the country*...

She'd stopped. Looking up to her right. He felt that bang of the heart: thinking *Here we go....* She'd swung round, shouted something, but he didn't catch the words. Ears muffled.... He began to run, poling hard and running, skis thumping into the crust as he clattered up towards her. Then he saw them – two skiers traversing down from higher ground on the right, straight down towards her. He shouted to her, 'Here! Come *here*!'

Because she had the down-gradient, could make it a lot faster than he could get up to her. She'd heard, was on her way. He stopped, dug his poles into the snow in front of him – crossed, each pole through the other's leather wrist-strap. Unslinging the Swedish gun, he pushed the selector switch from 'safe' to 'semi-automatic'. Fairly sure they'd be Lapp herdsmen, but not taking any chances on it. That one on the snowscooter had been a Lapp herdsman, after all, Isak could hardly have been the only Lapp on that side. Sophie christie'd to a stop beside him. He was standing, cradling the gun, but if those two came on now he'd kneel, using the crossed poles for a rest and put a warning shot over their heads. If they still came on after that you'd know you had trouble.

So would they.

They'd stopped, though. Gazing down in this direction. Sophie said, 'Only Sami. With this big herd. I'm sorry, I thought—'

'Better safe than sorry.' He switched to 'safe' and was about to sling the gun on his back again when an idea hit him. 'Hang on. Let's take a look up there, just on the off-chance. . . .'

'Climb up there? Ollie—'

'I know. But it might be worth it.' He jerked his poles out of the snow, put them both in his left hand. 'Come on.' He began to herring-bone up towards them. They seemed to be waiting for him; and in better perspective you could see they were short, squat men, leaning on their ski-poles. They'd see the gun – if they hadn't already, and Samis – Sutherland had mentioned, after Isak had reacted badly to the sight of the AYA – didn't like firearms, except in hunters' hands. He had its sling over his right shoulder, the gun itself in the crook of his arm, barrel outward from his body.

'You'll frighten them, with that. They'll guess we are – well, like—'

'I know. I want them to take off.'

Before he was halfway up they obligingly kick-turned and started away, passing from left to right upslope of him, heading down towards this side of the grazing herd. He grunted, climbing on and without much breath to spare, 'Won't waste time, you'll see.'

Regretting the use of time, all the same, knowing there were probably no more than two and a half or three hours of daylight left. He passed the place where the two Lapps had been standing, climbed on to the top of the slope, a sort of rounded plateau.

'Now, look here. . . .'

Both of them breathless – and seeing ski-tracks everywhere, tracks leading in all directions. Deer-tracks too, and droppings, like big sheep-droppings. The herdsmen must have been around here since first light, getting the herd together, bringing in strays. Ski-tracks radiated south, west, north, northeast. His eye followed the line of one pair of tracks that left the trampled area and led away westward – fresh-looking, and no others near them.

'That's the way to your deer-fence, right?'

She confirmed it. Beginning to catch on, he thought. The point being that anyone trailing them had been following two sets of tracks, not three, and there could be three from here on.

194

There was also a nice set of two skiers' tracks diverging northwestward. Such a change of direction wouldn't seem unlikely; at this point you had the Finnish border right ahead, while *that* way you'd stay inside Norway, near enough on course for Kautokeino.

He explained it to her briefly, and she laughed. He didn't see anything funny. He asked her, 'Five k's to the fence, would you say?'

'To the *reingjerde*?' She was still panting. 'I would guess three.'

'Even better.' There'd still be a lot of distance to cover, from there on. He looked around. Up here there wasn't even a deer in sight now. 'Let's try to make up some time.'

The *fjellstue* – mountain hut – was on the northeast shore of a lake, in a clearing with trees surrounding it, the trees being part of a big area of forest at that end of the lake. They stood blackly against a night-time whiteness of higher, snow-covered ground to the north and east, their branches shaken free of snow by a wind scouring down from that same direction. The light had gone. If Ollie hadn't decided to take a short-cut through the bulge of Finland instead of following the fence and the border round– the way that other ski-track had gone – they wouldn't have got here at all tonight. He'd made his decision at the deer-fence, where as it happened he'd also had to switch to a different map, a ground one instead of an air one, with more detail on it. The short-cut had about halved the distance.

It was too dark to see whether smoke was coming out of the cabin's chimney. But he couldn't smell any, and it was too dark to check the snow for tracks.

'Hang on here a minute. I'll take a look.'

'Don't be long.'

He squeezed her arm, and left her, ski'd out into the open. Wishing he had snowshoes here. The snow had a crust but a boot with a man's weight in it would have gone right through, you'd have been wading. So you were confined to skis, which weren't either very quiet or convenient at close quarters. He remembered a conclusion they'd reached, years ago, a result of some early tactical experiments during AWT exercises: *skis for the approach, snowshoes for the assault.*

Not that he was about to assault anyone. He hoped. He was expecting to find the place empty.

Close to the back wall of the *fjellstue* he listened, sniffing again for smoke or cooking smells, or others. Then he unclipped his skis and moved around to the lee side, close against the wall and under the projecting timber eave, where the snow was thin and hard as ice.

Crunch. . . .

It *was* ice. He waited, listening for reaction. There wasn't any. He was sure then – almost. . . .

No windows. She'd said the only opening would be the door. At the front corner he crouched again, running the palms of his mittens over the snow's flat, unbroken crust, finding no holes or indentations. Moving cautiously and slowly to the door, then, feeling his way. A porch roof projected over front steps, supported on timber posts bolted to the sides of them. Three plank steps. Down low again, eyes inches from the timber, he could see in close-up unbroken coatings of snow curving upward at the back of each step, as wind had blown it. And no human foot had trodden here, not since the last snowfall. Not unless someone had been very clever.

Like jumping all three steps. You couldn't totally discount it.

The door opened outward, and no lock, chain or bolt secured it from the outside, there was only a handle to be turned. With the gun ready, he reached from the side one-handed, turned it and pulled slowly, steadily. . . .

Then he was inside. Pulling the door shut so he could use his map-reading pencil torch.

Empty – and no signs of any recent occupation. Otherwise, it was just as she'd described it. Wood-burning stove, wooden bunks, an axe and a saw for the use of visitors. He switched off the torch, opened the door and called softly, 'It's OK, Sophie, come on in!'

She'd come by the same route he'd taken, in his tracks, leaving minimal evidence of this visit. He'd been thinking about it, didn't intend either to use the stove or to stay longer than they needed. He waited near the door, heard her take off her skis where he'd done it, then the scrape of her boots on ice as she came round the side. Wondering what humorous comment on this clandestine nightstop Gus might have made if he could have seen it happening – visualising the American's sardonic, lopsided grin, and mercifully having no way of knowing that by this time any grin on Gus Stenberg's face would be fixed, frozen, snow-encrusted, a grimace of death.

'Not even to heat a tin?'

'No fire at all. We've got tea left. And staying alive, getting the word out—'

'Oh, I *know*.' Shaking her hair loose. One flickering candle stub burned on the stove's cast-iron top. 'But I had – you know, a dream – loving, all warm and—'

Kissing. Her arms were round his neck and he was holding her, but he hadn't started the kissing and she hadn't either: kissing had commenced, self-initiated and now self-generating. Bulk of clothing, snow-cold in frozen candlelight, sweat drying cold inside. Knowing so well how it could and should have been, having had that same dream of – warmth. ... 'Don't imagine I haven't thought about it too.' About this cabin with the stove hot, warmth radiating, and Sophie. ... 'On and off all day I've thought about us being here.' Maybe even *all* the time, at back of the other minute-by-minute thinking. He heard her saying, words coming fast, muddled, as if from a swimmer, face momentarily out of water for a gulp of air, 'But you do not know yet, nor do I know—' He'd stopped her mouth again, guessing at what she'd been starting to say – that there might *never* be any realisation of that dream. He cut across it with, 'We'll have years and years to prove it, my darling.' Cruel – confusing the issue deliberately, trusting to her not having the fluency to sort it out: because such thinking was destructive, got you nowhere. Then they were apart, temporarily, both aware that they were physically spent, having probably broken a number of ski-trek records. Not spent to *that* extent – you'd need to be dead, he thought, frozen through to the bones – but – he was saying – struggling into practicalities – 'Cold food, then. Beans OK? Chew some meat with them?' The beans had been insulated in his sleeping bag but the reindeer meat was like frozen boot-soles now, but it was still meat, hadn't had a chance to go bad and there was nourishment to be had from it. 'Second course – for a real change – well, what about biscuits and—'

'Chocolate?'

'Then sleeping-bags on those bunks.'

'No. *One* bunk,' she said.

It would be a tight squeeze, with all the bulk of bags and gear. He was opening a tin. He told her, 'In olden times in England they called it "bundling". Pre-marriage custom, getting-to-know-you routine. Couple in bed all wrapped up separately, the girl actually *sewn* up and close supervision by Mama.'

'I'd have a pair of scissors.'

'Right.' He passed her the topless tin, started opening the other. 'But we're taking a risk, using this place. I don't want to stay long, just long enough to rest up enough to face the next marathon. Tomorrow night you'll have a hot meal and a soft bed in Kauto – think of *that*, to look forward to!'

'I won't have *you*. I'll wish I was back here, like now.'

'You're crazy.'

'And you will have that trek all over again.'

'Knowing the route now, I've some ideas to make it easier.' He meant *safer*, more than *easier*, but it was too cold to correct it. . . . 'We did incredibly well today, you know.'

'Don't you know we always will?'

'If you mean what I'm *thinking* you mean—'

'That, of course, I know even better than you do.'

198

'Expert, are you?'

'Not yet, but I will be.'

'*Bloody* soon.'

'Now, if you like. This minute. My God, who wants to *eat*—'

'You do and I do.' Holding her, hugging her. . . . 'You're – a baked bean. Taste, smell. . . . Sophie darling, we'd freeze. Anyway I want it perfect for you, like you never—'

'I never had it on ice and in wet clothes.'

'You won't now either. I'm just about dying for you, I can tell you, but—'

'Talk of dying, what if – what if there is never any other—'

'Don't think like that, Sophie. Just *don't*. I promise you—'

'You can't promise. You know, I know, there's no promising. They can be out there now, coming this moment – or when we leave, maybe—'

'Eat your beans.' He shook her, just gently. 'Hear me? I *do* promise, I'll make it come true, but right now just eat your fucking beans up, like a good girl.'

'And my fucking biscuits.' Small-voiced, shaky. 'Chocolate. Fucking raisins.'

'*Voia voia, nana nana.*'

She laughed, half crying. 'I love you, Ollie.'

'Big and lovely, best girl in the country.'

'I don't like that *big*.'

'I'll make you bigger, one day.'

'Heavens, that sounds like love!' Hugging against him, her mouth near his ear, teeth chattering and through all the gear he could feel her shivers. 'For a man to think of that, to *want* it—'

'Can't you believe things I tell you?'

Food for fuel, for generating internal warmth. Then the 'bundling'. Candle out, sleeping-bags crushed together on one timber shelf, heat building inside the bags de-freezing bodies and drying out damp clothes. He'd told her, 'Bundlers were supposed to make conversation. For instance' – he cleared his throat – 'are both your parents alive and well, Miss Eriksen?'

'Oh, yes. They have a farm near Kristiansund.'

'Must be a lovely place to live.' He thought, *I'm stupid. She's right, they could be outside there, this minute. Two covering the door, one to bust us out. . . .* Her murmur in his ear — relaxed, sleepy: 'Have you been there?'

'Once, years ago. Landed by helicopter, came in low over a lot of little islands, wooden houses on them. Summer, really beautiful.'

'And *your* parents, are they in good health?'

'We should have this conversation on tape, you know.'

'Answer the question, please. Also, do you have brothers or sisters?'

'Two sisters, both married. And my mother's alive. My father died a long time ago. He was an engineer, Merchant Navy, chief engineer actually. We're Scots, did you realise this important fact?'

'Does your mother live in Scotland?'

'Dorset. Down south. Royal Marine country, too. Home was in Edinburgh but she has arthritis badly, needs the warmer climate. She was a fine pianist in her day. I saw my father cry, once, listening to her play — and he was a tough nut, I'll tell you.'

'You're a tough nut too. Do you cry, ever?'

'I did when he died. I was twelve. That's the last time I remember.'

Not entirely true. . . .

Surfacing momentarily from sleep, reaching for that memory: of having to fight back tears — because it wouldn't have done her any good to see them — watching his mother trying to play the way she'd used to, her arthritic fingers clumsy on the keys and obviously hurting like hell. . . . Sophie was asleep, her body jammed against his on the hard, narrow bunk, bundled in insulation inches thick, but her soft breathing in that ear.

Sutherland's voice croaked, *Just because I'm fucked up, you don't have to sit around and get killed!*

Loud – and as clear in his ears – or brain – in the cabin's freezing dark as it had been when he'd uttered the same words yesterday.

Yesterday?

A struggle, then, to get time into perspective. Night *before* yesterday: when they'd been about to start excavating the snow-hole. So – *dream*, he thought, *just a dream*. . . . But no dream now: he was wide awake, alert to his surroundings, muscles tensed. Having been woken by – *what?*'

He had no idea how long he'd been sleeping. One hour, or six. . . .

Hum of wind in the forest. No other sound, yet. The middle step, he'd noticed earlier, creaked when weight was put on it. So you'd have warning, unless it was someone who'd been here before and knew it. But you wouldn't expect to hear anything for a few minutes at least. If he'd been out there himself and put a foot wrong – as he had for instance on that ice – he'd have been as still as a rock now, allowing the inmates time either to react or to go back to sleep. Having found the tracks at the back there, knowing there *were* inmates.

Still nothing. He unzipped the top of his sleeping-bag slowly, quietly, slid out of it and off the bunk, the submachine gun under his right hand as it touched the floor. Crack of light at the top of the door: moonlight. Clouds breaking up, then. So no snowing for a while, damn it. Boots: pulling them out of the sleeping-bag then out of the plastic and pushing his feet into them, the gun down on the planks beside them as he laced up their fronts. Ventile coat. . . . He picked up the gun, selected automatic fire, then crouched at the side of the door, reached left-handed to turn the handle and push it open, hold it against the thrust of wind.

Moonlight flooding in.

'Ollie?'

'It's OK. Just taking a look outside.'

Moonlight made it easy to see there was no one in the clearing, and to see from the snow's unbroken surface that there hadn't *been* anyone here either. Unless they'd come and gone – unlikely – on the same tracks, his and Sophie's, which were very clearly visible, so visible that he decided – having refreshed his mental powers with sleep now – that he'd been a prize idiot to have come here at all.

He knew why he had. Although for one reason and another it had obviously been out of the question once they got here, he'd brought her here with the same thought in his mind that she'd had in hers. Precisely what Gus Stenberg would have assumed, would have made his little snide comment about. He'd wanted a few hours alone with her – before they separated and maybe never saw each other again – a few hours with a door that shut and a stove providing warmth.

He had a pee, and went back inside.

'Sophie darling, we have to shove off now.'

'Was there something out there?'

'No. Nothing. But – look, please, get up, get ready. I shouldn't have brought you here, it's *bloody* dangerous.'

'All right.' Upheaval in the bag. 'Although I do not see why—'

'Because it's where they'd expect us to come. Anyone like us, without the time to spare for making a bivvy, *would* use ready-made shelter – if he needed his head seeing to, like I reckon I do.'

He heard her mutter something in Norwegian. She was out of her bag, rummaging in it for things that she'd been drying in there. 'I'm thirsty. Couldn't we make just a little fire?' She added in a squawk: 'My God, is it *moonlight*?'

She must have had her eyes shut or her head in the sleeping-bag when he'd opened the door a few minutes ago. He told her yes, moonlight, bright as day. And yes to her plea for a drink, a fire. They'd finished their Thermos tea last night, and you had to have a source of heat before you could drink even water, unless you were happy to eat snow. That would have done for him, at a pinch, but there was a limit to the privations he felt he could reasonably inflict on her. So as you had to have a fire anyway, you might as well make tea, enough to refill the Thermos flasks as well.

There were half-burnt sticks and bits of charcoal in the stove, and a small pile of cut wood in the corner. Plenty for

202

immediate needs. But paper to get it started. . . . He realised he'd have to sacrifice some of his small reserve of lavatory paper.

'I'll get snow in and make tea, you get dressed, Sophie. If you want to go outside, keep to the tracks we made last night.'

He led, navigating by his wrist compass, steering about due west but varying the course when necessary to make the best use of available cover. The moon was making it lighter than some days had been, combination of moonlight and snowscape producing a radiance of magnesium-type brightness. The clear sky was sending the temperature plummeting, too, it was *very* cold. . . . This westward track was the shortest route they could have taken, to reach the highway that ran up out of Finland to Kautokeino and thence north to Alta. South of the border it wasn't called Route 93, the Finns had their own designation for it where it led on down to their major northwestern town of Enontekiö. There'd be some long-haul traffic on it at night, he guessed.

They could alternatively have headed northwest to join what was marked on the 'graphic' as *vinterveg*, 'winter road', a cross-country track leading across frozen lakes and joining the highway about halfway up to Kautokeino. But there was at least one Lapp settlement right on it – at the northern end of the biggest of the lakes, a place marked as Suolujavrre. Sophie said she thought it would consist of maybe one farmhouse and a few *gamme* – turf huts – and it was just the sort of location Ollie guessed they'd have staked out. For one thing, it would have been a natural route to have taken from the point where yesterday he'd tried to confuse their ski-tracks by mixing them up with the Sami herdsmen's. There were other, equally small settlements they could have gone for – for instance, a place called Kivijavrre where Route 93 crossed the border, where there'd be a Customs post. Or, halfway up to Kautokeino, a main-road halt marked Oksal. But there was no point in

203

risking any of them when you could get to Kautokeino, the security of its police station and the certainty of good communications.

'See – if we followed that line – where I tried to make it look as if we might be going? That's how they'd have seen it, surely – and if I'd been in the other guy's shoes that's where I'd have sent a picket.'

'It is the way I would have chosen.' She nodded. 'Easier travel, Ollie.'

'But this way's shorter. As well as safer. Joining the highway about here – however that's pronounced. . . . Aiddejavrre?'

'There is a *fjellstue* there, like this one.'

'But we don't need —'

'I know we don't. . . . You think the highway will not be watched?'

'Depends how many guys they have available. But they can't watch every mile of it, can't flood the whole of Finnmark with bloody Soviets – not yet, they can't. . . . Besides, once you're on board some vehicle that's going north you're home and dry.'

'But *you* are not.'

'My darling, I told you, don't worry about me. . . .'

He'd explained: much as he loved to have her company, wouldn't want anything *but* to have her with him in any normal circumstances, once he had only himself to look after in that wilderness he'd be like a fox, she truly did *not* have to worry.

The 'winter road' started right down at Enontekiö too, but it took a course quite separate from the highway's. He guessed it would have been an old Lapp migration route. Except that in April and October the herds would have been driven around the lakes, unless they'd swum or waded over. But, for centuries, freight would have been hauled over the snow-road in sledges drawn by reindeer, and at migration times it would have been quite a spectacle – herds, and the men on skis, entire households on sledges and pack-reindeer. . . .

He and Sophie crossed the *vinterveg* well south of the bigger lakes. They'd seen deer grazing, and tracks left by motor-scooters, but no Lapps. They'd all be snoring their little heads off, he guessed, since with snowscooters they could virtually commute to the job.

Maybe ten kilometres to go. He had the map photographed in his memory. Between the south shore of a large lake and the north end of a small one: across open ground and into forest for a while, then in the open again with a river to cross and, on the far side of it, a really big expanse of moonlit, dangerously open *vidda*, after which they'd have woods again right up to the highway. The map showed that the wooded area had a river bisecting it, linking two lakes.

It would be a relief to get that far, back into cover after the long exposure on open snowfields. It wouldn't be dense cover – judging by indications on the map – mostly sparse, probably birch, thin stuff that was shadowy enough to hide in if you made the best use of it. But the moon was a menace. High clouds were so thin that even when they covered it the scene was bright. Snow reflected any light there was, magnified it, and ski-tracks could show up from miles away, particularly from the air or from higher ground, the harsh light creating shadow inside the depressions so that they looked black as railway lines across the brilliant whiteness.

They were nearly over the last, biggest open stretch when shots cracked out, wrecking premature hopes. The shots had come from high ground on the left – the south – two shots with about a three-second pause between them. By the time he heard the second one he was already flat in the snow, pulling Sophie down beside him.

There was no cover really close. The best bet was some woodland a few hundred metres off to the north of what had been their line of advance. He'd unfolded the butt stock of his gun and pushed the sights up to their maximum setting – four hundred metres – and the selector to semi-automatic: spotting the ambusher as he settled, squirming into a firing position, elbows in the snow, wishing to God he'd had a chance to zero this thing in. . . . He had him in his sights, squeezed off a single shot. About maximum range, he guessed. But like an echo then, another shot from out there somewhere – the south again

205

but not the same, farther away. A signal?

He muttered, 'Like fleas on a dog's back.' Slight exaggeration. But guessing they'd been heading to get between him and the highway, and this one had opened fire early because he'd seen he wasn't going to make it, and now his buddy was telling him, *Hang on, I'm on my way.* . . .

'*Sophie*.' Pointing north of east. 'Into that wood. It's a downslope, you should make it fast enough. River inside the wood – over it, pick a route to the highway through trees all the way. One and a half, two k's at most.'

'Go *now*?'

'That's my girl. While he's got his head down. If he puts it up and shoots at you, dodge. When you get there, stop anything that's going north. Don't wait in the road though, stay hidden until you hear one coming. OK?'

The slopes were empty now, his eye wandering over them constantly and the gun ready. That sod was most likely just over the rise, hull-down, waiting for his chum. Or he might be trying to filter round to the front: but if so, he'd have to come into sight again any moment now, over the fold in the snowfield that would be hiding him now. . . . '*Sophie, darling – go!*'

Flat, ready, watching for them to show, scared rigid that one or both might choose the next few seconds to poke his head up. If one did, you'd have to be damn sure you killed him because otherwise he'd see Sophie departing, and if he could get over the brow of that low hill eastward and fast enough he'd stand a chance of heading her off. One's own job meanwhile was to stay put and play Aunt Sally, hoping they'd think there were still two targets here. The hole she'd made when she'd flopped down might help, shadowed dark in moonlight. . . . But then, at the right moment, take off southwestward. There was a wood of sorts down there, surrounding the north end of yet another lake. Induce them to follow into that scrub while she was making it to the road?

A shot cracked over from his front. Same guy back on the job. Another from the left – forty-five degrees left. He saw the flash of that one, heard the *blip* of a small-calibre bullet passing close. So the range was OK: whether that was good news, or bad. . . . Man on the right getting up. Bending low, poling a few times, slanting down to the right — slaloming, zigzagging down, obviously to put himself between here and the road. Rapid fire from the left, short bursts in automatic, an attempt to pin one down here while the other shifted his ground. They obviously thought they had it made. The moving target was the one to hit, get *that* bastard. . . . She was away now, well out of sight and he didn't think they could have seen her go. In semi-auto now, single shot, sights still up at the four-hundred-metre setting, which had to be near enough right for this. The target was slaloming to make himself hard to get: so catch him on a turn, in one of the moments when he'd effectively be static. Like—

Now. . . .

Crack!

Arse over tit, sprawling, skis arcing like a windmill's sails. No time for cheers, though. Ollie twisted to his left, shifted into automatic, knowing he'd have only half a dozen shots left in the magazine, the first of which had been used to kill Isak. These magazines being twenty-round, not the more usual thirty. Enough, he found, for two very short bursts, aimed a little high, discouragement more than much hope of hitting, knowing the guy was there but not at this moment having him in sight.

Then he was up and moving — flat out, southwestward. . . .

She'll be OK. She'll make it now.

Not that it was a hundred per cent guaranteed yet — with one of them still alive. Could be others too. Also traffic on the road might be sparse, this time of night, not every driver prepared to stop for a lone skier thumbing. . . . A new idea hit him and he didn't hesitate, slanted to his left immediately — because although he had two spare twenty-round clips for this Swedish firearm it wasn't such a lot considering (a) he hadn't finished here yet, (b) he'd be some time in Finland after this, maybe with heavy opposition. And the man he'd felled had a gun, some kind of automatic weapon, possibly even *this* kind — logically you might expect them to be similarly equipped. He was on the level now and running: then uphill, driving himself up the hard-crusted slope to reach the sprawled body higher up. His mate would be up and coming on now, of course. . . . Skis thumping into the crust, body lunging, arms and legs working like pistons, lungs pumping, breath loud in his own ears like it could be sometimes under water. She'd be at least halfway to the road by now. Halfway or better. *Good luck, God's speed, my darling*. . . . A crackle of shots from behind – remote, his own man-made noise enclosing him, moonlight stronger as he came up into it again, finding the body, skis and poles widely scattered, snow churned deeply. He'd had his knife ready but the man was dead, face-down in snow dark with seepage from a head wound. Dragging him over on his side. . . . It *was* another MKS, with its strap around the Russian's neck tight enough to strangle. He used the knife – quicker than finding zips or other fastenings – slashing the coat open to get at inner pockets, finding among other items three full magazines. By their weight they felt full, anyway. He loaded one immediately, discarding the empty, then re-slung his own weapon, sheathing the knife and snatching up the dead man's gun, dropping flat in the snow with the body as a rest and slight protection, facing back to discourage the other one again.

Better still, to kill him. The fewer left on their feet, the better. But for the moment—

There. . . .

He was following Ollie's tracks, maybe at this moment still just outside effective range. . . . Glancing right, he muttered aloud, *Oh, shit*. . . . Another of them – higher up, black against moonlit snowscape, traversing down this way. More or less this way – actually moving left to right. . . . He switched to semi-auto for single shots – however many there'd be in this magazine. Working at getting his breathing into control, meanwhile. Should be a few rounds left, although it was hard to remember how many had been fired at him at the start of this action. Raising himself a little, elbows cushioned on a dead man's ribs: then steady squeezing, rhythmic firing of single aimed shots: four – five – six – *click*. . . . The target had dropped out of sight. Either hit — by fluke, at that range — or taken cover. He flung that gun away, lobbing it spinning end-over-end to fall into deep snow, and shifted around, crouching while he got his skis lined up, his gun slung on his back, poles in hand — pushing off southwestward with a downslope but poling too, doubled in the hope they wouldn't see him leaving. He wanted them to follow, but not too soon — better if they weren't certain he'd gone until they found his tracks, so he'd have time to prepare for them. As long as they trailed *him*, not Sophie. . . . Thinking of her, that she should certainly be at the roadside by now, he heard the truck, some heavy vehicle grinding up from the south. By the sound of it, the highway couldn't be more than a kilometre away, closer than he'd imagined. Even less than a kilometre, maybe. This was the first motor he'd heard: one solitary northbound lifesaver — *please*. . . . Then, like an instant, miraculous answer to that plea, he heard it braking, slowing. . . .

She could hardly believe her luck. At the same time, she hated it: having no option but to take advantage of it, leave. . . . Hydraulic brakes dragging the big truck to a stop, its enormous multiple tyres gouging inches deep into the hard-beaten dirt-stained snow that layered the road. She'd removed her skis at the roadside, left them there and retreated into the trees' shadow, climbing over the single strand of a flimsy deer-fence to get there. Then she'd barely had time to whisper a prayer — not for herself, not for *this* — when she'd heard the distant rumble. . . . Over the wire again, running out into the road: she saw the lights as a blur at first, then rising and clarifying as the heavy vehicle ground up the incline, coloured pinpricks of light above its cab and lower down the headlights blazing yellow, funnelling along the khaki-coloured, snow-ridged surface of Route 93. She was waving but simultaneously backing out of the road, not really expecting this first one to stop, and in any case preoccupied with other thoughts.

209

It was what he'd told her might happen, and prepared her for. More or less. She hadn't imagined it being quite like this, though. There'd been some flurries of rifle shots and automatic fire, but since then nothing – only her own hard puffing breath and pounding heart.

The driver wound down the window on the left side of the cab and poked his head out into the cold: 'OK, chum, hop in, quick!' He'd spoken in Norwegian, but he was a Finn. Sophie called, hurrying, 'Justing getting my skis. . . .'

He'd know she was a woman now, not a 'chum'. He leant over, opened the other door, grabbed the skis one-handed and she climbed in carrying her poles, There was room for the skis at the back of the seat, crosswise. She pulled the door shut, and he wound up the window: it felt like getting into a Turkish bath.

'Late out, aren't you?'

Typical young Finnish male. Thickset, with fair hair showing under a fur-lined cap on his bullet head. Frank, open expression, friendly smile. She nodded. 'Ski-trekking. Thanks for stopping.'

'Going to Kautokeino?' He was getting the truck moving. She confirmed. 'Kautokeino – yes. . . . I'd be grateful if you'd drop me near the *Lensmanskontor*.' It meant literally 'sheriff's office', but effectively 'police station'. 'Do you know where it is?'

'Must be where the flagpole is.' He nodded. 'Before the Esso station, but on the right.'

'*Right.*'

'Are you in some kind of trouble?'

'Not now.' She forced a smile. 'Thanks to you.'

'Not so good for a young lady to be out alone.' He glanced at her again. 'Lonely out here, and there've been some funny rumours going around lately, eh?'

She said, 'I love the *vidda*, and I am a good skier.'

Please God, let him come out of it all right.

'Want some coffee?'

'*Coffee?*'

She'd more or less gasped the word. It had such huge appeal.

210

As if one had forgotten that such a thing existed. . . . And the contrast – to be sitting here in warm comfort, having left him back there. . . .

His shots or theirs, those last ones?

As far as this end of it was concerned, he'd won, he'd triumphed, she was – quoting his own words – 'home and dry'. The word *would* now be passed out, disaster averted. *He*'d achieved this, and in the process he'd saved her life. *So please, God. . . .*

'Right there. Thermos on the ledge there. Use the cap, I have my own mug here. In fact you might pour me some, while you're at it.'

'Sure.' She took the mug from him. Hearing Ollie's voice assuring her *On my own it'll be easy, I'll be like a fox. . . .*

'Hungry?' Pointing again: 'You'll find some sandwiches in that box. I've had all I can eat, my wife always makes too many and then they go stale. Do me a favour, help yourself.'

Rumbling northward, at a steady seventy kph. The last shots would be the ones that counted. *How long before you'd know who'd fired them?* Coffee indescribably marvellous: incredible. . . . Headlights boring a tunnel, yellowish glow through watered milk. The driver was telling her they'd had a lot of snow down where he came from, days and days of it. Quite a sharp change tonight, wasn't it, this moon, the clouds breaking up so quickly? With luck tomorrow would be a fine day. Cold, but fine. The weather made a lot of difference, in his line of work. You took it as it came, naturally, and if you had your head screwed on right you always expected the worst, but all the same, a sunny day now and then. . . .

'Hey, hey. . . .'

Braking.

Sophie's eyes opened: her thoughts had been back there with Ollie. There was someone in the road ahead, right in the middle with his arms spread, signalling to the driver to stop. Not moving, confident he *would* stop. Bulky in heavy gear: no Sami, though, not throwing *that* length of shadow. The Finn muttered as his tyres gripped and the truck ground and slithered to a halt, 'He'll have come up by the *vinterveg*. Here's

211

where it joins, see.' The winter road – she could see the line of it southeastward. The driver said, 'Never mind, there's room for one more, can't leave a man to freeze.' The door on Sophie's side was wrenched open, and the man in the roadway stared up at her. Big man, stubbled face, dark eyes aslant over prominent cheekbones, cap with fur-lined earflaps dangling. . . . The driver called, 'Climb in, don't let all my warm air out!'

Ignoring that request: still holding the door, staring up at her. He asked the driver in heavily-accented Norwegian, 'Where did you pick her up?'

'Not far back. Why? Are you—?'

'She tell you what she's doing here?'

Not a Finn. No kind of Scandinavian either. The gun in his hand, as she saw it now for the first time, didn't surprise her, only sickened her. Her own stupidity. . . . Something like this had occurred to her when she'd opened her eyes and seen him standing there, and she'd dismissed it as a product of her overwrought imagination, paranoia. She knew now she should have urged the driver *Don't stop, put your foot down*. . . .

11

Motionless, among the litter below the tree and part of the tree itself, mixed in the pine's straggly bottom branches. Needles and sticks broke up the whiteness, ice-particles clung to the dead lower parts of the tree and he was an element in this confusion, prone, facing back to and across his own ski-tracks, thirty yards clear of them. Waiting – waiting happily because he'd heard some heavy vehicle stop and a door slam before it had ground on northward, noisily shifting gear. It had left him with a feeling of victory and *great* happiness – Sophie safe and away, the news on its way to Grayling. Like having played poker all night, trebled your stake and locked most of it away, playing on now with nothing to do but win.

Still a few hands to play, of course. This one now, and then the Yanks to be extricated. By that time things would be humming elsewhere. Hot lines busy, deployments on the Northern Flank no longer prefixed 'for exercise'.

So thank God for great mercies. Although it might take a little while, the high-level stuff. Oslo, Brussels, Washington, London, Helsinki would all have their hands in it. Her message had to be received, understood at the point of receipt, flashed to the summits who'd then presumably confer – electronically

213

no doubt but also man to man, voice to voice – before wheels could begin to turn.

Hours? *Days?*

The Soviet strategic concept for the launch of conventional war in Europe was said to be based on the primary essential of reaching the Channel in five days, the basis for this being an estimate of five days as the time it would take for NATO to react with a nuclear response, the one type of reaction which the Soviets dreaded. In this case – touch wood – you wouldn't be reaching for a nuclear response, so surely decisions would be reached far more quickly: say *one* day – having Norwegian forces immediately available as well as 3 Commando Brigade already deployed?

Movement two hundred metres along the trail. . . .

It was a downhill section, down to the lake, and the man was stemming, skis wide, thrusting outward in a pumping action and with his head up to watch the trail as far ahead as he could see it. He was in and out of sight as trees and undergrowth intervened, appearing and vanishing like intermittent frames in an old black-and-white movie or those little books you flicked through for the effect of movement. The other one might be off to the side, moving parallel to the line of the path. He might be following behind the one who was in sight – it would be nice if he was just following – but they might be playing it more craftily. It was an important thing to know. One might assume that Spetsnazi would possess all the skills, but they might also be careless if they hadn't guessed they were hunting a quarry who was at least as skilful as themselves. They might be under the impression that they were running down some tourist or anthropologist. OK, he'd demonstrated an ability to shoot straight, but that wouldn't necessarily have told them much. . . . Watching through the frieze of litter and pine foliage – brown, not green, dried-out and frosted although it still smelt strongly of resin when you had your nose in it – watching the skier as he came on with his legs pumping as a brake – hundred and fifty metres now, near enough – one was hoping he'd provide some clue as to his colleague's whereabouts.

214

Selector to semi-automatic. . . .

The other one might have picked up Sophie's tracks and followed her. Then it would be a while before he got to the highway and realised she'd got away. He'd return this way, presumably. Not necessarily, but—

He'd glanced back, raising one hand with the pole swinging from it.

Thanks. You can go on by.

Keeping very open order, as this pair were doing and as he and Sophie had done yesterday, did complicate matters for an ambusher. Since there were only two of them and he'd picked an ideal location he could handle it – he hoped – but it was less straightforward than it would have been if they'd been in close company. He wasn't sure yet which of them he'd hit first; he'd decide when the moment came, when he saw it – the principle being to hit and stop (maybe kill but anyway stop) the more distant target with a single, aimed shot, then rapidly shift target and blast the nearer one in automatic. Because obviously you could only hit one at a time, and the farthest away had the best chance of escape if you either missed or allowed him some warning. Then he'd be on the loose, and you'd have problems.

Face-down in snow and pine rubbish, listening to the first one passing, the scrape of skis in crusted snow and the bounce of trailing poles. Now head up slowly, by centimetres rather than by inches, to see the next one coming into sight on what was now a broad, smoothed-out path. The gun's sights were set on two hundred metres. Extended butt-stock snuggled into his shoulder. This character was stemming too, maintaining his distance astern of number one. You'd get in this single shot – catching him in one of his appearances between trees – and the other would then be – well, much closer anyway, having only just gone by. So the problem had resolved itself, and the time for action was—

Trees in the way. *Next* appearance. Holding a breath. . . .

Now.

He saw the man hit, crumpling as he veered sharply off the track. Ollie span round with the *crack* of the shot loud in his right ear: but the front-runner was hidden, a clump of firs in the line of sight. A second and a half later he was back in view – falling, stopping himself by falling down, about the smartest way he could have reacted. Ollie gave him the rest of the magazine's contents with the gun's snout depressed to aim at ground level which was where the target was by that time, but the Russian got off a burst of his own as he fell – *hitting* – impact like whiplash and a *knock* effect, muscular reaction left side and in that arm: he was changing the magazine as he ran, knowing he'd been hit by one or more rounds, sprinting to the track and diving into it with a clear view along it and the gun jabbering in his hands. The Russian had been crouching: now he swayed over, falling sideways and dropping his gun. He had one ski on, one off. With his free hand he'd been working frantically to unclip the bindings, but the odds had been against him although he'd started well with that fast reaction and the accurate snap-shot at a target which he could only have seen in about the same instant he'd opened fire. Once he'd rid himself of the skis he'd have been fighting on equal terms – or better, having already scored – but Ollie had grasped this as well as he had himself, killed him while he was still anchored to one of them.

Pain burnt in his forearm and side. Extending the arm to the position it had been in when he'd been hit he guessed at one bullet having creased its way up the inside of the forearm and then sliced into or through his side at waist level. He could feel the sticky warmth of blood, and reckoned he'd been lucky; but also that he'd muffed it, should have timed his first shot so that when he shifted target the other *would* have been in sight. But then, if he'd hung on for a better chance he might have made even more of a mess of it. . . . Anyway – priorities now had to be (1) check these two, that they were dead, (2) check for any others in the vicinity, (3) inspect the damage to oneself and apply field dressings, (4) get skis on and the hell out.

And be joyful, meanwhile, for Sophie having got clear away. That was what *really* mattered.

So – on foot, first, back through the trees, parallel to the track but clear of it, stopping in the edge of the forest to look for signs of enemies. The moon was on its way down, he guessed there'd be a few hours of darkness before dawn. Then maybe a *real* dawn for a change, a visible sunrise into a clear sky. Meanwhile the moonlight was hazy, casting long shadows, contrasts of black and white, depressions in the snow like bruises, ski-tracks shaded in grey pencil. They were where he'd have expected them, converging with his own near the point of entry to the wood, and the three sets were all he could see. There might have been others, a third man could have been left out there while two of them drew the covert, but on as much evidence as was visible he thought it was safe to assume the whole team had been accounted for.

He was aware that he was taking a lot for granted. Such as the fact that his own ski-tracks would emerge in due course from this wood, and the two Russians' tracks would not. And that there was a third lying dead out in the open, and a fourth – who'd died from a slashed throat – on a Finnish mountainside. He'd been lucky: but there was no surprise in it and certainly no self-congratulation, only recognition of the fact that not for the first time he'd had the luck on his side.

But everyone had *some* luck: not everyone made use of it. Training came into it – and field experience, and fast reaction. For instance, the second Russian had had his own stroke of luck when he'd scored a hit with that snapped-off burst while still in mid-air: but if one had been in that position oneself one wouldn't have thrown it away by allowing oneself to be caught in the open five seconds later. One would have been in cover and ready to shoot again, skis or no skis.

On present showing, in fact, the opposition hadn't done very well. Although you'd have expected them to be the best the Soviets had. He'd have to take care, he told himself, not to be lulled into *expecting* second-rate performances: others might well be more professional, or less over-confident.

Heading back through the trees, winding up this post-mortem on recent action, he recognised that in getting Sophie away he'd been *very* lucky. Unquestionable, genuine luck – to have been allowed that small space of time while the man had had his head down for some reason – signalling to his buddy,

217

or filling a magazine, whatever. More than just luck, it had been a gift, and more crucial than anything that had happened in the wood. OK, you could argue that she'd have been in the clear now anyway because he'd wiped them out, he'd have been escorting her to the highway to thumb a lift; but this was only on the assumption that if she'd been with him it would have turned out the same. You couldn't assume it; as he'd explained to her, there were big advantages in operating solo.

Now the bodies. Whether to pull them off the trail, hide them. . . .

The only point in doing so would be to deceive the enemy, if there were more in the area, let them know as little as possible about what had happened here. The less they knew, the less efficiently they could handle themselves. In particular they shouldn't be allowed to know their quarry had got away, leaving tracks they could follow.

Their weapons were Israeli Galil 5.56-mm SARs – short assault rifles – with folding stocks and 35-round magazines. No point in switching; he was used to the MKS now. But the shells were the right calibre, and lengthwise they fitted the Swedish magazines, so he filled a pocket with loose rounds. He also took a frozen half-apple from an outer pocket – of the second man – whose white-fleshed face with embryo red beard was reminiscent of a Van Gogh self-portrait. A scent of apple hung around him; he must have only recently been eating the other half. Ollie muttered, 'Thanks, Tovarisch . . .'. He had no way of knowing that he was addressing the mortal remains of Sergeant Aleksandr Borisovich Gerasimov of HQ Company, 23rd Spetsnaz Regiment.

Better leave them in the open, he decided, and leave all the tracks to tell their story. After Sophie had made her report in Kautokeino, Norwegian police or army would surely come down here to see what had been going on, and they might as well find evidence to support her story. There was no reason to believe other Soviets were around. These three had been arriving from the south: only just arriving, and not quite in time to put a stopper on the highway route. Some luck in that timing, too – if his guess was right.

His own wounds now. He stripped down to his thermal undervest to get at them, under layers of other bullet-torn, bloodstained clothing. There was a long groove up the left forearm, and a shorter, deeper gash in his left side where the bullet had torn through flesh and muscle under the lowest rib. More luck — that it hadn't been aimed as much as one inch either side, smashing the arm or doing *real* damage. Also that the cheese-faced marksman had been using the Galil and 5.56-mm shells and not the dumdum-effect 5.45-mm ammo they fired from their AKS-74s. He washed the wounds in antiseptic, taped impregnated dressings over them and put his clothes back on again. Holes and rips, undesirable from the point of view of insulation, could be mended later with the repair kit he'd left with other gear in the snow-hole.

Which was now his destination.

The door of the truck stood open, the heavily-built man in the road keeping a hand on it while he stared up, studying her intently.

The Finnish driver would still have stopped for him, she thought, even if she *had* screamed at him to keep going. He was that kind of person — a *Suomi* Samaritan. . . . She heard him stammer an answer to the question which had been aimed, she realised, at establishing her identity. . . . 'No. Well — yes, ski-trekking. Wanted a lift to the *Lensmanskontor* in Kautokeino. . . . Why, what—'

He'd told the stranger exactly what he'd wanted to know, of course. A humourless smile opened a crack among the black stubble. Breath plumed like smoke in the iced air as he growled, 'Tell you what. You're going to turn this thing round. Up the road, place called Oksal, there's room to turn. Then you'll take us all south, OK?'

'South to where?'

'What's it called. Ai'jav'ri, something like. Then you can go

219

where the fuck you like. Deal? Or do I pull you out and do it myself?'

The driver's expression was turning mulish. He glanced at Sophie, then at the open door, which the big man wasn't actually holding now. He muttered out of the side of his mouth to her, 'Shut it. . . .' He couldn't have understood what he was up against, to have thought he had any chance of getting away with it. The man saw his hand moving towards the gears, and he brought his gun up. It was close in front of Sophie's face and she had no doubt he was about to shoot the driver in the head. Throwing herself against his arm – the Russian was half up into the cab – she was deafened by the shot close to her ear, then in agony as his other hand clamped viciously on the back of her neck and dragged her out. Painful impacts here and there: the worst of them was a near-paralysing blow on the hip as his knee helped her on the way. She hit the road semi-stunned and with a photographic impression of the driver slumped forward, left hand clasping his right shoulder. A second or two ago, she realised, she must have seen that. Her ski-poles were still in the cab, she was dazed and ready to vomit but getting up, launching herself back at the open door with the intention of snatching one of the poles for a weapon. She wasn't thinking, at this stage, wasn't working things out, she was simply reacting, fighting for her life and for the driver's. The Russian saw her coming, hardly bothered to turn – just enough to aim a kick at her, savagely and contemptuously, putting her out of his way for a moment, swinging back for a second shot at the Finn. After which he'd kill her. Attending to the Finn first in case he got the truck moving. She'd been knocked down again by that kick, felt pain like fire in her hip and elsewhere, and that thought – that he'd surely kill her now – just as the pistol fired, point-blank at the driver's head – woke her to some degree of rational thinking, to Ollie's *vital thing is one of us gets there*. . . . She scrambled half up, running – over the snow-covered verge, to get to the trees beyond the reindeer fence. As she got to the fence she remembered – she had a gun in an inside pocket, the automatic Ollie had taken from the man he'd killed with a knife. She was fumbling for it as she stooped to duck under the wire and the Russian fired at her. She saw the flash out of the side of her eye, heard the explosion and fell sprawling, under the wire – guessing he'd only missed with that shot because she'd happened to duck just at that same moment, guessing also that trying to get away now – to get up and run – would be suicidal. Lying in the snow, groping inside her smock, getting fingers to the zip of her anorak and wrenching it down; remembering how Ollie had killed that man, the one who'd shot Isak. The difference was that it was herself *this* killer was coming to finish off, not some third party. The third party would be already dead, in the truck's cab. Her hand closed on the gun's butt, and she was remembering something else from Ollie, what he'd taught her about it. It was Swiss, a SIG or some such name, and it had no external safety-catch but an internal automatic one which meant that the pistol was safe all the time, you could drop it and it wouldn't go off, but you had no catch to bother with and you didn't even have to cock it, you could simply pull it out and fire it. She'd got it out, had it in her gloved hand, was forcing it through the snow under her breasts from right to left, the right side of her face numb in the snow and eyes three-quarters closed, trying to look dead while she watched him coming over with his own pistol ready in his hand – coming to see whether he'd killed her or if she needed another bullet. Like that other one put into Isak. He was on the verge now, ankle-deep in the crust and about three metres away from her, looming huge against the red glow of the truck's tail lights. She was scared of shooting too soon and missing but even more of waiting one second too long and letting him do his shooting first. Forcing herself to keep her eyes slightly open as she squeezed the trigger – very light double-action trigger mechanism, Ollie had told her – her head jarred from the crash – and again as he staggered, his gun coming up, at her. . . . She'd rolled sideways, fired twice more, aiming these shots properly with the gun in her right hand, right hand supported in the left, the way she'd been taught although she'd told them it was pointless, she'd never use a gun, never intended carrying one. The Russian lurched

221

forward, down on his knees as she fired a fourth bullet into him: she held the gun on him, ready to shoot again, watching as he collapsed forward on to his face.

Knowing where the herds were now, he made all possible use of their trampled grazing grounds. On some stretches, especially up to and near the *vinterveg*, there were snowscooter and ski tracks as well. The moon set at about eight, and in the two hours between then and sunrise he travelled by compass, checking progress by the rivers he crossed and other remembered topographical features. He was skiing straight into the rising sun when the loom of it began to show above the *fjells*; and then in daylight he took pains to be either on ground cut up by the deer, or on Sami herdsmen's tracks, or – when possible – in woodland.

Sunrise was brilliant, in shades of rose that flushed the snowscape pink as well. He'd have liked to have had Sophie here to enjoy it with him, Sophie with her love of these barren, wide-open spaces. But cloud gathered during the forenoon and long before dusk the overhang of cloud was total.

He passed wide of the mountain hut where they'd sheltered. Others might well find the *fjellstue* attractive. He'd been foolhardy, he thought now, to have used it, put *her* to such risk. Crazy – to have taken her to the one focal point for trekkers that existed in that enormous area of *fjell* and forest.

The apple had to de-freeze slowly in his mouth before he could force his teeth into it. He ate biscuits and chocolate frequently, and drank tea. Thinking about Sophie, and imagining her in Kautokeino. Or elsewhere: they'd send a helicopter to pick her up from the Kautokeino airstrip, he guessed. But he could hear her on the telephone to Grayling, after she'd reported first to her own bosses: and Grayling baffled, not knowing whether or not to accept this strange female's story. In any case it *would* take time, before you could hope to see action on the ground, and meanwhile Sutherland

and Stenberg were on their own and extremely vulnerable: even if the Spetsnazi *were* second-rate, by British special-force standards.

The westward transit had taken him and Sophie about twenty-four hours, including five in the *fjellstue*. Considering the journey had involved as much uphill work as level trekking, and precious little downhill running, that had been very good going. But now with only himself to look after, and cutting out any night stop, he was hoping to do it in about eighteen hours or less. Eating and drinking on the move, stopping only for reconnaissance purposes when there was a good perspective from high ground. It was more probable, he thought, that Spetsnazi might be waiting ahead than that they'd be trailing him, on this trip.

He was in the valley at the bottom of the wooded hillside below the snow-hole within a few minutes of midnight on Day 2 – having started from the snow-hole with Sophie just after 0400 on Day 1. So the trip had taken less than two days in all, instead of the three in which he'd told the Americans he'd *hoped* to make it. But this return trip hadn't been as fast as he'd hoped: and it had taken just about all his strength. He still had the climb, too, up the steep, thickly-treed hillside, and it would take at least an hour, maybe more. They'd slid and ploughed down in it in about twenty minutes, he remembered.

He found the same line of tracks – deep and hard-crusted now. If Spetsnazi had searched here, they couldn't have helped finding this steep trail. His heart was thumping hard, and he hadn't even begun to climb. He told himself, *Forget it. They'll be there. You're a day ahead of schedule. . . .*

Climbing. Skis on his back. No glimmer of moon tonight. The snow was hard-crusted where their floundering descent had broken through it, crunching under his Lundhags boots, but in the drifts when he blundered into them – sightless, seeing only the blur of white and black uprights and diagonals – it was waist-deep. He was exhausted – he could admit it to himself because this was journey's end at last – and also scared. For the Yanks, what he might find, as he climbed higher and closer to the moment of truth. Remembering Gus

223

Stenberg's flat statement of *I'm a desk man*, and the sharp disappointment he'd felt when he'd heard it. After the near-miss of the avalanche, when Gus had produced a hand-gun and taken charge of Isak in a quick, business-like manner, he'd had hopes of him, relief in the thought that he was about to get some help. Then that admission. And Gus's humility – as if it could have been *his* fault they'd unchained him from a desk and sent him on this mission without any preparation. None of it was anyone's fault: no-one had known they were going to war.

He stopped climbing, rested with his back against a tree. He hadn't made the transit any faster on his own than he had with Sophie, but obviously having done it non-stop must have taken its effect. Also it had been the return journey, more than eighteen hours' yomping on top of the first nineteen, and without much sustenance. . . . Leaning back, in pitch black-ness and a wind like razor-blades cutting through the bare trees, he could have let himself fall asleep. He felt the desire to sleep, temptation to shut his eyes, allow the brain to fold in on itself and nurture the start of a dream that was partly delib-erate, wishful thinking – Gus Stenberg crouched at the snow-hole entrance behind that bullet-stopping wall: 'That you, Ollie? Back this soon?'

He'd begun to slide down the tree, he realised. Could have ended sitting at its foot, freezing into co-identity with the iced environment, only to de-freeze with spring's white torrents rushing. . . . Catching himself again in the act of slumping, mind wandering: he pushed himself off the trunk, forced himself to resume the climb. It was heavy going now, seemed a lot steeper going up than it had been coming down. Telling himself, *About halfway now. They'll be there, you'll see. . . .*

It would be best to get Sutherland out by night, he thought. It wasn't going to be easy, with just himself and Gus to handle the ski-stretcher. You'd need the help of darkness, when you were hampered like that. Unless there was more snow to come, of course – heavy snowfall would be ideal, much better than night travel. . . . Cramming raisins and broken biscuit into his mouth, he decided that the first thing he'd go for, inside the snow-hole, would be a mug of strong, fresh tea. And then hot food. There'd be some beans left, at least, and they couldn't have eaten *all* the reindeer meat yet. Tea – food – sleep. . . .

Carl's leg. The doctors would very likely have to separate the tendons, if they'd begun to mend in the wrong places, and re-set it properly. Presumably you could do that to tendons, same way they'd break a bone that hadn't set as it was supposed to. Or Carl might be lucky, it could have joined up correctly just by chance. He'd weathered the shock of it extraordinarily well, better than one might have expected. . . . Climbing, panting into the frozen darkness, re-hearing Carl's muttered, *I have to convince myself this is me here.* . . .

He whispered aloud, 'With you in two shakes, gents.'

The trees thinned here, ended not far to his left. So this was the top at last, he was close to the snow-hole. Where he'd started down with Sophie close behind, one of her hands on his shoulder as they'd begun wading down through the snow which at that time had been soft and fresh with none of this crust on it.

A branch snapped.

He'd stopped. Stopped breathing too. Straining tired ears and eyes. Allowing himself a spurt of optimism in the guess – or hope – *Stenberg, outside the hole for a look-round or a pee.* . . .

The wall they'd built could only be a yard or two ahead. The whiteness that looked like a patch of open snow-slope might be it. He was still motionless, watching and listening: seeing in his imagination – that dry rustle – snow falling from an overburdened branch that had broken, somewhere to his right. It might have been no more than that.

Moving on, very slowly, cautiously. Wondering if it could have been his own weight snapping a fallen branch buried in the snow underfoot, and aware that the uncertainty was a symptom of his condition of exhaustion, loss of judgement. He'd reached the wall, though, a mound of hard-crusted snow hip-high and retaining the curve, the way he'd shaped it to protect the entrance to the snow-hole. He pulled the headover clear of his mouth, called softly, 'Carl? Gus?'

Not expecting an answer. Because they'd be inside. But just

225

in case – Stenberg could be outside, with the shotgun and tight nerves. He called more loudly, 'Gus?'

Ice-crystals rattled down through bare branches. He was creeping to the right, to get round the end of the low barrier. Then he was on snow as hard as rock, beaten hard and icy between the wall and the entrance. He crouched, taking his skis off his back – to leave them here, come and fetch them and take them inside after he'd contacted the others. Then inching forward and feeling left-handed for the opening, gun unslung and in his right hand, just in case. . . .

'Gus? Carl?'

He'd called their names with his head actually inside the entrance. There was no glimmer of candlelight from inside: there should have been a reflection of it in the tunnel's walls. Its absence revived earlier fear. He slung the MKS back on his shoulder, fumbled in his coat for the pencil flashlight. Then starting forward, crawling on his elbows, needing to be well inside the dip of the tunnel before he switched the torch on. Pausing, taking care that he had it pointing in the right direction. The small beam created a dazzling cone of reflected light between the curved, ice-gleaming sides and roof – a weird effect, blinding after the solid blackness. Then as his eyes adjusted to it – hearing the harsh intake of his own breath, seeing – ahead of him, instead of a vertically oblong opening into the chamber, some dark blockage. Hardly needing to focus on it to know what it would be. A body across the opening. He knew the worst, the truth carrying nightmarish impact all the more savage for its being compounded of truths he'd recognised and chosen to accept as risks. No real surprise in any of it: only a sensation of nausea – part exhaustion as well as part horror. . . . Worming in through the dip and closer to Gus Stenberg's body. The visible part was the torso, shoulders and face, and there was a bullet wound in the centre of the forehead, a black crust of blood around it and one frozen solidified trickle vertically downward. The body was on its side, facing this way, and across the entrance so as to hide whatever was behind it.

Up close, he saw the string.

They'd fixed it so that it passed under the body and up across the chest to the top of the left arm, where it had been knotted. Brown string, dark enough not to be noticeable – would have been invisible, without the flashlight beam directly on it – against the American's waterproof coat. It was string he'd bought in Karasjok. If he'd pushed his way in, hadn't seen this, his entry would have turned the body over on to its back and jerked the string taut. It wasn't difficult to guess what the other end was tied to. He edged to his left, cramming up against the side of the tunnel, up as close to the body as he could get without any danger of moving it, and shone the torch through the space above.

The shotgun was on the snow-platform that had been Carl Sutherland's bed, and Carl's body was lumped across it, holding it in position. Carl's face and head were mostly gone, blown into pulp probably by that same gun at close range. Ollie, peering over Stenberg's body, was looking directly into the AYA's twin barrels, and the string from Gus's body led round a ski-pole dug into the far end of the platform, and back to the triggers, noosed round both of them. Tug that string, you'd get a double load of number four shot in the face.

What you might call a Spetsnaz welcome mat.

He was glad he'd had the flashlight with him.

It was as well to have something to be glad about, too. Having left them here in order to get Sophie out. He'd had to choose, he'd chosen: now, he was looking at the outcome of that choice.

But – not only to get her out. Primarily, it had been to get the message out. And there was something else to be glad for – that you hadn't left her here too, made a dash for it on your own. It had been an option that he'd considered, at some point.

Breath short, heart pounding: forcing himself to think and act logically, controlling emotion and ignoring physical weakness. Sighting over Gus's body with the beam probing around the chamber, making sure there was no back-up to the booby-trap. He needed to get inside, in the hope they'd left the food and his gear; and there could be another string, another stage. . . . He didn't think there was but he wasn't in a state to trust his own judgement, made himself check it again, double-check. . . . And it was OK. If you could call such a scene 'OK' in any sense. . . . The gun end of it was the place to look, and the string they'd led around the gleaming ski-pole was the only one, with no others leading to it. No other strings anywhere in sight either – leading to other weapons, grenades, whatever.

He used his knife to cut the string, sheathed the knife, reached over the hard-frozen body to jerk the loose end of string from under it and toss it clear. The shotgun still menaced him as he pushed through into the chamber. Sutherland would have had this view of it – the twin black circles like empty eye-sockets – in his last moments. . . . Out of the line of fire at last he didn't bother to unload it, only pushed back the safety-catch, then used it to lever the deep-frozen corpse up from the snow-bed to which it had become rooted, so he could then pull the gun away from under it and put it down beside the body on the platform. Its barrels pointed towards the tunnel again and he could grab it quickly if he had to. He thought they most likely *would* be back. Having set a trap, you'd surely want to see whether or not you'd caught anything. He found a candle end and lit it, pocketing the torch. An idea was forming, in connection with the likelihood of Spetsnazi returning to this hole. Enough of an idea to persuade him to leave the bodies as they were; until this moment his intention had been to behave conventionally, arranging them in more dignified positions.

But first – gear, and stores. It looked as if it was all there, untouched. Either the Spetsnazi had all the supplies they needed or they'd been pressed for time. Probably the latter. Having found these two here, they'd have been in a hurry to find two more: or to report the situation, or – whatever. . . . They'd have set the gun-trap in the belief that one or both of those others might be coming back – not an illogical conclusion, since the two Americans had been just sitting here, obviously waiting for *something*, and one of them immobilised.

He re-packed his bergen with the items with which he'd lightened it for the westward yomp with Sophie, and with most of the rations – meat, cans of beans, chocolate. . . . The bivvy-bag he'd let Sophie use; also the pulk's tarpaulin cover, the naptha stove and one fuel flask. One shovel. . . .

Going *where*?

The answer was obvious – north, into Norway, the way he'd have gone if he'd had these two with him. There was nothing he could do now, down here in Finland – except vanish, as rapidly as he could make it. . . . He began to take some of the rations *out* of the bergen, realising he couldn't possibly need so much. Two, three days trekking, and only himself to feed. The thought of another journey and the need to get started soon reminded him of his state of weakness and depletion, consequent lack of concentration. Accompanying this, renewal of the longing for a hot drink, food and rest.

Take a chance – set up the stove again, make a quick brew and *then* move out?

It wasn't a chance you *could* take – he thought. . . . He wasn't sure, wasn't confident he had all the factors entirely straight in his mind, but he felt he ought *not* to chance it. For instance – well, anyone outside there would smell a fire, or cooking, at least a mile away. . . .

The shotgun had moved.

It had swung round, turning its barrels away from the mouth of the tunnel. He'd caught the movement in the periphery of his vision as he stooped over the bergen, delving to extract some of the heavier items. Light had gleamed on the dull metal of the barrels as they turned, swivelling until the stock met Sutherland's body and stopped the movement. A first reaction – after one frozen spasm of fright – was to dismiss it as hallucination deriving from the fact he'd come so close to his limits.

Then: 'Christ . . .'

Grabbing for the gun. But the creature in the tunnel spoke sharply – in Finnish, Lappish? – tilting up the barrel of his rifle, lining the sights on Ollie's eyes. He'd used that rifle-barrel a moment ago to poke the AYA so it wouldn't point at him. He rasped the same thing again – comment, instruction, whatever it had been – in the same snarling tone. . . . Russian?

Not Russian, surely. Candlelight glittered in blue slits of

eyes set in brown, deeply-lined skin, skin like parchment. Grey straggly beard – sparse bristles, more than beard – and bared, yellowish teeth. Fifty or sixty years old maybe. You could see the tension in him – readiness to shoot, to kill. . . . The rifle was an Armalite AR-7, the civilian version of the old AR-5. A gimmicky weapon, as one remembered it, with the unusual property of being buoyant. He wondered if he was dreaming, if this was nightmare, in which case he might wake up to find Sutherland and Stenberg alive, grinning at him, asking him *what* in hell he'd been dreaming. . . . Crouching under the low, vaulted roof of hard-packed snow, hands out from his sides as he faced whatever this was: the rifle-barrel was lower now, pointing roughly at his heart, the old guy tight-nerved, almost quivering, ready to kill and as secure in the tunnel as a rat in its hole.

'*Amerikaner?*'

He knew enough Norwegian to shake his head and answer, '*Brite.*'

'Hunh!'

Whether that had been an expression of surprise, pleasure or disgust was hard to tell. His glance flickered over Stenberg's body, the severed length of string, the AYA. A hiss of breath accompanying some kind of thought process. . . . Then the blue eyes had fastened on his own again: '*Sprechen Deutsch?*'

He nodded. Surprised at the question but not sure enough of his own judgement to know whether or not surprise was warranted. Lowering himself slowly into a squatting position: this was more or less a reflex, an instinctive move to reduce the tension, the chances of that old rifle being used. '*Ja.* I speak some German. I'm British and my name is Lyle. Are you a Finn?'

'Finn.' The sparse beard jerked sideways as he spat. 'Sami, Suomi. Both. I'm called Juffu. . . . These were Amerikaners?'

He nodded. 'I was sent here to look after them.'

'Protect them from the Ruoša-Tsuders?'

'From anyone. From you, maybe.'

'What d'you mean?'

'I don't know what *you* mean. I never heard of a Ruoša-

230

Tsuder. But they didn't know they had enemies here at all. That one was a professor, he was studying Samiland and the Sami people – history, culture, and so on.'

'Helped by that shit Isak?'

'Isak was supposed to guide us. He tried to have us killed.'

He felt dizzy, thought he might pass out if this went on much longer. On top of tiredness, thirst, cold and hunger was a growing sense of unreality. It was the second stage, he remembered, in the list of six symptoms of exposure in the order of progressive deterioration. *Feeling of weakness, muscle incoordination, slow stumbling pace, mild confusion. . . .* Next would come *stumbling and falling, slow thought and speech*. Or maybe that was the stage he'd reached already. He'd considered himself fit, for God's sake! Because he always had been fit, he supposed he'd taken it for granted. But there'd been months in the medics' hands, then the period of living it up in Brighton with – whatever her name was. . . .

Where did *loss of memory* appear in that list of symptoms?

Juffu had lowered the rifle. He was pulling himself out of the tunnel, into the chamber. Spare, stringy – when you allowed for some layers of protective clothing including the reindeer-hide outer garments. He said in fluent though accented German, 'Isak loves the Ruošas. Or he likes the promises they make him. To make him king, maybe. There never was a Sami king, you can forget those old fables. . . . What will you do now they've killed your Amerikaners?'

'Go north, back into Norway, after I've rested.'

'They kill your companions, you only walk away?'

'What else can I do?'

'They murdered my nephew. A young boy. Martti. He was a soldier. I taught him his lessons, all of it. To shoot, trap, track, live in the forests. They've killed him, so I'm the end of it now. My own half-uncle was Turi, Johan Olafsson Turi, who with my other distinguished ancestor – his name also was Juffu – was the hero of the stupidity in Kautokeino.' He turned to spit again. Then: 'They will come back here soon. At least one of them will come.'

Ollie stared back at the hypnotic blue glare. Having to think

231

hard to distinguish history from immediacy. He nodded. 'I was thinking I'd leave a trap for them.'

A glance down at the AYA. . . . 'With that?'

'Yes. A way I think they'd fall for it.'

'I know all there is to know of traps. If you want my advice on it.'

He explained his idea. Juffu watched his face all the time, frowning as if in faint disapproval, but then agreed: 'You're right. It's good.' The frown deepened. 'But it won't count for Martti. This will be yours, for one of the Americans.'

'All right.'

No point in telling him he'd already killed four of the Spetsnazi. In fact he'd given it some thought, during the long eastward trek, and he'd decided it might be sensible never to mention it to anyone. If it came out eventually, all right, it would come out, but—

'Martti gave me this.' Juffu was gazing down at the Armalite, stroking it like comforting a cat. 'He had one of this kind, and I admired it, since my own rifle was very old, the barrel worn. . . . A month passed and he visited me again, bringing this as a gift. His *vanrikki* was with him—'

'*Vanrikki*?'

'*Leutnant* . . . They were asking questions I couldn't answer. I knew nothing of this business then, I'd been resting. I pan gold in summer months you see.' His chin jerked southward. 'On the Lemmenjoki, I have a cabin there. . . . But they let me keep this rifle, despite my inability to help them. Then the Ruošas killed him – and the *vanrikki* also, and another by name Santavuori – slaughtered them like butchering reindeer!'

'So that was your nephew. I'm sorry.'

'Set your trap. I'll wait out there. If you hear a whistle – put out the light, come quickly.'

He began pulling himself backwards down the tunnel. Ollie stopped him, passed him the bergen: 'Take this with you?' It vanished slowly, towed out behind the old Lapp. Ollie, alone again in the snow cavern, death chamber, hollow with shock, and surprised as well as ashamed at having come so close to the end of his tether. A year ago he'd have been ready to make that trek again – *now*, and back again.

232

And these two had been in his charge, his care.

Booby-trap now. Concentrate. . . .

Or you'll blow your fucking head off.

The ball of string, first. He tied its end securely to the ski-pole, down at snow-level. The pole was firmly planted, they'd driven it deeply into the snow-platform and it had subsequently frozen in there solidly. OK. . . . Now the bodies. They both had parts to play in this. He didn't think either of them would have objected to such use being made of them, in the circumstances and in view of the manner of their deaths.

Move Carl first. Gus had to stay here inside the chamber in more or less his original position. So get Carl out first.

He dragged him out through the tunnel. Juffu was out there, close by the hole: he didn't move or make a sound, but he could smell him. Ollie left Carl's rigid body outside, went back in and rolled the ball of string out down the slope into the tunnel's dip. Then he brought out the AYA — loaded but on 'safe' — left it lying on top of Carl and went in again to blow out the candle, snuffing its wick between gloved forefinger and thumb. The smell of wax would be enough to alert a visitor to danger, but it wouldn't last long. Feet-first into the tunnel, then, reaching into the chamber to pull Gus back into his station across the entrance, at the same time clearing the string so that it wasn't trapped under him but lay across his torso.

Now the tricky bit. Not manoeuvring Carl back into the tunnel: that was easy, since the body was as stiff as a log and could be pushed to slide as easily as a pulk — but wriggling in beside it, into a space designed to accommodate one man's width of shoulders but not two. And also to have your arms free, to do the work. Carl's boots outward, right out in the entrance, the shattered remnants of his head inward, his rather short arms stretched — it was a wrenching effort, achieving this — as if reaching to the body in the chamber, the position he'd adopt if he was trying to shift the obstruction. Achieving even this much was a major effort, and it might have been claustrophobic to anyone susceptible to such phobia — which fortunately one was not, could not have served in the SB Squadron if one had been. . . . But the shotgun now. It had to go inside the leg of the trousers, the splinted leg, and be lashed

233

with string to the leg itself. He cut off lengths of string for this, also cut a hole in the material, a slit up on the back of the thigh, to facilitate the operation and then to pass the end of the string in and tie it to the triggers, a loop which he tightened around both triggers inside the guard. The safety-catch was on, so it was all right to take up the slack on the string – by inching Carl's body backwards, against the pull of it on the ski-pole inside – without danger of firing the gun. But once you'd taken the safety *off*, any further backward pull on the body would discharge both barrels into the puller's face.

He removed one glove again, reached in through the hole in the trouser leg, found the safety-catch and slid it forward. Now the trap was live and extremely sensitive. He put the glove on again and backed out, worming out backwards very, very cautiously so as not to risk setting the body sliding back. It wouldn't take much of a pull. Some Soviet coming to check the trap *he*'d set would find a body in it, apparently blasted in the act of crawling in. He'd want to pull him out – take a look at him and check whatever might be in his pockets, maybe reset the trap. The only way he could attempt it would be by grabbing hold of the boots – raising the legs would incidentally also raise the gun, pointing the barrels directly at himself – and pull. . . .

The viscous liquid burnt its way down, heat radiating outward through gut, flesh, bone and muscle, maybe even reaching into the numbed recesses of the brain. The drink was something Juffu had cooked up: strange, unpleasant taste but miraculous effect. The fire was a glow of red in a central core of smoke that rose to hang thickly under the roofing of timber. They were on a flooring of timber too, a foot-deep mat of branches with reindeer hides on top of it. Breathing smoke, absorbing warmth, while meat and beans de-froze and cooked on a fire fuelled largely with dried reindeer dung smouldering like peat.

From the snow-hole, Juffu had led him down on the same

track by which he'd climbed up to it, about an hour earlier he guessed. The track he and Sophie had made. Then off it eastward, through trees growing so thickly you had sometimes to force a way between them, ducking under branches. In normal conditions you'd be using a machete to clear a way through. Then after a few hundred metres they'd been climbing – climbing for ever, it had begun to feel. Mind wandering, mostly to Sophie in an attempt to anchor himself to consciousness and sanity – as if *she* was the guide. . . . A long, long climb, up through the wood and out of it, over the high bare shoulder of the mountain in a rising wind and a wetness in the freezing air that could have been a threat of snow. This bunker-like refuge was high, on the southern slope of a ridge linking twin peaks. It was one of a chain of pits which Juffu said his ancestors had dug two thousand years ago, reindeer traps. In those days Lapps hadn't farmed the deer, there'd been no need to because there'd been vast herds all over Lappland; they'd hunted them and lived from them very much as the American Indians had lived from their teeming buffalo herds, and one way of trapping them had been to drive them into places like this one. They'd lined the sides of the pits with stones so that the animals who fell in had no chance of finding hoofholds and climbing out again; and this particular antiquity of a hole in the ground was one Juffu had selected as one of his homes-away-from-home. He had others elsewhere, he said, although usually he lived above ground, only liked to have refuges that he could use in the very worst of the winter storms. And sometimes so that he could disappear. There were so many regulations now – what a man could hunt and what he could *not* hunt, when, where, how – and one such as Juffu had still to live, the only way he *could* live.

When they'd been still in the wood, ten minutes away from the snow-hole, Ollie had been hit by a thought that had stopped him dead. He'd called, 'I have to go back, Juffu!'

The old guy had halted. He was on skis, although Ollie had been carrying his on his back. Juffu's skis were very long and narrow, with points at both ends.

'For what?'

'Because I should've fired a shot for them to hear. Without it how can they believe the trap was sprung?'

Brain must have been bloody frozen. Nothing else for it – go back, unrig it, fire a shot, set the whole damn thing up again. . . .

'The sound would be muffled in that hole.' Juffu's tone was flat and scornful. 'Even from here you wouldn't hear it. And there are no Ruošas close to us now.'

'Can you be sure of that?'

He hadn't bothered to answer. Only started forward again, grunting, '*Kom . . .*' He was completely at home in this wilderness, part of it, as natural an inhabitant as wolf, bear, fox or wolverine. He'd understand them, too – by instinct, not by learning or calculation. And of course it was safe to light a fire up here – which was another thing Ollie had surprised his host by querying. The wind howled and boomed across these mountain heights, there'd be no taint of smoke or cooking at lower levels. No smoke visible outside either, even in daylight; it hung inside, permeating the thick roofing of branches and the snow overlay so gradually that it somehow became absorbed there. It choked and blinded you, but in the short term that was only a minor discomfort.

He'd asked him, 'Won't they find our tracks, trail us up here?'

'They'll see the track that leads to the snow-hole. That's why they'll be sure to go there and to fall into your trap. That's a deep track, a whole week of snow won't hide that one.'

'Are you saying there's snow coming?'

'In two hours. Or one. At most, three.'

So then all other recent tracks would be wiped out, and you could move reasonably safely. Back into Norway, where by now large-scale deployments should be in progress. Naval deployments and air as well as ground, he guessed.

And Sophie there. The foot of the rainbow. Incredible. . . .

'Juffu.'

The eyes opened: sparks of blue through cracks in the brown skin.

'Is Ruoša-Tsuder a word for Soviets?'

'Very old word.' He nodded. 'Russians from Karelia and thereabouts. My half-uncle Turi wrote of them in his book, how in olden times the Sami people were forced to live in the ground – like *this*, as we are now – because of the Ruoša-Tsuders. They were very cruel – all over Samiland raiding, burning, killing and stealing, bands of them like wolves. . . .'

'If you'd allow another question – how come you talk German so well?'

'I worked for them, in the war. Fighting, on their side. Many did. They made me a corporal.' He pointed eastward: 'Fighting the Neighbour has been a tradition, natural to us Suomi. Do you know that when this last war ended we'd been fighting the bastards for five centuries?' He didn't wait for an answer. Leaning forward to look into the stewpot he muttered, 'And now they're acting up again. God knows what they're at. I knew nothing of it when Martti and his *vanrikki* came. It seemed not to be my business – which is hunting, and the gold in summer. But – they killed him.' He was poking at the pot's contents with his sheathknife. 'It's ready, we can eat it now. . . .'

Waking – however many hours later it was, which he didn't know because his watch had stopped – he found the blue eyes fixed on him. So this character was real, he hadn't dreamt all that.

'Is it day now, or still night?'

'Dark. And snowing hard enough to fill tracks quickly.'

Collecting thoughts and memory, re-tasting the meal and also that peculiar drink – made, Juffu had told him while they'd been eating, from some herb which he called *juobmo*. It was cropped in summer and then cooked and mixed with reindeer milk – which was thick, heavy, full of rich protein, only about a cupful obtained at each milking. The mixture was left in a reindeer's stomach to dry, and to make a drink of it he'd added boiling water. Ollie felt sure it had done him good:

237

he felt as if he'd just woken from some long illness, still weak but on the mend. There was a sense of loss, too: visions of Carl Sutherland's pulped face, the black hole in Gus Stenberg's forehead. . . . Focusing on Juffu, he was peering through a haze of smoke that was nothing like as thick as it had been before; the fire still glowed and emitted warmth but it hadn't been built up or fanned as it had been earlier for the cooking.

The meat in the pot, which he'd expected to be venison, had turned out to be ptarmigan. Juffu had explained that in hard winter conditions ptarmigan moved down into the fir forests and stayed there until spring, and were easy to trap at this time. The meat had been gamey enough to suggest that this particular bird might have been trapped last winter, but he'd been hungry enough to enjoy it.

It was good news that the snow had come, as predicted. But maybe it would be good for the Spetsnazi too.

'You mentioned one Russian in particular, some big guy you're after?'

'A man I know has seen him. Nobody is speaking of these matters, they're frightened, but to me this one did. Because I'm who I am. . . . They call me the old wolf – and you know what is said about the wolf?'

'No, I don't—'

'That he has one man's strength and nine men's cunning?'

'I don't think I ever did hear that.'

'Well, it's true.'

'What did your friend tell you about this Russian?'

'He's their leader, gives them their orders. So he'd have given the order to kill Martti.'

'And – you're looking for him. . . . D'you have any idea where to find him?'

'Where to go—' a nod '—where he may be or may come soon – yes.'

'You were watching the snow-hole, though.'

'He was there, before.'

'Did he kill the Americans?'

'Martti was first. I have first claim.'

'All right. What is this place?'

'I was told by the same person. A store — a secret, hidden place.' The eyes shifted, blue lasers on Ollie's. 'Explosives. And—' Glancing down again, as he moved the pot on the fire. It was half-full of water, melted snow he must have collected while Ollie had been asleep. He added, 'Fuel, ammunition, is what one might suppose.' Ollie reached into his bergen for tea, powdered milk and sugar, and biscuits. Tea would be the thing now — strong and very sweet. What the old Lapp had just told him matched a conclusion he'd arrived at on his own before this, a guess that they might well have some kind of forward base, near the border, where they could refuel and stock up with ammunition and other essentials. It had stemmed from his thoughts about bridging equipment; but that material would be stashed near the major river crossing points, and as it would only be needed for an advance later in the spring he'd also guessed that such dumps might not have been set up yet.

'How far is it from here, Juffu?'

Not close, presumably. Or Isak would hardly have been ordered to lead the American party into this area. Except that as the intention had been to kill them, this mightn't have bothered Isak's bosses much.

Juffu told him, 'A day and a night. Or two days. . . . But also, lately there have been tracked vehicles coming and leaving by night, hiding in the forests by day. From the same person again I was told this.'

Nodding: eyes glittering, fixed on Ollie's. Solitude, more than madness — Ollie hoped — would make a man odd in his mannerisms and speech, no doubt. . . . He wondered how far an elderly but wiry Lapp would travel, presumably on skis, in a day and a night or two days. Maybe between sixty and a hundred kilometres? Tracked vehicles, though. . . . Sophie would have told them — told her people, and Grayling — that the assault was scheduled for end March, early April, the end of the NATO exercise; he'd said nothing to her of his own doubts on that point, because he'd had nothing solid on which to base them. But would they stock a forward ammo dump in foreign territory eight weeks before they were going to need it?

The water was boiling. He dropped teabags into it. Wind-howl overhead where snow was falling meant blizzard, white-out on these high, exposed slopes. Ptarmigan gave warning of blizzards, Juffu had mentioned during their meal. When they laughed raucously in the depths of the forest, you could expect the worst. But – assessing one's own options and motives now. . . . Awareness of failure, loss, smarted worse than the soreness in his arm and side: the Americans were *dead*, it had happened, was permanent, irrevocable. . . . Also, with his mind somewhat clearer now he recognised that his impulse to go north over the border into Norway was roughly ninety-five per cent urge to rejoin Sophie and the rest an interest in personal survival – and the second quotient might spring at least partly from the first. Whereas he was now face to face with a new concept – a job still outstanding here in Finland, and a sense of deepening personal involvement. Compulsion, even. Stirring the tea, he muttered, 'I think I won't go north. Might tag along with you, d'you mind?'

12

Sophie said, '*One* spoon of sugar, please.' The pink light of dawn showed through an uncurtained window behind the general's desk.

She was at Reitan, near Bodø, at the headquarters of COMNON, Commander North Norway. In this comfortable, well furnished office cum reception room the degree of comfort was far from matching her state of mind, although from her appearance at least she was a lot more composed now than she'd been twenty-four hours earlier when she'd brought a Finnish thirty-tonne truck thundering up Route 93 into Kautokeino, dragged it into a swaying, tyre-screeching swerve on to the side road that ran down past the *Lensmanskontor*. Even at that pre-dawn hour the Norwegian flag had looked calm and dignified on its pole outside, loftily untouched by any threat to the values it symbolised while she'd hammered on the police-station door, 'raving' – police description, later – 'like a crazy woman. . . '. Having no idea whether Ollie might by that time have been alive or dead or dying in the snow, but having a dead Finn with her in the truck's cab and screaming at the astounded, half-awake *politi* that they'd find the body of the Finn's killer – a Russian, whom *she*'d shot – on the roadside somewhere between Oksal and Aiddejavrre.

They'd been inclined to lock her up, but they'd allowed her to call a government telephone number in Oslo, and remarkably quickly the Army had then sent a helicopter to pick her up from the military airfield just outside town. The police had taken her out there to meet it, and had insisted on getting an army signature for her, but in the interval she'd been brought up to date on recent events, including the brutal murder in Alta of a Sami by the name of Nils Aikko – who had previously been in police custody, assisting in their enquiries into the cause of the Tromsø air disaster – and the apparent suicide by hanging of a young Sami girl in Karasjok. The dead girl had been the niece of a well-known Sami author and exponent of *yoik*, a man known as Isak, who'd simultaneously vanished, was believed to have taken a party of American tourists into central Finnmark.

A colonel – he and the general were both Norwegians – told her now, 'The three individuals found shot dead within a few kilometres of the highway *were*, going by various indications as well as by what you've told us, Soviets and Spetsnazi. Their weapons were Israeli Galil assault rifles, and they'd all been killed by bullets of the same calibre. A fourth Galil has been found behind the stove in the *Statens fjellstue* near Aiddejavrre, along with other equipment including a short-wave radio. Probably stashed there by the man who shot the truck driver and tried to kill *you*. But as to the other three – what might have happened down there – well. . . .' He shrugged. Then glanced at her enquiringly, as if hoping for some explanation from her, for that litter of foreign bodies. She'd been told earlier, in fact, about the three dead Soviets, and her relief had been tremendous; none of the descriptions had come anywhere near a picture of Ollie, and the three dead men's skis had been of East German manufacture, whereas Ollie's Royal Marine skis were Norwegian-made. But none of it was any guarantee that Ollie was alive now, or would be tomorrow. Another aspect of it that kept her from making any comment was that when no war situation existed, killing was homicide even in self-defence. She'd given them a detailed report of

242

everything that had happened, but the only death she'd mentioned had been that of Isak.

'One must assume that Captain Lyle fought his way out of a Spetsnaz ambush.' The general was studying his cigarette as he spoke. 'And will now be in the process of rescuing the Americans. He does seem well able to look after himself.' He looked at Sophie now, half smiling. 'Your concern is entirely understandable, Miss Eriksen, but – well, by and large I believe you could afford to relax now, wait for him to surface with his Yanks in tow.'

'He's one man alone, General. With those two to look after, and one of them can't walk. . . .' Heaven knows how many Spetsnazi there may be – but they tried to kill us, they *did* murder Isak. . . . If you won't ask the Finns for help, couldn't you send in a small rescue party, a group of good skiers – including a doctor perhaps – maybe by helicopter?'

'Miss Eriksen—'

'*I* could guide them. I'd be only too happy, to—'

'Would you listen to me for a moment, please?'

She waited, looking at him. He was a nice man, he was reasonably sympathetic, very likely a fine soldier too, but that had damn-all to do with it. Most sympathetic of them all, genuinely sharing her concern for Ollie, was Major Grayling, the Royal Marine officer who was the only foreigner on this staff, at this moment leaning sideways to put down his empty coffee-cup.

The general went on, 'I would say there's no doubt that Captain Lyle has taken precisely the best options that were open to him. In doing so he has also demonstrated a remarkable ability to evade and outwit these infiltrators, and with your own *very* considerable assistance he has succeeded in alerting us to this threat while at the same time doing as much as could have been done to safeguard the Americans. Personally I have every confidence that we'll hear from him, and them, in the next day or two. I should add that by now our patrols will be all over the border regions – keeping low profile for the time being, but they've been told to keep a sharp lookout for that party and to render any necessary assistance –

243

short, that is, of crossing the border. Eh?'

The colonel gave him a nod of confirmation, and he went on, 'But your suggestion that we alert our Finnish neighbours – at this juncture, Miss Eriksen, I'm sorry, but it's not possible. In the context of decisions taken at the very highest levels. This is for your ears only, now. To start with, the only way to face a threat of this nature – and from the Soviets of *all* people – is from a position of strength. And ignoring for a moment the NATO exercise deployments – which have barely got under way except for the British 3 Commando Brigade Royal Marines – although, as you would have expected, such other elements as are immediately available are being rushed to us – well, for example, look at our own two hundred kilometres of frontier with the USSR. It's a light fence, as I suppose you know, not fortified in any way on our side, and to guard it we have one rifle company of a hundred and fifty men, drawn from a garrison of five hundred men based a few miles away, the other side of Kirkenes. Whereas the Soviets face us across that fence with fifteen hundred MVD border troops backed by two motorised infantry divisions, one brigade of naval infantry, two Spetsnaz brigades, powerful air support and of course *enormous* naval power just along the road.' He cocked an eyebrow. 'See what I'm getting at?'

'Are you saying we can't defend ourselves?'

'Certainly not. We can, and will. I'm explaining that our dispositions are designed to maintain a state of peace – with a deliberate imbalance, taking the greatest care not to offer them the slightest provocation. So until we have deployed our own reserves as well as standing forces, and also much larger forces than we have available in Norway at this moment, we would not be so idiotic as to invite an immediate attack. Doesn't this make sense?'

'We pretend we don't know anything's happening, until we're ready for them.'

'Right.'

'But the Soviets are already in Finland. How can we *not* inform Helsinki?'

'Frankly, that's an equally sensitive situation. I'm speaking

244

in the most strict confidence again, Miss Eriksen. The point is that we can't be certain that such information, if passed to the Finnish government, might not – well, go forward into the wrong hands, thus bringing about exactly the situation we're determined to avoid. As soon as we're ready – *then*, of course—'

'I understand, but—'

'Deployments are in progress. Even from – well, far away. Movements not only of troops but of air and naval forces, at this stage all under cover of preparation for the forthcoming NATO exercise.'

'Does it have to take so long?'

The general glanced covertly at his watch. Grayling stared at the ceiling. The colonel said, 'Forty-eight hours isn't so long, particularly when care has to be taken not to attract attention to what's happening. But also, bear in mind that you yourself have told us we have almost eight weeks in hand?'

'Captain Lyle may not have eight *hours*!'

'Well.' Grayling stirred. 'While I'm totally in agreement that the sooner he's out of Finland the better, I'd support what the general said just now, that he's an extremely competent, expert operator, to the extent that I'd guess the Spetsnazi should be more worried than we are.' He smiled at her. 'But as I mentioned, sir – the Americans have expressed concern for the safety of the professor and his assistant. I told them – this was last night, Miss Eriksen, after we'd studied your report and also one from the Kautokeino police, and obviously Oslo had been in touch with Washington – I told them Lyle had gone back into Finland to bring them out, that they'd be in his extremely capable hands; and as they know, obviously, of the policy decision as outlined by the general – well, *they* seemed more than satisfied—'

'They may be.' Sophie's fists were clenched in her lap. 'They are a very long way away, they haven't any idea at all how it is down there, how it *was*, how it must be for him now. I am *not* satisfied, I want him *out*!'

'As we do.' The colonel nodded. 'Him and the Americans, and the sooner the better. But he'll *come* out, we don't have to fetch him – which is just as well, because we *can't*.' He glanced at the general, then back at her. 'I'm sorry, Miss Eriksen, but you really do have to *accept*. . . .'

She said to Grayling – in his office, after they'd left the general, who had yet to shave and have some breakfast – 'I could have been talking to the wall. Once you people have your minds made up.'

'I know how you must feel.' He offered her a cigarette, and she declined it. He went on, lighting his own, 'In fact I'm entirely with you. But I also see that the arguments they were giving you are extremely cogent, in all the circumstances. And I do feel very sure that Lyle's competence, already well demonstrated – for heaven's sake, those three Spetsnazi didn't kill *themselves*, did they – leaves little reason to doubt that he'll emerge with his Yanks very soon now.' He picked up a telephone.

'Yes. Absolutely. . . . Yes, all right, I'll be there in—' glancing at a clock '—say fifteen minutes? Fine.' He hung up. 'Sorry. But it's all your doing, this, *you* started it all, didn't you? Actually, thanks to the fact that everything is now in hand and rolling faster every minute, this is by far the quietest it's been since your call came in and electrified us all, about this time yesterday. As you'd already been on to your department in Oslo, we had them, London, Washington *and* Brussels all yelling at us at one and the same time. Confucius he say, 'Instant satellite communication mean total bloody chaos'. . . . But the show's on the road now, things may *seem* to be moving in slow motion but you really would be surprised.'

'I believe you, Major. But I'm concerned only for one person.'

'Quite.' He nodded. 'Am I right in thinking it's – very personal?'

'Even if it were not—'

He'd snatched up another ringing 'phone. 'Grayling here.'

Listening, making a note. . . . 'Right. Got it. Thank you.'

He hung up. Feeling his unshaven jaw, and turning his mind back to *her* problem. When MoD had dumped this Lyle thing on him he hadn't thought of it as anything important. Now it had blown up into major earth tremors and, potentially, if it wasn't handled very, very skilfully, could become the start of World War 3. And Lyle in person was still so to speak *his* baby. He began – feeling his way, sympathetic but wanting her off his back now because there was a lot going on in which he was involved – including the possibly imminent arrival of 4 MAB, Marine Amphibious Brigade, six thousand US Marines under a two-star general and with all their own transport and artillery – 'I can really only advise you as the general did – to be patient, *try* not to worry, trust in his turning up very shortly, complete with Yanks. There really isn't anything we can do *except* wait. NATO simply can*not* go barging into neutral Finland, you see. . . . Actually I'd like to persuade you to go and have a good rest, you've been through the hell of an ordeal and it's hardly surprising you're maybe a little overwrought. Frankly, you ought to be tucked up in a warm bed!'

She thought – almost said aloud – *Yes. With Ollie.* . . .

The shotgun blast was a thudding punctuation in the wind's howl. But it was recognisable. He was in the fringes of the wood, with the snow-hole thirty metres away: and seeing a man appear reeling, staggering and then falling sideways on to the low wall, struggling along it and sidling bear-like around its end, into the open. Arms clasped across his belly. . . . Ollie crouching in the straggle of birch, releasing the skis' bindings; then, as he straightened, pushing the selector-switch of the MKS to semi-automatic. This would be a mercy killing: having devised the trap that had done *that*. The Russian was bent double, forearms clamped over his lower abdomen in an attempt to hold himself together or simply clasping pain, blood literally flooding down. His face turned upward, staring up and forward like a blind cripple begging – for release, for the impossible – his mouth a black hole, no sound audible except the wind's. Ollie sighted, point of aim the forehead: he was on target and about to squeeze the trigger when he heard what he realised later was the metallic *thwack* of a steel crossbow firing, and the head in his gun's sights shattered as if something inside it had exploded. The Russian toppled – his weight had been well forward – his arms opening, limp, as he collapsed on his face and the mess of his own stomach.

Ollie lay flat in the snow, facing downslope, searching through trees and blizzard, knowing the crossbow artist couldn't have seen *him* either, certainly hadn't before he'd fired that shot. . . . Mind on the search, but also wondering where Juffu might be – he was out there somewhere, having gone ahead, an old fox sniffing out its territory, snuffling for any intruder's scent. *Probably passed wide of the snow-hole: leaving it for me.* . . .

A shot cracked over. He heard the shot itself – from his right? – and had guessed there might be a suppressor on that weapon, before the bullet whipped past his head with an unmistakable 'down-range' crack which again suggested reduced muzzle velocity, reinforcing the suppressor theory. Crossbow first, then a silenced rifle, and the shootist had him in sight, obviously, which made for a situation that wasn't tolerable, so *move*. . . . Sprinting – baboon-type lope, the only kind soft snow allowed – for the cover of his own custom-built wall. Built for others, not for himself, but they wouldn't be needing it now. Dodging, before he got there and dived in behind it, and a burst of automatic fire raking the trees, then raising snow-fountains along the top of the mound. Shifting into automatic and crabbing rapidly to the wall's far end. Russian blood all over, orange-looking in this light. From the end he'd work his way out close to the ground, try to get some sight of wherever this threat might be. Over Carl's legs: smell of scorching as he passed.

A gun – MKS, like this one – was propped against the inside of the wall. The Russian would have put it down in order to have his hands free to grab hold of Carl's boots and haul him out. . . . He had his own gun ready: hoping to be lucky, catch the Spetsnaz shifting *his* position. . . . Edging out from the wall – flat, *in* the snow, but a blare of automatic fire came so instantly that the Russian must have *known* this was where he'd show himself, might have been sighting on this spot and ready for him to show; but also he'd have to be up on his feet, even up on a branch, to have enough height of eye to get a view of him from downslope. Wherever he was, *this* was no second-rater.

Back in partial cover of the wall he was straining for a glimpse of him through the blinding effect of blizzard when there was one quite different-sounding single shot – from the right, up in those trees. An *entirely* different sound, and he guessed *Juffu*. . . . Well timed, at that, with luck an end to the frustrating business of being shot at without knowing where to shoot back. Part of his own slowness could have been psychological, the image still vivid of that shambling creature virtually gutted. You could think of yourself as case-hardened, but there were limits. He was in the open again, clear of the wall, half up to search for his enemy, hoping he might be preoccupied with Juffu but not taking anything for granted, having respect for this Spetsnaz man's fast reactions and marksmanship. Snow driving horizontally from left to right, all white and grey with the blackness of the trees behind, daylight growing but nothing like grown yet. . . .

There.

Movement, a flitting from one tree to another. Ollie knelt with his left shoulder against the end of the wall; back in semiauto, sighting on an apparent swelling of the lower part of one birch trunk. He fired, fired again at a blur of very swift movement, and heard the Armalite bark again from his right. And the target was suddenly in full view. For a half second. . . . He'd shifted to automatic and squeezed off a short burst but the Russian had gone – into trees, bark splinters flying where he'd vanished. Ollie had squeezed off a longer burst, the end of it wasted except for the hope of a fluke shot, the target already out of sight: he must have crashed out into the open snowfield and would have gone straight down, no doubt.

Or stopped, in trees a short distance down, hoping to be followed?

Juffu had fired twice, was reloading on the move, ski-skating away through the wood in long, swaying lunges. Following the Russian out into the open – for Christ's sake.... Ollie yelled at him: the sound was lost in the welter of wind and snow. Changing his magazine.... Then he floundered to his skis, twenty or so metres away, passing close to the whitening body. Guessing that the big man – who might be the guy Juffu had talked about, which could partly account for Juffu's extreme rashness – had decided odds of two to one were unacceptable and therefore ducked out of it: and Juffu was now offering him a grand slam.... Ollie forced his bindings shut and pushed off across the slope, twisting between trees with the storm's force at his back. The edge of this wood was as far as he was intending to go: if the old fool had chased, gone on down – well, Christ....

He'd picked a pro, too, who might *well* be the one he'd talked about, Spetsnaz leader, thus a red rag to the bull. Still, a very unwise bull: a wolf lacking *one* man's cunning, let alone nine.... Skidding to a stop, outside the trees, to have some kind of view, but close to them. Visibility about five, six metres. He saw two sets of tracks. One would be the Russian's, the other where Juffu had stem-turned in the soft surface snow to point his skis straight down the hill, narrow twin tracks converging where he'd brought his planks together to race down parallel to that other set. Visibility faded into whiteout where hillside and blizzard merged.

Nothing you could do. Except throw another life away.

Confirmation came immediately: from down the hill, a short burst of automatic fire, half a dozen rounds in one heart-stopping ripple of destruction; and no doubt at all *whose* heart would have stopped. Only the wind's noise then. In his mind Ollie had an image of that brown, tough-skinned face, eyes like blue sparks in narrow slits, and snow patching his furs as it might an old wolf's pelt.

Thinly against the wind, a single shot. Head-shot at close range, and *goodbye, Juffu*. Only this morning, drinking tea

250

and chewing reindeer meat, waiting for daylight and the old guy rambling on with stories about trapping and hunting; he'd mentioned that a bear would nearly always double back and lie in wait beside its own tracks if it came to realise that it was being followed. Apparently it hadn't occurred to him that a Ruoša-Tsuder might have a brain as good as a bear's.

He headed back through the trees. Finding it difficult to accept that what had just happened *had* happened. But there was nothing to be done about it — except to get on with it now, alone. He'd been alone before, he was on his own again now, and thanks to Juffu he *knew* something, had an objective. The big Russian wouldn't climb back up here, he guessed. He'd wait in cover near Juffu's body for a while, in the faint hope that where you'd found one idiot you might get another. But not for long. . . . He *might* come back up. You couldn't take much for granted, not knowing his priorities or how his mind worked. He must have come here to check the trap — *their* trap — and obviously he'd have a strong interest in eliminating survivors of the Sutherland expedition. But now instinct suggested he'd have other fish to fry, that he'd be weighing those priorities. He'd have been unwilling to get pinned down here because of such other commitments. Maybe it felt like this not only because of the way he'd pulled out of the action, but also Juffu's story of tracked vehicles coming and going from the dump. Suggesting that action might well be imminent.

What might the Finns be doing meanwhile? Turning blind eyes?

People — Sami people — were scared to talk, Juffu had said. None of them knowing who was behind it, which fellow Samis might be involved. And if you opposed the movement and it won, you might wish you hadn't. On that sort of basis and in this vast emptiness the Spetsnazi would only have to bribe or frighten a few herdsmen into either cooperation or silence and non-interference, he guessed.

At dawn, less than an hour ago, he and Juffu had climbed out of the reindeer pit, returning here not only to see whether the trap had claimed a victim — it hadn't until about the moment of his arrival, and this wasn't necessarily all that much of a coincidence if the Spetsnazi had also been waiting for daylight – but also, if he'd found the trap still set, to disarm it. He'd had visions of some innocent Lapp herdsman passing by, seeing a tourist with his head and shoulders in a snow-hole, trying to pull him out. . . . Juffu had argued no, it's a good trap, leave it, if the Ruoša-Tsuders didn't come today they'd come tomorrow, and no herdsman would be endangered meanwhile because where the only growth was birch there'd be no reindeer moss, therefore no grazing herds.

But there might have been some individual passing. This was a wilderness but life did exist in it and pass through it. Even tourists, ski-trekkers, and even in the depths of winter although it seemed there were none *this* winter.

Proof of the trap's effectiveness was now snow-covered except on its lee side. Humped, with the snow building up on it, and the orange stains fading under that deepening white shroud. There was no need to touch it. No doubt there'd be a couple of spare MKS magazines in the pockets, but he had enough. He'd take one off the gun, and refill his spares with the loose rounds salvaged from that other firefight. He'd bring the gun itself along too, also the AYA and its boxes of cartridges from the snow-hole, as far as Juffu's pit. Might strip the Swedish gun and take along some of its parts for spares.

He cut the string from the shotgun's triggers, and the strings binding it to Carl's hard-frozen leg, pulled it out of the scorched trouser leg and ejected the two empty cases. Safe as houses for the time being, he thought; the one who'd killed Juffu couldn't get back up here in less than forty minutes – minimum – even if he had any intention of returning. Which seemed unlikely. But in any case he didn't want to hang around here longer than necessary, only long enough to attend to a few essentials. Like hauling Carl back in through the tunnel, then getting him and Gus back up on to their platforms. Working as fast as he could, actually, panting with the effort – knowing that guy *could* be back up here and maybe sooner than one thought. He was conscious of being alone again: having got used to that strange creature's company.

He took three cans of beans which for some reason he'd left

behind yesterday. The taste of baked beans reminded him now of Sophie.

Forget her. She's for later. Right now, mind on the job. . . .

First, back to the reindeer pit. For some more hot tea – the last for quite a while, maybe – and food. Repack the bergen and refill magazines. Study the maps, work out – from as much as one could remember of Juffu's talk this morning – where to start looking for his 'secret place'. Weather conditions weren't ideal for ski-trekking, except for the advantage of tracks not lasting long. The crossbow expert knew he still had one enemy on the loose.

Lieutenant-Colonel Jimmy Boyers, the Commando CO, jumped down from the Gazelle helicopter that was his personal transport and hurried towards his *hutte*, a timber bungalow containing both living quarters and office space. He'd been at a meeting at Bardufoss; his brigadier had been there, and senior Norwegians, the CO of the other Commando – they'd moved up from the south now, were in tents at Evenes – and representatives of a US Marine brigade and of the ACE Mobile Force – ACE standing for Allied Command Europe and the brigade including Canadians, Italian Alpinis and the British 1 Para. Those units were on immediate standby, ready to be flown in on call, but intelligence advice now was that actual deployment might not be necessary, that there was reason to believe the Soviets would abort their invasion plan when confronted. Against this background it had been decided that if the new deployments could be avoided, 'provocation' would be minimised and risks of escalation thus considerably reduced. So meanwhile the weight was to be taken by 3 Commando Brigade RM, with the Dutch marines attached to them, and the Norwegians themselves, and for this Commando it meant one of two alternative redeployments on which a decision was to be signalled very shortly.

Tam Ellworthy, HQ Company Commander, was waiting in

253

the entrance to the *hutte*, in company with several others including Jack Hillyard, Boyers' second-in-command. Ellworthy, whom the others were permitting to have first go at him, wanted to talk about Ollie Lyle, for God's sake.... Boyers was aware of Lyle's recent activities, but couldn't see how it was any part of his business, especially at this of all times. ... 'I know, by all accounts he's done a fantastic job. But what we have to concern ourselves with here and now—'

He stopped, mouth still open, in the doorway of his own sitting-room, astonished to find a girl here, a civilian. Rather striking-looking too, his second glance told him; and he guessed who she might be, but he didn't want this, didn't have time for whatever involvement or potential involvement was about to be insinuated on him, or attempted.

The girl had with her a Norwegian officer he'd met a few times before, one of the liaison team. Boyers nodded to him: and the check to what he'd been saying was only temporary. He continued, turning back to Ellworthy, 'Immediate concern is *this*.' Handing him a file of paperwork, but his glance took in the second-in-command as well. 'Much as we expected, but it still could be one or t'other.' He turned to the girl. 'This is a pleasant surprise, but—'

'Excuse me.' The Norwegian told Sophie, 'I should introduce Colonel Boyers.' He ushered her forward. 'Miss Eriksen, sir. This is the lady who was with Captain Lyle in Finland. She brought out the information on which – well, all this which is happening now—'

'Yes, indeed.' Boyers clasped her hand. She was looking at a man in his early forties, an easy, friendly smile temporarily camouflaging urgency, impatience.... 'If I may say so, Miss Eriksen, you don't look anything like an Arctic warrior. But most sincere congratulations on your remarkable achievements.'

He hadn't been given all that much detail – there wasn't time for gossip – but he knew that in company with Lyle she'd made an impressively fast yomp out of Finland and not only survived an attempt on her life but personally killed the Spetsnaz thug who'd attacked her. She said, getting her hand back from him, 'Thank you, but – well . . .'

She'd glanced at Ellworthy. He put in quickly, 'She's very deeply concerned for Lyle, sir. They were being hunted by Spetsnazi when she came out, they were on his tail when she left him – on *his* insistence, so one of them would get out to us – and he was going back in there to try to evacuate some Americans.'

'So I heard.'

'She reckons he could be badly up against it. One Yank lame, and—'

'Please sit down, Miss Eriksen.'

The fast way to get rid of this was to take it head-on, have done with it. Boyers waved the Norwegian towards another seat. . . . Sophie seeing clearly that he didn't have time for her, that he was about to listen to whatever she had to say, then murmur a few reassurances and push her out, quick. She jumped in, therefore, with a ploy aimed at short-circuiting that kind of brush-off routine. . . . 'Ollie told me that the Royal Marines always look after their own people. Is that so?'

'Well.' A glance, notable for its lack of expression, at his 2 i/c. Both of them thinking it was most unlikely that Lyle would have said anything of the sort. It was the sort of thing you saw trotted out in crap about the Foreign Legion. On the other hand it wouldn't be easy to answer *No, we don't give a shit*. It wouldn't be true, either, but either way she'd have you.

He told her, 'We're in a somewhat special situation at this moment, as I'm sure you realise. After all, *you* sparked it all off. And we owe you a lot, Miss Eriksen, don't imagine I'm not aware of it. But any minute now we'll be moving out, and – well, this Commando consists of forty officers and seven hundred NCOs and Marines, and every one of them has at least as much as he can cope with at this moment. Much as I wish I *could* help—'

'You cannot, and – and that's all there is to it. It's also too bad for Ollie.'

He frowned.

'Why me, Miss Eriksen?' He looked at the liaison officer. 'Why this Commando?'

The Norwegian gestured rather helplessly, glancing at her, and she said, 'You were Ollie's company commander when he was a young lieutenant, he told me. He said Captain Ellworthy was also an old friend. We had many hours for talking, in our snow-hole which I helped him dig. He said if I needed help, I should – well. . . .' She'd sighed, spreading her hands, the gesture indicating *So much for old friends*. . . . She added, 'Didn't he visit with you here when he arrived in Norway?'

Ollie hadn't mentioned either of these characters. The Norwegian liaison officer had given her all that stuff. He'd known it all because a fortnight ago Ellworthy, begging a lift for Ollie Lyle in Norwegian Army transport from here up to Alta, had stressed how much of a favour the liaison officer could do for himself and for Lieutenant-Colonel Boyers.

Boyers was now pointing out to Sophie that for serving NATO personnel to cross into Finland would be out of the question. Even if there'd been a single man to spare – which there was not. If there'd been any way he could have helped, he'd have bust a gut to do so: but unfortunately, in the circumstances. . . .

'All right.' She accepted defeat. 'I know all you say is true. I'm sorry to have wasted so much of your time. I'll – go and try some place else, I—'

'For chaps to be sent into Finland?' He shook his head. He was on his feet, not wanting to detain her. 'It couldn't be done, you know. Really, it's inconceivable, particularly right now. But – he'll come out of it, I'm *sure* he will. . . .'

This was the bullshit coming, and she didn't want it, she'd had enough of it already from her own people. She held out her hand. 'Thank you for listening to me.'

Alone with his second-in-command, Boyers murmured, 'Lucky old Ollie Lyle.'

'Absolutely. If he *does* get out. It sounds like rather a sticky wicket down there, though, wouldn't you say?'

'And a bloody shame, there's damn-all we can do about it.' Boyers pointed at the chair Sophie had used. 'Sit, Jack, we have a few points to finalise and this is the best time for it.'

'There is one possibility. If you'd consider it.'

Boyers glanced at him, frowning: interrupting a fresh line of thought, surprised to find they were still discussing Lyle's predicament.

256

'Well?'

'The Special Boat demo team, Mike Brabant's lot. Their job's finished, they've been dumped here and we were supposed to deliver them to Evenes to fly home on tomorrow's Charlie one-three-zero.' Tomorrow's RAF Hercules to Lyneham, Wiltshire, that meant. 'But the flight schedules are shot to hell now, and what's more we probably won't be here. I was going to try persuading the Cloggies to look after them, with accommodation and transport.' By 'Cloggies', he meant the Royal Netherlands Marine Corps' commando unit that was currently billeted down the road at Trollhogda Camp. 'But you see, there's no employment for Brabant and his boys. The bigger SBS detachment who were at Ramsund have gone north – to whatever skulduggery they were earmarked for, anyway they've *gone*—'

'Are Brabant and his team AW trained?'

'Not Mike himself, he missed it, but—'

'Who's his number two?'

'WO2 Beale. Tony Beale. The demo team comprised Brabant, Beale, and six others. Some of them have done AW training, some haven't.'

'You've been working on this, evidently.' Boyers glanced at him sharply. 'Did you say anything about it to that girl?'

'*No*, sir.'

Frowning, thinking about it. . . .

'They'd have to volunteer. And I'd have to get an OK from Brigade. They'd need to wear civvy Arctic gear, I suppose – as much as shows on the outside.'

'I think the Norwegians might help with that.'

'Then transport – preferably helo. If there's anything to be achieved at all. . . .' He nodded. 'Right. Get Brabant and Beale over here, let's talk to them.'

13

A couple of times it had stopped snowing altogether, and conditions were better generally because the wind had eased off quite a bit. He was skiing straight into it, though, and he was still masked and goggled, with the headover pulled up over the lower half of his face, and his hat's earflaps fastened down. He thought he had about two hours of daylight left, and he intended to keep going for as long as possible, then not waste time digging in, just find some sheltered place and make the best of it.

Studying the map – 'Graphic (Ground)' – in Juffu's reindeer pit, and putting together such clues as he'd let drop about his so-called 'secret place', accepting what seemed to make sense and discarding whatever didn't, also combining what was then left with his own ideas, where for instance *he*'d have sited a supply dump for a fast move up towards Karasjok, he'd settled on an area about fifty-five kilometres NNE of the snow-hole and ten to twenty east of the border. This still left an area of roughly eighty square miles; but some of it was high, bare ground, and it was only forest that counted, obviously. There were other clues as well – for instance the proximity of mountain slopes had to be relevant, since Juffu's informant had been a reindeer herdsman, one of a *siida* wintering their herd somewhere close by.

He had an image in mind of Lapps in the postures of the three wise monkeys — seeing, hearing and speaking no evil. Except *that* one had spoken. Maybe he'd felt safe enough gossiping to Juffu, who for months on end probably didn't converse with any other human being, sharing more of his life with foxes, hares and ptarmigan than with people.

Had done. The past and pluperfect tenses applied now.

Ought to have gone down the hill after him, backed him up?

He knew for certain he should not have. But the old hunter was dead — as were the Americans. And in Juffu's case, he himself had stood waiting for it, expecting it, then hearing it. Natural enough to think now that there should have been *some* damn thing he could have done.

Survivor's guilt complex. But you could recognise that, and still feel it. It was a fact that the old Lapp had acted like an idiot, had thrown his own life away and there'd been no way to stop it happening: but you could still feel you should have *tried* to save him.

Crazy. And a crazy old character, too. Some of his yarns had been bizarre in the extreme, but he'd talked as if he'd believed in them. For instance, a wolf grabbed a hunter by the wrist before he could stab it: the hunter, knowing a thing or two about wolves, didn't try to pull his hand away, he cleverly thrust it down the wolf's throat and strangled the animal from inside. . . . And then the talk of bears, bear talk seemingly for ever. It had included an assertion that the male bear was extremely chivalrous. If 'Uncle Woolly' met a Lapp girl in the forest she had only to lift her skirts by way of proof and he wouldn't lay a paw on her.

Willows grew among the birch here. He'd come down some way, to stay in cover while it lasted, although a more distant view had shown him that before long he'd either have to go right down into the forest — which would make progress slower — or risk a long transit of bare, open snowfields.

The snowing amounted to no more than occasional flurries on the wind now. Maybe an hour and a half in hand. By nightfall he hoped to have covered about two thirds of the distance, which wouldn't have been bad, in these conditions; not good *enough*, but not bad.

The wound in his side hurt quite a lot now. It was the lunging action, the unavoidable exertions of ski-trekking, and probably no more than bruising or torn muscle, but it was still irksome. The wound was clean enough, he'd washed it and the other one with disinfectant again and taped clean dressings on, before he'd left the reindeer pit. Those had been the last of the dressings, incidentally.

Movement: on the facing hillside, across the valley. Like an ant crawling on white-gloss paint. He pushed up his goggles. Could be a reindeer. . . .

Except it wasn't. He didn't stop, because if that happened to be a Soviet it might be better if he didn't know he'd been spotted – for the time being, anyway, and on the principle of keeping one's options open. . . . That hillside, like this one, was lightly wooded, but the moving figure was in a more open area where the treeline dipped to what looked like a gully. Like shadow slanting down: the ant was moving more slowly, reaching that point now. *And joining another* – who'd crossed the stream – or whatever that was – ahead of him. In the greyish slant of the gully were places that seemed greenish, faint green aura on the hill. . . . Ice, he thought. Ice surfaces at angles that reflected light although elsewhere they didn't. Farther along, on the other side of it, the sparse growth of trees thickened and climbed again.

Standing with binoculars at his eyes, that first one?

He'd moved on now, as the other joined him. It was the posture, more than any detail or actual sight of glasses. Or it could even be a touch of paranoia: *imagining* those as Spetsnazi keeping pace and watching.

It would be unwise not to assume that they were hostile. *And* observing him. So, all right, assume it. The next possibility being that they'd come from the area of the snow-hole, that one of them was the man who'd shot Juffu, who'd also know Juffu had had a companion there who'd got away. It was a lot of supposition, but this wasn't Oxford Street, there weren't such huge crowds of people wandering around that it would be coincidence, exactly.

The way to mislead them would be to make a feint towards Norway. Slant left, northwest, let them see one heading for the border.

They might swallow it, particularly if they didn't know he'd seen them. And he was in the right place for it. To get to that frontier one *would* have come this way, most likely. Having passed round the mountain range that was now on his left and ahead, continuing around it he'd be heading about NNW – to cross the frontier roughly where he'd come south with Sophie and the Yanks, and the wretched Isak. That would be the route they'd expect him to take, surely, if he was getting out.

Which in the circumstances anyone with any sense *would* be doing.

One hour, about, to sunset. Dark in say eighty minutes. No need to go far off-course. So, OK. . . .

He'd go down then, he decided. After he'd let them see him turning away he'd move down into the forest and lay up for the night, continue through low-level forest when he pushed on in the dawn. Having disappeared towards the Norwegian border. . . . He couldn't see those people now, but the trees were thicker where he thought they must be now; he was in denser cover too, might be out of their sight too at this moment, but they'd have a clear view of him when he was crossing the mountain's shoulder. Even if they hadn't seen him yet, they would then.

Darkness was coming as he made his way down through forest on a long, east-facing hillside. Glad to have got this far: over that high part he'd found himself traversing about three kilometres of avalanche slope, with a convex, steeper part above him and a towering cornice above that, all covered in fresh snow over a hard-crust base. Like playing Russian Roulette: he'd increased the steepness of his traverse, to get it over quickly. . . . But down now into the valley, using the last of the day's light, side-slipping through clumps of fir with his skis, sometimes clattering over fallen, half-buried branches, the litter of last night's and this morning's strong winds. The trees' branches sagged under the weight of new snow.

Very nearly dark. Even on the crests the day would be fading, but down here it was as good as over, deep shadows speeding its demise. Partly for this reason he turned north again when he was about halfway down. Navigating by compass and contours then: looking forward to stopping, shedding the weight of the bergen and relaxing strained muscles.

He found a place that would do. Thick brushwood for cover, and he'd use the tarpaulin as a tent-sheet, slinging it over the nylon tow-rope set up between two trees. It would be adequate, well enough hidden for the dark hours, and before dawn he'd be moving on. He took off his skis, thankfully lowered the bergen to the ground. Cold beans now, biscuit and chocolate, and there was still some tea remaining in the Thermos.

He'd heard the wolves howling. They must have been wolves, not dogs, there was no Lapp settlement so close. And Lapps didn't camp with their herds these days, or even very near them, snowscooters had changed all that, allowing them to live in village houses and commute, returning nightly to home comforts. Juffu had said, rambling on in the deer-pit this morning while they'd waited for the dawn, that this led to inefficient husbandry of the deer, so the animals turned semi-wild. Where *siidas* relied on scooters, he'd said, the deer were neglected, the early-warning signs of disease often not seen in time.

Carl Sutherland should have met Juffu. A week or two with him, he'd have had a new book to write.

He was awake suddenly, lying still in pitch darkness, knowing he'd *been woken*.

Movement, outside the shelter. Very slight, cautious, barely audible under the sigh of the wind. Then again. . . . Spaced-out movement like a man placing one foot after the other with immense care at long intervals, listening in those intervals for reaction. . . .

Half up – at least as cautiously – weight on an elbow, arms clear of the bag, MKS ready and switched to automatic. Hearing the same sound again, and closer. Then catching the smell. . . .

Extraordinarily familiar odour.

Juffu?

That *was* the connection. The first time he'd smelt it had been in the snow-hole, and later it had become an integral part of the atmosphere in the reindeer pit.

Snuffling. A soft panting. Then again snuffle, snuffle.

Wolf?

He moved – suddenly and loudly: 'Fuck off, you—'

Convulsion, against the side of the shelter, something crashing into the side of it and a scrape of claws before it broke away through the brushwood. Then nothing except the ululating moan of wind.

He'd caught on to the connection with Juffu. The answer was damp fur. *That* had been the smell. Wet animal – wolverine, whatever – and Juffu's wet furs. All his hunting gear he'd made himself, he'd said, either from reindeer hide or out of the pelts of other animals he'd trapped. And maybe those furs and hides were still closer to their original state than they'd have been if they'd been bought in a shop. In any case, it had been the smell of animal, not of man.

Couldn't have been a wolf. A wolf would surely have sounded heavier. More likely a fox, or wolverine. He snuggled down into his sleeping-bag again, with a need to regenerate warmth lost during that short hiatus.

Long before dawn he was up and preparing to move on. He'd decided, having thought about it in the night, to risk using the naptha stove, making sure the tarpaulin enclosed it completely so no light could show out. Not that it gave out such a lot of light — except when you were getting it going, before it was in control; in fact a cooking smell was the greater hazard, quite faint scents being easily detectable over considerable distances in this unpolluted environment. But remembering the state of exhaustion he'd been in when he'd got back from his trek with Sophie he also thought it would have been taking a chance to have begun the day *without* some warmth under the belt. In the Thermos too, for later. He made tea, and heated a can of beans. It still wasn't light outside, wouldn't be for quite a while, so there was time to take it slowly, absorbing several mugs of the hot, sweet nectar.

The Sea King from the Naval Air Squadron at Bardufoss came racketing down into the river valley, lowering its camouflage-painted shape into the dawn shadows, dropping out of sight among the trees that filled the shallow depression on both sides of the frozen river. The helo was out of sight then of any ground observer more than a few hundred metres away, and particularly from the nearby Finnish border and points south of it. Thunderous noise, downrush of wind whipping up a snowstorm as the machine settled its skids gently on the ice. Ice needed to be twelve inches thick to take this much weight, and there was at least three times that thickness. In the moment of touchdown the cabin door was open, three men tumbling out, turning to receive the gear that was thrown down to them: then all crouching, heads together, arms on each others' shoulders, the down-draught practically flattening them as the machine thumped its way up into the air. No one at any distance could have known it had landed. Hearing, if they'd known their helicopters they'd have identified it from its sound as a Sea King, but they'd only have seen it dip out of sight, dipping towards the river, then reappear as it soared up again, banking away from Finnish air space as if the pilots had suddenly realised how close to the border they'd been flying. The second pilot, looking down and seeing their three passengers climbing off the ice, throwing their skis up on to the bank ahead of them, saw one of them wave. He muttered, 'And the best of British to *you*, old chum.'

It was Tony Beale who'd waved. He and the two Marines were on the river bank now, having stashed their Clansman PRC 320 radio actually *in* the bank, with a shovelful of snow over its waterproof cover for camouflage. Now they were getting ready to move off, adjusting their gear. Skis, face-masks, headovers, oiled-wool hats and their outer garments were all Norwegian products, civilian style; their back-packs were all different, but similar to any other ski-trekking tour-ists' packs. Their haircuts weren't noticeably 'military' either. No weapons were visible, although in shoulder-holsters they were carrying Finnish-made Jati submachine guns borrowed from the Norwegian Army. Neat little weapons – newish, the Norwegians had had them only for evaluation – fifteen inches long with forty-round magazines of 9-mm parabellum.

Beale was a big man, six-two in his thermal socks, but spare, bony-faced, with deepset eyes and a big nose. Married, three children, the last one born only a few months ago; the Beale home was in Hampshire. Gerry Simmerton, from the West Riding of Yorkshire, was shorter and of heavier build. Blunt-faced and usually genial, he'd been a Bootneck for six years but had only done just over one year in the SB Squadron. The third member of the team, Bill Howie, was an entirely different type again: he was a Celt, black-haired and blue-eyed, barely five-foot eight but built like a greyhound and – over a good distance – faster. He was from Brechin in Angus. He and Simmerton were bachelors, and both had the SB qualification of swimmer-canoeist third class. Tony Beale was an SC1.

Looking up at the lightening sky. It was going to be a clear day, by the looks of it. High cloud, wind about force three from the northwest, ground temperature minus twenty. . . .

'Fit, are we? Want to check the map again?'

They didn't. Meaning they had it photographed in their brains. As they needed to, since any one of them had to be able to see the task through if the other two came to grief. Their destination was a snow-hole, presumed to be still in existence, its location marked on Beale's map from a grid reference contained in a Norwegian bird's report. This was all they had to go on, for starters. But with luck they might run into Ollie Lyle and his two Americans before they got very deep into Finland. Ollie had been supposed to be bringing these Yanks out, one of them on a ski-stretcher probably, and the more-or-less straight line between here and the snow-hole was (a) the shortest route, (b) the route Lyle had told the Norwegian bird he'd be taking.

'He might even turn up before you start in.' The Royal Marine major from COMNON's staff – he'd flown up to Elvegardsmoen to brief this SB team – had told them, 'And we want them out double-quick. Because apart from obvious considerations, we don't want problems with the Finns. Any minute now we'll be blowing the whistle and we *think* the Soviets will turn about and go home. What they're preparing – apparently – is a sneak invasion, infiltration, so once they know we're on to it and ready for them – well, it's a new ball-game and please God not the game they want to play. But by then we'll have tipped off the Finns too, so they'll be deploying – at the least, they'll have patrols out pretty smartly. And your Captain Lyle—' Grayling had hesitated, '—well, reading between the lines of this rather economically-phrased report, and taking certain other indications into account, I'd guess he's been throwing his weight about, in that neutral territory. He'd have had no option, I'm sure, but all the same. . . .' Frowning, pursing his lips; he'd finished, 'What it comes down to is we want him *out*, Mr Beale.'

He had a feeling he'd been here before: looking out from trees across rising ground at a confluence of frozen streams, a bivouac, three men whom he was assuming to be Spetsnazi. Soviets, anyway. Fur-clad, indistinguishable from each other in size or shape. One had just crawled into the bivvy, one was outside doing something – like waxing – to a pair of skis, and the other was moving around, collecting firewood.

This was an apex of the trees through which he'd come from the south. Open ground in front, a small branch of the spider-web of streams out on the right and joining the main stream at right angles. A bulge of the forest close to the junction was where they'd put their bivvy, with its back to the trees. They could sit in its entrance – one of them might be there now, but he couldn't see – and have a view in most directions.

A detour westward would be the answer. His object was to move northeast, but he was going to have to retreat and then go west – about two kilometres – and circle round, pass round to the north of them. The map showed forest there and one of the branches of this complex of iced-up streams running into it. If there was a stakeout *there*, of course, one might have new problems, but you wouldn't know until you got there.

They could be hunters – wishfully thinking. . . .

But apart from a different lie of the land and the fact they'd built themselves a bivvy instead of putting up a tent, the set-up looked so familiar, so much like the lookout post he and the others had nearly run into on the day Isak had been killed, that he felt almost sure these must be Soviets too – trained the same way, working to the same patterns. And he *hoped* they were – because their presence would indicate there was substance in Juffu's information. There'd be no other reason for them to have been stationed in this remote neck of the woods.

They'd pass themselves off as tourists on a hunting trip, he guessed, to any other trekkers who might come by.

He went back through the trees, half a kilometre back over his own tracks. Then west. It would take about an hour of the precious few hours of daylight, this walkabout. But if it was taking him to the target – and this was the only way to get through to it. . . .

If *he*'d been running the show for them, he thought, he'd have had patrols inside the forests as well as lookouts in the open. Then you *would* have it sewn up. But maybe they didn't have the manpower to spare.

Circling north, then northeast, maintaining roughly the same distance in from the edge of the forest on his right. It was level going here, on crust with only a few inches of fresh, fine-grained snow covering it. From the point where he'd now turned northeast, the map showed, he'd have a trek of about five kilometres through forest and then a section of open ground to cross. And no way to avoid crossing it except by another much longer westward detour. Too far, too time-consuming. . . . And there was bound to be a lookout post there: if this added up to anything at all. . . .

Sophie would be worrying, by now. If he'd found the Americans alive he'd have had them across the frontier before this. She'd know something had gone wrong. So would Grayling. But Grayling would have a lot on his plate, right now; and she'd most likely be down in Oslo, they'd have wanted her down there for de-briefing. So she'd be waiting for news from Grayling, probably telephoning him several times a day.

Maybe he should have headed straight for Norway, from the snow-hole. Nobody had asked him to hang around down here or look for ammo dumps. And if poor old Juffu hadn't hinted at the existence of one he *wouldn't* have been here. That was all it had taken, one barmy old Lapp's supposition!

A Royal Marine general had told him he was a 'pig-headed bloody idiot'. And he'd heard his own mother say on numerous occasions, 'You always were strong-headed, Ollie.'

OK, but he'd had those two Yanks in his personal care, and—

Forget it. . . .

Forging on. Somewhat fearful that they *might* have patrols inside the forests, that as one approached the target their security would get tighter. Having to be very watchful, there-fore, while also anxious to push on as fast as possible. Munching chocolate occasionally, but sparingly now because stocks were running low. Raisins had run out yesterday. And supplies had only lasted this long because they'd been intended to feed five people. Three of whom were dead. Incredible — when one thought back to the start of it, to Carl Sutherland telling him over the supper table in Alta that evening, 'Escort, in a sense, but I didn't mean an armed guard, for heaven's sake. . . .'

A chauffeur-handyman, butler, maybe.

He was expecting to come to the end of this reach of forest at just about the moment that he saw it coming – a whiteness ahead, the ground rising, bare, to a rounded hill shown on the map by a single ring of orange contour-line. It touched the forest's edge on both sides of the open strip at about the strip's narrowest point, where it was about one kilometre across.

Then from the edge of the trees, with the hill's summit to his right, he saw a tent perched on it. A hemispherical mountaineers' tent like the ones they'd abandoned with the pulk.

There was no sign of life around it, no lookout in sight. But there didn't have to be, there could be one inside the tent and he'd have a perfectly good view. Checking the map again. . . . From up there you'd have a view northwestward of about six to eight kilometres, and eastward about five. That post covered virtually any approach from southerly directions, in fact.

No mileage in trying to detour eastward; the forest looped back there, you'd have another high-up snowfield to cross. And you could bet they'd have that under surveillance too. Westward – well, it would take the rest of the day to get round that way. *And* there'd be another crossing of open ground eventually. Except *that* piece might be negotiable in the dark. It would *have* to be, this had to be the answer now: more delay, but if it was the only way to get there – even as much as an extra day. . . .

They'd have picked the site for their forward supply dump – which he now *knew* must be here – with the advantage of these open areas in mind. There was another which the map showed about seven kilometres north of here, curving protectively around the intervening area of forest. That bit of forest would be *it*. In there, somewhere, Juffu's 'secret, hidden place' had to be. Protected on three sides, and a route westward through forest all the way to the Norwegian border.

Still nothing to be seen up there. But the tent wouldn't be there for no purpose.

He started westward, inside the forest but with its edge in sight. Hating the need for this new detour and the waste of time. But there'd be no point trying to save a day and blowing the whole thing. Once they knew they had a visitor: and the guy who'd killed Juffu could be here already, could have been one of that pair he'd seen: they might be watching, waiting for the survivor to show up.

Might. . . .

He'd gone to the edge of the trees for another look across at the other side. So close, and the detour such a waste of valuable time. Then, turning to commit himself to the long trek round, movement caught his eye – off to the left. Reindeer, grazing. The ground fell away at that point – which he hadn't noticed until this moment – not very steeply but enough for the animal he was looking at to be as it were hull-down, its body in sight but not its legs. There were others not far beyond it of which he could see even less: and beyond them, a pair of antlers showed for a moment and then vanished as the beast put its head down.

Falling ground – *dead* ground. Only that short stretch of it: a hundred metres beyond it, more deer were grazing in full view. The question was, from that tent, with its higher perspective, might it *not* be dead ground?

He told himself, *Only one way to find out.*

'See what's under that.'

Beale gestured towards a snow-covered hump out in the open, a few metres from the long mound that fronted the entrance to the snow-hole. Simmerton ski'd over to it, his skis barely indenting the new snow already frozen into a hard crust. He got out of his skis then, dumped his back-pack and detached the shovel from it. Bill Howie watched from the trees above and to the left, a position from which he had all the open ground in view and also some depth of vision into surrounding woodland. They'd been out as far as the edge of the trees and seen that the snowfield there was also trackless, that nothing and nobody had been here in recent hours. All the same,

Howie's Jati was cocked and ready. (The front cocking handle, unfolded as now, put the gun ready to fire; folded back, it set it to safe. And there was no selector-switch: first pull on the trigger allowed for single-shot use, fully back gave you the works.) They'd arrived here through the forest, well spread out; Howie had been on the right of the line, had investigated the mound which must have been built as a screening wall, found the tunnel opening and called to Beale, who'd told him to hang on, *he*'d take first look inside.

Simmerton was shovelling fast, cutting hard snow away from that other heap and tossing it away. Beale stooped, crawled into the tunnel, torch in one hand and Jati in the other, and with a sharp lookout for booby-traps. Howie surveying the surroundings with tense concentration. The fact there were no tracks here didn't mean they had the whole mountainside to themselves.

Simmerton growled, 'This is a bloke. Or fucking *was*.' Then Tony Beale came out of the tunnel backwards, muttering, 'Camera ... Fucking hell ...' Delving into his back-pack, where he had a 35-mm Olympus. He told Howie, 'Two guys inside, both greased. Not nice at all. Reckon they must be the Yanks. Not Ollie Lyle, for sure.'

'Happen *this* could be, then.'

Simmerton was using the side of the shovel to remove crusted snow from the corpse of a man in reindeer-hide outer clothing, face down, humped in a lot of frozen mess. Beale half-turned, hesitating: then decided to finish one job at a time, and wormed back into the snow-hole. The Yorkshireman's face was twisted into an expression of distaste as he forced the shovel in below the body; it took a lot of effort, levering upward in several places, to detach it from the blackish ice that had glued it to the ground. He could turn it over now, expose its face.

He'd turned away. Shaking his head. 'Tone ...'

'Yeah.' Beale came from the snow-hole. Praying this was *not* Ollie Lyle, but scared it most likely would be. Muttering, 'Not a snow-hole, it's a fucking mortuary. One with his head blown off, other geezer shot in the head too but a rifle did it.' He'd

272

taken photographs. Slinging the camera over his shoulder as he scrunched over on his Lundhags boots and stopped beside Simmerton, staring down at the body. Breath pluming like smoke in deep-frozen air, Simmerton asking, 'Him, is it?'

'Nothing like.' Readying the camera. Then he stooped, got the dead Russian's face in focus in close-up, snapped it. 'Nothing *like*.' He added, 'Shotgun again, though, could've been the same one.'

'So what now?'

He'd been thinking about it, and it hadn't taken many seconds to see there was only one answer. *Out*. Back to the border, and report in, over the Clansman. Two stops en route: one very shortly, back in the trees there, for a quick hot drink and snack. Then another stop up on the mountain's shoulder. He'd had a look round from that height on the way here, and over a huge area of snow-covered wilderness seen nothing moving, but he'd stop there again and look harder. Then the last bit of the yomp back would be in darkness, probably. But there was nothing you could do here: there were no tracks, no message had been left in the snow-hole – he'd searched, and drawn blank – there was nothing to give any lead at all.

14

He was scared the reindeer might stampede. If they did and there was a goon up there in the tent to see it happen, he'd wonder what had scared *them*. Then take a closer look. They weren't going to stand still, that was for sure, but they might be induced to shift naturally, just move along. . . .

All but one were moving, almost as soon as he began his ski-crawl. He paused to give that one time to get the message; but the stupid animal still grazed. He crawled on a few metres, stopped again and tried a few low-toned obscenities.

Deaf as well as blind.

He was satisfied that from the tent this was dead ground. It wouldn't be if he stood up, and out in the middle where the ground rose to a central ridge he'd have to really hug the snow.

The reindeer flung its head up, sprang away. Snow flying from its scrabbling hooves as it galloped clumsily after some others, who also then began moving faster — trotting with their heads raised, obviously with the wind up. He crawled on, because there wasn't anything else he could do. Beginning to think he shouldn't have started. Nose down to the trampled snow, imagining the Soviet lookout in that tent with his binos up, alerted.

Reindeer droppings. Ugh. . . .

Left ski, right ski: laboured, stealthy crawling, a technique acquired years ago in AW training. Telling himself it was probably over-optimistic to hope to reach the target – target *area*, say – tonight, when there wasn't so much daylight left. It would obviously be best to check the place out in daylight – having first located it, of course – so as to work out some plan of action that would include withdrawal afterwards. How well guarded and/or patrolled the place might be, only reconnaissance would reveal. Connecting with that, another thought about Juffu's alleged Spetsnaz leader: if he hadn't heard anything from the team who'd been trying to block the southern approaches to Kautokeino – and he wouldn't have, not unless there'd been survivors or *a* survivor, more than those three – then maybe he wouldn't know that Sophie had got past them?

Supposition: based on the fact that having killed Juffu, that guy knew there was one he *hadn't* killed, and would be very keen to put that right.

Halfway over. Or maybe not quite halfway. There was a slight up-gradient, so the central ridge must still be ahead. He stopped, lay flat, looking to his right. Until now he hadn't dared to, having no option anyway but to continue crawling. But he couldn't see the tent, still couldn't see it when he got up again, to crawl on. *Creep* on. . . . Feeling as if he'd been at it for hours; and the trees on the far side didn't seem to be any closer. Reassuring himself – *Saving most of a day. Get there tonight, lie up, recce by daylight tomorrow, hit it at dusk.* . . . Promises, promises. Hit it how, with what? And get *where* tonight?

It wasn't easy to keep down as low as he knew he must. When you tried to hurry it, there was a tendency to rise up – risking a bullet, or bullets plural, maybe the 5.45-mm variety, little ones with little hollows in their noses. . . . He'd stopped again: with snowscooter tracks right under his eyes. Nothing very surprising in this – there were reindeer here, so there'd be herdsmen at times, and they'd use scooters presumably because there were several Lapp settlements within about twenty-five kilometres – for fuel supplies and maybe homes to commute *from*. But it stimulated hope. Juffu's informant being a mountain Sami, reindeer herdsman, one of a *siida* supposedly wintering their animals in the immediate vicinity of the 'secret, hidden place'. Juffu's voice like a distant echo in his Finnish-accented German: *Nobody is speaking of these things, they're frightened. But to me this one did.* . . . It wasn't exactly confirmation that this was the right place, but it seemed the furnishings were right, it fitted the background as sketched by the old Lapp. There had to be a *siida* close by, Sami herdsmen who were in the know – because having eyes and ears they'd hardly *not* be – but who'd have been coerced into silence.

Entering the wood, at long last!

Half a minute later he was right inside it, on his feet, easing strained, cramped muscles. Ski-crawling used muscles you didn't need in any other activity. That was how it *felt*. . . . His watch wasn't accurate, he'd had no way of resetting it after it had stopped not long ago, so at first light this morning he'd set it to 0945, which wouldn't be all that far out, he thought. On that basis he now had about two hours of daylight left. So he'd saved several hours and a lot of wear and tear, he was in what *might* turn out to be the right area and he had that much time in which to reconnoitre.

Map. . . . The 'graphic' was looking distinctly dog-eared now.

Northeast. That was where logic pointed. When he got to the river that ran through the bottom of the valley he'd know he was getting warm – figuratively speaking. So now – downhill through this forest, bearing left, to avoid rising ground that should appear on his right. He put the map away, and his skis on. The snow's surface was a crust, recent falls cemented, and he gave a thought to the idea of continuing on foot – for the sake of caution, the possibility of the alleged Spetsnaz 'leader' being here ahead of him, maybe with patrols out hunting. On the other hand safety might lie in speed, getting there before he was expected. And they might imagine they had security sewn up, with their lookout posts as well as tame Lapps around to serve as insulation.

277

Skis were noisy on the hard snow, in the forest's pervading silence. Animal tracks were visible all over the place. He was looking all ways at once – picking a route between the trees and simultaneously watching for movement and tracks other than the animals', forewarnings of the presence of patrols. The last thing he wanted now was any confrontation: one shot, one shout, he'd never get to any target.

Or away from it.

On his right – sure enough, now, rising ground. A small hill, in fact, shown on the map by a couple of contour rings and a central dot, no height indicated. A stream came down it – steep, narrow, rock-strewn, heaped with ice; in spring and summer it would be less stream than a series of waterfalls. Crossing it near the foot of the hill he guessed that from where it vanished into the forest it would wind down to join the river that was somewhere down to his left. And *his* river couldn't be far ahead now.

By April, this quiet forest would be thunderous with the rushing torrents. The thought reminded him of Sophie, of their talk about a fishing holiday on the Teno. Tana – whatever. They'd hardly known each other, he thought, when they'd made that somewhat tentative arrangement.

There.

Stemming. Then side-slipping, stopping ten metres this side of it. The trees crowded to the river's banks, but the frozen river itself looked open, dangerous. He took his skis off and went forward cautiously, having learnt how they tended to keep watch on open spaces.

Tracks. He'd stopped breathing: could hardly believe he was seeing this. . . .

Tank tracks!

Correction. Controlling excitement, forcing the brain to work calmly: not tanks, but BMPs. BMPs being a range of Soviet tracked vehicles, infantry combat vehicles – armed, amphibious, varying forms of the same basic. These would be load-carriers, or adapted for freight.

If you followed these tracks now, wouldn't they lead to the dump?

It seemed like such a gift. So easy. But where the hell *else* might they lead?

Three and a half metres wide: that was BMP width, all right. They'd churned the river's ice from as far to the right as his view extended, and at about thirty metres' distance to his left they climbed out of the river, flattening the bank on its far side. There'd be nowhere for them to go, except to the dump. And — *some* time — on to the frontier, and over it. . . .

So — OK, leave skis here, continue on foot. Come back for them maybe if it turns out there's far to go. He dumped his bergen too, hiding it with the skis and poles in undergrowth.

Crossing the ice — conscious of the need to get over quickly, back into cover, but also feeling incredibly mobile and unhampered without the bergen's weight — and climbing the bank. . . . He had the MKS slung over his right shoulder, that hand on the gun and its selector to automatic. In the trees now, he started cautiously on a line parallel to the churned track. More roadway than track: and it was solid confirmation, if any were needed now, of the accuracy of old Juffu's information.

About a hundred metres beyond the river he stopped, crouching in cover and looking into a cleared space about the size of half a tennis court. Parking area, unloading area? Empty at the moment. . . . Creeping closer, he saw it was floored with the sort of metal trackway used sometimes for emergency aircraft runways. He thought, *I'm here.* . . . The suddenness of arrival was bewildering. But the approach road was the same; he hadn't been close enough to see it, until now. They'd have track-laying vehicles for that job, laying the stuff section by section, mile by mile. Combat Engineers' department, in the Soviet Army organisation. And there was no surprise that there was no transport here at this moment: they'd unload by night, start back in darkness. . . .

Exactly as the old guy had said, in fact.

So what are we waiting for?

The dump had to be on the other side of that open space. There was certainly nothing *this* side of it.

Except a Russian walking along the roadway. . . .

He'd ducked lower. He could only see the man's fur hat. Hearing from a distance a snowscooter's high snarl – unsilenced, ear-splitting, somewhere outside the forest but shattering its deep silence. The Russian was now crossing the parking area. Submachine gun on his back, fur hat with earflaps down, black boots showing below a heavy topcoat – that was as much as he'd noted before he ducked down again. But a voice called now – Russian. . . .

Up a bit, slowly. Spotting this second guy appearing out of the trampled, snowy forest floor. Facing the first one, therefore facing *this* way. Consequently one didn't exactly jog around. . . . Voices continued, but there could be a third one in the conversation now, he thought. Head up again *very* slowly, centimetre at a time. Two of them with their backs this way, both the backs with guns slung on them, this pair in conversation with a third at whom they were looking *down*.

Up higher. . . .

The one facing this way now was where the second one had come from – at a lower level, in a hole of some kind. This would be it, he guessed. Tunnel or some such entrance to whatever. . . . He was coming up steps now, this guy: Ollie lowering himself equivalently. . . . Then all three were walking – slowly, from right to left – in a close group, along the far side of the vehicle park. The one who'd risen from the earth wasn't visibly armed. The drone of their voices faded as they turned away – to their right, heading away into obscuring trees.

Where they'd gone was the far side of some kind of dugout, he thought. There was nothing to be seen – from here – so it had to be under the ground, and they'd changed direction as if turning a corner. Further details might now be ascertained – since they'd departed, and while there still was some daylight in which to attempt a little reconnaissance. Crawling. Crabbing along slowly, cautiously. The broken ground was easier, being all trampled, than terrain he'd had to cross recently, snowfields where he'd been wishing to God he'd brought a Royal Marine issue white cotton smock, which he could surely have proff'd during that brief stop at Elvegardsmoen. But he hadn't dreamt he might have any need for such a thing. . . .

Now, he had to pass around the side of the clearing and get up close to the tunnel or – well, steps, whatever that guy had come up from. And as he was going to have to move around here later in the dark, he had not only to see what was what but also to memorise distances, bearings, landmarks.

Now. In a position from which he might get a good view of things: using a tree-trunk for cover, hugging it, raising himself slowly. . . .

Juffu's 'secret place' was a very large hole in the ground. Not reindeer-pit style, but rectangular and much, much bigger. Three times the size of the parking area: tennis court and a half, roughly. He was off to its side and about fifty feet from it. It had a humped roofing of some material like netting over which branches, dirt and snow had been scattered. Well, the snow would have scattered itself, of course. From overhead – aircraft or satellite – he guessed it wouldn't be visible at all, but from this angle what gave it away most obviously was that here and there rectangular shapes were visible under the covering. He couldn't see any kind of entrance on this side.

Cut a way in?

He dropped: and lay flat, motionless in snow and forest litter. Three Soviets were approaching, up this side of the rectangle, having passed down the other side and around the far end. One of them was doing all the talking; by the sound of it, he was either lecturing them or telling a story. And they were going to pass so close and so easily in mutual sight that it wasn't – wasn't *tolerable*. . . . It would only take one of the three to glance this way: let alone step off the path for a pee. In any case they might not keep to that path, might come through the trees – as they did, at times, the state of the snow showed it clearly. . . . He lay like a corpse, listening to the single Russian voice steadily increasing in volume as the trio approached.

As it reached about maximum gain, it cut out altogether.

Silence. Ollie thinking, *Bugger's seen me. Pointing me out to the others.* He wasn't even breathing. But he was ready to roll violently sideways, shooting as he moved. Then *up*, and running, dodging. . . .

That same voice now uttered one short sentence. Punchline

of the boring story, timed carefully for effect. For a couple of seconds it wasn't getting the expected response: but quickly then the loud, obviously forced laughter. Even in that incomprehensible language it had obviously not been very funny. Ollie wasn't moving yet, he was waiting for the decibels of the conversation, which was now general again, to be considerably reduced by distance before he did so. When he did lift his head, with tortoise-like slowness, he was looking at their backs again and they were crossing the vehicle park, still three abreast, towards the roadway that ran south to link with the frozen river.

And there might never be a better moment.

The cover was plastic, like a rick cover, with cam net thrown over it, assorted muck on that, snow as a top dressing; he was crouching, trying to pull up the plastic, which at ground-level was buried in the snow.

No joy. Buried in earth as well as snow, he guessed, and the earth subsequently frozen into its present rocklike hardness. They'd have excavated this hole and covered it in the summer, at any rate before the freeze.

He could have cut a way in easily enough. But not easily in a way that wouldn't show.

Use the entrance? Chance it? Creep up, then dive in, hoping to find oneself alone in there?

Bloody dangerous. It wasn't only a matter of getting in, there was also the problem of getting *out*.

Five or six yards to his right he saw an edge of the cam netting. A join, overlap of two sections. Obviously it couldn't have been all in one piece. He guessed the plastic wouldn't be either. But if you could flap the netting back there, cut a slit in the plastic under it: then the weight of the net would hold it down afterwards and hide the slit?

He couldn't see any snags in that. Checking the other way meanwhile, seeing the three Russians' backs identical except for the absence of a submachine gun on the one in the middle. Some distance away now, pacing slowly up the trackway.

It took only half a minute to get inside. You couldn't put the net back in place behind you, *that* was the snag, during the time that you were in the hole the entrance route would be visible to anyone passing near. . . . *So be quick*. . . . Under the covering and over the top of a stack of wooden crates, pulling himself over them with the weighted cover pressing on him. Forcing himself through, he slid down over the edge into a gap between rows of crates and boxes.

Pencil flashlight. Battery weak, but still adequate. He was in an alleyway about one metre wide between the stacks. Close on his left where he landed, though, was an earth wall – as if the pit ended at that point, but it did not: so this was a barrier, separating this part from the end where the steps led into it. There'd be a way through somewhere. Unless there were two distinct parts of the store, and another entrance at the far end. But for the loading or unloading work they'd surely want access through the near end. . . . Stooping, looking around, with economical use of the torch. . . . The excavation was about five feet deep, its covering material raised in a longitudinal ridge over a wire jackstay down the centre, a few feet higher. He wondered what they'd done with the earth they'd dug out of here. . . . In some places, taller stacks of boxes pushed the roof up – as he'd noticed from outside. They'd covered the ground in here with the same kind of heavy trackway as they'd used for the roadway and parking area, with timber slats as well under the bottom layers of crates.

Ammunition boxes, these. The Russian markings meant nothing to him but it was obvious what they were. He moved along the aisle to a cross-passage; all the way to the corner the boxes were the same. Feeling his way around the corner in darkness. Rough timber crates, rope handles. More ammo, he guessed – from their shapes – and for his purposes not a hell of a lot of use. It would all help, later, but it would need – well, encouragement.

The crates here were of a different size and shape. On the right, in the cross-passage. A quick use of the torch showed (1) that this whole stack was of one kind, and (2) entirely different markings from the first lot. Rifles? The shape suggested it. They'd be AK-74s, then. But why would you need them? Every man who came up this way would have his own personal weapon, surely. Also, measuring the crates by using his fore-arm as a ruler – an AK-74 was slightly under 950 millimetres long overall, and these were half as long as that again.

Mortars, maybe, or missile-launchers. Either would do very well. He unsheathed his knife, felt for the edges of one lid, slid the blade in and levered, prising it up. Then by hand, the lid squeaking as the nails wrenched themselves out. Flashlight, as he peeled back tarred paper lining the inside.

SAM missile-launchers, ground-to-air, NATO designation SA-7 *Grail*s, fired from the shoulder. Mach 1.5 and sup-posedly capable of hitting aircraft up to fourteen thousand feet. Lovely. Better than a mortar would have been, in fact. The *Grail* was a heat-seeking missile, but there was no prob-lem in that either, one had only to provide it with some heat to seek.

As long as they'd stashed some missiles here as well as launchers. Which they surely would have. He lifted one launcher out. Basically it was a long tube in which the missile would be inserted – the barrel – with a shorter lower part containing the firing mechanism and trigger, and the sights were on the top of the barrel. He put it down on one of the lower stacks, and shut the lid of the box it had been in. He was looking for SAM missiles now. But by chance he found some cases of grenades first, stopping to investigate them because the markings weren't in Russian but in German. The grenades inside were also German – West German, at that, Diehl DM-51s. He guessed these must be Spetsnaz private stores; regular Soviet forces would be issued with hardware from Warsaw Pact munitions factories, surely. But grenades might come in handy, he thought, if there were problems later. As there might be. He helped himself to a couple, anyway. The basis of the feeling that he might need some was that as yet he had no idea how he'd get away, once he'd completed this job. In fact, the lack of any plan for withdrawal was beginning to worry him. Withdrawal had to be a stage in any plan of attack that didn't involve suicide. . . . A new idea occurred, suddenly, a possible good use for some grenades, an old dodge that might come in quite handy. But it was too late to go back for more, he'd already been in here too long, with the cut in the plastic so visible.

He found SAM missiles. They were on the other side of the stack that had the launchers in it, cases back-to-back with those. And one would be enough. He didn't want to be cluttered with more stuff than he was going to need.

Voices. He'd switched off the torch, pushed it into a pocket. A mumble of Russian, from the direction of the entrance, and a reply that might have come from outside. Couldn't have spotted the hole he'd cut, they'd have sounded more excited than that, surely. . . . He'd been dithering slightly – with the missile box still open, wondering whether to pull out some of the paper lining and wrappings for later use. He did have an alternative procedure in mind, he'd been weighing one against the other when these voices had warned him that the staff were back. Which made his mind up, to the extent that he left the combustible material in the box and shut it, put it back up where it belonged. The voices by this time were louder, closer, and he guessed there did have to be a passage through from where they were into this larger section.

Heavy objects were being thumped around, in there.

Smell of petrol. Quite strong, suddenly.

Fuel storage at that end? It might account for the separation, the earth wall, safety precaution. Even if there was a way through, maybe over on the other side. In any case it wasn't much of a safety measure, between very large quantities of such highly explosive and inflammable materials, it wouldn't keep a *real* fire from warming-up that gasolene.

And there was going to *be* a real fire. With any luck. . . .

A Russian voice called, from a distance, and a nearer one answered. Then a blare of noise: radio switched on, music gushing, very loud and very Russian-sounding, Red Army choir-type, defenders of communism on the march for Mother Russia, earth-mother, heroes of the revolution goose-stepping under scarlet banners with hammers and sickles on them instead of black ones with swastikas. He shut his mind to it, got on with what had still to be done. He was going to have to come back in here, to set it up – after dark, when he'd be able to move around more easily, and if they kept that frightful noise going it might help. Meanwhile he was taking the launcher and one missile. Simplest way being to load missile into launcher, thus having one burden instead of two.

The petrol store occupied his thoughts while he was doing this. Noise of Moscow Radio deafening from beyond the earth wall. He was relieved to find the missile did fit, and that the mechanics of the launcher were as simple as he'd expected. But the petrol seemed so obvious, such a close convenience that not to make use of it seemed like looking a gift horse in the mouth. Except it would mean getting into that other part, which might be tricky, since that was where the action seemed to be. Maybe the supply of weaponry and ammunition had been completed, and fuelling was the final stage. All this having been in progress for weeks or even months while Spetsnaz teams staked out the border area to grease anyone who saw or heard of it.

Like three Finns, two Americans, two Lapps: and those were only the ones one *knew* of.

Simple enough, and helped by the trusting attitudes of Norwegians and Finns. And it would have worked if the CIA hadn't thrown a spanner in the works. Blindly and expensively, in terms of two innocents sacrificed, but sending them here *had* scotched it. Or would have – touch wood. As those two would have put it, *knock on wood*. . . . He was manoeuvring himself over the top of the ammo boxes, where he'd got in, dragging the launcher beside him. Pockets weighted with the Diehl grenades. Successful visit to the supermarket; now, one had to avoid the check-out. Initially, getting out from under the netting and then folding it back over the knife-slit in the plastic to cover it and hold it down, with a scattering of snow over it as a finishing touch: then, sneak back to where he'd left his bergen. But if there happened to be a Soviet there to notice the cover bulging and wait to see whether whatever finally squeezed out had four feet or two. . . .

There wasn't. Luckily. That form of exit had been a total gamble: out into the daylight blindly as a newborn babe. Successful delivery, as it happened: he was hunched down, clutching the launcher against his chest, studying the surroundings. Then away: leaving the massed choirs behind him and trotting, bent double, into the trees.

Knowing where he was going now and how to get there, the return journey was faster than the outward had been. Despite having to stop and wait in cover while the three Soviets who'd left the dump a quarter of an hour earlier came striding back along the trackway and through the vehicle park. They were marching, swinging along in the tempo of the music. . . . One of them went down the steps into the hole while the others marched on down its far side, where they'd gone before. Ollie thinking, *Five of them here now. Five at least.* Might be others with their heads down. Also, there probably *was* an entrance at the other end. A loading area too, quite possibly; if the BMPs could drive on round, down the side of the dump where those two had just disappeared. If there was an entrance/exit down at that end it seemed likely the earth wall did extend right across.

Not that it mattered, really.

He was measuring distances in paces, in preparation for his return in the dark. He reached the frozen river – effectively now a road, there'd no doubt be other lengths of river-road in similar use between here and the Finnish-Soviet border – and crossed it on the BMP tracks, looking and listening from cover first, then quickly over to find the bergen and skis.

Two hours, say, to lie low. Or rather, high – up on that hill. It would be dark or getting dark in about *one* hour, and any time after that would do, according to what might be going on here. If BMPs rolled in, for instance, and the staff got busy, there'd be no reason to wait, but if there was no activity tonight then it might be better to let them settle down. With luck they'd keep their radio going. He wondered *where* they'd get their heads down. In bivvies maybe, somewhere down near the other end. Or even inside the hole, the far end of it? He thought, *My God, what a way to wake up.* . . .

About thirty below zero, he guessed, maybe thirty-five, on this hilltop. There was very little shelter from the wind, as the firs grew rather sparsely up here. On the other hand there was reason to put up with that much discomfort, because on top there'd be a lot less chance of passers-by, unfortunate encounters. That wouldn't be a good way to be woken either. Not that he intended to sleep, but it could happen. . . . And if they had any sense they *would* take a look up here occasionally. The main danger might be the guy who'd killed Juffu. If he was here, or coming here, knowing Juffu had had a companion who'd got away — and possibly identifying the pair of them as the two (Ollie and Sophie) who'd got away from the snow-hole a jump ahead of him two days earlier?

Nothing to do but take your chances, anyway. And not long to wait now, thank God.

He'd hidden the SAM launcher and its missile near the river, down below. There'd have been no point lugging that weight up here, then down again. But he'd brought his other gear — skis, poles and bergen.

When he'd finished the tea that was in his Thermos, that was *it*, so far as anything hot was concerned. He'd given wishful thought to the possibility of flashing-up the bluey, particularly since from this height no odour could have reached the Soviets down below, with the wind carrying it straight off the hill. He could have hidden the small flame well enough too; he had the tarpaulin slung from a branch to provide some shelter, and it could have been used to shroud any cooking operation. But the crucial factor was that he had less than a pint of naptha left, and an essential use for it.

He wouldn't be able to melt the frozen baked beans. He could have thrown the full tins away but he had a better idea. He removed the lids completely, not leaving them as flaps, and dug out the frozen beans with his knife. Now he could put the empty tins to good use: to make a booby-trap that might help to cover his withdrawal up this hill after the dump was blown. At least it ought to delay pursuit, allowing him to move into stage two, escape down the hill's east-facing side. This was the best scheme he'd been able to evolve, so far. He'd seen from the map that there was a stretch of more or less open ground below the hill and on that side, and he'd heard at least one snowscooter from that direction – confirming the same thing – so almost certainly they'd have an observation post down there, but he thought that at night it should be possible to slip past it. Particularly with major confusion reigning, as he hoped it would be.

A six-foot length of string would be about right. He cut a length from his now much-depleted ball of it. Six feet would span the width of the track up beside the rocky stream. He tied the ends of the string to the two German grenades, pushed the grenades into the empty bean cans – which they fitted as if they'd been designed for it – wrapped the loose bight of string around both cans and stowed the whole assembly in an inside pocket.

He knew it wasn't so much a withdrawal plan as a gamble on what he *might* be able to get away with. You couldn't plan effectively, when you had no idea at all how many Soviets there'd be on the ground, whether they'd have patrols out, or what.

Engine noise woke him.

Dragged out of what must have been more doze than sleep, he thought, *Diesel*. . . .

BMP engines were diesels. Oddly enough. They must have found some additive to prevent it freezing. But another puzzle out of that: what the petrol might be for, in the dump. Some other kind of vehicles, obviously. Or BMPs fitted with different engines. The ones he was hearing now were surely diesel. For helicopters maybe. . . . Anyway, who cared, it would all burn. . . . He was already moving: he'd been fully dressed inside the bivvy-bag but he was out of it now. Leaving the tarpaulin shelter rigged, leaving also his bergen, skis and poles. Because he'd be back here – passing through – please God. . . . En route to Norway and to Sophie. But for now, forget her: *concentrate*. . . .

He was taking the naptha container with him, and the MKS with one full magazine in it and one spare in an outer pocket. Checking by feel that it was there: and the knife in its sheath. OK.... Moving cautiously to the stream, the ice-fall, he started down beside it – feet-first, the main effort being to prevent oneself slithering down too fast.

Down into the blare of Moscow Radio, faint and not unpleasant at first but louder with each metre of descent. There could have been a dozen BMP engines rumbling down there, you couldn't have heard anything but the radio now. At one stage a light flickered through the trees, lasted a few seconds then was gone, either switched off or lost through its movement or his own. BMP arriving along the river-road, maybe: visualising it as it lurched up away from the ice, crawling over the bank on to the trackway.

It was good that they were keeping the radio on, and loudly. Fill their ears, dull their sensibilities, if any. With luck they'd be busy, too, with the arrival of these vehicles. Or vehicle; but he guessed there'd be a convoy of them.

About three-quarters of the way down he stopped, peered through darkness at ice and rock, trees crowding in on both sides to make it even darker. This was about the right place for the grenade-trap, it would be as good as any other. Anyone coming up by this route would have to be this side of the ice at this point: otherwise they'd be mountaineering, whereas here they'd only be clambering up a steep incline. He pulled out the pair of canned grenades, stashed the assembly where he thought he'd find it easily enough on his way up. Setting the trap would take only a few seconds. It mightn't be needed, but if there was any close pursuit – and if there was, chances were that it would be on his own tracks – it might hold them up just long enough to make a difference.

Starting down again. The music began to quieten. A voice rose in its place – loud, haranguing tone, political rhetoric by the sound of it. It went on for about two minutes, hitting a note of triumph and then the music was swelling again, taking over. Ollie was leaving the stream then, picking his way down towards the river.

By stealth, by guile....

Plus — as he'd more than once thought to himself at moments akin to this one — a little nerve and a lot of luck. Or the other way about.

The vehicle park glowed with light. But it was a diffused light, not the beams of headlights. He could see the glow of it through the trees on his way to where he'd left the missile-launcher. Recovering it now, cleaning snow off it.... He balanced it on his left shoulder and moved on, down to the edge of the river, the ice-road. He was right-handed and right-eyed, so when the time came he'd fire from the right shoulder, but right now he needed that hand free for the MKS.

The line of the ice was dark and empty: he crossed over, and trotted into the trees on its other side. He wasn't anticipating problems at this stage, but ready for them and with some emergency moves in mind in case things didn't go quite as they should. For instance, this missile would home-in on a hot BMP engine readily enough. That would be better than nothing, would create confusion, maybe also create a fire, an explosion of fuel that might then spread. Confusion and panic were allies, the best a small attacking force ever had.

And you wouldn't get a much smaller attacking force than *this* one.

He could see three tracked vehicles in the park, and the illumination came from numerous lamps, oil-lamps, which had been dotted around, all over. A dozen men were unloading jerrycans which were being slung from hand to hand, a human chain from the BMPs to the steps at this end of the dump Twelve men — fourteen — *fifteen*.... As he watched — satisfying himself that they were all fully employed, so he could get on with *his* job — another Russian came up the steps from the fuel-store, against the direction of the flow of gas-cans, and strolled round to the rear of a BMP. An officer, presumably. Tall, burly. That BMP's rear hatch was open and he must have been talking to someone inside.

Juffu's killer?

It *could* be him. But from this distance you couldn't be sure. And take any fairly large guy and dress him up in Arctic gear, that was what he'd look like. He could be that one, and he could have been one of the pair on the hillside – or might have no connection with either, and it made no difference, except he'd have liked a chance to square things up for Juffu and the old guy's nephew.

He went back to the river, to put the launcher where he'd need to have it. Then saw, looking towards the target from this point, that it wouldn't do at all. There were too many trees much too close to what would be the line of flight. The whole point of pandering to the SA-7 missile's heat-seeking predilection was that if you aimed it like you'd aim a bullet there'd be a good chance of missing. The missile would tend to weave in flight until it picked up something that attracted it – namely, heat – and before that stage was reached it could hit a tree. Or be drawn to impact on a warm BMP engine, for that matter.

It took about two minutes to find a more suitable spot. Still at a reasonable distance from the target but with no trees near enough to the intended trajectory to matter. He hid the launcher, made sure he had the place marked down so he could come straight back to it. There wouldn't be much cover here, unfortunately, but he couldn't have it both ways.

The big Russian had gone back to stand near the entrance to the dump, where the loads were being passed down. They were working on the second of the three BMPs now. Ollie slunk to his right, into the cover of trees and through them to the side of the dump, opposite his earlier point of entrance. There were no Soviets anywhere round this part; they'd have all been put to work, he supposed. He spent about half a minute making sure of this, then ran forward, crouching, jerked the camouflage netting back to uncover the slit in the plastic, wormed in over the stack of crates.

He was in. On hands and knees – as he'd landed – still now, listening. And *not* having been shot at – which during those few seconds in the open and illuminated by the glow from the unloading area, he'd been aware could happen. . . . The radio music, slightly less loud because of the earth wall's insulating effect – made it unlikely you'd hear any other sound in this pit, even if it was close by. But there was no light in this part. . . .

He re-slung the MKS, to have his hands free. The bottom layer of crates would be the best for starting fires in. Flames spread upward as well as sideways, and he wanted the fires to take a good hold before they made themselves obvious. Giving him time to get out of here, too. Fires plural because by starting several you'd be playing safe, making it more likely you'd get at least *one* that caught.

Starting with one near the barrier – as near as it could be to the petrol – then one in the SAM missiles, and one or two among the ammo boxes. By which stage he'd be back near his exit hole, and evacuating.

In each place he lifted the upper tiers down and poured naptha over the lower crates, spilling it over the wood and seeing it run inside, into the packaging. Then re-stacking, but leaving access for ignition. There wasn't much naptha left for the last one, but the first three looked good. Even the last – well, he wouldn't have wanted to hang around and watch it. . . . He went back to the first, struck one of his few remaining waterproof matches. Flames spread quickly over the wood and into the gaps between the boards, so quickly that from there on he really hurried. Smoke was thickening in the confined space by the time he'd lit all four. He climbed out – again, ready for trouble as he made his swift and sudden emergence: but nothing had changed. Glow of light from the working area, Red Army choir giving tongue, and a smell of burning, acrid smoke leaking as he pulled the cam netting back over the ripped plastic.

The unloading was still in progress. He'd only been inside there about four minutes. He found the launcher, put the MKS down and lifted the heavier weapon on to his shoulder. He'd already checked over its firing mechanism and it was pretty much the same as other types of launcher. Feeling for the sights, he clicked them up on their hinges. That Soviet officer – or he might be an NCO – was still in the same place, still watching the jerrycans flow past him and down into the store, but another Soviet had just gone over to him – from one of the BMPs. Ollie watched – in fact he was waiting for more heat, wanting to make sure this came off properly, knowing he

293

wouldn't get any second chance. He had the launcher ready, most of the length of its barrel – the upper tube – behind his shoulder, balanced by the heavier forward section – which had the trigger at its rear end, close to his chest. The big guy was walking towards the BMP from which the other man had run over to him. Reaching up, having something passed down to him. Radio – radio-telephone, some kind of voice-link. And the music was switched off; sudden silence came as a shock, after that volume of sound.

Somewhat disconcerting, too. He'd needed that noise, he'd been counting on it.

Wait until they switched on again?

He wanted it to cover the noise of the launcher firing. If they didn't hear it they wouldn't have to know a missile had fired, or even that there was an intruder here. They'd have an explosion and fire in their ammunition dump, cause unknown. Some fool's cigarette end, maybe. Accidents did happen around explosives.

But if he waited, the fire was going to burst through. He could smell it even from here now. The wind was this way, of course. . . . Conference still in progress, Spetsnaz officer talking to head office. Ollie sighted on the area where fire was not yet visible but soon would be, and where surely it would be hot enough by now. The launcher was in balance on his shoulder, needed only steadying by his left hand lightly supporting its forepart; his right hand was folded around the trigger.

A bright spot appeared in the plastic cover and immediately expanded, a smoking circumference of it flaring back in a ring of fire and black smoke before flames gushed up through the centre. He heard Russian shouts as his hand tightened on the trigger, then arrested the launcher's violent tilt as the missile ignited and ripped away, explosion deafeningly close to his right ear. . . . He let it fall, stooping to snatch up the MKS, still crouched in that motion when the dump erupted. The blast threw him sprawling backwards and heat scorched through the trees, singeing them, turning snow and ice to slush. Multiple explosions with matching bursts of flame, objects whirring over: he was up and running, magnesium-bright light from a new mushrooming of fire behind him, the whole scene lighter than daylight, roar of flames still punctuated by explosions. He had no idea what might be happening around the vehicles but he guessed the men working there wouldn't have had much chance, that close to it. In the moment of firing he'd been floodlit by the fire, as the plastic cover had caught and burned: now he was running, crouched and dodging – out of habit, training, more than expectation of pursuit, and it was a surprise when he stopped and looked back – from the river's north bank – to see human figures moving, in silhouette against the huge blaze. Those must have been inside the BMPs, in behind them, shielded. Except *he* hadn't had any shield, and he'd survived. But nothing like as close. . . . Running on again, uphill into darkness the way he'd envisaged escaping, though not with a lot of confidence. He was thinking, *Done it, actually bloody well* done *it*, in the belief that he was also virtually in the clear, getting away from it unscathed, when something kicked his leg from under him. A hammer-blow from behind, an extraordinary sensation, a bang and then the leg folded, he was falling, aware of some brilliant light on him, also from behind. He hadn't heard the shot, or shots, it would have been part of that uninterrupted medley of explosions. Having fallen, smacked into the ground, he was twisting himself around, with the leg like a log of wood attached to him and impeding the movement but not hurting, getting no feeling from it at all – getting round, and with the submachine gun in his hands, seeing in the centre of dazzling light a man running, bounding up the slope towards him. There was another behind him, but diverting to the right; and that light was on a BMP, they'd managed to turn it and that was its single headlight glaring up through the trees. He was curled on his left side, the side of the useless leg, selector-switch to automatic, sights wavering for a moment or two – cursing at his own unsteadiness – then *on*. He'd squeezed off a three-round blurp, and saw his man go down. Now the light. In semi-auto, one carefully aimed shot: bull's-eye. As it *should* have been, for Christ's sake: but it was dark up here now, light downhill where the fire still blazed but explosions were less frequent. He remembered there'd been another guy behind that one—

So don't just fucking lie there, you wimp. . . .

The only way to move was crawling, dragging the left leg. No nerves working in it, no feel at all. Even if he'd had the time, or light to see by, he wouldn't have wanted to look at it. He was crawling uphill to where it was darker and so that other one wouldn't have him pinpointed. Also watching for him, staring into the gloom for any movement. Not with much expectation of getting away now, only of not becoming dead if he could possibly avoid it; and the event might at least be delayed by knocking off that other guy. *Then* think about what, if anything, might be done thereafter. There'd be others of them surviving: for instance, *someone* had turned that BMP around and switched its light on. Searching the darkness, gun ready and on auto, aware that this was a lousy time and place to have been immobilised: then a rifle cracked, a ringing percussion not far behind him, up the slope. One shot, and the ringing was still in his skull as a man's voice cried out, a shout of pain, anger or despair – whatever – but also close, and then the thump of a body hitting the ground, smashing of undergrowth as it rolled or slid into it. Ollie had a shadow in his gun's sights, would have fired in the next second if it hadn't spoken, a harsh, urgent croak – *in German*. . . .

'*Brite* – Ollie? Where're you hit? You done for?'

It had to be a dream. And of course, that was the answer. All he had to do was wake up, maybe with cramp in that leg. . . . The shadow slid closer, down the slope towards him, then was lit up for a moment, light flaring from below on the heels of a new explosion, leap of flame blinding as darkness clamped down again blacker than before but leaving him with that vivid image – dark, creased face, slitted eyes blazing blue. . . .

'Juffu? This can't be – *Juffu*, how the *hell*—'

'Thought I was dead.' A grunt. Up close, actually in contact, the smell of wet dog stronger than ever. Juffu muttered, 'Now maybe *you* are.'

15

and

EPILOGUE

The old wolf's instincts were probably right. Ollie saw it clearly in that moment—not analytically, but in the round, as if he was out of the running now, immobilised and therefore finished. He wouldn't have acknowledged it if Juffu hadn't said what he had said, but he thought now, *Well, too bad, but you got away with a lot more than your share, nobody goes on for ever.*

Juffu supported him as they made their way to the stream. He had to crawl from there on, though, the track not being wide enough for the two of them in tandem and anyway too steep for any way up except by crawling, dragging the leg which was still leaking blood despite the tourniquet he'd put on it.

He'd stopped to set his grenade trap. Working by feel in the darkness, removing the pins then pushing the grenades back into the cans, then reaching to position one in an ice crevice in the stream and the other to stand upright, its open end upward, on the outer side of the track. The string was then a few inches above the ground at one end and about two feet up at the other.

Juffu muttered, 'You set good traps. I'll remember you for that.'

'You're great for morale.'

Then he'd repeated the question he'd gasped out before but which Juffu hadn't bothered to answer effectively: 'How the hell did you get here?' They'd been staggering along together at that stage, Juffu holding him up on the side of the useless leg, and he'd only growled in his heavily-accented German, 'Found your gear on the hill, came to find you.... Now save your breath.' Trying again before they started uphill, he asked him, 'That Spetsnaz leader, the big guy you chased after – can't he shoot straight, or something?'

'I shot *him*.'

Juffu had been hurtling directly downhill when the shooting had started, and he'd let himself collapse – somersaulting, cartwheeling, floppy as a dummy just as gravity and impetus took him. Convincing enough for the big Russian to have had no doubt he'd killed him and consequently to fall for the age-old snare of a live corpse with a rifle in its hands. Juffu added, 'I could tell you a story of a hunter who lay just so, and the bear snuffed him all over – his nostrils and his armpits, his bottom, everything – and was satisfied to leave him.... Now – do *you* want to live?'

Crawling on up. He was beginning to get some feeling in the leg, enough to wish it could have stayed numb and to know it was going to be a lot worse soon. The fire was still blazing down below them, across the shoulder of the hill with the trees in silhouette against the loom of its glare and ammunition still popping off, but up here there was only a rosy glow, a haze of radiance reflected downwards from the clouds. They'd heard at least one BMP on the move, presumably departing. It wouldn't have much to hang around for. . . . At least, he thought, dragging himself up the steep, icy track and the leg really hurting when it hit things now – rocks, ice, fallen timber – at least one had achieved that much. Although it was surely only a matter of time, now. It was natural and necessary to keep trying, keep struggling, but he thought Juffu's instincts on the subject of survival – or non-survival – were most likely very sharp, like an animal's. The pain was getting worse, he'd lost a lot of blood and was still losing it, and there were waves of nausea and dizziness. It wasn't easy to see how one could hope to get off this hill even if one succeeded in getting up it.

Then he was at the top, crawling to the tarpaulin shelter. He was halfway to it when the grenade exploded. Grenades, plural, he thought at the time, assuming they'd fired simultaneously. And that had been the only point of defence; the next guy who came up would *get* here.

Juffu rolled up the blood-soaked trouser-leg for him and examined the smashed knee, using Ollie's pencil torch and with an eye on the darkness surrounding them, rifle close to his hand, and the MKS in Ollie's. It might not be a bad thing, he thought, if the leg did freeze. After one glance at it he didn't look again. That was how it was, there was nothing to be done about it except tighten the tourniquet and then wrap the mess of flesh and bone in a bandage soaked in disinfectant.

The trouser-leg was sopping wet with blood, but in the hope the flow might stop now he let Juffu roll it down, to give it a chance of drying. Then with a lot of help he got into his sleeping bag with the bivvy-bag outside it, but only up to his armpits because he needed to have his arms free to handle the gun. The temperature was about minus thirty, he guessed. Being incapable of much movement one needed to be as well wrapped-up as possible, and there was no way he could leave just that leg out. Juffu, having fixed him up, roamed about, going frequently to the head of the stream to watch and listen, moving as quietly as any wolf could have moved. The pinkish light was less actual *light*, it seemed to Ollie, than a tinting of the darkness. Or maybe his sight had been affected. But Juffu was either close by or he was somewhere distant, he didn't ever see him come or go.

There were other routes by which this hill could be climbed, he thought; they wouldn't *have* to come up the line of the stream. They'd only be more likely to come that way because it was the easy way up and they'd be led to it by the blood-trail he'd provided. But then again, if they started up that way and found one of their own people dead or dying from the grenades, if they weren't stupid they'd try another way.

He had his bergen behind him as a bolster, and the MKS on his lap on top of the bivvy-bag, and he kept exercising his hands inside the gloves and mittens in the hope they'd work when he needed them. The pinkness in the dark was less and less noticeable as fires died down.

Juffu was here again. Ollie felt as if he'd slept, woken to find him close against him, actually in contact. Throbbing agony in the knee. Trying to get his thoughts together, concentrate. . . . 'Make a fire? Tea? Stove's no good, I used all the naptha, but there's tea and stuff.'

'I'll make a fire.'

It couldn't do much harm. If there were any Spetsnazi still around they'd know where they were, by now. He heard his own voice muttering, 'Tea would be marvellous. . . . But then you clear off, Juffu, while the going's good. No point both—'

'*Ja.*' Juffu was gathering wood. 'You're right.'

'Tea's in my pack here. Pocket on that side. Sugar's in there too.'

Talking seemed to make the leg hurt more. Or maybe it was just hurting more all the time. It throbbed, pain seeming to travel through the bone while drumbeats kept in step with it in his skull. The thigh felt as if it had ballooned, and if it had been easier to get out of the bag he'd have looked to see if the bleeding had stopped, so he could have loosened the tourniquet. Juffu had begun to talk to him again: '*Juobmo.* . . . And if I had a bear's gall I'd put some on that wound, you'd see how the pain would go. You don't believe me, but you'd see. The old folk knew many useful things that are now forgotten.' He seemed to have been talking from some distance and through ice-water, and Ollie knew his own voice wouldn't carry that far so he didn't bother to reply. He remembered that *juobmo* had an unpleasant taste but a strengthening effect, and if that was what the old guy wanted to give him, OK, no problem, and you could ignore the bit about the bear's gall. He seemed to have some kind of fixation about bears. There was an interval of silence then, possibly a long one, before he became aware of a fire's light and warmth and a broad-shouldered, ape-like figure hunched over it, a face like a yellow mask with two chips of broken glass thumbed into it as if into clay. He was stirring something in a pot. *Juobmo*, that would be. He had Ollie's mug there too, must have extracted it from the top part of the bergen without waking him.

'That's a strange-sounding language, yours.'

'What?'

He'd been raving in his sleep, apparently. It didn't surprise him to hear this. The leg was hurting very badly indeed, really insufferably, and he told Juffu he thought the best thing might be to amputate it. However painful the process might be it couldn't be any worse than it was already. Then he'd be mobile, too, he'd be able to hop along on the good leg, using a ski-pole to support himself on that side. He couldn't see why this shouldn't work quite well, although Juffu told him he wasn't thinking straight. Ollie insisted: he had a very good knife, razor-sharp carbon steel. . . .

'Rubbish. You don't know what you're saying.' Moving closer. 'Here. . . .'

Juobmo. He'd forgotten how foul it was, and it made him retch. When the spasm was over Juffu held the mug to his lips again: 'Drink it *all*. If you don't you won't hear the cuckoo.'

That was an expression he'd used before, meaning, 'Won't live out the winter, won't see another spring'. And he did want to live that long, at least, to see Sophie again. There were a lot of things he wanted to say to her, and there was also the prospect of that fishing trip. So he drank the *juobmo*. He thought Juffu very likely did have wolf's blood in him. He said, 'Could have sworn the Ivan I shot down there was the guy you were after.'

'I told you, I killed mine. But if you hadn't shot the one you

301

did shoot, he'd have had you with his next bullet.' Juffu touched the bivvy-bag in the area of the shattered knee. 'It was a bullet from him that did this, *nicht wahr*?'

It might have been. He was probably right. That one downslope behind him, etched black against the glare of burning. 'I suppose. . . .'

'You truly believed me to be dead?'

'Sure. When you went after him I expected it, then I heard the shooting.'

'If I'd thought, I'd have brought you proof, I could have worn his face.'

Gibberish — and darkness like black water. Face — nose, mouth — only fractionally above the icy surface. If the wind got up at all you wouldn't have a prayer, you'd drown. He heard Juffu telling him that in the old days it was the custom, the way ritual demanded they should go about it.

'Go about *what*?'

'The hunter who had ringed his bear and then speared it—'

'Christ. On about bears again. . . .'

'—would receive certain honours.' Juffu refilled the mug with *juobmo*. 'Drink this, while I describe the form they took. The women, to start with — they'd chew alder-bark and spit the juice at him, also at the dogs and the other people so that it stained them. Clothes, faces, everything, people and dogs alike. And the men could not have sex with their wives for three days, the hunter for five days—'

'Some honour.'

'—and the hunter would cut off the bear's muzzle and tie it to his own face, so *he* became a bear, for that time. The remainder of the animal would be cut up and cooked, to provide a feast that would last three days. The greatest delicacy, which would be offered first to the hunter, would be the soles of the bear's feet. Then the blood which had been collected would be smeared on the tents, dogs, people—'

'Oh, Jesus *Christ*. . . .'

The knee was throbbing like an engine, pumping pain through the leg, and the drumbeats were so violent they were shaking his whole body. He was having to fight impulses to

302

scream. He thought he probably did make some noise. Juffu was telling him – rasping into his ear, close up against him – 'When it begins to get light we'll start down, and from the *siida* who are close by I will obtain a *pulka* and a draught-reindeer to pull it. In the meantime since you don't like to be told about bears I will speak of wolves and of the different ways there are of hunting them. To start at the beginning – well, it was accepted by all our people in the old days that Baergalak made the wolf. Baergalak is our name for the devil. He made him, and Ibmel – who is God – breathed life into him through his nostrils. . . .'

Tony Beale's SBS team, as well as others in the border area, had seen the dump blow up, in their case from a distance of about sixty kilometres. They'd had the big Clansman radio with them for communications with COMNON, and the same Sea King crew flew them in, not landing because even over-flying Finnish territory was a breach of that country's neutrality and of NATO regulations. But this was an emergency, a far from normal situation, and the helicopter's first pilot – whom the Marines called a 'jungly', their parlance for a flyer who's been everywhere, a term originating in the Borneo confrontation of 1963 – this 'jungly' agreed to take them in but he didn't want to land if it could possibly be avoided, so the three of them abseiled in from a hover at fifty metres. And in fact as the machine hammered across the frontier in the steely glimmerings of that dawn they'd seen Finnish Army units already deploying, heavy transport all the way down the highway from Karigasniemi south to Angeli.

(The other area of intense border activity was in the west, south of Kautokeino and around the border crossing at Kivilompolo, which was where the other thrust of the invasion would have come, up to Kautokeino and on from there to Alta. The Soviets had set up a forward base there as well, and in that sector one Kola Lapp, a Spetsnaz conscript, crossed alone into

Norway and surrendered, requesting asylum. He'd been a member of the team which A.N.Belyak had brought up with him – into the Karasjok district initially – after the murder of the three Finnish special force men, and in a later series of debriefings a lot was learnt not only about recent activities but also about Spetsnaz organisation, training and operational procedures. The *Lopar* was also able to identify photographs and in some cases the frozen corpses of former Spetsnaz comrades.)

The SBS men who abseiled into Finland in the first hour after dawn found a blackened acreage of forest and in the centre of it a smouldering crater which had been an ammunition and fuel dump. There was one burnt-out *Boievaya Machina Piekhoti* and a number of bodies. Some of these would only have been recognisable to their dentists, but two were later identified (by that Kola Lapp, from photographs) as Spetsnaz troopers Pereudin and Kunaiev. Continuing the search, Beale found tracks which were copiously bloodstained, and followed them across rising ground to where a rocky stream led up to the summit of a hill. The stream was still solid ice; this part of the hillside faced southwest, so the heat of the blazing dump hadn't got to it.

There was a track leading up beside the stream, and they could see that the wounded man had begun to climb here, although it looked as if he'd been losing even more blood than he had lower down. In fact Tony Beale concluded at this stage that if the man they were trailing was Ollie Lyle they were almost surely too late.

Two hundred metres up, they found a body sprawled across the ice. He'd been of average height, with dark complexion, narrow face, black beard, and he smelt of onions. Beale took a photograph, and the *Lopar* defector later identified this one as Yuri Dmitrovich Grintsov, a Spetsnaz *leitnant*. He'd been killed by a grenade, and nearby was a baked-bean tin with another grenade still in it, short length of string attached. The ring and split-pin had been removed, so if the grenade had been pulled out of the tin it would have exploded as the other had. They'd been linked by string, and both should have gone than if I were to turn your Northern Flank adventure into a novel I'd name *you*.'

'Right.' He nodded. 'But obviously I can't give you more than just the bare bones of it, right here and now.'

'Well, sure. But if we then decided to go on with it – well, I'd fit into your schedule, whatever time you could spare.... Incidentally – why would you want to do this?'

He'd like to see it in narrative form, on paper and between covers, he told me. Partly as a surprise present for his wife. They hadn't been married long, she was Norwegian and she'd played a major part in the action, apparently.

'But anyway – posterity, you know. Like *What did you do on the Northern Flank, Grandfather?*'

'Even though it would have to be presented as fiction.'

'Absolutely. From *my* point of view it would have to be.... And we'll need a fictional name for me, I suppose. How about Oliver – Ollie for short – for the first name?'

'All right.'

'Don't want to bore you with domestic trivia, but the fact is my wife – call her Sophie, shall we? – well, she's—' he smiled '—if it's a boy we're calling him Oliver, and if it's a girl, Sophie.'

'Arrival of one or other being imminent?'

'Not long now.'

'Congratulations.'

'Thanks. And for a surname, how about Lyle? Open Champion, 'eighty-five? Connection is that I have ambitions in that direction. Golf's one of the few sports I can aspire to, with this plastic knee.'

At that stage I was attributing his limp to the parachute accident. Soon after he'd begun his story I'd realised this wasn't the case, but only near the end had he mentioned that it was a Soviet 5.45-mm bullet that had smashed his knee-joint into pulp. That tiny slug has an airspace in its nose, shifting the centre of gravity right back so that on impact it tumbles, with viciously destructive effect.

But now he'd made this statement about his wedding, and the old Lapp hunter attending it. . . .

'Did you say Juffu came to your wedding?'

'Right.' He grinned. 'We borrowed a car from Sophie's brother, drove up there and tracked him down. Car, then boat. He has a shack on the Lemmenjoki river where he pans for gold, and we more or less kidnapped him. In the summer, this was. I was still on crutches, Sophie did most of the work. Long trip – the wedding was down in Kristiansund, where her parents live. Her brother says his car *still* smells of wet dog.'

That might be a happy note on which to finish. But it leaves a contrastingly sombre question smouldering.

How long before they try again?

Maybe the deal touched on this. There must have been a deal. Neither side wanting war, they'd have settled for speedy withdrawal in return for no public humiliation. It would explain the hush-up; and some assurance for the future may have been included.

May have. But on the 196 kilometres of the Norwegian/Soviet frontier there are still only 150 Norwegian riflemen facing 1500 border guards, two motorised infantry divisions, one brigade of naval infantry and two brigades of Spetsnazi.

And a second question – which has occupied a lot of minds over the past fifteen years – might well be linked to the first. *Why do Spetsnaz-manned midget submarines intrude so frequently in the northern fjords?*

We had no answers, only theories. I said finally – and lamely – 'We'll just have to wait and see', and 'Lyle' added, 'Let's hope it's a long, long wait.'

SAM LLEWELLYN

DEAD RECKONING

Picturesque Pulteney, a charming fishing village and a yachting haven for the wealthy on the south coast, is home to whizz-kid boat designer Charlie Agutter. But beneath the gleaming hulls lurks deadly treachery. For someone is out to get Charlie. Someone who doesn't care who else gets hurt in the process. Charlie's brother is dead – and everyone is blaming Charlie, designer of the revolutionary new yacht that killed him. Charlie knew it had to be sabotage.

It looks like a personal vendetta. But with the Captain's Cup approaching fast, and serious money at stake, something more sinister is bringing the surf to the boil. Charlie will have to move swiftly if he is going to save his career and still win the race . . .

'The Dick Francis of ocean racing' *Sunday Express*

0 7474 0086 5   ADVENTURE THRILLER   £2.99

A top secret SBS mission during the Falklands
War soars into explosive action . . .

SPECIAL DELIVERANCE

ALEXANDER FULLERTON

In the war-torn, storm-swept South Atlantic, a small band of
highly-trained SBS experts embark on a vital secret mission: to
sabotage Argentina's stock of deadly Exocet missiles.

The dangers are unthinkable: the coastline is exposed and treacherous,
the missile base is surrounded by vast tracts of open land, they must
infiltrate and destroy without ever being detected. Some say it's
impossible . . . but no one underestimates the SBS's lethal capacity.

And one man, Andy MacEwan, an Anglo-Argentine civilian recruited to
the team as guide and interpreter, has more than the success of the
mission on his mind. His brother is a commander in the Argentine Navy
Air Force and there is no love lost between them . . .

*'Good rollicking stuff – full of tension and highly authentic on SBS
technique'*
TODAY

'The action passages are superb. He is in a class of his own'
OBSERVER

0 7221 3719 2   ADVENTURE THRILLER   £2.99

From the bestselling author of DEATH WISH comes . . .

HOPSCOTCH
BRIAN GARFIELD

Before his enforced retirement from the CIA, Miles Kendig
thrilled to the cut-throat strategy of pursuit, the
red-blooded rapture of out-witting his opponents, the
subtlety of human conflict. Now, with the demands of
everyday life so easily accomplished, he felt empty, lifeless
and unwanted.

'You belong in the rubber room' they told him. But Miles
knew he was the best. He would show them. Both East and
West were terrified by his crazy plan. And this was going to
be Miles Kendig's last chance blaze of glory . . . if they
didn't nail him first!

'Brian Garfield is a natural storyteller'
NEW YORK TIMES

Also by Brian Garfield in Sphere Books:
NECESSITY
DEATH WISH

0 7221 3820 2   ADVENTURE THRILLER   £2.99

A STUNNING, INTERNATIONAL SPY THRILLER OF CHILLING PLAUSIBILITY

CEDAR

JAMES MURPHY

Political in-fighting inside Her Majesty's Secret Service has forced Joseph Mercer, head of Russia Section, to resign. But his superiors will not let him go until he has paid their price . . .

Then comes the news that a leading member of the Soviet Politburo is working for Britain under the codename CEDAR. Mercer is suspicious and sets out to discover the man's identity. But his search is cut short by the betrayal of his own networks inside Russia.

Suddenly Mercer becomes the prime suspect – accused of a crime he didn't commit. He's fighting for his life in a nightmare world where truth counts for nothing, and friends are deadlier than foes . . .

'Remarkable conviction and pace . . . brought together with a tight clarity of style and subtle touch of scepticism' DAILY MAIL

0 7221 6313 4   ADVENTURE THRILLER   £2.99

The aftermath of a war game that
went terribly wrong . . .

THE FIFTH ANGEL
A ONE MAN KILLING MACHINE

DAVID WILTSE

Sergeant Stitzer, said the officer who'd trained
him, was a hero. He was also one of the most
dangerous men ever to wear a uniform.

These days, they kept Stitzer in the cell at the end
of the corridor. TV cameras watched him night
and day. A broken yellow line on the floor marked
the point of no return.

Five years on, Stitzer had still not surrendered. In
his crazed mind he still had a mission to fulfil. And
the major knew that while Stitzer had breath in his
body he'd find a way to carry out those orders.
And not even the most secure military hospital in
the world would hold him back . . .

'Pacy, original and very readable' THE TIMES

0 7221 9107 3   ADVENTURE THRILLER £2.95